Praise for *Something Like Happy*

"Filled with beautiful life lessons of love, loss, friendship, and
forgiveness, *Something Like Happy* i...
A warm, funny, thoughtful nove...
and charged with e...

—**LORI NELSON SPIELMAN**,
bestselling author of *Th...

"Simply irresistible."

—*LIBRARY JOURNAL*

"Delightful page-turning awaits readers.... Polly is a wonderful
character with a positively infectious attitude—memorable and
magnetic, with a healthy dose of gallows humor. Joy shines through
the tears, as this novel is a life lesson that should not be ignored."

—*PUBLISHERS WEEKLY*

"*Something Like Happy* is inspiration in a bottle.
Author Woods uses her novel—inspired by a social-media hashtag—
to explore the exhilaration of new friendship, the power of loss,
and the evergreen tendrils of hope."

—*BOOKLIST*

"Inspired by the '100 Happy Days' challenge,
Woods presents a hilariously uplifting and heartwarming story
of hope in the midst of despair.... This is an enjoyable read
that needs to spread far and wide."

—*BOOKPAGE*

"Woods is a great option for fans of Graeme Simsion,
Gabrielle Zevin and Marian Keyes."

—*LIBRARY JOURNAL*

"Heartfelt and charming."

—*KIRKUS REVIEWS*

"I read this recently and loved it SO much.
I cried buckets, but it's ultimately a really positive,
uplifting book about making every day count."

—**CLARE MACKINTOSH**, *New York Times*
bestselling author of *I Let You Go*

"Entertaining, funny and full of wisdom. I loved this book."

—**KATIE FFORDE**, bestselling author

something
like
happy

something
like
happy

a novel

eva woods

GRAYDON
HOUSE

GRAYDON
HOUSE

Recycling programs
for this product may
not exist in your area.

ISBN-13: 978-1-525-81199-9

Something Like Happy

BookClubbish.com
GraydonHouseBooks.com

Printed in U.S.A.

To Scott (SP), with all my love

You can't always pinpoint the precise moment that your life goes wrong. Most of the time it creeps up on you, year by year, moment by moment, until one day you look around and realize you're so far from who you used to be you don't even feel like the same person. It's usually a gradual collapse, sneaking; a stone there, a pebble here. A slow erosion of who you are, bit by bit, piece by piece.

But other times you can say exactly when it was your life fell apart. When all your carefully placed cards tumbled down, and your house collapsed, and you knew in that moment nothing was ever going to be the same again. In that moment, you weren't sure if you would even survive, or be pulled under forever. But you did. Somehow.

DAY 1
Make a new friend

"Excuse me?"

No answer. The receptionist carried on clacking the computer keys. Annie tried again. "*Excuse* me." That was a level-two "excuse me"—above the one she'd give to tourists blocking the escalator and below the one reserved for someone with their bag on a train seat. Nothing. "*Sorry,*" she said, taking it to level three (stealing your parking spot, bashing you with an umbrella, etc.). "Could you help me, please? I've been standing here for five minutes."

The woman kept typing. "What?"

"I need to change the address on a patient file. I've already been sent to four different departments."

The receptionist extended one hand, without looking up. Annie gave her the form. "This you?"

"Well, no." *Obviously.*

"The patient has to change it for themselves."

"Um, well, they can't actually." Which would be clear if anyone in the hospital ever bothered to read the files.

The form dropped onto the counter. "Can't let another person change it. Data protection, see."

"But…" Annie felt, suddenly and horribly, like she might cry. "I need to change it so letters come to my address! She can't read them herself anymore! That's why I'm here. Please! I—I just need it changed. I don't understand how this can possibly be so difficult."

"Sorry." The receptionist sniffed, picked something off one of her nails.

Annie snatched the paper up. "Look, I've been in this hospital for ten hours now. I've been sent around from office to office. Patient Records. Neurology. Outpatients. Reception. Back to Neurology. And no one seems to have the slightest idea how to do this very simple task! I haven't eaten. I haven't showered. And I can't go home unless you just open up your computer and type in a few lines. That's all you have to do."

The receptionist still wasn't even looking at her. *Clack, clack, clack.* Annie felt it swell up in her—the anger, the pain, the frustration. "Will you *listen* to me?" She reached over and wrenched the computer around.

The woman's eyebrows disappeared into her bouffant hair. "Madam, I'm going to have to call security if you don't—"

"I just want you to look at me when I'm speaking. I just need you to *help* me. *Please.*" And then it was too late and she was definitely crying, her mouth suddenly filling with bitter salt. "I'm sorry. I'm sorry. I just—I really need to change the address."

"Listen, madam…" The receptionist was swelling, her mouth opening, no doubt to tell Annie where to go. Then something odd happened. Instead, her face creased into a smile. "Hiya, P."

"He-ey, everything okay here?"

Annie turned to see who was interrupting. In the doorway of the dingy hospital office was a tall woman in all shades of the rainbow. Red shoes. Purple tights. A yellow dress, the color of Sicilian lemons. A green beanie hat. Her amber jewelry glowed orange, and her eyes were a vivid blue. That array of color shouldn't have worked, but somehow it did. She leaned toward Annie, touching her arm; Annie flinched. "So sorry, I don't mean to jump in front of you. Just need to very, very quickly make an appointment."

The receptionist was back clacking, this time with a jaunty beat. "Next week do ya?"

"Thanks, you're a star. Sorry, I've totally queue-jumped!" The rainbow beamed at Annie again. "Is this lovely lady all sorted, Denise?"

No one had called Annie a lovely lady for a long time. She blinked the tears from her eyes, trying to sound firm. "Well, no, because apparently it's too hard to just change a patient record. I've been to four different offices now."

"Oh, Denise can do that for you. She has all the secrets of this hospital at her fabulous fingertips." The woman mimed typing. There was a large bruise on the back of one hand, partly covered by taped-on cotton wool.

Denise was actually nodding, grudgingly. "All right, then. Give it here."

Annie passed the form over. "Can you send care of me, please? Annie Hebden." Denise typed, and within ten seconds, the thing Annie had waited for all day was done. "Um, thanks."

"You're welcome, madam," said Denise, and Annie could feel her judgment. She'd been rude. She knew she'd been rude. It was just so frustrating, so difficult.

"Brill. Bye, missus." The rainbow woman waved at Denise, then grabbed Annie's arm again. "Listen. I'm sorry you're having a bad day."

"I—what?"

"You seem like you're having a really bad day."

Annie was temporarily speechless. "I'm in the bloody hospital. Do you think anyone here's having a good day?"

The woman looked around at the waiting room behind them—half the people on crutches, some with shaved heads and pale faces, a shrunken woman hunched in a wheelchair in a hospital gown, bored kids upending the contents of their mums' bags while the mums mindlessly stabbed at phones. "No reason why not."

Annie stepped back, angry. "Listen, thank you for your help—though I shouldn't have needed it, this hospital is a disgrace—but you've no idea why I'm in here."

"True."

"So, I'm going now."

The woman said, "Do you like cake?"

"What? Of course I—what?"

"Wait a sec." She dashed away. Annie looked at Denise, who'd gone back to her blank-eyed keyboard stare. She counted to ten—annoyed at herself for even doing that—then shook her head and went out down the corridor, with its palette of despair blue and bile green. Sounds of wheeling beds, flapping doors, distant crying. An old man lay on a trolley, tiny and gray. Thank God she was finally done. She needed to go home, lose herself in the TV, hide under the duvet—

"Wait! Annie Hebden!"

Annie turned. The annoying woman was running down the corridor—well, more sort of shuffling, out of breath. She held a cupcake aloft, iced with wavy chocolate frosting. "For you," she panted, thrusting it into Annie's hand. Each of her nails was painted a different color.

Annie was speechless for the second time in five minutes. "Why?"

"Because. Cupcakes make everything a little better. Except for type 2 diabetes, I guess."

"Uh…" Annie looked at the cake in her hand. Slightly squished. "Thank you?"

"That's okay." The woman licked some rogue frosting off her hand. "Ick, I hope I don't get MRSA. Not that it would make much difference. I'm Polly, by the way. And you're Annie."

"Er. Yeah."

"Have a good day, Annie Hebden. Or at least a slightly better one. Remember—if you want the rainbow, you have to put up with the rain." And she waved, and skipped—was it the first time anyone had ever skipped down the Corridor of Doom?—out of sight.

Annie waited for the bus in the rain, that gray soupy rain that Lewisham seemed to specialize in. She thought what a stupid thing it was the woman had said. Rain didn't always lead to rainbows. Usually it just led to soaked socks and your hair in rattails. But at least she had somewhere to go. A homeless man sat beneath the bus shelter, water dripping off his head and forming a puddle around his dirty trousers. Annie felt wretched for him, but what could she do? She couldn't help him. She couldn't even help herself.

When the bus came it was rammed, and she stood squeezed up between a buggy and a mound of shopping bags, buffeted by every turn. An elderly lady got on, wobbling up the steps with her shopping trolley. As she shuffled down the bus, nobody looked up from their phones to offer her a seat. Annie finally snapped. What was wrong with people? Was there not a shred of decency left in this city? "For God's sake!" she barked. "Could someone let this lady sit down, *please*?" A young man with huge headphones slouched out of his seat, embarrassed.

"No need to take the Lord's name in vain," said the old lady, tutting disapprovingly at Annie as she sat down.

Annie stared at her feet, which had left grimy marks on the wet floor of the bus, until she got to her stop.

How had her life come to this? she wondered. Losing it in public over a change of address? Weeping in front of strangers? Once it would have been her raising her eyebrows as someone else had a meltdown. Offering tissues, and a soothing pat on the arm. She didn't understand what had happened to that person. The one she used to be.

Sometimes it felt to Annie like her life had changed in the blink of an eye. Eyes shut—she was back in the bedroom of her lovely house on that last sunny morning, and everything was good. She was filled with excitement, and hope, and slightly exhausted joy. *Perfect*. Eyes open—she was here, trudging back to her horrible flat, catching the bus in the rain, lying awake full of dread and misery. One blink, perfect. Two blinks, ruined. But no matter how many times she closed her eyes, it never went back to how it used to be.

DAY 2
Smile at strangers

The doorbell was ringing. Annie woke up with a jerk, her heart shock-started. What was it? The police again, the ambulance…but no, the worst had already happened. She sat up, registering that she'd fallen asleep on the sofa again, in the clothes she'd worn to the hospital. She couldn't even remember what she'd been watching on TV. *Tattoo Fixers*, maybe? She liked that. It was always comforting to see there were people who'd made worse decisions than she had.

Riiiinnnngg. She moved aside the blanket Costas must have laid over her. As she stood up, crumbs and tissues and a remote control fell out of her clothes. It was as if she'd come home drunk, but drunk on misery, on grief, on anger.

Riiiiinnnnnng! "All right!" Jesus. What time was it, anyway? The TV clock read 9:23 a.m. She had to hurry or she'd miss visiting hours. Costas would have left ages ago to do the breakfast shift, in and out without her even seeing him. A feeling of shame rolled over her—the Annie of two years ago would never have slept in her clothes.

"Annie Hebden! Are you in there?"

Annie winced. Through the door chain she could see a blur

of jewel green—it was the strange woman from the hospital. Polly something.

"Er, yes?"

"I've got your hospital letter." A hand appeared in the gap, this time with silver nails, and waved an envelope under Annie's nose. It had her name on it, but a different address. One in a nicer part of town. "You probably got mine," said the woman cheerfully.

Annie looked at the pile of letters on the mat. Bills. A subscription to *Gardening Monthly*, which she really should have canceled by now. And a bright white envelope addressed to Polly Leonard. "How did that happen?"

"I guess Denise got mixed up when you changed the address. I called her to switch them around, no harm done."

Was the hospital supposed to give out her address? "So you came all the way here, just to give me this?" It would have taken more than half an hour from Polly's home in Greenwich to Annie's in Lewisham, especially at rush hour.

"Sure. I've never been to this part of town before, so I thought why not?"

There were a million reasons why not. The area's soaring crime rates. The monstrosity of its seventies shopping center. The fact they'd been digging up the heart of it for years now, creating a traffic-clogged hellhole full of thundering drills and melted tarmac.

"Well. Thanks for bringing it." She stuck Polly's letter out the gap. "Bye, then."

Polly didn't budge. "Are you going to the hospital today?"

Every instinct told Annie to lie, but for some reason she didn't. "Oh, yeah. I will be, but—"

"Appointment?"

"Not exactly." She didn't feel up to explaining.

"I'm going in, too. I thought we could travel together."

Annie had been known to stay in the office for an extra twenty minutes some days, just to be sure her colleagues were gone so she wouldn't have to catch the bus with them. "I'm not dressed," she said.

"That's okay. I can wait."

"But...but..." Annie's stupid brain couldn't think of a single reason not to let this annoying, overly colorful stranger into her home. "I guess...okay, then."

"So this is your place." Polly stood in Annie's drab living room like a Christmas tree. Today, she wore what looked like an ankle-length cocktail dress in crème de menthe satin, and underneath it, biker boots. A fake fur jacket and a knitted hat completed the look. The hem of the dress was damp and dirty, as if she'd just walked through Lewisham in the rain. She looked like a model on an urban fashion shoot.

"I'm not allowed to decorate. Landlord won't let me." The tenth-floor flat still had its depressing laminate floorboards and seventies knobbly walls. It smelled of damp and other people's cooking. "Um, I need to shower. Do you want—you want tea or anything?"

"That's okay. I'll just stay here and read or something." She looked around at the shabby room, the laundry on the rack—Annie's overwashed pants and leggings—which had dried all crispy. Polly picked something up from the dusty coffee table. *How to Obtain Power of Attorney.* This looks interesting." Was that sarcasm? A slim pamphlet with a sad stock photo of someone holding an old person's hand. When really getting power of attorney was more like grabbing that old person's hand and tying it to their side before they could hurt themselves. Or someone else.

"Well, okay. I won't be long."

Annie went into the bathroom—rusty mirror, moldering shower curtain—and wondered if she'd gone mad. There was a strange woman in her house and she was just letting it happen. A woman she knew nothing about, who could be crazy, and quite likely was, judging by her clothes. Maybe that was why they'd met in the neurological department. Maybe she'd had a blow to the head and it had turned her into a person with no boundaries, who came to your flat and read your depressing private pamphlets.

Annie had the world's quickest wash, what her mum would have called a lick and a polish. For many months after her life fell apart, the shower used to be the place she cried, her fist stuffed in her mouth to muffle the sound. But there was no time for that today, so she threw on a near-identical outfit to the one she'd worn yesterday. No point in looking nice. Not for a place where people were either dying, or wished they were.

On her way out—no makeup, wet hair bundled up—she heard voices from the living room. Her heart sank. He must be on a short shift today.

"Annie!" Polly beamed at her as she went in. "I was just meeting your lovely friend here!"

"Hiya, Annie!" Costas waved. Costas was Greek, gorgeous and had abs you could crack eggs on. He was also twenty-two, had turned Annie's spare room into a festering rubbish dump and hilariously enough worked in Costa Coffee. At least, he thought it was hilarious.

"He's my flatmate. I need to go now."

"In a minute. Costas brought back some pastries!"

"Boss says I should take away. Still good, though!" He was holding open a brown paper bag full of croissants and Danish pastries. He smiled at Polly. "You come to Costa sometime, I make you special Greek coffee. Strong enough to blow off your head!"

Suddenly Annie was angry. How dare this woman come here and lift the lid on Annie's life, the sordid flat, the unwashed dishes? "I'm going now," she said. "Costas, could you wash up your pans? You left green stuff all over the baking dish last night."

"Spanakopita—needs to soak."

"Oh, I love spanakopita!" cried Polly. "I backpacked in Greece when I was eighteen. *Kyria!*"

"*Kyria!*" Costas gave her a thumbs-up, and his widest white grin. He was always smiling. It was very wearing. "Very good, Polly."

Annie put her coat on, as passive-aggressively as she could. "I'll be late."

"Oh! Right, let's split. Lovely to meet you, Costas-Annie's-friend."

"He's my *flatmate*," she said, opening the door crossly. She wasn't entirely sure why.

"Ladies and gentlemen, the bus will now stop to change drivers. It will take, er…we don't know."

The bus filled with a gust of sighs. "I'll definitely be late now," Annie muttered to herself.

"Bloody wasters," grumbled an elderly man behind her who was wearing a hairy suit that smelled strongly of damp. "Two pound a journey for this. Lining their pockets, they are."

Polly said, "Well, it gives us a chance to look around." Annie and the man exchanged a quick incredulous glance. The view out the window was of a large Tesco and a patch of waste ground with a burned-out car on it. "Or chat," Polly went on. "Where are you off to, sir?"

"Funeral," he grunted, leaning on his stick.

"I'm sorry. Friend of yours?"

Annie shrank into her seat. A man in paint-stained jeans was already rolling his eyes. What if people thought she was with the woman who talked on the bus? The most dangerous London pest, worse that urban foxes or Japanese knotweed.

"Me old mucker Jimmy. Had good innings, though. Fighter pilot in the Blitz, he was."

"Oh, how fascinating. How did you meet?"

A woman in a headscarf removed one earbud and tutted loudly. Annie cringed.

"Grew up on the same street. Old Bermondsey. He was RAF, I was navy. I could tell you a thing or two, love." He gave an emphysemic chuckle. Annie picked up an abandoned *Metro* and began to ostentatiously read about gangland stabbings, as the old man droned on.

"And then Jimmy, he 'id in the wardrobe till 'er 'usband nodded off, then he nipped out the window..."

"This is so sad," Annie said pointedly, waving the paper. "Three stabbings this month alone."

"Bunch of 'oodlums," said the old man. "Jimmy and me were the terror of the streets but we never did no stabbings. A punch in the face—now, that's civilized. Gentlemanly."

Annie closed her eyes: she could not endure another second of this. Luckily, the bus started to move, and Mate-of-Jimmy's got off at the next stop, seizing Polly's hand and planting a wet kiss on it. "Nice speaking to you, young lady."

"I've got some hand sanitizer," offered Annie.

Polly laughed. "He'll probably outlive me."

Annie raised her paper again. Everyone else on the bus had headphones in, like decent people. Only Polly insisted on staring around her, waving at babies and dogs, making eye contact all over the show. If she carried on like that, there was a good chance they'd be arrested by the London Transport Police and not even make the hospital.

But they did make it. The homeless man was still sitting by the bus shelter, and Annie wondered if he'd been there all night. His head was bowed. Polly hunkered down to him, as

Annie cringed again and stared off into the distance. "Hello. What's your name? I'm Polly."

He glanced up slowly, clearing his throat. His voice was like sandpaper. "Jonny."

"Is there anything I can bring you when I come out? Hot drink?"

Annie was blushing on Polly's behalf. Wasn't it patronizing, to offer a hot drink instead of cash? He looked surprised. "A coffee would be nice. Anything hot, really."

"Sugar?"

"Eh, two, please. Cheers."

"See you a bit later, then. I've got to go in there now."

"Oh. Good luck."

Annie was already walking off, deathly embarrassed. Once inside, she did her best to shake Polly off. "I'm going this way, so—"

"Me, too. Good old Neurology." Polly tucked her fur-clad arm through Annie's. "It's the best department. I mean, it's your brain. Everything you are is in there. Much better than stupid hearts or legs, or the worst, *dermatology*."

"Yeah," Annie said with heavy sarcasm. "It's great when your brain starts turning to mush in your head." They'd stopped outside the inpatient ward. "Well, I need to go in there."

"Okay." Polly didn't move.

"I mean, only one person's allowed at a time. So I better just..." Why wouldn't she go? If she didn't leave soon, then she might see—

"Hello. Hello!"

Annie flinched at the high, nervous voice of the woman tottering toward them in a hospital gown. She was pointing a bony finger at Annie. "You. Miss. Are you the nurse?"

"So sad," murmured Polly. "Can we help you, madam?"

Annie tried to block Polly off. "I don't think we should—"

"I'm looking for the nurse." The woman was barely sixty, but looked eighty. Her face was sunken, her hair gray, and under her hospital gown her legs were bruised and wasted, one wrapped in a bandage. "I need—oh, I don't know what I need!"

"I'm sure it'll come to you. Shall we go into the ward?" Polly was taking her arm, which was mottled with scars that never seemed to heal.

"I don't think you should do that." Annie wanted to scream.

"Oh, come on, Annie, she needs help."

"Just leave it, will you?" snapped Annie. "Go to your own bloody appointment!"

The woman was staring at her. "You. I know you, don't I? Are you the nurse?"

"I, uh…" Annie's voice was dead in her throat. Polly was staring, too, her forehead wrinkled. "No, I'm—"

At that point a harassed-looking nurse dashed out from the ward. "Maureen! Come on, back to bed now. You can't walk on that leg."

But she wouldn't leave. She was still staring at Annie. "I know you. I *know* you!"

Too late to pretend. "Yes. It's me, Mum. It's Annie. I was just coming to see you."

Charity—one of the nicer nurses, even if she did insist on praying over the patients—gave Annie a sympathetic look. "Come on now, Maureen. Your daughter will be in to see you soon."

As the ward doors swung shut, Polly looked at Annie. "That's why you were here? You're not sick yourself?"

"No. Mum, she—well, she has dementia. Early onset. She had a fall at the weekend, trying to get a chip pan out of the cupboard. Even though she hasn't had a chip pan since 2007.

But they'll probably discharge her soon and then—I don't know what then." Annie took a deep breath.

Polly's expression hadn't changed. Interest, understanding, but no pity. "I guess that explains your attitude of barely suppressed fury."

Something broke inside Annie. "Look. I don't know you, and you've got no right to say that. My mum's not even sixty and she has advanced dementia. Why wouldn't I be furious? I should be furious. So why don't you just butt out of my life, okay? What gives you the right to…to…come to my house, and interfere and…" The rest was drowned in sudden, inconvenient tears.

Polly reacted strangely to this tirade, which left Annie gasping for breath. "Come with me," Polly said, grasping her hand. Hers was cold, but surprisingly strong. She dragged Annie down the corridor.

"What? No, I don't want to— Let go of me!"

"Come on. I want to show you something." They'd reached a door with a sign on it that read Dr. Maximilian Fraser, MD FRS. Consultant Neurologist. Underneath it someone had Blu-Tacked up a sign in green ink: No, I Am Not a Supplies Cupboard. Polly threw open the door. "Dr. McGrumpy! It's your favorite patient."

A voice from the dark said, "Come in, Polly. It's not like I'm in the middle of a highly confidential patient review or anything."

"You're eating a Crunchie and watching cat videos on YouTube," said Polly, which was true. The room was tiny and gloomy—not much bigger than a cupboard, in fact—and one wall was covered in dark glass. Behind a computer sat a burly man in scrubs, his thick dark hair sticking up as if he'd been running his hands through it, several days' worth of stubble on his chin.

"What do you want now?" He had a Scottish accent. Annie saw his eyes rest on her, so she looked at her feet in their shabby black loafers.

"I want to show the scan to my new friend Annie."

"Not *again*. Do you think I've nothing else to do, is that it? You think hospital funding is so luxuriant I'm basically your personal AV monkey?"

"Come on. You know I'm your best patient."

"*He's* my best patient. No hassle." Annie saw he was nodding to a glass jar that held a floating human brain. "Go on, then." He sighed. He clicked his computer and the wall screen glowed into life, revealing another brain, the ghostly image of one this time. White, spongy. One side of it was darker, tendrils of black curling through it.

"That's my brain," Polly said proudly.

"Oh," Annie said, not sure what she was seeing.

Polly went over and tapped the glass. "Fingerprints," grunted the doctor. She ignored him.

"That's my tree. Glioblastoma—it means 'branches,' see."

Annie looked at the doctor for guidance. "No one knows what that word means, Polly," he said.

"Well, let me explain. That's my brain, and this lovely tree-like growth here—well, that's my brain tumor." Polly smiled. "I call it Bob."

"Take deep breaths."

Annie sucked in air. She was sitting on the doctor's wheely chair. He was kneeling in front of her, peering into her eyes. His were brown and intelligent, like a kind dog. "Can you follow this?" He held up a finger.

"Of course I can," she said irritably. "I'm fine. I didn't even faint." She didn't understand why she'd freaked out. She barely knew Polly, brain tumor or not.

Polly had gone to get "hot sweet tea," as she'd brightly an-
nounced. "Isn't that what they did in the war?"

The doctor said, "You didn't know, I take it. You never
wondered why she'd so many appointments?"

"We only met yesterday. And she's acting like we're, I don't
know, teenage pen pals."

"That's Polly. It's quite hard to avoid being friends with
her." His accent rolled hard on the r's. He sat back on his heels.

"So…she's sick."

"Very sick."

"Can you…do anything?"

He stood up again, wincing. "Christ, I'm getting old. I
shouldn't really tell you. Confidentiality. But since you just saw
her brain scan I guess I can take that as patient consent. Because of where Bob is, there's a strong chance removal would
damage her brain." Annie remembered what Polly had said.
About the brain being everything we are. "She's had chemo,
which bought a bit of time. We're keeping an eye on it. Lots
of MRI scans. Costing a bloody fortune. If it goes near the
front cortex, well, that's game over, and it's very aggressive.
Quite advanced already."

"If?"

"When."

"How long?" she asked.

He scrunched up his face. "For the record, doctors really
hate that question. We're not clairvoyants. But we've told her
about three months."

Annie gaped. So little. An academic term. A financial quarter. A season of an American TV show. Imagine if that was
all you had, to cram a whole life into. "Oh," she said. In the
circumstances, it was all she could think of.

The door banged—"Don't bring the bloody house down!"
he shouted—and Polly came in with a paper cup.

"Whoops!" She spilled some, licking her hand. "Here, drink this." Annie peered into the cup. It looked disgusting, like soapy dishwater. Suddenly it was overwhelming: the tiny dark room and the strange woman with the tumor, and her own mother in the ward nearby, with her brain also dying inside her. Annie stood up, her head swimming.

"I'm sorry… I'm really sorry, but I can't do this. I'm sorry you're ill, Polly. I really am. But I need to go." And she rushed out, slopping the tea onto the floor as she went.

DAY 3
Make time for breakfast

"Morning, Annie Hebden!"

Annie had never been a morning person, not even when Jacob would wake her in the early hours, and she'd hold his warm body next to hers, feeling his soft breath on her neck. Lately, she wasn't a night person, either. There was sometimes a window around 4:00 p.m., after many cups of bitter coffee from the manky not-washed-since-2011 machine in the office, when she didn't feel entirely horrendous. But 6:00 a.m.—that was pushing it for anyone, surely. She padded across her living room to the front door, which Polly was hammering on. "Is it morning? It's pitch-black."

"It's lovely out." Polly didn't sound remotely tired.

"It's *not*. It's 6:00 a.m. on a Wednesday in March." And why was Polly at her door so early? Why was she at her door at all?

"Well, okay, but it'll be lovely soon, and I have coffee and croissants, so let me in!"

Two mornings in a row of being woken up by Polly, even though Annie had run out on her the day before. For a moment she thought about pretending the door had become stuck in a freak locking accident. Then she sighed and opened it.

She didn't bother with the chain this time. Twenty-four hours and she'd learned Polly could not be kept out.

Polly was wide-awake, today wearing jeans and a T-shirt that said Yes We Can. On her feet were cherry-red cowboy boots. "How do I look?" She shook her head from side to side. "Hannah Montana dying of cancer?" With her short fair curls tied back, a large bald patch was visible from chemo, the skin mottled red.

Annie said, "Ha." She hadn't got used to Polly's cancer jokes. She hadn't even got used to the cancer.

Polly held up a tray of paper cups. "Coffee! Do you have some nice cups? It's a shame to drink from plastic lids."

"I'll do it. You should sit down."

"I'm not dying right this second, Annie. Cups?"

Annie gestured at the kitchen as she sank into her nasty faux-leather sofa with the rip in the side. "Do you ever sleep?"

"Oh, I don't have time for that. I have three months to live!" That phrase had surely never been said so cheerfully. "Or so Dr. McGrumpy tells me. That's what I call him."

"Yes, he did seem…grouchy."

Polly inspected, and discarded, a mug with Cartman from *South Park* on it. A gift from Annie's work Secret Santa, despite the fact she had never watched an episode of *South Park* or expressed the slightest interest in it in her life. "Bless him. He's your traditional grumpy Jesus-complex-but-can't-save-everyone doctor, but he's the best there is." Polly's voice echoed from the cupboard. "Honestly, Annie, we need to talk about your crockery choices."

It seemed that in Polly's world, the cups were a problem, but the cancer was just a fact of life. Finally, she found some old floral-print ones that had been a wedding present to Annie's mum and dad. "Ooh, vintage?"

"No, just really old and crap." Annie gave a yawn. "I need

to go to work today. They would only give me so many days off for Mum."

"That's why I'm here early. So we can make a plan."

"What plan?" Annie didn't have the strength for anything today.

"I'll explain. Here we are." She'd poured the coffee into the dinky little cups, and arranged the croissants on a flowery plate, showering flakes onto the floor, which Annie saw was already sprinkled with dust and toast crumbs. She was really letting things slide. Costas had grown up with seven sisters, and before moving to England had barely had to boil water for himself, so housework wasn't his strong point. "So," Polly said, settling herself. She'd taken out a notebook, a hot-pink one with silver edges. "As you know, I have three months to live. So obviously, when I found this out, it was a bit of a shock. You know the drill, crying on the bathroom floor, desperate denial, staying in bed for a week…"

Annie did know the drill. She'd practically written it.

"But I realized, eventually, I'd been given an amazing opportunity. I don't have to bother with any of that rubbish we spend our time on—bills, pensions, going to the gym. My life, or what's left of it, is now intensely concentrated, thanks to good old Bob the tumor. And I plan to make the absolute most of it."

Annie reached for a croissant. "Don't tell me you've made a bucket list."

"It is the standard 'three months to live' behavior. But no, it's a bit more complicated than that. I don't want to just tick stuff off. Swim with dolphins, check. Go to the Grand Canyon, check. I mean, I've done all those things, obviously."

"Obviously," muttered Annie, mouth full of pastry.

"I don't want to just…go through the motions of dying. I want to really try and change things. I have to make some kind of *mark*, you see, before I disappear forever. I want to show it's possible to be happy and enjoy life, even if things seem awful. Did you know that, after a few years, lottery winners go back to the exact same levels of happiness as before they won? And people in serious accidents do, too, once they've adjusted to their changed lives? Happiness is a state of mind, Annie."

Annie gritted her teeth again. The things that had happened to her weren't a state of mind; they were very real. "So what's the plan?"

"Have you heard of the Hundred Happy Days project? One of those viral internet thingies?"

"No." Old Annie would have liked such things, posted them on Facebook, shared inspirational quotes. New Annie was scornful of projects and plans and lists. It all meant nothing when your life had truly come crashing down around your ears.

"It's simple, really. You're just meant to do one thing every day that makes you happy. Could be little things. Could be big. In fact, we're doing one right now."

"We are?" Annie looked around doubtfully at her shabby living room.

"Breakfast on nice plates. Seeing the dawn in with a friend." Polly raised a cup to the reddening sky out the window, and Annie thought, *Friend?* Was it as easy as that? And how could something so small make any difference at all? "Now, I reckon if I'm lucky—lucky in the 'I have cancer' sense—I've got another hundred days left in me, so I'm going to do the project. And I want your help."

"Me?"

Polly set down her cup. She had a line of foam on her upper lip, and her hair was suddenly burning red with the sun that had decided to come up, bloody and bright and beautiful. "Annie—I hope you don't mind me saying this—you seem kind of the complete opposite of happy."

Annie blinked. "I've been having a tough time recently. You saw my mum."

"That can't be it," said Polly. "An attitude like that takes *years* of work."

"Well, I live in a crappy flat full of plywood and mold, which I share with a Greek child who'd never washed a cup in his life before."

"Costas? He's adorable."

"Maybe. But tripping over his dirty pants and chipping cheese off all my dishes—less so. Look." Annie rooted around under herself on the sofa, bringing up a pistachio shell. "He leaves these all over the place. Drives me crazy. And I haven't even got started on my job, which I hate, and I'm going to be late for if I don't leave soon."

"Okay. So you're miserable. That's why I want you to do this with me. What do you say? For the next one hundred days—if I make it that long—we'll think of one happy thing every day, and write it down. We can backdate it to when we met, shave a few days off—Time's winged chariot and all that. I want to prove that happiness is possible, even when things really suck."

Annie thought of how to reply. "But… I'm not sure I believe that, Polly."

"You could try, though. Why not?"

For a moment, Annie almost thought about telling her—explaining how much worse it got than a sick mother and an unwelcome flatmate and crappy flat—but she couldn't. Polly was a virtual stranger. Instead, she said, "There's plenty of reasons why not. I need to go to work now, or I'll be late. Again." She stood up, chucking down the remains of her frothy coffee (admittedly a big improvement on the bitter instant stuff she usually made). "Look, Polly, it's nice of you to ask me to join your project—" (bloody interfering more like) "—but it's honestly not my thing. I have a lot on my plate right now. Thanks for breakfast. I'm sure we'll see each other around the hospital sometime."

DAY 4
Make the most of your lunch break

Much as Annie hated going to the hospital, she had to admit there was something strangely comforting about it. That hushed hum of activity, the sense the staff had things in hand, and you could just sit and wait and soon they'd come to take your blood pressure or scan you with their machines. All those notices about hand washing and crash carts—life in there was serious. There was no point getting upset about stupid things.

Unlike at Annie's office.

"Annie—9:08. Just so you know, for your time sheet."

Annie gritted her teeth so hard she was surprised she didn't spit out bits of enamel. "Right. Thanks, Sharon."

"Just make sure you note it down. That's a quarter of an hour docked off, rounding up." Sharon, a bitter woman who lived off chips and Appletiser, was the only person in Annie's office who didn't hate the new time sheets. Once, Annie had approved of the system, too. She'd even helped to bring it in, in her role as finance officer. Sure, she was sympathetic when people had sick children or late trains or broken boilers, but it was a workplace and they all had a job to do. Back then she'd worn smart trouser suits, or dresses with belts and cardigans, and she'd brought her lunch with her in Tupperware and she'd helped organize the Christmas do.

Until everything changed.

She sat down at her desk—dust and sandwich crumbs lodged in every crevice, no pictures, nothing nice. The plants she'd once tended had turned brown and dusty, and she'd thrown her wedding picture in the bin two years ago, shattering it. She switched on her computer, hearing it groan as it tried to come to life. She wondered if Polly still worked. She bet it had been somewhere with shiny clean iMacs, and plants that everyone watered, not just Sharon, who passive-aggressively let them die, then prodded their desiccated corpses like victims at a show trial. Where everyone wore dark-rimmed glasses and had creative brainstorming sessions over table football.

"Coming for the team lunch today, Annie?" asked Fee, the office manager, scratching at her eczema. "Only I need everyone's choices in advance."

Annie shook her head. She'd once made an effort to join in, but really she didn't have anything in common with Sharon, or Tim, who blew his nose onto his sleeve, or Syed, who never took off his massive headphones, or— "Annie?"

"Hi, Jeff." She pasted on a weak smile. He was her boss, after all.

"Can I have a word?" He mimed a mouth flapping, as if Annie didn't understand English. Jeff didn't seem to realize that he worked in the world's saddest office, where enthusiasm was about as useful as opening a vein right onto the floor. His office was plastered in motivational posters and Post-its with slogans like Quitters Never Win, Winners Never Quit. His bookcase was crammed with business books. *Get Rich or Die Trying. Rich Middle-Manager, Poor Middle-Manager.* Although how you were supposed to get rich running local government waste-processing services, Annie didn't know.

"Do take a seat in the Chat Area." Jeff, who owned about thirty-eight suits from Top Man and was trying to grow a beard, was a big fan of the "Chat Area"—two spindly chairs and a table with fanned-out issues of the local government magazine, *Inside Lewisham*. "Annie. How are you?"

Shit, she thought. Awful. Dying inside. "Fine."

"Because I've noticed you've been...not so present this week?"

"I took some days as leave."

"Yes, yes, but—when you're here, you don't seem to engage with people?"

Why did he turn everything into a question? "What do you mean?"

"Well, people have mentioned that you don't really chat in the kitchen, or go out for lunch, the old watercooler moments, you know, ha-ha!"

"That's because I'm doing my job! And we don't even have a watercooler since the budget cuts!"

"Well. You know what I mean." He leaned forward earnestly. He was five years younger than Annie, she knew, yet he spoke to her like she was a stroppy teenager, which, admittedly, was how she felt right now. "Thing is, Annie, an office is more than just work. It's a team. Friends, I hope. Like the crew of a ship." He mimed something that she gathered was meant to convey pulling on rigging. "So what's the harm in a bit of chitchat over a nice cuppa? And it might help if you smiled more. People find you a bit...unfriendly?"

She felt the ache of tears in her nose again. "My mum's ill. You know that."

"I know. I know. I'm very aware you've had...a rough time of things the last few years. And we're fully committed to a family-friendly, er..." Jeff trailed off awkwardly, perhaps remembering that Annie no longer had a family. He knew, of course. Everyone knew, and yet they still got upset about the franking machine and who'd used all the milk. What was the matter with them? "I know it's been hard. But we have to bring a positive attitude to work, no matter what's going on. PMA, Annie!" He made a gesture as if he was swinging an imaginary baseball bat. "You know, there's going to be more redundancies this year. We'll all have to fight for our jobs. So…if you could just join in a bit more, smile, you know, ask after people's kids and so on. I mean, it's been two years, hasn't it? Since…everything?"

Annie stared down at her hands, humiliated beyond words. But she wouldn't cry in front of him. She would wait until she could slip into the loo and sob her heart out there, as she had done at least once a week for the past two years. Through gritted teeth, she said, "I'll try. Can I go now?"

Annie stood in the work kitchen, waiting for the silted-up kettle to boil. The air smelled permanently of tuna, and in the sink there was a spill of what was either vomit or instant pasta. Sharon had prized it off with a fork, like a food crime scene, and left one of her trademark notes about it. *It is NOT the cleaners JOB 2 wash up ur FOOD.* There had to be more to life than this. Dragging herself here every day, on a bus full of angry commuters. Sitting in this office that was never cleaned properly, with people she would literally cross the street to avoid. As the kettle snapped off she felt a cold nugget of certainty settle in her chest. *There has to be more than this. There has to.*

"There's someone to see you."

Annie looked up from her screen a few hours later to see Sharon hovering. Sharon only seemed to have five outfits, which she wore in strict rotation. Today's outfit was number two—a red cardigan covered in dog hairs (she had four) and an ankle-length skirt with a misshapen hem. "Who is it?"

Sharon sniffed. "Some woman. Dressed like a *mad* person."

Oh, no, that sounded like Polly. When there'd been no knock at the door that morning, she'd thought she was safe. Polly was clearly dealing with her diagnosis by seizing life, but would it last? The trouble with seizing life was eventually you had to pay some taxes or get your hair cut or regrout the shower. Why had she latched on to Annie, who wasn't seizing life so much as hiding from it at all costs, crying in the loos? Maybe she could head her off.

Too late, she saw Polly was already barreling into the office, waving. She wore a red trilby and a big cape-like coat, and was carrying a cardboard box.

Annie jumped up. "What are you doing here?"

"I thought we could have lunch."

"I don't have time for lunch."

"Annie! Are you paid for your break?"

"Well, no, but—"

"So they're getting an extra hour out of you, unpaid, every day?"

"Keep your voice down," Annie hissed, looking about her. Her coworkers were hunched at their desks, eating sandwiches or slurping up tinned soup, staring at their computers. "How did you know where I worked?"

"Oh, you're on the website. I brought you a care package!" Polly shoved the box onto Annie's desk. A silver photo frame, a mug that said You Don't Have to Be Mad to Work Here But You Probably Are. Sachets of tea. Biscuits, sparkly pens, wet wipes, a little plant. A notebook with a blue silk cover. "Just a few things to brighten up your work space. I bet it's all dirty and nasty."

"It is not!"

"You sure?" Polly ran a finger over the base of Annie's computer and brought it back, black with dust. "Everyone's work desk is filthy. We spend so much time at them and we don't even try to make them nice. Little things can really make a difference."

Annie sighed. "Come on, we should go out. We're not meant to have visitors." She hustled Polly out the door, past a goggling Sharon, who had finally found something more interesting than *Farm World* to look at.

Polly looked at the building—hideous seventies concrete plonked beside ten lanes of traffic—with a critical eye. "I don't blame you for being miserable. This place would bring anyone down."

"Exactly. And I have to work here every day, doing something I hate, so how will adding some tea bags to my desk help?"

"It'll help. A journey of a thousand miles begins with a single step."

"You're not going to suggest I open up and get to know everyone in the office, and learn that we're all the same under the skin, no matter how much skin there is?"

Polly laughed. "No. Some people are just awful. And some things need to be run away from, very fast, like an exploding bomb. You should quit."

Annie felt anger build again—who was this woman, telling her what to do? "I can't. I need the money."

"You can do something else," Polly said cheerfully.

"There's a recession on."

"Excuses." Polly waved a hand. "Everyone uses that one, Annie. Oh, everything was always better in the past! Things are rubbish now we're not allowed to send our children down the mines! It's just a cop-out."

"But—"

Polly grasped Annie's arm. "I know you're cross, but I'm sorry—cancer card. You'll see I'm right, in time. Now come with me. We're doing something for our hundred happy days. It's a pretty simple one—take a lunch break."

"I never said I'd do the hundred days. And, anyway, I do take a lunch break."

"And what do you do? Go on Facebook? Run errands?"

"Sometimes I buy a sandwich."

"In a nice place?"

"There is nowhere nice around here. Tesco usually."

"Do you at least leave your desk to eat it?"

"And go where? The loos? The traffic island in the round-about?"

"What about here?" Polly stopped, opening her arms wide in the manner of a Las Vegas showgirl.

Annie looked skeptically at the square of grass they'd ended up beside. "The park? I'm not going in there—we'll get kid-napped by drug dealers!"

Polly was already pushing open the gates. "Hello, hello, anyone here selling drugs? I really want to buy some crack! See, nothing. I think we're safe."

"It's freezing."

"I have blankets." Parking herself on a bench, Polly took two heavy Slankets from her tote bag.

"I feel ridiculous." Annie was glad at least that the blanket partly covered her face. What if someone from work walked by and saw her picnicking in the cold, dreary park beside all the dog poop? They'd think she'd finally snapped her last thread.

Polly whipped out two small cardboard boxes. "You're not vegetarian?"

"No, but—"

"Then eat up!"

In the box was a crumbly piece of cheddar, a juicy sliced pear, a thick slab of pink ham and a hunk of crusty bread. All topped with jewel-red chutney.

"You didn't get this around here," Annie said accusingly. "It's all chicken shops and kebab vans." She tried a mouthful of the cheese, sharp and salty and crumbly in her mouth. Oh, God, it was delicious. And to think she'd been planning to eat some Easy Cheese singles.

Polly took a few bites, then set down her own box. "Here," she said, taking something from her bag. "A list of ten things to do at lunchtime within ten minutes from your office. Yoga. A singing group. A street market."

"I can't take a lunch break every day!"

"Er, why not?"

Annie didn't have an answer for that. "I'll think about it."

"It can just be tiny things. Look at this place, for a start. Isn't it nice? There's a football pitch—you could come and watch hunky men in shorts. There's dogs to pet, and even a little coffee kiosk. Not to mention this play park." She nodded toward the swings, where kids were being pushed on swings and down slides, bundled up against the cold. Annie winced and turned away; she tried to avoid playgrounds.

"I said I'll think about it."

Polly leaned back, closing her eyes against the faint spring sun. "Don't be your own worst enemy, Annie. There's plenty of other people for that. Remember—today is the first day of the rest of your life."

Annie rolled her eyes, but she had to admit the fresh air and good food had lifted her mood somewhat. Better than a Cup-a-Soup while Sharon snooped over her shoulder and every-one talked about *Strictly Come Dancing*. She realized that Polly had now been to her office and her home—where she spent about 96 percent of her time these days—and she knew noth-ing about the other woman, except for her eccentric wardrobe and the fact she seemed to have swallowed the *Little Book of Inspirational Quotes*. "So, are you feeling okay?" she ventured.

Polly opened one eye. "I'm still dying. But within the con-text of that, yes, I'm okay. My energy levels are good, probably because I'm on so many pills I'm surprised I don't rattle. Dr. Max is paranoid the thing will grow a millimeter and I'll start drooling." Annie winced, but Polly was still smiling.

"And…have you given up work?"

"Of course. I was in PR, you see. Who cares about campaigns for a new lipstick when you have three months to live?"

Annie didn't ask what she was doing for money. Only posh people were called Polly. Her head swirled with questions. Was Polly married? Did she have any kids? And most of all, why had she chosen Annie? "This project," Annie tried. "Are your friends doing it?" She almost said, *your other friends*, but she and Polly were hardly that yet.

"Oh, they'd love it. They're all about Instagramming their morning avocado and blogging about yoga holidays. I don't want that. Anyway, they've got kids and jobs and marriages and stuff. They're busy."

And Annie barely had one of those things now. "So, why did you ask me?"

"Because. I want someone who doesn't believe in it. I want to know if it's possible to make yourself happy, even when things really, really suck. I need to know death can have some meaning. Like it isn't all just totally random bad luck. You see?"

"Um, I guess."

Annie wasn't someone who had a lot of friends. She preferred a small group, people she could trust, though this had backfired somewhat now that she could never speak to Jane again. So there was no denying it—there was a gaping hole in her life, which had once held the people she loved most. Mike. Jane. Jacob. And her mum. Maybe, just maybe, it would be nice to make a new friend. But Polly was unpredictable and posh, and, for Annie, a silly project would have been like putting a plaster on a severed arm. So she forked up bits of her lunch—so sweet, so crunchy—and said she'd better get back. "Can I pay you…?"

"Don't be daft. I'll stay here for a bit," said Polly, swaddled in the blanket. "I bet there's some cool little shops."

"If you like fried chicken and stolen bikes," said Annie, but her heart wasn't really in the gibe, and she realized she did feel better. Refreshed, unlike when she sat at her desk with a sandwich in a plastic triangle from the corner shop.

On the way back to the office, she passed the receptionist, who recoiled. "Shit, are you okay? Are you sick or something?"

"No, why?"

"Because, like, you just sort of *smiled* at me."

Back at her desk, Annie unpacked Polly's box. She put the pretty stationery into the dusty desk-tidy, then on second thoughts wiped it down with her sleeve. God, it was filthy. She put the sparkly pens in a mug with Cotswolds Wildlife Park on it, where they'd taken Jacob on his first ever day out. His last, too, as it turned out. For months afterward she'd played it over in her mind. Had he caught a chill? Picked up an infection? She placed the plant beside her monitor, touching the thick green leaves. Hyacinth, bright pink. She'd grown ones just like it in her little garden. She wondered if Mike and Jane were looking after them now.

Sharon sniffed loudly, which was her way of getting Annie's attention without having to say her name. "You were late back from lunch. That's ten minutes."

Annie sighed. "I'll put it on my time sheet."

"And you should answer that message. I don't have time to be taking your personal calls all day."

"What message?"

"Left it on your desk. Some foreign woman rang."

Annie hunted around, eventually finding the scrap of paper

under the desk, alongside a sizable dust bunny. She shot Sharon a dirty look, but her colleague had gone back to her very important work (*Farm World*). She unfolded it, and for a moment a thrill of horror went through her. This was her fault. She'd taken a break, let herself feel all right for a moment. And now look. She shot up, fumbling for her bag.

"Where you going?" shouted Sharon. "You've got time to make up!"

Annie ignored her. She really couldn't care less about the time sheets right now.

It was nearly forty minutes before she reached the ward, panting and sweating into her nylon top. "My mum...she's taken a turn for the worse?"

"Who?" The receptionist didn't even look up.

"Maureen Clarke. Please, is she all right?"

"Hang on." She tapped at the keyboard while Annie's blood boiled. Why were all these women so unhelpful?

"Annie? Is that you?" She turned at the sound of the Scottish accent, to see Polly's neurologist. He looked as if he hadn't slept in days, his curly hair sticking up and his white shirt creased.

"I got a message, my mum..."

"Aye, she had us a wee bit worried there, but she's okay, don't take on so."

"What happened?" Annie's heart gradually slowed. "Why are you treating her—aren't you Neurology?"

"Polly asked if I'd take a look at her chart. Not really my area, of course, but I know a bit."

"Oh." Was Polly planning to infiltrate every area of Annie's life?

"Your mother was..." He sighed. "Well, she was a bit agitated. Thought we were keeping her in prison. Look, why don't you come with me. I want you to meet a colleague of mine."

Annie followed him down the corridor, which was painted the color of baby puke. She noticed people nod to him as they passed—orderlies, porters, cleaners. "Afternoon, Dr. Fraser. Hi, Max." And he nodded back, not breaking his stride. They'd reached a door now, and he swiped his pass over it.

"Mum's locked in?"

"For now. Annie, we thought she might hurt someone."

Her mother was in the bed, wearing just a hospital gown, shivering as if she was freezing cold, looking around the room with hunted eyes. Annie started to rush forward, then stopped, horrified. "She's chained up!"

"Och, Annie, it's just a standard restraint. I know it looks bad, but trust me, it's keeping her safe." Her mum's wrist, thin as a child's, was encased in a foam band attached to the bed. Worse, Annie could see from the way her mother's eyes skipped over her that once again she did not recognize her daughter, her only child. That, in this moment, Annie meant as much to her as the padded hospital bed and the yellow sharps bin and the beeping monitor she was hooked up to.

The door opened again and in came a tall man in a spotless white coat. "Who is this?" he said crossly. Annie couldn't place the accent. "Mrs. Clarke should be kept in isolation, I said."

"That's why she's bloody terrified." Annie felt angry tears in her eyes. "Please. Did you have to tie her up, like an animal?"

The man—she could now see he was frighteningly handsome, with smooth olive skin, slicked-back black hair and the kind of cheekbones models would kill for—raised an eyebrow. "Dr. Fraser? What's going on here?"

Dr. Fraser rubbed a hand over his tired face, making his bushy eyebrows stick up. "This is Mrs. Clarke's daughter, Sami. I thought you could explain some of the treatment options to her. Why don't we go into your office?"

Annie protested. "I can't leave my mum like this!"

"Dr. Fraser is right. Your presence is upsetting her. Please." The other doctor ushered them into a small side room. Annie caught a glimpse of her mother's terrified, confused eyes as the door shut behind them. *She doesn't know who I am. She doesn't know me.*

"Sit down, please." Dr. Handsome motioned to a plastic chair and Annie sat, broken by anger and sadness. "Miss Clarke…"

"It's Ms. Hebden." Why would he assume she wasn't married? Did she just have that look about her?

He frowned at the interruption. "Your mother is very ill. She had what we call a dissociative episode and threw a chair at one of the nursing staff. Luckily no one was hurt, but we can't take that risk again."

Stunned, Annie looked to Dr. Fraser for confirmation. He shrugged uncomfortably: it was true. "But…she's tiny."

"People can be very strong when in the grip of dementia. I'd like to take your mother onto my service. I'm the new consultant geriatrician here, Dr. Quarani. We need to talk about options."

Annie nodded dully. "Is there anything you can do?" She was staring hard at his desk, trying not to cry. On it was a framed photo of a beautiful woman with red lipstick and a headscarf, two young children hanging off her. A perfect family.

"There's a clinical trial. A new drug. It's been quite effective for certain forms of dementia."

Annie looked up. "It might help?"

"We believe it can slow the progress of the disease in early onset cases like your mother's, calm the patients down somewhat. It works by regenerating some of the neurons in the brain. You understand we can't reverse the damage that's already been done?"

Annie knew the disease had already done its work, twisting and tangling her mum's brain synapses, mixing up her memories like a drawer dumped out on the floor. "But you could maybe stop it going further?"

"Slow it, perhaps. But Ms. Hebden, there are side effects, as with all medications. It's experimental. Do you understand what I'm saying?"

"You can think about it if you want, Annie," said Dr. Fraser.

Dr. Quarani frowned again. "Mrs. Clarke should start the protocol as soon as possible. I want to move her to the geriatrics ward today. I'd like to keep her in for observation during the trial, so I can monitor the progress of the treatment."

Geriatrics. Annie's mum wasn't even sixty yet, and she was being lumped in with old people, the ones with no time and no hope. "If I say no, what will happen?"

"She'll have to vacate the bed in a few days and be released to your care. I would suggest you think about a care home."

And how much would that cost? Would she be able to find somewhere decent? Annie nodded dully. "I think—I think it sounds like a good idea. The trial. If you're sure."

Suddenly, he smiled, and Annie blinked. He was dazzling. "Thank you, Ms. Hebden. I'll find you an information pack. Please." He held open the door again and, rather stunned, Annie went through it. Her mother was lying there, small and quiet, only her eyes moving.

"Don't mind Sami," said Dr. Fraser, closing the door behind them. "He's a good man, even if his bedside manner is a bit...brusque. Just not used to the way British patients want your arm and your leg as well as everything else."

"Is it a good idea?"

"It's the only chance. Doesn't mean it'll work. But...she's not going to get better like this." They both turned to the woman on the bed, who stared at them as if she might be able to work out what was going on, if only she concentrated hard enough.

"You two…"

Annie waited.

"Are you my lawyers? Because I didn't do it, I'm sure. Whatever it was."

"No, Mum," Annie said wearily. "You aren't in prison. You didn't do anything wrong."

"But I think I did." She heaved in a big panicky breath that turned into a sob. "I just don't know what it *was*. Can you call Andrew, please? Call him to come and get me?"

"Mum…" Annie stopped herself. Not this again. "I'll call him. I promise."

"We can give her a shot," Dr. Fraser said gently. "Let her sleep for now, and you can have a think about what Sami said. If you have any questions, just ask me, okay? I'm a neurologist really, but there's a lot of crossover with Geriatrics, unfortunately."

"Thanks." Annie wanted to go to her mother, hug her or something, but she knew her skin would feel like ice, the pulse fluttering underneath it like a frightened bird. And it would be terrifying for her, to be hugged by a total stranger. "I better get back to work. I'm already in trouble."

"They'll understand, surely?"

"I wouldn't bet on it. Thank you, Dr. Fraser."

"Please, call me Max. Dr. Max, if you want."

"Okay. Thank you."

Going out, trailing back down the misery-colored corridor, she passed Polly. She was sitting on a gurney, chatting to a cleaner who was leaning on a mop, laughing. "Annie!" she cried, jumping down. "We have to stop meeting like this."

Annie swallowed her tears. "How come you're here again?"

"Well, basically the MRI machine is massively overstretched, so I sort of hang about most days and wait for a gap so I can have my scan." Polly must have seen her face. "Oh, Annie! Are you okay? Is it your mum? Come here, sit down."

Annie collapsed onto a waiting room chair, noticing the rip in the plastic covering. Spilling its guts, just like she felt. "She—she's having a bad day. Doesn't know who I am. She got very upset—they had to restrain her."

"I'm so sorry. That must be awful."

There was this woman, this virtual stranger with more than enough problems of her own, patting Annie's arm. As if she really cared. How did she manage that? Annie took in a bubbly breath. *There has to be more than this.* Something was clearly working for Polly, whatever it was. And she was too tired to fight now, too tired to hold out against the one corner of color and positivity in her life.

"That hundred-days idea?" she heard herself say. "I'll do it. I mean, if you want me to."

"Of course I do. We both have to keep coming here...we may as well try to enjoy it."

Annie couldn't even begin to imagine how she'd ever enjoy this—how she'd ever not hate every second of it. How she'd find anything at all to be happy about in her life. But as with the drugs trial, when there was no other option, you had to do something rather than nothing. "Okay," she said. "I'm in. Just as long as I don't have to swim with dolphins."

"You don't want to swim with dolphins?"

Annie shuddered. "I can't think of anything worse."

"But dolphins! Everyone loves them."

"I don't. They always look like they're planning something. Nothing that smiles that much can be trusted."

Polly burst out laughing. "Oh, Annie, you're hilarious. I promise, not a sea creature in sight. Why don't you come over to mine on Saturday—we can compare our lists for the week, okay?"

It was years since Annie had been around to someone's house. Since she'd made a new friend, or socialized at all. The idea was terrifying. But she made herself say, "Okay. I'll be there."

DAY 5

Get active

Annie stood over her chest of drawers, holding the swimsuit she'd unearthed. Tastefully substantial, in black-and-white stripes, she'd bought it for a holiday in Greece with Mike. It was supposed to be their last just the two of them, and in a way it had been—they'd never gone on holiday together again, and now never would. She held it to her briefly. The smell of salt and sun cream lingered in the fabric, reminding her of when she'd been happy. Turquoise seas and the whisper of the ceiling fan and waking to squares of sunlight on the wooden floor.

It would have been so easy to put it back, give up on the cold public pool with its grubby changing rooms, but she wanted to have something to tell Polly the next day. And so she packed the suit into a bag, along with a towel and an old-lady swim cap covered in plastic flowers. And when she blundered into the pool at lunchtime, she found herself smiling at an over-sixties water aerobics club attired in similar headgear, and they waved at her, and she waved back shyly, wondering if she might be able to take her mother to something like that one day, if the trial worked. Realizing that without her even knowing it, hope had somehow lodged itself in her heart again after years of being AWOL.

DAY 6
Celebrate your body

"Oh, God! Sorry, Annie, I forgot you were coming."

Annie blinked at Polly, who was standing in the doorway of the beautiful three-story house she'd said to come around to. Her jaw fell open. "Um, should I go?"

"No, no, come on through. I'm really sorry. It's just Bob, you see. Makes me forgetful."

Annie stared at the floor, which was tiled in a blue-and-white mosaic. Did Polly realize? Maybe this was a symptom of the cancer. "Um, are your family in?" She knew this was Polly's parents' house, though not why Polly was living there.

"No, they're all out."

Thank God for that. "Um, Polly…"

"Do you want tea or something?"

"Thanks, but did you—?"

Polly spun, her bare feet padding on the tiles. "Did I what?"

"You're, uh…" Annie could only gesture.

Polly looked down. "Oh. I totally forgot! Ha-ha. I bet the neighbors got an eyeful." So even though she realized she was entirely naked, she wasn't planning to put any clothes on. Annie felt her shoulder blades constrict.

But when they went through into the kitchen, she realized what was going on, as an older woman with glowing
white hair was there holding a camera. "I'm having my picture drawn," explained Polly. "In the buff. Just something I
always wanted, and I'm never going to look any better than
this." As it was she was marked all over by her treatment,
bruises like inky fingerprints crawling up her legs and arms.
She was so thin, too, every vein and bone standing out under
skin stretched paper-thin.

Annie had been ushered into a large light-filled room, half
conservatory and half kitchen, a glimpse of the Thames visible from the large back garden. An ache began to take hold
of her heart. This was her dream kitchen, the one she'd read
about in design magazines, where she'd pictured her children
running barefoot, stealing fruit from the bowl, bringing her
their drawings, their bumps to kiss better. Now she would
never have that.

"We're finished, dear, if you want to put your clothes on,"
said the artist, who Polly introduced as Theresa.

"Seems a shame. It's really quite freeing." Polly spread her
arms, making her breasts jiggle. Annie averted her eyes. "Hey,
Annie, you should get one done, too. My treat."

"What?"

"Get a picture. Since Theresa's here and all. She works
from photographs, see." Theresa was nodding encouragingly.

"I really don't think—"

"Come on, Annie! To cross the ocean, you need to lose
sight of the shore! Do something every day that scares you!"

Oh, God, these inspirational sayings were going to be the
end of her. "No. Sorry. I really can't." Annie could hear the
anxiety in her own voice, which surely was a bit pathetic when
Polly was actually dying? When she'd had needles poked into
her spine, cameras peering inside her, a probe in her brain

even, how could Annie get upset by the idea of taking her clothes off in front of people?

"Oh, come on," Polly coaxed. "What's the worst that could happen?"

"I just can't," she said again. "I'm sorry." It was years since she'd undressed in front of anyone. Even at the hospital they were tactful about it, left you behind a screen when you had your examinations, waited for you to cover yourself with a blanket. They were good about discretion there—tissues and slipping away as you wept, inconsolable, in the dingy little rooms where your heart had broken.

Polly's face fell. "All right. But will you look at the photos with me? I'm kind of nervous."

"Of course I will." Polly had her shoulders slightly bowed in the pictures, as if she was trying to protect her body, when it had been through so much. You could see it all—the bruises, the scar from the cannula on her hand, the bags under her eyes.

Polly's voice thickened. "I just—I wish I'd had this done years ago, you know? I always wanted to, and I was healthy then, and I was—oh, crap, I was hot. I can say that because I have cancer. I was a hot babe, and all I did was moan about my cellulite and thread veins and talk about getting Botox. I used to spend three hundred pounds on face cream! What was I thinking? I should have taken a naked picture every single day. I should have covered my house in them and walked down the street in the buff." She sniffed. "Oh, bollocks. This is it, isn't it? Even this is as good as I'm ever going to look again. I'm only going to get worse and then I'm going to die."

Annie looked at Theresa in alarm at Polly's sudden mood swing, but the artist was placidly packing up her photography equipment. She looked down at own body, hidden under her baggy jumper, and bit her lip as fierce tears unexpectedly burned her nose. No, she wasn't going to cry, over her own saggy stomach and barrel thighs, her yellowing toenails and cracked feet, which hadn't seen a pedicure since her wedding day. Polly's body had let her down in the worst possible way—the least Annie could do was not hate her own healthy one. She pushed back her (lank, greasy) hair. "All right, then. Maybe just a few pictures."

"Lovely. Could you push your chest forward more? Shame to hide those fantastic bosoms!"

Annie blushed and shuffled forward. Somehow, for some mad reason (Polly), she was lying on a blanket-draped couch in a "draw me like one of your French girls" pose, totally naked. Everything was on display, from her unwaxed pubic hair to the ridges her socks had left around her ankles. Only instead of Leonardo DiCaprio on board the *Titanic*, she was being photographed by a seventy-year-old lady.

To Theresa she said, "Is there any way you could, uh...this scar? Sort of hide it?"

"I like to draw people exactly as they are, Annie," Theresa said gently. "Trust me. No airbrushing here. What was it, a cesarean?"

"Um, yeah." She avoided Polly's eyes. "I wish I'd had time to go on a massive diet first," she said hurriedly.

"You look great, silly," said Polly. "Like a painting by Rubens. Voluptuous."

"Who?"

"You know, the painter...in the National Gallery? Never mind. I'll take you sometime."

Annie blushed again. She was so clueless. "Isn't *voluptuous* just another word for *fat*?"

"I'd rather look like you than me," Polly said, extending a bony leg.

Annie tried, "But you look great. You're so slim."

Polly burst into laughter. "Oh, Annie. For God's sake. I'm slim because I have cancer. I'm dying. Hey, does my tumor look big in this?"

"Sorry, sorry." Annie sighed, knowing she'd messed up.

"Nurse! Is this chemo low-cal? Toxic chemicals are soooo fattening!" Polly twirled around the room, high-kicking her thin, bruise-marked legs.

Theresa was peacefully snapping away. "Is this your first experience of cancer, dear?" she said to Annie.

"Er, yes."

"Then don't worry. It's normal, this kind of up and down. It's all the emotions, you see, hitting her at once like a wave. Trying to live your hardest at the same time you're dying. The old rules don't apply anymore. You just have to strap in for the ride."

DAY 7
Spend time with family

Bing-a-ling-a-ling.

Even the doorbell was upbeat. Annie stood once again on the doorstep of Polly's parents' house, nervously wiping her hands on her jeans. She'd spent ages choosing a bottle of wine, bewildered by the choice in Sainsbury's. Rioja. Sauvignon. Chablis. In the end she went for one at eight pounds, thinking it had to be decent at that price.

She wasn't sure why she'd said yes to Polly's casual invite, intended to "make up" for the surprise of all the nudity: "Come around for Sunday lunch tomorrow. Mum and Dad like to make a big thing of it." Manners, probably. Or the idea of spending yet another Sunday alone. They were always the hardest—the day when she and Mike used to go to the pub for lunch, or take Jacob to the park.

The door was opened by a young man with dark-rimmed glasses and a scowl. "Yes? You're not one of Mum's God-botherers, are you?"

"No, I'm, um, Polly's friend?" It felt presumptuous to say the word.

"Oh. Shall I take that?" He examined the bottle, holding it away from him. "Hmm. Okay."

"Is that Annie?" A woman in a purple wrap dress came out into the hallway. Chic and slim, with bobbed gray hair and glasses on a jeweled chain, which she put on to peer at Annie. "Darling. We're so glad Poll has a new friend. You *are* brave."

Annie didn't like the sound of that. She wasn't up for anything brave. Polly's mother looked at the wine, too. "How lovely! My favorite."

"Chardonnay?" the young man said doubtfully. "Really?"

"Shh, now. There was a piece in the *Obs* food just last week about how it's coming back in."

Annie looked between them. Had she brought the wrong thing?

"I'm Valerie, darling, and this naughty boy is George, my son. Georgie, get Annie a drink. We have a Sancerre, or a Malbec, or we could even scare up some Riesling, I imagine?"

Annie had no idea what those things were. "Um, whatever's open, thanks." Valerie led her in—she smelled of some exotic musky perfume that made Annie think of orange groves and desert moons. Her own mother had always smelled of cooking and Hall's soothers. Now she just smelled of the hospital.

"You mustn't mind George," Valerie whispered in her ear. "He's very protective. This nasty business has brought all manner of people out of the woodwork. Grief tourists, you know. It's horrible, the way they want to gawp at Polly being ill." Did they think she was a grief tourist, too? Annie looked behind her at the door—if only she'd changed her mind and not come, after all. This was going to be a disaster; she could just feel it.

Polly was perched on the arm of the pink Indian-print sofa, talking to an older man in a navy jumper and slacks.

"You see, the problem with the euro is…" He had a booming voice and was sloshing back a giant glass of red wine.

Polly saw Annie and jumped up. She was in dungarees, her hair tied back with a red scarf. Annie felt drab in her jeans and hoodie. "Annie! Thank God you've come to rescue me from this hellish discussion of finance. I don't care, Dad! I didn't care even when I was going to be around to see the consequences."

Annie tensed, but Polly's father just tutted, as if she'd made an off-color joke. "Like it or not, Poll, the outcome of the referendum has a lot more impact on the future than what type of shoes you're going to wear."

"But the shoes bring me joy. And other people joy." She waved one foot, which was shod in an embroidered teal slipper, its gold thread winking in the sun. Annie hunched down slightly to hide her own scuffed Converses.

"Roger Leonard," the man boomed, crushing Annie's hand. "What about you, Annie, do you have any burning thoughts on the state of the EU, or indeed on my daughter's footwear?"

"I like the shoes," she ventured.

"Another one." Roger knocked back more wine. "I gather you met Polly at the hospital?"

"They are wonderful there," said Valerie, who was stirring something on the stove. "When P was first poorly we thought we'd have to go private. We were all ready to chuck money at it, weren't we, darling! But she said no, she'd tough it out on the NHS. Little trooper. And they have been *marvelous*."

Annie nodded along. Did they realize some people had no other option than to "tough it out"? She'd no idea how she was going to pay for a care home when her mother came out of the hospital.

Polly sat down at the table, tipping her chair so it wobbled on three legs. "Especially Dr. McGrumpy. Mum *loves* him."

"He is terribly dishy. That accent."

"He looks like someone wearing a Chewbacca costume."

Valerie said, "Oh P, you do exaggerate. He's just *manly* is all."

Annie quite liked the way Dr. Max was hairy. It made him seem cuddly, like a giant friendly bear. As they sat down, she wondered again about Polly's domestic situation. Why did she live with her parents, and had she ever been married? Did she have a boyfriend or anything? Annie imagined that terminal cancer was a bit of a barrier to dating.

"Here we are," Valerie said, setting down a steaming terra-cotta dish.

George groaned. "Dear God, Ma, not couscous again? You know I'm on a low-carb diet."

"Bad enough your sister's got so thin, without you wasting away, too."

"I'd love to waste away. I'm well jel of how skinny she is. I'll just have the chicken."

So that's what it was. Annie was struggling to identify the contents of the food, a sort of yellow stew with a strong spicy smell. She let Roger slop some onto her plate. "Valerie does love her Moroccan."

She prodded about in the mix, trying to find something edible. That was a tomato, she thought. Tentatively, she put it in her mouth, only to turn red and let out a small yelp. Not a tomato.

George was smirking. "Mum likes to load her tagines up with Calabrian chilies. Be careful."

"Get her some water, Georgie," said Valerie. Annie gulped it down, feeling embarrassed. Everyone else was perfectly at home, eating the red-hot stew, drinking wines with different complicated names, discussing stories from that day's papers. She tried to piece together what they all did. George, she gathered, was an aspiring actor who enjoyed trashing all the stars in accompanying magazines. "Look how bald he is. She's had Botox." Roger, it seemed, worked in the city, and Valerie had been the head of a girls' school and was now retired. The table was covered in papers and magazines, even academic journals with titles such as *Advances in Oncology*. As they ate, they bandied about medical jargon.

"We really think P would benefit from alternative therapies," Valerie said, eating daintily. "There's a lot of studies now about acupuncture, and Chinese herbs seem to be quite effective. I'm going to a talk on homeopathy next week, too."

George groaned loudly. "Please, Mum."

"What? There's plenty of evidence about the power of positive thinking. What harm can it do to try things?"

"McGrumpy says it's all hokum." Polly had once again only taken a few bites of her food.

"Yes, well, it's not in the hospital's interests to fund non-medical therapies, but we think there's every chance. Don't we, Roger darling?"

George rolled his eyes. Roger had his eyes on his food and just said, "She's a trooper, aren't you, P? She's going to fight this thing."

Annie was puzzled—Dr. Max had told her there was no hope for Polly. She had nothing to add to the discussion, so she ate around the chilies in her food, and felt boring. Why had Polly even asked her? She could have been in bed, watching a boxset of *Grey's Anatomy* while listening to Costas talk loudly in the next room. He always rang his mum on Sundays. She was suddenly shot through with a longing to do the same. Just to have her mother know who she was, discuss her life, dissect the week's soap operas. Such a little thing to ask for.

George pushed his plate away. "Right, I'm off."

"Where to, George?" Polly asked innocently.

He shot her a look that Annie didn't understand. "The gym."

"Oh, yes, anyone special going to be there?"

George said, "Hey, Poll, speaking of special—are you ever going to call Tom back? He's been texting me again asking about you."

Who was Tom? Valerie and Roger exchanged a quick panicked look, but Polly ignored the comment, toying with her tagine. "Have fun with all those bench presses, bro."

Valerie wailed, "But you haven't had pudding! I made clafouti!"

"Um, no carbs and no sugar, remember?"

"But, Georgie—"

"Not now, Ma. I'll be late." He pulled on a leather jacket. "Will we be seeing Annie again?"

Annie blushed. Polly said, "Don't be so bloody rude, G. She can hear you."

Roger ignored this tension, sloshing more wine into Annie's glass before she had time to say no. She'd hardly been able to eat any of her food—she'd be drunk at this rate. Valerie was staring ahead of her, eyes suddenly blank.

"All right, Mum?" said Polly.

"I think I'll go for a little nap, darling." She fixed Annie with a bright smile. "I'm so lucky having both my children at home with me! Are you close to your parents, Annie?"

"My mum's not too well just now. She's in the hospital."

"I'm sorry to hear that. What about your father?"

Annie could feel Polly's eyes on her. "Well, he's—he's not really in the picture."

"Oh, what a shame." Valerie looked vague again. "Perhaps you'd get the dishes, Roger darling. I think I'll just..."

"Hmm?" Roger was looking at his phone, peering over his glasses. It vibrated suddenly, making everyone jump.

Valerie's voice soared and broke. "I do wish you'd put that thing away. It's family time. *Family*, Roger." She stood up, scraping her chair. "You can clear up. I'm going to lie down."

Polly stood up, too, scraping out a slice of clafouti, which turned out to be a sort of custardy pie. "Come on. I'll show you the garden, Annie." Annie trailed out after her, aware of some undercurrent of tension and with a vague niggling worry it might be something to do with her.

"Sorry about George. He's gunning for an Oscar in the role of Most Bitchy Brother, I think."

"That's okay." Annie was still trying to take in the garden. She could have fitted her entire flat into it twice over. It meandered down the hill, full of green nooks and wrought iron furniture, fruit trees and little statues. "Did you grow up here, then?"

Polly looked around, disinterested. "Yeah. Didn't expect to find myself back living here at thirty-five, though. I guess you grew up not far away?"

Only two miles or so. But worlds apart. "Is that the Shard?" She could see the wedge-shaped skyscraper soaring through the gap in the trees, across the wide gray ribbon of the Thames. Annie had a sudden stab of jealousy again. Imagine if she'd grown up here, with this garden, with the shops and cafés of Greenwich just around the corner, instead of on her Lewisham council estate, doing her best not to get pregnant before she left school.

"We should go up it," Polly said, taking a running jump and leaping onto an old wooden swing that was tied to the branch of the apple tree. It looked like a photo shoot, her carefully chosen outfit, the disheveled garden behind and the view of the city across the river. Something Instagram-worthy, a picture of a perfect life.

"What, the Shard?"

"I have some tickets I bought a while back for me and George and his boyfriend and…anyway, he split up with his boyfriend, thank God, because Caleb's awful, so we never used them. Fancy it? Another happy thing? Bring your flat-mate, too."

"Costas?" She got enough of him singing Mariah Carey in the bathroom and melting cheese all over everything. "I suppose I could see if he's free."

"George thinks it's tacky." She smiled. "Annoying my brother is another thing that makes me happy, I have to say. Do you have any brothers or sisters, Annie?"

"Not that I know of," she said. She might have any number of half siblings, of course.

"Oh, right, you said your dad wasn't about. Where is he?"

"I've no idea. As far as I know he buggered off when I was two days old. Couldn't handle it, the whole family thing." Leaving Maureen Clarke, twenty-four and broke, alone with a new baby in a drab council flat. Stunned, lonely, wondering what happened to her life. It was all so different from this family, with Polly's successful father and stylish mother, her confident clever brother, this beautiful house, like a sagging-down wedding cake, the garden full of fruit trees.

"That's rough."

"Not really. You can't miss what you never had, after all. I hardly think about him."

Polly gave her another irritating inspirational look. "Life's too short for regrets, Annie. Maybe you should try to find him?"

"I did the happy-days stuff," Annie said, changing the subject firmly. "I wrote down some things, anyway." Swimming, walking, visiting her mum—it didn't seem a lot. "How's yours going?"

Polly didn't answer, and Annie saw she'd stopped swinging, her face pale. "Are you okay?"

"It's just… Oh, crap. I shouldn't have had that pudding." And she lurched forward onto her knees and threw up on the grass with a retching sound.

Annie ran to her. "Polly! Are you all right?"

Polly sat up, shaky, wiping her mouth. "It's just Bob. It happens all the time. Sorry you had to see."

Annie helped her up, feeling how hard Polly was trembling. "Why don't you go and lie down? I'll see myself off." It was easy to forget how ill Polly was, but underneath all this cheer there was no escaping the fact that the tumor was gnawing away at her, a little bit every day.

DAY 8
Walk to work

No. No, please. He can't be. He can't be—

Annie sat up in bed, panting, her body clammy with cold sweat. It was the dream again. That morning, back in the old house. The slice of sunlight across the floor. The brief second of happiness before it all shattered, Mike's footsteps in the hallway, and then his terrified voice shouting for her. *Annie! Annie, call an ambulance!*

But it was just a dream. It wasn't real, it wasn't now. She got her breathing under control, slowly bringing herself back to the world. Monday morning. She was sorely tempted to roll over and go back to sleep, but she dragged herself up, listening carefully at the door to make sure Costas was out. It was irrational, but bumping into him in her pajamas could make her want to explode with rage. She'd once had her own lovely home with its spare room and window seat and garden full of flowers, and now here she was flat-sharing again. She washed in the moldy shower, brushed her teeth in front of the toothpaste-stained mirror and got dressed in her usual black attire. The dream still clung to her like cobwebs, an under note of panic in her breathing that she knew made no sense. It was years ago. It was far, far too late for panic.

Since she was up early, Annie set out to walk to work. At the last moment, feeling how cold it was when she opened the front door, she almost balked. But she thought of the packed bus, and remembered that she'd have to have something to write down in her notebook. So she went. One foot in front of the other, walking away the past, step by step, until her breath came quicker because of the exercise rather than the dream, and her head had cleared. The walk was perhaps not the most beautiful in the world, but the morning sun was pink on the concrete, and when she arrived at the office she was slightly puffed and glowing. She was even early, since she hadn't been stuck in traffic on the bus. Sharon helpfully commented that her face looked "all red and sweaty," but Annie barely even cared.

DAY 9
Write down your thoughts

Annie sucked the end of her pen as she regarded the blank page of her notebook. On the other side of her bedroom wall, she could hear Costas talking on the phone in loud Greek. Another person who could just ring their mother up for a chat whenever they felt like it, without worrying whether said mother would know who they were or not. She tried to block out the noise.

So far, in just over a week, she'd made a new friend—or a new whatever Polly was. She'd got naked in front of people for the first time in two years. She'd exercised. She'd taken a lunch break. It wasn't much in the scheme of things—no dancing in the rain or trekking the Inca Trail—but it was more than she'd done in a long, long time. But what could she put for today, and tomorrow, and the next day? Hearing a loud clattering noise from the kitchen, she opened her bedroom door to find Costas washing up, clanking and splashing.

"Annie, hello, I do the washing like you ask."

"Great. Thanks. Um…" She could have asked him not to spill water everywhere, but instead she said, "Listen, do you want to come up the Shard with me?"

"The big building?"

"Yeah. My friend has some tickets. There's a nice view or something."

"I would love to, Annie! Thank you! Thank you so much!"

"It's not that exciting," she muttered, withdrawing to her room again. She'd broken the precedent of chatting to him now, so she'd have to stay in there all night unless she wanted to hear all about his mother's ear syringing and his cousin Andre's goat business in Faliraki. But at least she had asked, and that made her feel just marginally like a slightly nicer person. Perhaps that would do as a happy thing for today.

DAY 10
Make tea for your office

"Did you put sugar in it?" Sharon sniffed suspiciously at the cup Annie had offered her.

"Two sugars. Is that right?"

"I only have one now. I'm on a diet."

"Right...the sheet in the kitchen still says two."

"Fine, I suppose I'll drink it."

Annie didn't rise. She passed a coffee to Syed, their hipster social media officer, who was wearing a cricket jumper and yellow cords. He removed his large headphones and she heard banging music leak out. "Wicked, thanks, Annie." Thumbs-up.

"Green tea for you, Fee." Annie sat the cup on the office manager's desk, and she looked up with a start.

"Oh! Thank you."

Fee didn't look good, Annie realized (though she knew this thought was somewhat hypocritical). Her lips were chapped and her hands shook as she lifted the cup.

"Um, everything okay?" Annie hoped it was so they wouldn't have to have an uncomfortable conversation about emotions. In this office it was okay to talk about TV, beverages and the failures of the IT system, and nothing much else.

"Oh! Yes, yes. All fine. Totally fine."

Annie took a seat at her own desk, with the mug Polly had bought her. Unlike the other office ones it wasn't yet irreparably stained with tannin. She tipped a little water onto her narcissus plant, and ran a finger along her computer stand. No dust. And although she was still stuck in the office and hating pretty much every second, she found that with a clean desk and not feeling like quite so much of an antisocial troll, she hated it just a tiny fraction less.

DAY 11
Give someone flowers

"Aren't they pretty! Peacocks!"

"Peonies, Mum," Annie said gently. "Do you like them?"

"They're ever so nice, dear." Annie felt a lump rise in her throat. Her mother had always loved flowers, scrimping to buy a bunch from the market on payday. When Annie used to bring Jacob around to visit, every Friday, she'd always taken a big bunch of flowers, too, grown in her own garden. She hadn't done that for a long time.

Her mother spotted Dr. Quarani coming across the ward, crisp and clean in his white coat. "Look, Doctor. This nice lady has brought me some peacocks."

He didn't smile. "I need to take your pulse, Mrs. Clarke."

"She seems a little better," Annie ventured as he stood with her mother's thin wrist in his hand. "Calmer, anyway."

"Her mood was stabilized somewhat, yes. As I said, it's important not to get your hopes up."

"I won't." And yet despite this warning, despite herself, despite two years of misery having stamped on them in steel-capped boots, Annie could feel that her hopes were ever-so-slightly up. Like a drooping flower when you put it in water. She had to be careful with that. She knew only too well that hope was not to be trusted.

"Annie!" On her way out of the hospital, she turned at the sound of her name. A man's voice.

"Oh! What are you…? Are you all right?"

It was Polly's brother, George. Sitting in the ER holding a bandage to his face. He grimaced. "It's nothing. Banged my head at the gym. What are you doing here?"

"I'm seeing my mum. You know, she's been ill." She stared at him. There was a spot of blood on his white shirt.

He stared back, coolly appraising, taking in her cheap scuffed bag, her straggling hair, the polyester slacks that were making her sweat. "Listen, Annie. My sister's very sick."

"I know that."

"And she's also kind of…magnetic. She collects people. Waifs and strays." Annie bristled. "She was always like that, but now she's sick it's even worse. They sort of latch on. She thinks she may as well give away everything she has, since she has 'three months to live.'" He scowled. "We don't know that, okay? People live for years sometimes with cancer."

Annie was so tired. Tired of this hospital, tired of her mother not knowing her, tired of her pokey little flat and tired of her life. "Look. I didn't 'latch on' to Polly. She was the one who literally turned up on my doorstep. But she was nice to me, and she asked me to help with her happy-days project, and—well, I don't see how I can say no. Okay?"

He nodded slowly. "Okay. I believe you."

"I wasn't asking if you believed me. Who would try to con a woman with cancer, for God's sake?"

"I'd have said that, too, before all this. Honestly, Annie, we've had to stop her giving her money away so many times. She just doesn't believe people lie. Even her friends—this girl she was at school with tried to get her to invest in a jewelry business, which basically doesn't exist, and one of our cousins wants funding for a charity that is pretty much just them going on safari in Africa, and God, people really *suck*, you know?"

"You don't have to tell me that," said Annie.

"All right. Well, I'm sorry if I was a bit—"

"Rude? Unwelcoming?" She was too tired to be polite anymore.

To her surprise George smiled. "I was going for 'icily enraged,' like an offended Southern belle. I should have thrown a drink in your face." He moved the bandage, gingerly. His left eye was purple with bruising.

Annie winced in sympathy. "That looks sore."

"It's okay. It'll mean no auditions for a while, though. Not that I'm exactly inundated." He glanced up at her. "Listen. Would you please not mention this to my sister? I don't want her worried. I just had a stupid accident."

Annie shrugged. "Sure."

"Thank you. I'm sorry I was a twat. I'm just so angry, you know? Like all the time. I should be sad and supportive and all I can feel is totally and utterly enraged that this happened to Poll."

"I understand," said Annie, who knew that feeling well.

"I'm really sorry. I'll see you for this supertacky trip up the Shard?"

"I guess so. Well, bye, then." She stopped in the doorway. "Cucumber slices," she called.

"What?" George had his eyes closed.

"It helps with the swelling. Freeze them, then put them on the eye. Just a tip." Something you discovered when you spent most of your time crying.

At the bus stop, the homeless man—Jonny—was there again, reading a paperback with the cover missing. Annie waved at him, tentatively, feeling embarrassed when he smiled back. His teeth were terrible. What was the point in waving if she couldn't do anything to help him? The bus came and she got on it, feeling vaguely that she had failed, but not quite knowing why.

DAY 12
Tidy up

She was naked. Every bit of her on show, stripped down, displayed for all the world to see.

Annie sat on her sofa, a cup of tea cooling in front of her. Her nude drawing was propped up on the chair, brown paper wrapping hanging about it like the folds of a dressing gown. It had been waiting for her when she came home.

For a long time, she just stared at it. It was her, unmistakably her—the scar on her stomach, the mole on her shoulder—but at the same time it wasn't. Somehow, the curves and folds of her body, which caused her such angry tears when she looked in the mirror, had been transformed into something different.

This was her, Annie Hebden, ex-wife of Mike, ex-friend of Jane, mother of Jacob. She could never stop being that. Daughter of Maureen—something else she would always be, no matter how far into the darkness her mother disappeared. There was no one like her on the whole of the planet, no one who had ever lived or ever would. There was not a single other person with her fingerprints, with her memories, with the blood beating in her veins. She was herself, and she was alive right now, despite everything. This picture proved it.

Annie got to her feet, restless. What could she do? She'd let her friends drift away, turned down offers from colleagues, stopped going out, and gardening, and making her home nice, and even washing her hair. She stayed in every night with TV and sugar for company. It was time to stop. In fact, it was time to start.

In a burst of activity, she tore the ratty blanket from the sofa, exposing the ripped pleather underneath. A shower of pistachio shells clattered out. *Bloody Costas.* Next the sofa covers, then the shabby rug on the floor. All of them dusted in crumbs, splashed in ketchup and tea. She bundled them into the washing machine and set it going. It occurred to her this was a small, happy thing—the sound of clothes spinning, getting clean. It reminded her of Mondays after school, when she'd come home to find the machine whirring and her mother watching *Countdown* with a cup of tea and packet of orange Club bars. And they'd sit together, working out answers on the back of the *Radio Times.* Her mother, who loved word puzzles, had always beaten her hands down, calling up words from the depths of her memory. *Adamant. Vivacious.* These days, she often couldn't remember her own name.

Trying to stay one step ahead of grief, Annie flung open her fridge and larder, blitzing the out-of-date food, the peppers with mold sprouting on them like hipster beards, the ready meals that were iced into the freezer, the packets of pasta and rice spilling all over the shelves. Soon she'd filled a huge bin bag. She started making a list. *Wash windows. Re-cover sofa.* She took all the cups out of the cupboards and scoured the insides clean. Polly was right: her taste in crockery was truly abysmal. She filled another bin bag for the charity shop, putting everything in except her mum's nice china. She added to the list: *Buy new spoons. Get a spiralizer. Ask landlord to have walls painted in color that doesn't look like dog poop.*

Next, the bathroom. She looked with distaste at the old moldy shower curtain. She'd buy a new one, in cheery colors, that didn't wrap around your legs like a slimy alien ghost. She'd get a new bath mat and some nice towels. She threw out dried-up lipsticks, flaky mascara, bottles of shower gel with only an inch of scum in the bottom. God, it was moldy. How had she let things get this bad?

By the time Costas came back off his late shift, he could barely open the door because of the pile of bin bags blocking it. He looked around, confused, and cocked his head at Annie singing along to Magic FM as she scrubbed the hob. "Annie! Is this because I leave cheese on the dish? Because I promise, I wash! I wash them good! Do not kick me out, please?"

Annie burst out laughing. "Oh, bless you, no, I'm not throwing you out. I'm throwing *myself* out. Or at least, some of the mankier bits of me."

Costas looked puzzled.

"I'm sorry it hasn't been nicer for you here," she said. "I promise, from now on, I'll make this a better place for both of us to live. I mean, we could both do that. Keep it a bit tidier? What do you say? Not so many pistachio shells in the sofa? Grease the dishes before you bake cheese in them?"

He knit his brows, frowning. "Annie? You are feeling okay?"

She considered it. She hadn't cried in the shower for almost two weeks. Her flat was cleaner than it had been when she moved in. Her mum was getting better. And she had actual social events, with actual people, in her diary. "Actually, Costas, you know what? I'm not too bad. Not too bad at all."

DAY 13
Take a higher view

"He's delicious," Polly said, peering at Costas's bum as he read the display on the wall. "Tastier than a whole box of baklava."

"He's twenty-two," Annie whispered reprovingly. She wished Polly would lower her voice. "Also, pretty sure he's gay." He'd never actually told her this, but the fact he went all-night clubbing in Vauxhall three nights a week was a fairly strong indicator.

Polly sighed. "I should have known. Nobody straight has eyebrows that neat. Ah, well. Maybe George and he will hit it off."

Annie doubted it—George hadn't addressed a word to him since he mentioned what he did for a living. She'd seen him wrinkle his nose as Costas enthused about all the different drinks he could make. "Latte, skinny latte, flat white, not-flat white…"

"How long is this going to take?" George complained now. "We've been waiting for, like, an hour already."

"We've been waiting for ten minutes," Polly scolded. "And it'll be worth it."

"I can't believe you're making me a do a tacky tourist thing. What next, Madame Tussaud's? The zoo?"

"The zoo is a great idea! Let's do that next week. I could even adopt an animal, name it after me. Something to live on when I'm gone. Unless it's a mayfly, I guess."

Costas was staring around him, rapt. "In Greece we have nothing this big. We lost all our money instead and set fire to our capital." He said it cheerily.

"That's the spirit, Costas," Polly said, rubbing his shoulder. Annie tensed. She really had no sense of personal space. "It's a modern marvel. You can see all the way to Kent on a good day."

"The question of why we'd want to see Kent remains unanswered," George muttered. The bruise on his eye was still livid, but he'd shaken off Annie's attempts to ask about it.

They were now in the lift, alongside a tubby family in tracksuits, who all gawped at Polly's choice of ensemble—a red ruffled skirt showing her long frail legs, a pink sparkly cowboy hat, such as might be worn by drunken hen-do attendees, and a jacket made of purple sharkskin. Annie would have looked like a clown in it, but Polly was drawing admiring stares along with the puzzled ones. "Isn't she that one off that telly thing?" Annie heard one of the Tracksuit Family hiss.

"Going up high has always inspired people," Polly declared. "Look at Wordsworth. Coleridge. They used to wander in the Lake District, high on nature, spitting out poetry."

"High on opium more like," said George. "Is there any of that up here?"

The lift stopped, and they got out into a wide expanse of glass, filled with people milling around. Annie blinked as light flooded her eyes, London spread out beneath them. Like a Lego town, with green patches and boxes of buildings and houses and little cars meandering along. A real-life Mo-nopoly board.

Polly had barged her way to the concession stand. "No opium, but pink champagne all around!"

George tutted. "Cheap pink fizz? Are you serious?"

But Polly was already carrying a tray of four glasses. "Shut up, George. You're the most god-awful snob, you know. I remember when your favorite food was spaghetti hoops. Just drink it."

"As long as no one finds out," he said. "Is Costas even old enough to drink?"

"I am twenty-two," Costas said reproachfully. "Thank you, Polly. This is very kind of you. Thank you for the pink cham-pagne and the trip in the big lift and the view of your lovely city."

"You're very welcome," she replied, once again patting him. "It's nice to be here with someone who isn't a snobby misery-guts, frankly."

"Pink fizz up the Shard," muttered George, who was none-theless tossing his back. "What next? You want to go around M&M'S World wearing a Union Jack hat?"

"There is a world of M&M'S?" Costas took a sip and sneezed.

Polly ruffled his hair. "Adorable."

Annie reached for her drink, tentatively. It was a plastic flute, filled with bubbling liquid, the color of old pinky-gold. She'd seen a dress that shade once, in a ball gown shop, when shopping for her school prom. It was expensive—a hundred pounds, nearly—but she'd saved up from her Saturday job in Boots and dropped loads of hints, and her mum had been giving her lots of coy smiles and it was her birthday coming up, so on the morning she turned eighteen Annie had rushed downstairs to find a dress bag hanging over the door. It had to be it. The dream dress, lace and silk, with a long swishy skirt and a bodice that somehow held in Annie's wobbly bits and made her chest look like a glamour model's.

When she'd opened it, she'd thought it was a joke. "What's this, Mum?"

"Oh, I went to see that dress you wanted, but it was far too expensive, so I made you this one on the sewing machine. It's exactly the same."

It wasn't the same at all. It was the color of gone-off salmon, and the lace wasn't lace at all but scratchy polyester, and the bodice had boning that stuck into Annie's ribs, and she looked like a giant blancmange in it, and in the end she'd gone home early from the prom and watched *Frasier* instead. Another not-so-happy memory. But now here she was, drinking champagne up the Shard. She lifted her plastic flute to Polly's. "Cheers."

"Cheers." Polly took a gulp. "Dr. Max will kill me. I'm not supposed to drink before my MRIs. I spend so much time in that machine I'm thinking of having it wallpapered. Come on, let's go up to the outside deck."

Outside, the wind was stronger, the sun dazzling in Annie's eyes. Deciding now was not a good time to mention her mild vertigo, she stayed as close to the wall as possible, while Polly spun off toward the railing, pointing out landmarks below. "Somerset House! The London Eye! Big Ben!"

"British Museum," Costas said happily. "Where you are keeping all the priceless statues you stole from my country's Parthenon and you refuse to give back!"

"I suppose it's not so bad up here," George said grudgingly.

Annie looked at him from the corner of her eye. "How's your face?"

He squinted against the sun. "Fine. No harm done."

"I'm sorry about your boyfriend."

"What?" George scowled. "What's that supposed to mean?"

"I just meant…you were supposed to come here with him, weren't you? Caleb?"

"Caleb and I are just friends." The tone was light, or aiming at light, but Annie recognized the difference between pretending to be over something and really being over it. Sometimes she thought she'd never manage the latter. She let it drop.

Annie looked out as the wind blew her hair in her face. From up here, it wasn't the London she knew, of dog poop and roadworks and damp, expensive flats. It was a shining city, full of millions of lives, every single person thinking they were the most important in the world. A city where hundreds of people slipped away every day, dying in hospitals or nursing homes or even on the street, and hundreds more arrived in maternity wards and birthing pools and sometimes accidentally on tubes. So what did it matter if, among all that, Polly was going to die, or Jacob already had? She felt the weight of it crush her, all those dreams being shattered and hearts being broken.

"I feel so small," George said, almost to himself.

"I was just thinking the same thing."

"I mean…all these people, who don't even know I'm alive. How the hell will I ever be an actor when there's so many other people out there wanting the same? I may as well just give up."

"But on the other hand," said Annie, "at least if we really screw up our lives, probably no one will ever hear about it or care. We could just die, peacefully unknown."

George looked at her. "I like you, Annie. You're a good antidote to my sister's irritating positivity. I mean, when she got cancer I was prepared for depression and crying and awfulness, but instead she's become some kind of walking self-help bible."

Annie didn't quite get it. "You're all so kind of…matter-of-fact about it."

George shrugged. "The show must go on, right? You're still living right up until you die."

"I guess."

"This is what she wants. No moping, no misery. And Mum and Dad… I don't think they believe it's going to happen. I can't blame them, really. I mean, look at her. You see why we think there must be some hope?"

Annie did. Polly was smiling, happy, her face flushed with the heat of the sun and the wind on her face. Yes, she was thin, but that wasn't unusual among London women. She didn't look ill at all. She looked radiant.

"Come here," Polly called, beckoning them over. The sun was piercing through the clouds, warming Annie from head to toe. "Look, there's London Bridge. Have you any idea how many hours I've spent there, freezing my arse off on the platform, cursing and complaining? But look how peaceful it is from up here."

And it was. Trains looped into the station on their interweaving tracks, like ducks gliding over the water. Tiny people, with all their tiny worries and dreams and hopes and fears. Polly said, in hushed tones, "I bet this is how God sees us."

"*God veto!*" shouted George. "You don't even believe in God, Poll, you massive hypocrite. You can't start just because you get cancer, that's cheating."

Polly was sticking out her tongue. "Okay, okay. Whatever you want to call it, then. The universe. The great spaghetti monster. Maybe that's how I'll see you all from heaven."

"Optimistic," said George. "I remember what you were like as a teenager. You might not get in."

"If there is an afterlife, I'm going to tell God about the

time you cut all the heads off my Barbies and tied them to my bunk bed."

"He'll understand. He'll have seen how annoying you were."

"*She*, please."

"Do you believe in God, Annie?" Costas asked quietly as the siblings bickered. He did, she thought. She'd seen his crucifix and bottles of holy water. She'd never wanted to broach the topic—because how could a gay man belong to a church that hated who he was?—but she knew he sometimes came in from clubbing on Sunday mornings, dance music still ringing in his ears, and went to the Orthodox church in Camberwell. One of the many ways she would never understand people.

"Um, I don't think so." Otherwise, she'd have to believe in a God who let Jacob die and allowed her mother to waste away. "You're religious, right?"

He shrugged. "In the Bible, it says that what I am is sinful. To be...gay, you know." He looked at her shyly, to see if she'd known or minded. Annie arranged her face in an expression of complete tolerance. "But then I see things like this—" waving to the sky above, streaked blue and silver and peach "—and I meet such kind people who take me to the tall buildings and give me pink drinks, and I think, there must be something. Just something more. Even if it is not a person or a thing or a place. Do you know what I mean, Annie?"

"I think so, yes," she said. She'd lived with Costas for a year now, and this was the most they'd ever talked. He'd never even told her outright that he was gay. They'd slept with only a wall between them, virtual strangers, and now here they were. And they stood and watched the sun blaze out over London, and it was as beautiful as pink champagne and prom dresses and new friends.

"Polly! For Christ's sake." She looked up from her reverie, startled, to see Polly climbing on the railing around the viewing platform. George was grabbing her around the waist as a security guard rushed over. Annie's own heart lurched, vertigo making her head swim.

But Polly was laughing. "Oh, don't be so boring, George. I want to see farther!"

"Ma'am, you can't climb on that. It's too dangerous."

"It doesn't matter if it's dangerous, I'm dying!" She was laughing, but Annie saw her face was also streaked with tears, and as George got her down, jerking his head to the lifts to indicate it was time to go, she realized he wasn't just grouchy all the time—he was really, really scared.

DAY 14
Do nothing

Annie! Annie, call an ambulance!

Annie was in her old house, the sun coming in the white curtains of the bedroom. She held Jacob in her arms, but then she looked down and he was blue, his skin almost translucent, a web of veins showing through. He was so cold, and he was so still—a wax doll that looked exactly like her baby. It was a dream. She knew it was just a dream, and she struggled awake through the layers of sleep that held her down. *Not real. It's not real.*

She sat up in bed, looking at the clock. Sunday again. Costas hadn't come back from clubbing, and the flat was quiet. Annie made herself tea and a poached egg on toast, arranging it on a nice plate, bearing in mind Polly's comments on her dishes. She sat on her now-pistachio-free sofa, noticing that the fall of sunlight no longer illuminated dust and crumbs everywhere. That was something. A small something, but something all the same. She admired the food on the plate, which was edged in lilac flowers. The yellow of the yolk, the pale green of the avocado. Before she knew it, she'd picked up her phone and snapped a photo, stopping herself as her finger hovered over the Facebook button. No way. She could *not* become the kind of person who posted pictures of her breakfast.

There was a message from Polly, cheerful and upbeat, about going to the National Gallery that week. Annie still felt troubled by what had happened at the Shard, the way she'd climbed so recklessly on the railings, reaching for the sky. Polly was clearly more sick than she'd realized, taking risks, going too far. With anyone else Annie might have tried to dodge the meet-up, replying with something vague about work. But Polly didn't have time for a brush-off. If Annie postponed her, there might not be any time left. So she said yes, despite her misgivings, and then settled back to enjoy the peace of her Sunday doing nothing.

DAY 15
Finish a task

"And so, to celebrate the completion of the fly-tipping fines project—finally!—we're going for drinks at the Shovel after work," Jeff said, trying to sound natural while reading off index cards. "I must stress that in accordance with council diversity policy these will have to be self-funded and attendance is not compulsory. If you have any special dietary requirements, please let us know and we'll try to move the venue. This project was a real team effort, with everyone contributing to its success and..." Annie tuned out. She'd already spent much more of her life thinking about fly-tipping than she could ever have imagined. She was surprised they were going to a pub—the council were so keen to avoid possible cultural offense they'd moved the Christmas do to January, when no one felt like celebrating at all.

"Are you going?" Fee was standing in front of Annie, whispering over Jeff's drone.

"Oh! I don't know." She'd routinely avoided all work events for years now. "You?"

Fee had dark circles under her eyes. "Well, I suppose...if you were going..."

Annie thought about having to make awkward conversation with Jeff, who only talked about going to the gym and work, and pretend she didn't loathe Sharon, and veer away from Tim's halitosis. But on the other hand, she had no other plans. "I suppose we could. Just for one."

"Just for one," Fee agreed. She smiled, the strain on her face melting away. "It's worth celebrating the end of it. I don't know about you, but if I never hear the phrase *fly-tipping* again, it'll be too soon."

DAY 16
Take in some culture

"I love this," Polly said, bouncing up the steps of the museum. Today she wore a lemon-yellow summer dress, in honor of the sun that was bathing London, turning the Thames to a slick of silver. Because it was March, she wore it with purple tights, green snakeskin stilettos and a vintage coat with a fur collar. People gazed at her wherever she went, and no surprise, because she spoke at stadium volume at all times. "I did my degree in art history. What did you do, Annie?"

"Nothing," Annie said, whispering to compensate for Polly's loudness. "I went straight into work." There hadn't been much money about, and her mother had convinced her she'd be better off getting a job, some security in life. *Don't wish for the moon, Annie.* Sometimes she wondered if there was another Annie out there in a different world who'd sat in libraries and discussed literature and politics while wearing knitted scarves, kicked up autumn leaves under the spokes of a bike.

"I guess it was kind of a joke degree, mine. I just looked at beautiful things all day. I have this theory that if you only look at nice things, and smell nice things, and hear nice things, you'll always think good thoughts and be happy."

Annie was doubtful. It wasn't possible to only surround yourself with nice things. There would always be grimy buses, and the shriek of a pneumatic drill like the one digging up Trafalgar Square outside, and there would always be death. It was impossible to make death lovely. "How much will it cost—the gallery?" Her monthly budget wouldn't last long if she kept going along with Polly's schemes. She'd had to take the afternoon off work for this, and Sharon's eyebrows had plenty to say about that.

"It's free! Haven't you ever been before?"

"I can't remember." In the old days, she and the girls—Jane, Miriam, Zarah; the fantastic foursome as Jane tried to get them calling themselves—used to come into town every Saturday. An exhibition, or some shopping, or a meal out. Since they were no longer speaking, Annie had let the habit lapse. She felt vaguely ashamed. Here she was, with so much culture on her doorstep, and all she ever did was watch TV.

Polly seized her arm again, dragging her in. "Come on, I promised I'd show you some nudey ladies."

Annie trailed behind Polly, cringing wildly as she shouted, "And here's Degas, such an old perv, but look at these lovely redheads. I wish I'd been a redhead, don't you? I feel I just would have had more adventures that way. Look at the beautiful way he drew their backs—so vulnerable. And look, Rubens—that's what I wanted to show you."

Annie stared. An expanse of dimpled bottoms, stomachs that curved out and luscious white thighs. Polly was right. They did look like her. Minus the limp hair the color of blah. "So, this was considered beautiful then?"

"They thought being skinny meant you were poor. Or sick." Polly waved a hand at her own spare frame. "I mean, not to skinny-shame anyone, either. I just wanted you to see

that what we think of as hot now totally wasn't hot in the Re-
naissance. Ideals of beauty change all the time."

"I'm in the wrong era, then," said Annie. She couldn't stop
staring at the pearly tones of the skin. Nothing fake-tanned
here, just pinks and creams and ivories. The folds of flesh were
glorious, plump living bodies that you could just tell had been
fed on honey and cream and sides of venison. The way the
women held themselves, proud and coquettish and ravishing.

"This is my favorite," Polly said, pulling her in front of
another nude, this one of a reclining woman seen from the
back, staring into a hand mirror and out at the viewer. "*The
Rokeby Venus.* I just love that pink she's lying on. I tried to
get that exact shade for my bridesmaids' dresses, but I didn't
know what to call it."

Annie's head swiveled around in surprise. This was the first
she'd heard of Polly being married. *Ask her. Ask her more.* But
she chickened out again, afraid to spoil Polly's sparkling mood.

Polly was still looking at the painting, as if she was trying
to remember every inch of it. "You know what I wish? I wish
I'd come here once a week and just looked at this. Because I
don't think I could ever get sick of it, but instead I just looked
at lots of stupid things—work colleagues I hated and the inside
of dirty trains and stupid internet stories about which celeb-
rity got fat. Always rushing around to meetings and worrying about getting the mascara account and whether I should
take up Pilates. I wasted all that time, Annie."

Annie didn't know what to say to that. "I bet you've seen
some beautiful things, too."

"Oh, I have." She sighed. "Sunsets over the Grand Canyon
and the Taj Mahal and the Alps in the snow and so on. But it
wasn't enough. How could it ever be enough? I want to see
everything. I never want to stop looking."

Afraid Polly might cry, Annie put her hand gently on her

friend's arm. She didn't say, *It's okay*, because it wasn't. "We're here now, though," she said. "We can look at it now."

Polly took a deep breath, and smiled. "You're right. We're here, looking at it. It will be here long after both of us are gone, still hot as hell. Right, Annie. I think what we need now is the most essential part of all museum visits—gift shop, then cake."

On the way out, Polly stopped on the steps, causing a pileup of Chinese tourists behind her. "What?" Annie felt a dart of worry. Was she going to be sick again, or climb a high building, or take her clothes off? Apparently any or all of those things could happen at any time.

But Polly was smiling. "You ever see that film *La Dolce Vita*?"

"Oh. Yeah." Annie's mum's favorite film. A dream of handsome Italian men, and gelato in sunny squares. A world away from her mother's actual life. "Why?"

"Are you thinking what I'm thinking?"

"Um, probably not?"

Polly pointed. "Fountains! Dancing in!"

"Are you crazy? Imagine how dirty that water must be."

Polly was already walking, calling back over her shoulder. "Oh, no, I could get sick! What might happen then? Come on, Annie. Life isn't about avoiding the storm—it's about learning to dance in the rain. Where's your sense of adventure?"

It was lost, terminally lost. In fact, she wasn't sure she'd ever had it. "Polly!" She was moving toward the fountains with their icy gushing water, the smell of a public swimming pool. Annie dashed after her. Polly'd reached the edge now, and was pulling off her coat.

Annie panicked. "I'm pretty sure you're not allowed to do this."

Polly rolled her eyes. "Good. I hope I get arrested. That's something else I never did."

"But—"

"Come on, Annie! Have you ever danced in a fountain before?"

Of course she hadn't. The only ones she'd ever come across were ill-fated urban art projects full of cigarette butts. "Oh, God."

Polly was barefoot now, her toes thin, her nails painted silver. Her legs were bruised, sticklike. But she was laughing, plunging in. "Christ, it's freezing! Come in!"

Annie couldn't think of anything worse than getting into a cold dirty fountain. What if she caught polio? Was that still around?

A rectangular man in a yellow tabard was approaching, talking into a radio. "Ma'am, I'm going to have to ask you to get out."

Polly was holding up her skirt, splashing about. "Why?"

He seemed thrown. "Um, health and safety."

"Oh, it's okay. I'm dying, you see. I'll sign something if you want."

He looked at Annie, who shrugged helplessly. "I'm sorry, she's really sick, and—"

"You'll have to get her out or I'll arrest her."

"Are you actually a police officer?"

"Well, not exactly, but I know some."

Annie had a feeling that right this moment was a very important turning point for her. She could stand back and let him stop Polly, who after all only wanted to paddle in a public fountain before she died, or she could...

"What are you doing?" the man said, looking panicked. "Stop that—stop it, ma'am!"

Annie was pulling off her boots, and then, shuffling around

under her skirt, her frumpy woolen tights. Then she, too, was plunging over the edge, wincing at the cold. "Jesus!"

Polly laughed, clapping her hands. "Go, Annie, go, Annie!" People were starting to take pictures, nudge each other. Annie cringed. Polly took her hands. "Can I have this dance, Ms. Hebden?"

"Oh, God, Polly, I really can't—"

"Come on! The idea is to *dance* in fountains, not just wade around in them." She yelled to the crowd. "Play us a song and we'll do a turn for you!"

"Oh, God, no, don't…"

Someone's phone started playing a tinny version of "New York, New York." "It's the wrong city!" shouted Annie.

"Never mind. Come on." Polly had her arm around Annie, high-kicking. Annie joined in halfheartedly, spraying no-doubt-infected water all over her skirt. There was a plop, and someone else slipped over the wall—a group of foreign-exchange students, jeans rolled up the knees, laughing and swearing in Spanish. Then parents started lifting in their kids, and the air filled with splashing and shouting and screaming. The song swelled to its end, people now singing along—"New York, New *Yoooooorkkk!*"

Polly bowed, breathless with laughter. "Oh, my God. That was hilarious." People were dispersing, clapping and laughing, the moment gone. A mere minute, two minutes, where Londoners had connected instead of going on their way. It had felt like an eternity to Annie.

Polly was still gasping for breath. "Are you okay?" Annie said, worried.

She coughed, nodding. "It was worth it. That was brilliant."

"Well, why don't we get you inside into the warm? Tea and cake?"

She coughed again. "Tea and cake…sounds…amazing."

★ ★ ★

"Are your feet dry now?"

Polly held up one bony foot, which was plastered over in paper towels. "I look like I'm peeling."

"Just let me know if you get too cold. Dr. Max said you had to be careful."

"I'm fine! Cheers." Polly raised her teacup. "You know, I wish I'd eaten cake every day of my life, too. All those salads and goji berries I choked down, and I'm going to die at thirty-five, anyway. What a waste, Annie. I swear those uneaten cakes are going to haunt me. From now on, at least two cakes a day. Working on my Boucher bottom."

Annie nibbled on a fondant fancy, iced in a silken pale pink that was almost too pretty too eat. "I'm the one who doesn't even know if she's been to the National Gallery before or not," she said. "What was I doing with my life? I can't remember the last time I even did something like this, just had tea with someone."

"I've been meaning to ask you about that. Where are your friends, Annie?"

She blinked. Polly's frankness took some getting used to. "I used to have some. From school, you know. But I guess I sort of let them drift." When everything burned to the ground with Jane, her other friendships had been sucked into the fire, too. At the time, she hadn't cared. It was like mourning a village when a city had been flattened. But she felt the loss now: every Saturday she stayed in alone, every time she thought about taking a holiday and balked because she didn't want to be that solo traveler on the Sad Single Women's painting trip. "Anyway, what about yours?" she countered. "I've not met any of your friends yet, either." Maybe Polly was ashamed of her.

"Well. To be honest, I've sort of been avoiding them."

"Why?"

"Oh, I don't know. Maybe because when I look at them I see how much I must have changed. And they treat me differently—like I'll break or something. I sort of wish they'd take me aside and tell me my outfit doesn't match or something, like they would have before. It just feels a bit…awkward."

"I've been avoiding my friends, too," Annie admitted. "For a long time now." So long she doubted they were even friends anymore.

"You've got time." Polly closed her eyes briefly in bliss as she swallowed a pistachio-green macaroon. "That's what this is all about, you see. I don't have much time left, so I want other people to do the things I didn't manage. Stare at art. Eat cakes. Oh, and this." She reached into her bag—which was sewn all over in little mirrors—and pushed a ticket over the table.

Annie read it. "*Fantasia on a Theme by Thomas Tallis.* What's that?"

"Only a concert of the most amazing piece of music ever. Something for our ears as well as our eyes. Can you come?"

"Oh, I don't know…"

"*Cancer card,*" Polly mumbled around a bite of Victoria sponge. "Please. I really love it, and this might be my last chance to hear it."

"Oh, all right, then. But you have to let me pay you back. Honestly, I feel bad." She thought of George's complaints about freeloaders.

But Polly just pulled a face. "Annie, I can't take this money with me when I go. I may as well use it to have a nice time with my friends, don't you think?"

Friends. All the while Annie had been thinking of lost ones, and now she'd found one instead. She'd thought this would never happen again—how would she make more friends at thirty-five?—but it seemed it had, in the unlikely setting of the Lewisham Hospital Neurology Department. "All right, then," she said shyly. "But you have to let me do some things myself, too, okay? I can't just keep tagging along on your happy days."

A bright smile lit Polly's face, and Annie suddenly realized she'd played right into her annoying life-changing hands. "Maybe you could start by looking up an old friend. After all, I won't be around forever."

But Annie didn't want to talk about that now. She wanted to stay in this moment—happy, relaxed, feeling like a real friend sat across the table from her. A real friend who wasn't already half-gone from her. "I'll think about it," she said.

DAY 17
Listen to music

"I didn't know it would be this dressy. Why didn't you tell me it'd be dressy?" The Royal Festival Hall was full of older couples in tuxedos and floor-length frocks, quaffing white wine and chatting loudly about Mahler. Annie had rocked up in her usual black slacks and a jumper, and was now feeling woefully underdressed. They'd also had to talk their way in, since Polly had forgotten to bring the tickets. Her cancer card (and her Visa card) had been pressed into service, however, and the situation was saved, salved with a few tears. Annie had hung back, embarrassed, and ashamed of being embarrassed. Now they were late, and people were staring as they pushed their way into the row.

Polly was wearing a dress with sprigs of cornflowers on it. "Oh, you're fine. Who cares about all that? We're here to listen, not look."

"And what is it we're hearing?" She'd planned to YouTube it beforehand, so she could at least seem knowledgeable, but Sharon had hovered by her desk all day and there hadn't been a moment.

"My absolute favorite. Vaughan Williams. It's so dramatic

and beautiful. I guess classical music snobs would say it was a little schmaltzy, but who cares."

There were snobs even within classical music? Annie's exposure to live music had consisted of a trip to see *Phantom of the Opera* for her hen-do, and one Take That concert in the O2. As she recalled, Jane had organized both of those. As they took their seats—very near the front; how much had this cost?—she felt itchy with nerves. The mood was reverential, hushed. She opened her bottle of Diet Coke and earned herself several black looks from the old people around them as it fizzed. Chastened, she hid it under her seat and resolved to be thirsty for the rest of the show. It wasn't like a musical. No one had drinks, or sweets, and no one was flicking through Facebook on their phones. The hush died down even more as the orchestra filed on, all in black, and took up their instruments, tuning up and settling their sheet music. They looked impossibly glamorous, intensely focused. Annie began to feel wildly nervous. What if she had to cough? She might need to cough in a really important bit. Would they lynch her?

"Here we go," Polly whispered, even those three quiet words drawing more dark looks. Annie gripped the edge of her chair. She needed to sneeze. Oh, God, she really needed to sneeze. She crinkled up her nose as the first note sounded.

Oh, wow. It was... Annie felt herself frowning, biting her lip at the sheer power of it. The deep bass notes, the same refrain taken up by different instruments, over and over, layered with moments of silence where she felt herself shaking. The melody searing her ears, the lower notes making her stomach vibrate. She found she was gripping her seat. And the urge to sneeze was completely gone.

Twenty minutes later, a storm of clapping erupted. Annie was wiping her eyes. Polly turned to her. "Well?"

"It was good. I thought it was…good." It was the best thing she'd ever heard in her life.

"Are you having a *Pretty Woman* moment? Sorry, I can't take you anywhere in my private jet, but the upside is you don't have to have sex with me for money." Polly's voice sang out as usual, and a crumbling couple behind them tutted. The orchestra were shifting into place, getting ready for the next piece, when the auditorium was suddenly filled with the unmistakable opening chords of "Like a Virgin." Annie looked around, panicking, for the source of the noise—was it by some horrible chance her phone? No, it was Polly's. Everyone was staring. Even the orchestra were looking down in annoyance. Slowly, calmly, Polly fished it out and pressed Cancel, but not before Annie had seen the name "Tom" flash up. She looked at Polly, wide-eyed, and Polly just laughed. "I think we're about to get banned from the concert. Come on, let's get a churro and walk along the South Bank passing judgment on people." And they fought their way out, feeling the full strength of five hundred people's disapproval, but somehow, Annie didn't mind as much as she would have thought.

DAY 18
Make time to chat

"What's that you're listening to?" said Sharon, hovering by Annie's desk.

Annie took out her headphones, hurriedly. She'd been playing the Vaughan Williams over and over, the sound of it swelling in her ears as she looked out on the grimy strip-lit surroundings of her office. "Oh, nothing."

"We're not meant to have headphones in. What if I need you?"

Annie could have pointed out that Syed had his headphones in all day long, even going to the loo with them, but instead she said, "Just wave if you need me, Sharon. Or email."

Sharon sat down again, cracking her knees. "Never used to be like that. What's the point of being in the office if I have to email you? Antisocial, that's what it is." But Annie could hardly hear her, because she was drowning it out with the soar and sob of the violins, and she really didn't care anymore.

DAY 19
Get a pet

"Look! Isn't he adorable?"

Annie's eyes traveled to Polly's feet, which were clad in silver platforms, wobbly and shimmering. She seemed to be almost straining out of them, as if she was too impatient to be walking on the ground like normal people. "That's a dog."

"A puppy." Polly bent down to scoop up the wriggling tangle of limbs at her feet. The puppy was a boxer, Annie thought—snub nose, dark wet eyes. Emitting a strong smell of damp fur. "His name's Buster."

"But where did you—?"

"Oh, I just woke up and thought, you know what I always wanted?"

"Fleas? Rabies?"

"A cute puppy. So I went and got one from a guy on Gumtree. It was that easy."

"Um, how much did you—?"

"Oh, eight hundred or something." Polly was blowing kisses and making silly faces at the little thing, which was letting out a high whining sound.

Eight hundred pounds. That was almost a whole month's

rent on Annie's horrible flat. She tried not to roll her eyes. "Poll, you know you've brought a dog into a place full of sick people. You do realize we're in the hospital?"

"It's okay. I'm sure he won't catch anything."

"*Polly.* How did you even get him in?"

"I smuggled him in my bag." She was defensive now. "I thought he might cheer people up. It's so depressing in here."

"Yes, it is depressing on the *neurology* ward, but honestly. Look at him."

Buster, wide-eyed and wriggling, was now doing a small wee. Polly held him away from her as it puddled on the floor of the corridor, which funnily enough was the color of urine to start with. "Oops."

"I'm getting Dr. Max," said Annie.

She found him on his knees in front of the vending machine, his arm inside it and an expression of ferocious concentration on his face. "Are you okay?"

"Shh! This is a very delicate maneuver...aha!" A KitKat Chunky finally fell down and he pulled his hand out, victorious, clutching it. "Surgical hands one, bastard thieving machine zero." He saw Annie's look. "I paid for it! It just didn't come out. And I haven't had any lunch."

"I'm not judging. I just need your help with something."

"What?" he said, spraying chocolate.

Annie told him.

His face darkened. "Right. I'm not having this. Take me to her."

Ten minutes later, Dr. Max had dispatched a sulky Polly to her MRI with a lecture about all the types of infection you could pick up from a puppy, and was now on his hands and knees mopping up the wee with a roll of blue hospital paper. Buster was cowering near the wall.

"Can I…?" Annie offered timidly.

"No. It's done now. Bloody irresponsible puppy farmers. Turning dogs into breeding machines. Poor wee mite isn't ready to be away from his mum—look how scared he is."

"Why did she—"

"Disinhibition." He sat back on his heels, sighing. "It's a bad sign, Annie. It means the tumor's eating away at her. The bits of her brain that control impulse and judgment… You know how you airbrush a picture, with the little dots? That's what's happening inside her brain right now."

Annie nodded, a lump rising in her throat. "She danced in a fountain the other day."

"See? Loss of control. It's not good."

"But she seems so well. Happy, most of the time."

He tutted. "It's not happiness, it's euphoria. There's also memory loss, and mood swings, what we call emotional lability."

"But—"

"This isn't some inspirational 'making the most of life' movie, Annie. This is brain damage. That's what you're seeing."

"I danced in the fountain, too."

His bushy eyebrows twitched. "I didn't have you down for the fountain-dancing sort."

"I'm not. I don't really know what happened. I guess I thought I could stop her doing anything really over the top."

He nodded. "You're a good influence on her. Dancing aside. It seems to…distract her somehow from what's going on. Keeps her on an even keel."

"So it's getting worse."

"Aye. And it'll get worse still. Och, Annie, are you crying?"

"It's just…" She bit her lip as a flood of salt rushed to her eyes. "The poor puppy, away from his mum. It isn't fair."

He stood awkwardly, holding a wodge of wee-stained paper. "Come on, Annie. We get enough crying on this ward."

"S-sorry. Will Buster be able to go back to his mum for a while?"

"I'll try to bring him back tomorrow. Give that bloody breeder a piece of my mind. He can stay in my office for now. I'll find him a wee bed."

"Do you want me to come with you tomorrow, to the breeder?"

He looked surprised. "Are you no' at work?"

"It's Saturday."

"Oh, aye, I lose track of time in here." He smiled, his eyes softening. "Only if you do the punching. I need to save these surgical hands of mine for performing miracles. Have you a good right hook, Annie?"

"I can hold my own. I grew up on a council estate, you know."

"Och, well, then. I'll insist you come."

"It was so unfair of McGrumpy to take poor Buster away," Polly complained as they wandered to the exit of the hospital later. She kept stopping to wave at people, ask after them. "Hey, Paul, how's that ankle? Take it easy on the court next time! Mercy! Did you get your hair done?" Cleaners, admin staff, consultants, nurses—she seemed to know everyone. "I am too capable of looking after a puppy. He's got no right to say I'm not."

"How do you find time to meet all these people?" Annie asked as Polly waved at another porter.

"Oh, I've spent half my life here in the last few months. Waiting for scans, getting blood taken, chemo… I truly make the most of the NHS."

Annie had also spent a lot of time in the hospital, and she

didn't know anyone's name. Before Polly she'd always kept her nose in a book, or tried to answer work emails on her phone, feeling guilty about not being in the office. Awkwardly—going for casual but missing by a mile—she said, "You know Dr. Max?"

"The man who's had his hands inside my skull? I am familiar with his work, yes."

"Well...what's his deal? Is he...you know?" Annie felt herself blushing. She hated that. It was never a delicate rosy tint with her, rather an explosion of red like when you squashed a tomato. "Is he married or anything? I mean, he seems to practically live in the hospital."

Polly started laughing. "Annie, you little minx. You've got a crush on Dr. McGrumpy?"

"No. No, I don't. I was just wondering about their private lives. They work so hard." He didn't wear a ring, but that might be for hygiene reasons.

"Annie and Max, sitting in a tree—"

"Shh!" Annie looked around fearfully.

"I don't know if he's married. Married to the job, I suspect. But, Annie, we don't have time to fall in love. We've got living to do! Although he wants to stop me having any fun at all."

She thought of Dr. Max's advice. Keep her on an even keel. "Listen, Poll, I'm sorry about the dog. But there's other fun things we can do. What would you most like to try for the next happy thing?"

"Honestly, what I'd really love to do—please don't hate me for this—is give you a makeover."

Annie groaned. "Seriously? It's such a cliché. Is it going to change something fundamental if I stick on a bit of lipstick?"

Polly tucked an arm in hers. Annie hoped it didn't have puppy wee on it. "Look, I get what you're saying. I get that it's a bit patronizing to make someone over. But there are just so many different looks in the world. So many clothes, so many hair colors, so many types of makeup. And I spent most of my life up to now wearing the same things. Suits, shift dresses. Jeans, jeans and more jeans. Yoga pants. The same Barry M eyeliner. That's why I'm now trying to wear every random thing in my wardrobe, you see. You always wear black?"

Annie looked down at her outfit, trousers and a gray shirt she'd worn to work. "It's just easier. Saves time in the morning." Even as she said it she knew it was an excuse. And she'd once liked clothes, hadn't she? She'd bought so many maternity outfits when she was pregnant, loving the changing shape of herself, the promise of what was to come.

Polly wheedled, "It'd be so much fun. Why do you think I dress like this?" She plucked at the getup she was in today, a short pink frilly dress worn with orange tights. "I don't have a lot of time, Annie. I may never get to wear culottes or cowboy boots again. I have to do it now, or never. So, join me? Remember, if plan A doesn't work, there's twenty-five other letters to choose from."

"Is this where you play the cancer card?"

"I thought it was sort of implied."

What could she say? Polly was dying—that cancer card was real. The least Annie could do was put on a stupid dress. "Fine. Why don't you come over to mine and we can, I don't know, do our nails or something."

"Amazing. I'll bring brownies."

"We're not nine," Annie grumbled. "It's not like a sleepover where... Oh."

"Annie?" Polly turned back to where she'd stopped. "You've gone white. Are you okay?"

Move. Hide. Quick. Quick! But Annie's legs weren't moving. She was frozen, staring straight ahead, at the man sitting in the snack bar. She couldn't see what he was drinking, but she knew what it would be. Latte, one sugar. Half if he was trying to lose weight. He wore jeans and a green polo shirt, and his arms looked tanned and strong.

His voice shouting in from the corridor. "Annie, call an ambulance!" Fumbling in the bedsheets for her phone, struggling to dial the number as panic coursed through her...

Polly waved a hand in front of her face. "Annie? Are you okay? Hey, that's a song." Her voice was clear and piercing. Annie came back to herself and scuttled on by, until she was past the snack bar. Polly came swaggering after, in her impractical shoes, pausing to wave at a junior doctor. "Oh, hey, Kieran, working nights today? Don't forget to try those supplements I mentioned. Great for boosting melatonin."

Annie sank onto a seat—green plastic, the stuffing leaking out. The noises of the hospital washed over her, squeaking wheels and beeping monitors and hurrying feet. Lives being lost. Lives just starting.

"What's the matter?" said Polly.

"I... It was just...someone I hadn't seen for a while."

"Who? Your long-lost dad? Your one true love? Something's really upset you."

"No. No, I'm fine. I just—I didn't have any dinner. I better go home, I think."

She walked to the door very fast, head down, face half-covered by her scarf. Though she didn't think he would see her even if they passed; she was pretty sure he never thought about her at all.

DAY 20
Try an adrenaline sport

"Is this the place?" said Annie nervously. They were in Dr. Max's car, which like its owner was somewhat dented, and had mud and what Annie suspected was Toffee Crisp ground into the upholstery. They'd pulled up outside a salvage yard in Deptford, and no one was around. Piles of smashed masonry sat between burned-out cars, and from a small Portakabin a Rihanna song was leaking.

"This is where Polly said she got him." Dr. Max made a growling sound in his throat. "Can't believe she came down here on her own. Sometimes I think the lassie must be touched, brain tumor or no brain tumor."

"Should I go in?" Annie had Buster at her feet, emitting small squeaks as he chewed on the car mat.

"Let's both go. Not sure how safe it is here." They'd joked about getting into a fistfight, but Annie felt nervous as she climbed out of the car, Buster bundled in her coat. It was so quiet, except for the radio and the creak of rusting metal in the breeze. "Hello?" she called. Nothing.

Dr. Max strode over to the cabin. The back of his shirt was flapping out of his trousers. "Hello, hello, anyone there?"

The door creaked slightly and a sinister-looking man came out, wiping his hands on a rag. He wore a very tight black vest, showing off arms roughly the width of tree trunks. "What d'you want?" His voice sheered the corners off the sentence.

"Um, hello," Annie said nervously. "My friend bought this puppy from you yesterday but the thing is, she can't keep him—she's got cancer, you see."

"S'my problem?"

"He's far too young to be away from his mother," stormed Dr. Max. "Where is she, anyway?"

"Sold 'er."

"For God's sake. Do you even have a breeding license? You should be ashamed of yourself, pal."

The man shifted slightly on his feet, making his arms ripple. Annie began to back away, cradling Buster to herself. She could feel his heart whirring through her jumper, and her own matched it. "Dr. Max, maybe we should—"

"I'm not going to be intimidated. They're breaking the law here."

The man whistled, as if calling a dog, and two other men stepped silently out into the yard. Annie froze. "Er, Dr. Max..."

"A disgrace is what it is. I'll be reporting you to the RSPCA and I demand a full refund for my patient and—"

"*Dr. Max!*" She was already backing away to the car. "I think we should get out of here."

But Dr. Max was squaring up to them. He was stocky, but no match for the three hulking men now closing in on him. Annie had a horrified vision of him lying on the ground, his face beaten to red pulp. And it was a nice face, too. "Please!" she shouted, addressing the lead man this time. "He's just annoyed because my friend has cancer. He's her doctor, you see." Scary Man said nothing, but cocked his head at her, listening.

She went on. "He's a good doctor. Helps lots of people. Don't hit him. He's a surgeon—he needs to look after his hands."

"S'doctor?"

"Yes. Honestly, he works so hard."

"I am *here*, Annie, you know."

She shot him a look. "Shh! So, why don't we just go and take the dog, and we'll say no more about it?"

"Sod that, I'm not running away. I—"

"*Shut up*, Dr. Max."

One of the men was approaching. He was even larger, like the biggest in a series of Russian dolls. He had his hands on his metal belt buckle, and Annie didn't know what was happening—was he going to hit Dr. Max with it?—and then he dropped his jeans. "See this? What's tha'?"

Dr. Max blinked. He was being shown a mole on the man's hairy bottom. "Er, it's a mole."

"S'bad one?"

"I can't really tell." Dr. Max squinted. "It looks okay to me, if it hasn't recently changed."

"S'old."

"Right. Well, you'd have to get it checked out by a derma-tologist, but I don't see any obvious cause for concern, no."

He buckled himself up again, and an eloquent look went between the three men. The lead one went into the Portak-abin, then emerged with a handful of greasy cash. "S'half," he growled. "Can't take the dog back. Nowhere to put 'im."

"We'll take him," Annie said eagerly. "He can stay with me for a while. It's fine, honest." Though how she'd keep a puppy in a tenth-floor flat she had no idea. All she knew was they had to get out of here or she'd be scraping Dr. Max off the yard. "Please," she hissed to him. "Your patients need you. Polly needs you."

"I could take these guys."

"I know. I know you could. But should we just…leave it?"

His fists still clenched, he nodded reluctantly. "Can you really look after the pup? I would but I'm never home. It wouldn't be fair on the wee scrap."

"Of course I can. Please, can we just go?"

Finally, he turned, and Annie was back in the car so fast she could easily have won the hundred-meter sprint at school, rather than coming last as she always had in real life. Buster was still pressed against her, oblivious, his pink tongue hanging out. "Looks like you got yourself a dog," said Dr. Max, starting the engine. "Come on. We better find a pet store."

DAY 21
Have a makeover

"Are you ready for your close-up, Ms. Hebden?"

"Not even a little bit. But you better come in." Annie had opened the door to Polly dressed like a World War II recruiting poster. Petrol-blue jumpsuit, red lipstick, headscarf. Annie herself was in pajama bottoms and a hoodie. The hoodie had a crusting of something on the side—porridge, possibly. Maybe Polly was right. She did need a makeover.

"Help me with this, will you?" Polly was struggling with a huge suitcase. "Oh, look, there's my baby!" She fell on Buster, letting him lick her face.

"Should you be doing that?"

"Oh, not you as well. I'm dying, anyway. I'd rather go having cuddled this little darling." *Little darling* was stretching it, Annie felt. She and Costas had woken up ten times in the night to take Buster down in the lift to "make wee-wee," even though Costas had to be up at five to serve coffee. Despite this there had been several suspicious pools when Annie got up and she had to leave all the windows open to get the smell out, so the flat was now freezing. Luckily, Costas had taken enthusiastically to the puppy, and was already referring to himself as "papa," which Annie found worrying. Buster couldn't stay.

Annie began to feel alarmed by the suitcase. "We aren't going to just—you know, do pedicures and watch *Orange Is the New Black*?"

Polly laughed. "Nice try, Hebden. You know my motto. Go big or go home."

"I am home." But Annie knew her grumbling was pointless, and if she was totally 100 percent honest with herself, she was a little excited, seeing the fabrics Polly was pulling from her case. Faux furs. Silks. Patterns of red and green and purple.

Polly looked at her critically. "Right. Basics first. When did you last do anything with your feet?"

Ten minutes later, Annie was, with much protesting, wrapped only in a towel, her feet soaking in a bowl, an unmentionable burning cream spread over her lady bits, while Buster chewed her shoes in the corner. She'd tried to say her lack of beauty regime was a feminist statement, but Polly just raised her nonexistent eyebrows again. "Is it really? Or is it just that you haven't let anyone near you in years?"

"Both," Annie said sulkily. Now she watched as Polly approached, something like Sellotape in her hands. "What's that?"

"Nothing. Omigod, what's that over there?"

"What—aarrgh!" Polly had slapped something down on her leg and just as swiftly whipped it off again. "Mother of Christ! What was that?"

"Wax, duh. We better finish it, or you'll have one bald strip."

"I hate you," Annie muttered. There was more to come. Her feet were buffed into submission, her nails clipped, her fingernails filed.

Polly kept shaking her head. "How did you let them get

so bad? Didn't you see them every time you looked down at your keyboard?"

Annie wanted to say that it was easy to ignore things. You just closed your eyes, or looked at something else, and you told yourself it didn't matter in the scheme of things if your nails were bitten and your cuticles red and ragged. But she couldn't speak because her face was smeared in a plaster-like mask and she could hardly breathe for fear of cracking. Annie could feel her body fizzing with alarm, as bits of it that had rested in peaceful neglect for years were suddenly attacked, deforested, buffed and moisturized. "It's not about beauty," Polly lectured. "There's hundreds of different ways to look amazing. It's just about caring for yourself. If your hair is all greasy and your hands are sore and cracked, how can you feel good?"

Annie was having her eyebrows tweezed when the door went. Oh, no. Costas. She'd hoped he'd stay out tonight. He was wearing his work T-shirt and smelled of coffee, but his smile was wide. "Polly!"

"Hello, you." Polly and he exchanged kisses. "I'm making over your lovely flatmate."

Costas clapped his hands. "My sisters, they do this, too. I used to paint their hands!"

Another ten minutes, and Annie was staring at the ceiling in deep shame, while Polly painted her nails a sparkling gold shade, and Costas did her feet in silver. Her practically teenage flatmate kneeling between her ankles was not something she'd ever hoped for. Buster sat watching attentively, head cocked to the side. She said, "Are we nearly done? Only, *Grey's* is on at ten, and—"

"We're not remotely done," Polly chided. "There's still hair, makeup and clothes. Let me ask you something, Costas—what do you think Annie should wear?"

"Big skirts," he said immediately. "She is a—what do you

say?—curvy lady, so she needs the...you know." He flared
his hands out from his hips. "Big skirts. And tight here." He
cupped his hands in front of his skinny sculpted chest.

"Brilliant!" Polly nodded, sending splodges of varnish up
Annie's fingers. "Like a prom dress. That's a great idea. And
then I think something like a pencil skirt and blouse, big
heels, you know."

"Not the black slack-pants," Costas said darkly, as if he and
Polly had already discussed this.

Annie thought this was a bit rich from someone who wore
T-shirts so tight you could see what he'd had for breakfast
(protein shakes, mostly). "I can hear you," she said crossly.

Polly ignored her, jumping up. "Annie, don't move for five
minutes. We're going to dress you up."

A red silk skirt, with a frilly petticoat underneath. A tight
short-sleeved sweater, like something from the fifties. "Lean
on me." Polly shoved a red patent stiletto onto Annie's foot.
"Now the other." They were high, much higher than anything
Annie would ever wear, and she teetered alarmingly in them.

"I can't walk in these! How am I meant to get past that bog
around Lewisham Station?"

"Annieeee—you don't *walk* in an outfit like that. You get a
taxi, and glide regally up to the door of the restaurant."

"Can't afford taxis. Never go to restaurants." Not anymore, anyway.

Polly rolled her eyes. "It's for a special occasion. Something
worth dressing up for, making a fuss. You know?"

Annie couldn't think when she'd ever had an occasion like
that. Even on their wedding day Mike said they might as well
just drive their own car to the registry office. The house was
costing every penny they had and it didn't make sense to pay
extra. "Well, I can't wear this to the office. They'd laugh me
out of there."

"'Course not. That's why we have options. Costas!"

Costas, who was wearing a little pillbox hat with a face veil, began to produce outfits on hangers. "Casual day out." This was knee boots, a suede mini, leggings and a black jumper with a scoop neck. "Show off your bosoms, Annie!" Another flourish, another outfit. "Date night." ("Some chance," muttered Annie.) This, a printed red tea dress with frilled sleeves, which Annie had to admit was lovely, to be worn with a leather biker jacket. "Make it more tougher," he explained. "Like grrr, motorbike chick." Annie had never had anyone describe her as a motorbike chick. "Day at the races." A floral dress with wide straps, a stiff A-line skirt and nipped-in waist, in shades of yellow and pink. "Big hat also. Heels."

"I've never been to the races in my life," complained Annie. "What am I meant to wear for normal days? Work? Hospital?"

"Wear this red dress tomorrow," Polly ordered. "With the jacket, too. And boots if you have them—no higher than midcalf. Hair up in a big ponytail. Red lipstick. I'll show you how."

Annie's hair was set with big rollers. She felt like bits of her were being pulled off, changed and put back on again, like washing a dirty pair of curtains. But what was the point if you were exactly the same inside?

After some time, Costas looked as his retro Casio watch. "Time to go out!" It was half past nine.

"Oh, to be young again." Polly sighed. "I used to love going to G.A.Y. on a Sunday night. Have fun, darling."

"I can wear this hat?"

"Please. It looks fab. And you're wasted in that coffee place—you really know about clothes."

He shrugged. "Is just until I get something more. Bye, Polly, bye, Annie. Biker chick! Grrr." He got down on the floor to kiss Buster between his dark eyes. "Bye-bye, cutie.

Do not worry, Papa will be back to take you for wee-wee in the morning."

Annie really hoped he wouldn't get too attached to the dog. "I guess we should clear this up." She started scooping up armfuls of clothes, distracted by the flashing gold of her nails. "Where did you get all this stuff, anyway? It's not yours, surely." Polly was much slimmer than Annie and about a foot taller.

"I have a stylist friend, Sandy. She has entire rooms of clothes—it's ah-maz-ing. She says you can keep what you like. She gets sent loads of things from companies in the hope one of her celeb clients will get papped wearing them."

"Thanks." Not that Annie was planning to wear any of it. It was fun to play dress-up, but she wasn't about to succumb to the cliché of a makeover changing your life.

Polly was sitting down, as if she'd suddenly run out of energy. "So. Now I have you by yourself, are you going to tell me what all that was about Friday?"

Annie froze, a floppy straw hat in her hands. "Um, what?"

"That guy you were running away from."

Annie's hands constricted on the brim of the hat. "I wasn't running away."

Polly paused. "Annie. It's okay if you don't want to tell me. But don't lie, okay? Is it something to do with why you live here, and why you share with Costas?"

"I live here because I can't afford to buy, and I can't manage the rent on my own and I can't get anywhere better."

Polly examined her own nails, painted every color of the rainbow. "There's a lot of *can't* in that sentence, Betty Buzz-kill."

Annie flung the hat down on the suitcase with perhaps unnecessary force. "Look. My life wasn't always like this, okay? I'm just...having a bad spell. I used to like clothes. I used to get dressed up when I went out—jeans and a nice top and heels and my hair done—and I used to buy decorating mags and bake cakes and stencil my own furniture. All of that. I did own a place once—an actually nice place, that I loved— but that was with Mike."

"And Mike is?"

Annie sighed. She hated this bit. Hated the way people looked at her after they heard the story. "He was my husband."

"You're divorced! Chic. Or did he die horribly? Oh, God, I'm sorry if he died horribly."

"No, he's perfectly fine, as far as I know, and still living in our house with Jane."

"Mike and Jane, sounds like a kids' book. And Jane is...?"

"She was my best friend. Since we were five." Annie-and-Jane. Primary school, secondary school, visits to Jane at uni, interrailing around Spain, Annie's maid of honor. Until the day Mike came home and said, *Annie, I have to tell you something.* She'd only grasped snatches of that conversation; she'd been so in shock. *Fallen in love...didn't mean to...never meant to hurt you...*

"Ah, I get it." Polly beamed. "The guy at the hospital was Mike?"

"Yup."

"What was he doing there? Is he sick?"

"I don't know." There was another possibility for why he was there, but it was so awful Annie didn't even want to think about it.

"Sorry, it must have been crap, but I do love a good misery story. Your husband left you for your best friend! Does it get better? Meaning worse, of course. They got married?"

In response, Annie fumbled her phone from her pocket. She scrolled through Facebook until she pulled up a picture of a smiling blonde woman holding a pink cocktail on holiday. The bridge of her nose also pink—she never wore enough sunscreen, and Annie always used to nag her about it.

Polly peered at the phone. "Jane Hebden. It was his name? You didn't change back to Annie Clarke?"

"No." Annie wasn't sure why. Thinking she'd lost enough, maybe. Some kind of spite, not wanting to erase every trace of their marriage. Jane had taken everything else.

"And you're still Facebook friends with them both? So you can look at pictures of them and torture yourself?"

"Um, yeah." It was pretty much Annie's main hobby, stalking them online.

"Well." Polly stood up, which seemed to cost her some effort. "I'll hand it to you, Annie, that is quite the catalog of misery. Anything else? You better not have cancer, too, I warn you. That's my thing. You better not be trying to beat me in the 'world's most tragic story' competition."

For a moment Annie thought about telling her all of it— the blood on Mike's pajamas, the blue lights of the ambulance filling her living room, the sound of her own screams, coming from somewhere deep inside her—but she couldn't. She didn't think she could bear to say it out loud. "Just the crap job and flat and the divorce and the senile mother."

"Good." Polly stooped, helping her pick up the clothes, the chiffons and lace and silk and leathers. "We're quite the pair, aren't we, Annie Hebden? I'm dying, you probably wish you were dying."

"I did, quite a bit actually."

"Don't blame you. That's an almighty crapstorm. Question is…what are you going to do about it?"

"What do you mean?"

"Well, it's too late for me—I can try to enjoy my last hundred-or-so days, but I can't have any more. You've still got your whole life. What are you going to do with it? Remember, it's not about counting the days—it's about making the days count."

Annie said nothing. That was a question too terrifying for her. Her rage and pain had given shape to her life, the way a pearl forms around grit in the oyster shell. When she was no longer Annie, wife of Mike and mother of Jacob, she was Annie, who hated Jane and Mike. Who'd been hard done by. Who was angry, and unforgiving. What would she be without those things? If she let go of them?

"Big questions," said Polly. "What do you say for now we just watch TV and have a cup of tea?"

"I'd love that," Annie said gratefully.

"But tomorrow, Annie Hebden-Clarke, you will wear the red dress, and put on this lipstick the way I showed you, and do your hair nicely and you will do something positive toward changing all this. Agreed?"

Annie nodded. It was easier just to go along with it; she'd learned that now. "Let me wash this makeup off and I'll make us some tea."

Polly looked exhausted, despite her cheerful tone of voice. Her eyes were sunk into green shadows that had nothing to do with makeup. "Okay. I might just close my eyes for a sec."

In the bathroom, Annie hunted about for makeup remover. It was so long since she'd worn anything more than a slick of lip balm. She found it, then paused as she noticed something else in the cupboard. A little box of blister tablets, the name Maureen Clarke on the front. Sleeping tablets, prescribed for her mother when her symptoms first started, which Annie had hidden because she'd taken five one day, forgetting each time. Annie had a memory from then—everything lost, her husband and best friend living together in her house. The police coming around. *Ma'am, I'm afraid we've found your mother.* Walking in the street in her nightie, no idea who or where she was. Annie had stood in this bathroom and looked at those pills. Run her fingers over the little pouches in the silver foil, and imagined popping them out, and swallowing them, one after the other. Going to sleep, and not waking up from the crushing wall of pain that seemed to have fallen on her. She hadn't, of course—her mother needed her—but still, she hadn't thrown them away. She touched the box now, gently, then shut the door on it again.

In the living room, Polly was asleep, breathing slowly, Buster cuddled up in her arms and snoring gently. One of his ears was up and the other down. Annie covered them with a blanket, and settled in, flicking the TV on to *Grey's Anatomy*. If only Lewisham Hospital was full of beautiful people, like Seattle Grace. Admittedly there was handsome, stiff Dr. Quarani. And there was also Dr. Max, grouchy and disheveled, with his stubble and unironed shirts. Maybe she would wear that red dress tomorrow, after all. If she wore any more black someone might mistake her for a pedestrian crossing and walk right over her.

DAY 22
Flirt with someone

"Annie?"

Annie turned around from the coffee bar where she was buying her breakfast—a syrupy latte and a sticky bun. There was little else that could get her out of bed on a dark freezing morning. "Oh, hi, Dr. Max." She slid the coffee over in a vain attempt to hide the bun.

Dr. Max looked like he'd been up all night again. His blue scrubs were crumpled, and his hair was sticking up at various angles like he'd jammed his finger in a socket. All the same, the sight of him made some kind of warmth start to work its way out from her stomach, fanning to the ends of her toes and fingers and the top of her head. He frowned at her. "You look different. Did you do something?"

Annie was wearing the red dress, as instructed, and the leather jacket, and the boots. Her hair was still silky and bouncy from Polly's rollers, so she'd tied it into a ponytail. "Oh, I just—Polly gave me a makeover."

He rolled his eyes. "Honestly. That woman. Are you both twelve? What was wrong with how you looked before?"

She hated to admit it, but she had left the house with an

extra spring in her step that morning, feeling her hair bounce behind her. Costas, who was covered in glitter and getting in from clubbing as she left, had grrred at her again, which she took to be a good sign. And here was Dr. Max, looking at her properly. "It's a dress," he said finally. "Is that what's different?"

"Oh, yes, it's new."

"It's nice. I mean, a nice color. I mean…"

Annie felt red roll over her cheeks. She risked: "Do you want a coffee? I'm just grabbing some breakfast before work."

"Hmm. Well, I could do with a five-minute break. I have to operate on someone's brain in an hour and I'm so tired I might fall asleep with my hands in their cranium."

"That sounds awful."

"Par for the course. It's not a nine-to-five job, this."

He asked for a triple espresso, and took out a ratty tenner, but Annie waved it away. "I'll get this. It's the least I can do for you, now Mum's so much better." Even she had commented on Annie's new look, saying, "That's a pretty dress, Sally, can I borrow it for the dance?" Sally was some friend from her mother's youth, dredged up from forty years ago.

They sat at a small greasy table the color of bad news. Dr. Max downed his espresso. "That's good, but you know it might not last. Sami's tests are going well so far, but there's a limit to what the drug can do for her."

"I know. I'm just glad she isn't trying to throw chairs."

His eyes were tired. "It can't be easy. What about you? Are you looking after yourself? Getting enough sleep and so on?"

"I try. It's hard making it here every day and to work, as well, not to mention Polly's schemes. Plus, now I have Buster keeping me awake."

"How is the wee man?"

"He's so far eaten five books, three pairs of shoes and a

whole avocado. Skin and all." Not to mention the multiple trips up and down in the lift all through the night, in a vain attempt to prevent puddles of wee on the floor.

"He'll need shots and that. And you can't keep him forever, you know. Aren't you in a flat? And who's looking after him when you're at work?"

"Yeah. I know, I know. I've had to get a dog-walker in." Which was an eye-watering expense that Annie hadn't seen coming. "But it makes Polly happy."

He finished the coffee and frowned. Annie hid a smile: he had drips of coffee caught in his stubble. "Don't let her bully you. I know Polly's very fun and charming, but remember her brain is also in the process of imploding, aye? She may not always be rational."

"Oh, it's okay. I think I've been a bit too rational for a long time, if you know what I mean."

He sighed. "Sadly, if I ever have a rationality lapse, people literally die."

"Do you ever have time off? I mean, er, is it very busy?"

"There's only two neurologists in post at the moment, and we can hardly keep up with the work. We don't get paid to come in all the time, but if we don't, as I said, people die."

She ate the last bite of her bun, noticing lipstick smeared all over it. This was why she didn't bother usually. "I better go. Duty calls."

He checked his watch. "And me. I'm meant to be sawing someone's skull open as we speak."

And Annie had to...what did she have to do? Move some paper around, key in some numbers? It was embarrassing, how little her job mattered. She stood up. "Well, thank you again for helping Mum. And good luck with the brain stuff."

"Thanks for the coffee." He was still studying her. "It is the dress, I think. Nice."

★ ★ ★

On the bus, Annie sat down beside a teenage girl with loud pulsing headphones. Normally she would sigh and tut, thinking horrible thoughts about the person. But today she didn't mind so much. Her mum was all right, for now at least, and she had a nice dress on and she'd had coffee with a doctor. And it wasn't even nine yet. She started to wonder about her daily routine. It had been the same for two years now. Up, into the moldy shower, eat a bowl of muesli, get dressed in some form of black. Out the door. Wait for the bus, jiggling and sighing in the cold if it was late. Squeeze on, usually without a seat. Get to work, key in the door code, feeling her heart sink, because however horrible the journey was, it was paradise compared to being in the office. Sit at her desk. Turn on computer. Answer emails. Lunch at one. Sit at desk, eat sandwich, stalk Mike and Jane on Facebook. What if she did something different today? What if she changed?

The girl took out her headphones and went to get past Annie. "Cool dress," she said nonchalantly.

"Thank you!" Annie was still smiling long after the girl had got off.

When she reached her stop, her eye was caught by the bakery beside the bus stop, a shabby neighborhood one wafting out smells of icing sugar and melting chocolate. On impulse, she went in.

Ten minutes later, feeling self-conscious, she reached work. Someone else had to tap in the code for her, as she was carrying a large white box with buns in. "Thanks."

"Got something nice in there?" The man nodded to the box. He worked upstairs, she thought. She sometimes saw him having a cigarette outside in the rain.

"Buns. Um, would you like one?" Her heart began to race. He would laugh at her, think she was daft.

"Seriously?"

"Sure. There's loads."

"Well, thank you!" He was smiling now, whereas she'd only ever seen him looking miserable and damp. "Cheers very much. Another day at the coalface, eh?"

"Yeah." She rolled her eyes and smiled as he went to the lift, and she went past the receptionist, who was ogling the whole thing. "Bun?" Annie said.

"I'm on the 5.2."

"Oh, well, another time, maybe."

She opened the office door, seeing Jeff come out of the kitchen with a coffee in his usual stained mug, which had the logo of a software company on it. "Morning."

"Oh. Hi, Annie." His voice was flat. Did she always look as glum as everyone else in this building? "You're..." He glanced at her dress and makeup. "Special occasion?"

"Oh, no. I brought some buns. Would you like one?"

Jeff blinked. "Oh, that's—wow. Um. Do you have enough?"

"Sure." Annie carried the buns to the central table where they sorted the post, feeling everyone's eyes on her. It was unnerving. She knew most of them thought she was antisocial, and unfriendly, and too much of a stickler for expense rules. "Um, there's some buns here, if anyone wants..." She trailed off, suddenly sure everyone would be on some kind of gluten-free diet.

But Jeff was selecting a custard slice. "Thanks, Annie. This'll get me through that three-hour budget meeting." Then Syed came over, and then Fee.

Annie went to her desk, switching the computer on. "Hi, Sharon." May as well go all in on this "something different" idea.

Sharon had been watching the bun incident with narrowed

eyes as the rest of the office fell on the box like carrion crows. "Not very healthy, is it? Sticky buns." This from the woman who always ordered two portions of chips at lunch, one to eat and one to snack on throughout the afternoon. "Anyway, you've got work to do. That's another fifteen minutes off your time sheet."

Annie sighed and put aside thoughts of making the office a better place. Even if she did clean up the kitchen and bring snacks, she was fighting against the weight of apathy, which was heavier than bricks. Against the fact that not a single person in this building wanted to be there. Who would? Shut up in a lightless box, surrounded by people you didn't like, doing work that didn't matter, among dirt and debris from years of indifference.

She picked up her first invoice. Once, when she'd first started here, she'd almost enjoyed the work. The neatness of it, adding things up, pressing buttons to get people paid, producing clean sheets of numbers and facts. Having a paycheck, and being grown up. But somehow, coming to work had started to feel like death. Like she couldn't breathe, like every bit of her skin was coated in dust and grime and other people's misery. It was funny, but this office was actually more depressing than the hospital, where people came to get bad news. Maybe because in the hospital they really faced life down, instead of ignoring it, eyes glued to screens.

Around her, the sounds of the office blurred into one. Tapping keys, the drone of the copier, the buzz from Syed's headphones, where he was listening to episodes of the QI podcast. And the thought came to Annie again. *There has to be more than this. There has to be.*

DAY 23
See old friends

"Good morning." Annie's mum was awake, sitting up in bed with her hands folded in front like the queen.

"Hi, Mum. How are you today?"

"Very well, thank you," she pronounced in polite tones. "Who are you, dear?"

Annie's heart sank again. She hadn't even realized it had lifted. "I'm Annie."

"Oh, that's funny. I think my daughter's called Annie, too. She might be along to visit sometime."

Across the ward, Annie saw Dr. Quarani coming over, and she hastily wiped her hand across her eyes. "Mrs. Clarke," he said, slotting a pen into the pocket of his starched white coat. Annie wondered if he had a wife at home, doing all his laundry. "How are we feeling today, ma'am?"

Annie liked the *ma'am*. So many of the nurses called her "Maureen" or "love" or even "Mary." Her mother had always been a stickler for politeness. "I'm all right, thank you, Doctor." She stage-whispered, "This lady has come to visit me."

"That's kind of her." He took her mother's pulse and made a note on a chart. "You're doing well, Mrs. Clarke. Your vitals have stabilized and we've seen a big reduction in those moments of distress."

"She still doesn't know who I am," Annie said, swallowing down tears.

"No. I'm sorry. We might not be able to do anything about that, as you know."

"You're handsome, aren't you?" Annie's mum said loudly. "Where is it you're from, Doctor?"

"I'm Syrian, ma'am."

"Goodness, that's far away. Isn't he a handsome chap—oh, what was your name again? Do you think he has a wife?"

Annie blushed. "Mum, we can't talk to the doctors like that."

"It's fine." Dr. Quarani smiled—and he was even more handsome then. "I'll be back later to check on you. Bye, Ms. Hebden."

As he turned to go, Annie heard the loud click of heels on the floor and knew it was Polly. She'd tried to keep her mother away from her new friend—she couldn't bear for someone else to see how weak and confused her mum was, and didn't really know how to explain the friendship. It felt too early, too fragile, to even be called that.

"Hiiii!" Polly swept over. "Where've you been? I was looking for you. Had my old brain scanned again. I bet they've got more photos of it than anyone ever had of my face. Hello, I'm Polly." She stuck her hand out to Dr. Quarani.

He shook it politely. "Dr. Fraser's patient, yes?"

"Oh, yeah, that's me. Brain Tumor Girl." She seized his wrist suddenly and Annie winced for her. "A Fitbit? Are you into sport?"

He pulled his hand back. "I'm training for the London Marathon. Dr. Fraser and myself are doing it."

"You are? That's amazing. I did it five years ago. If you want any training tips I can—"

"Excuse me, miss. I must get on. Bye, Mrs. Clarke."

Polly watched him go. "I wish everyone wouldn't think of me as Dr. Max's patient. I mean, it's my brain, not his. Who was that?"

"Mum's doctor, Dr. Quarani."

"He is by far the most beautiful thing I've ever seen between the walls of this hospital."

"Polleee," Annie groaned. "Don't. He's a bit serious. Plus, he's married, I think."

Annie's mum said loudly, "You know, nearly every doctor I've had in here is foreign. People say it's a bad thing, but what I'd like to know is, who would be doing those jobs if they weren't here? Thank goodness they came, is what I say!"

"Have to agree with you there, Mrs. Clarke," said Polly. "We'd be literally dead without them, wouldn't we?" Annie thought of Dr. Max, British, but also far from home. Why did he work down here, battling every day with an enemy you couldn't see or touch? Polly was leaning over her mum, speaking clearly. "Hello, Mrs. Clarke, I'm a friend of Annie's."

Maureen was looking around the room again, with that unfocused confusion that stabbed at Annie's heart. "Oh, Annie, my daughter? She should be here soon. She never visits, far too busy with that husband of hers, I imagine."

She avoided Polly's gaze; she didn't want pity. "Mum, I think you're a bit confused, aren't you? I'm Annie."

"Don't be silly, Annie is my daughter. I know my own daughter, though she doesn't visit. I wish she'd visit. I'd really like some *grapes*." She said it plaintively, and Annie thought of the few times she had brought grapes, only to be told "she shouldn't have wasted her money."

She stroked her mum's hand, noticing how the skin raised

up and didn't stretch back down. She was barely sixty. How did she get so old, so helpless? "Mum, shh now. It's okay."

Her mother's face seemed to blank out, and she blinked and turned to Polly. Her voice was suddenly higher, girlish. "Miss, can you help me? I'm waiting for Andrew, you see."

"Who's Andrew?" Polly said, looking at Annie.

Her mum giggled, like a young girl. "Andrew's my special friend. He's going to propose to me, you know. I can just feel it. Sally, don't you think he will?"

Sally was Annie. "'Course I do, Maureen," she said heavily. "But don't you think you should rest now?"

Polly was looking at her quizzically. Annie mouthed: *Confused*, and then to her mum: "I'm sure Annie will be here soon, Maureen. And I'm sure she'll bring you lots and lots of grapes." She stood up. She had to go. There was a limit to how much she could stand on a daily basis.

Polly followed her out to the corridor. "Annie…"

"Don't." Her voice shook. "I know you've got questions, but please. I can't. Not now."

"Andrew's your dad?"

"Yes. She's…sometimes she doesn't remember he left her thirty-five years ago. She thinks they're still together, in love."

A long moment passed. Annie stared at the flecked lino beneath her shoes and willed herself not to cry. Eventually Polly said, "We don't have to talk about it if you don't want. I was actually coming to find you. I've got something to show you."

"Where are we going?"

"Med library. Did you know they had one here? You can get journal articles copied and so on. You see, there's lots of new research going on all the time. Sometimes we don't get the most up-to-date treatments in this country because of cost." Polly knocked on the glass door of the small shuttered office.

It was answered by a pretty woman in a pink headscarf. "Oh, hi, Polly. I've got those photocopies you wanted."

Annie hung back, heart hammering, fixing her eyes firmly on the ceiling. Was this a trick? Or maybe just coincidence? Maybe Polly didn't even realize. But of course she did. "Thanks, Zarah. In return, I've brought you a little surprise. Look who it is!"

Zarah saw her, blinked. "Annie! Oh, my... What are you doing here?"

"My mum's been sick. You...you work here?"

"Yes, I...got the job last year." And Annie would have known that once, because Zarah had told her everything. But she hadn't even seen her in almost two years. Since everything fell apart.

"You two should catch up," Polly insisted, grinning like she was Cilla Black on *Blind Date*. "Annie's here nearly every day, Zar. I'm surprised you haven't run into each other."

But even if they had, Annie would have fled the other way. "Er, how did you figure out we knew each other, Polly?" She was careful to keep her voice steady.

"We got chatting and Zar mentioned what school she was at. Small world, huh?"

"Not really, we went to school about a hundred meters from here." Again with the light tone. Nothing wrong here. She forced her face into a smile.

Polly went on. "Anyway, it's a sign, you both being here, so you have to meet up. You've got each other's numbers, yes?"

"Mine's the same." Zarah's voice was also cool, revealing nothing. Annie couldn't meet her eyes.

"Er, mine, too."

"Great, she'll text you, then." Polly was clutching Annie's arm, implacable. "See you later, Zarah!"

Outside, Annie pulled herself away. "Don't do that."

"Do what?"

"Push me into things. You could have just told me she worked here."

"And you'd have gone and talked to her? Because things are fine between you?"

"I might have."

"Seems to me that if things were fine, you'd already know that one of your best friends worked in this hospital."

"She's not—I mean, we used to be..."

"What happened?" Polly looked genuinely interested as she hopped onto the nearby reception counter, swinging her legs in their green patent Mary Janes.

"Ma'am, you'll have to get off—oh, it's you, P," said the receptionist. Someone else Annie had never seen before. Polly really knew everyone.

She took a deep breath. "Look, I know you're trying to help, but there's a reason Zarah and I aren't exactly friends anymore."

"Which is?"

Annie opened her mouth. Shut it again. She still wasn't ready. "Don't keep *pushing*," she burst out. "I already told you about my dad. I just—I'm not like you, okay? I can't just... open up."

"Fine. You don't have to tell me. But for God's sake, Annie. You miss one hundred percent of chances you never take, you know."

"What's that supposed to mean?"

"It means—text your damn friend. Drink a cup of coffee with her. What's the worst that could happen?"

DAY 24
Spend time with children

"Annie! It's so nice to meet you." She wasn't even in the door of Polly's parents' house when she was enveloped in a hug from Milly, Polly's friend. She had a chic dark bob streaked with purple, and sunglasses on her head, though it was nighttime. "Come in, come in, everyone's here." Annie trailed after, already wishing she'd stayed at home. Polly had finally organized a get-together with her friends, and had insisted Annie come "for support," but she was starting to feel like she was the one who'd need it.

Annie paused in the door of the kitchen, her dream kitchen, holding her bottle of wine. It looked like a scene from a catalog. Stylish, beautiful people—Polly, George, their parents, Milly, Milly's husband, Seb, who had trendy glasses and a cashmere jumper, and Polly's other friend Suze (mane of blond hair, sky-blue manicure, skinny jeans). She couldn't have felt more out of place if she'd tried. The red dress and boots felt too try-hard, and she knew she hadn't done her eyeliner right. She wanted to bolt, but Polly jumped up and put an arm around her. "Everyone, this is Annie, my hospital friend."

That made her think of puke and tears and linoleum. She

waved weakly. "Hi." She felt so awkward her shoulders were practically meeting in front of her chest. George gave her a friendly smile, but even that didn't help. He was one of the beautiful cool people, relaxed and confident.

Valerie, Polly's mum, was wearing some kind of stylish shift dress, with dark-rimmed glasses and recently blow-dried hair. "Hello, darling, nice to see you again." Annie's heart began to ache. Her mother was an old lady in comparison, though she was actually younger. Even when she'd been well she hadn't dressed like Valerie, thinking new clothes a waste of money when she could make her own. It wasn't *fair*. Why was it Annie's mother who'd had such a tiny portion of life? And then lost even that? Who couldn't even remember that her husband had left her a lifetime ago?

Valerie hustled Annie toward the table. "Now, why don't you sit over here beside George. I can see you two have been getting on well."

"Mum…" George was frowning.

"Remind me, Annie, you are single, aren't you?"

There was an awkward silence. "Well, yes, but—"

"Mum." George's face was tight. "We've talked about this, okay? Just leave it."

Mystified, Annie hovered near her seat. Polly squeezed Annie's shoulder and whispered, "Come on. It's not so scary."

Easy for her to say. Didn't she see not everyone could leap at life, grab it with both hands, be forced into meetings with old friends they hadn't spoken to in two years, made to dance in fountains and go for dinner with new people and admit they knew nothing about art or music or clothes?

Everyone was smiling at Annie. As if she was the poor relation they had to make a fuss of. Suze said, "So, Annie, I hear you've adopted Poll's dog?"

"Well, I'm just sort of looking after him for now." Meaning she was the one with the chewed shoes and no sleep and puddles of wee everywhere.

"George could help you with that," Valerie said, setting down a basket of homemade focaccia. "He loves animals."

George and Polly exchanged glances. Annie stared angrily at her slate place mat. She didn't understand what was going on.

Then things got a hundred times worse as there was a noise in the hallway like horses in a cavalry charge, and a wailing like a banshee, and Annie felt her chest close up in fear. *Children.* There were children here. Why had no one warned her? Two tiny blonde things erupted into the room, one in a pink dress and one in a Breton top and jeans. "Mummy, Harry did a poo in the loo!"

"Mummy, Lola hurted me. Put her on the naughty step!"

Annie watched, rooted in horror, as they threw themselves at Milly, one around each leg. Milly laughed helplessly. "Darlings, say hello to Annie."

They turned their little faces to her, curious, as if they might come over. Annie couldn't. She just couldn't. Their snub noses, their curling blond hair, the little shoes. How old were they? Three, four? Twins. She couldn't bear it. "I…"

Luckily, Polly must have understood. "Annie and I are just popping out for a moment. Er, secret hospital chat." And she propelled her out the patio doors into the quiet cool of the garden.

"Sorry, I just—it was a bit overwhelming, everyone at once." Annie was desperately trying to get ahold of herself.

"Don't blame you." Polly groaned, slumping on a patio seat. "They're exhausting, those kids. I don't know how Mill does it. I'm going to have to lie down for a week once they've gone home."

"Mmm." Annie sat down beside her, wiping the seat first with her sleeve.

"I mean, maybe it's for the best I never had any kids myself. Imagine how much harder it would be now, with all this."

"Did you want to?"

"I don't know. I always assumed I would. I mean, you do, don't you?"

"Mmm."

"But I kept putting it off. Told myself I'd try at thirty-three, or thirty-four, or thirty-five. And guess what, I'm out of time. That adorable little baby in the cheesecloth blanket, that's never going to exist. I leave nothing behind me."

A pause. Annie by now knew better than to say she was sorry. Polly hated that.

"But maybe it's for the best," Polly repeated. "All that screaming and not being able to go to the loo on your own, and look, chocolate smeared on your vintage Chanel." She held up the arm of her jacket. "At least I got to do things. Travel, and work, and...you know. And Milly changed so much—it was as if the life was sucked out of her. She used to be so fun—last one in the bar, always up on the news of the day—and now she sometimes doesn't even know what day it is. Of course, neither do I, but that's because my brain is being eaten by a tumor. Maybe that's what motherhood is. A tumor."

Annie gritted her teeth. "Some people would quite like the chance to have that tumor. I'm sure Milly's happy."

"I don't know. Would you be happy covered in baby sick and having to watch Peppa Pig ten times in a row?"

"I *was*," she snarled, instantly regretting it.

In the darkening garden, Polly was watching her. "I wondered when you were going to tell me."

"I wasn't. Necessarily."

"Thought not."

More silence. Inside, the rise and fall of children's voices. She'd never got to hear Jacob speak, but he used to babble, a rise of clear joyful sounds, like bubbles going up.

Polly waited. "I guess this is something to do with Mike and Jane?"

"Sort of."

"See? I knew there was more. Annie, you really are trying to knock me off the winner's podium for 'most pathetic story.'"

Annie breathed hard. "So you know about the divorce and my mum being sick and my friend running off with my husband. Would a dash of infertility help?"

"Always."

"I had three miscarriages before Jacob. One at three weeks—ruined the carpet. Blood everywhere. In my hair, in the bed, all over Mike's pajamas. One at ten—they found out at my dating scan, and I had to have a D and C. And the last at five months. You have to give birth when it's that far along. It was awful."

Polly left a moment of silence. "Then you stopped trying?"

Annie shook her head. She picked at her tights with shaking hands. "Um, Mike wanted to stop. But I... I couldn't. So I tried again. Pretended to be on the pill. He was *furious*. But then it seemed to work. Jacob was born full-term. Healthy."

"Lovely name," said Polly.

"Yeah. I always liked it. Then he—" She hitched in her breath. After all this time, the story still felt like a stone in her throat. "One morning Mike went to get him up. He'd slept through the night, we thought. I was happy! I thought things would be better from then. He didn't sleep well—we were all knackered. And I had this one moment of being happy—there was sun coming in the curtains, and I thought... I thought how good my life was. But when Mike went in, Jacob was— he was cold. Mike didn't want me to see but I—I pushed into the room, and he—he was already blue and he... We called an ambulance but he. Was gone. He was gone. Cot death, they said. Just one of those things." Though she'd torn herself apart looking for reasons. Had he been too cold? Too warm? Had he caught something and she'd just not noticed? She took another breath. "I went to pieces. It was like... I didn't know who I was anymore. I didn't know if I'd survive. I couldn't sleep, I couldn't eat. I used to just lie on the floor of his room all night and howl, like a dog. I didn't wash. I didn't change my clothes for two months. And Jane—well. She was my best friend. She was around all the time. Comforting me. Helping. Except she couldn't even reach me, no one could, so she comforted Mike instead, and then after a while he said he was sorry and it was an accident but they were really in love. I guess because she still got dressed and didn't cry all the time or refuse to throw away old cot sheets because they were all she had left of her baby." Annie breathed again. She'd said it. She'd said it and nothing had broken. The voices went on inside: Lola asking for some cake. The bird in the tree kept singing. The noise of the boats on the river kept hooting, mournful, like whale song.

After a while Polly fumbled for Annie's hand, and slapped it gently, as if handing her an invisible object. "Here."

"What's that?" Annie said shakily.

"My cancer card. You get to win for a while."

"I do?"

"Shit, of course you do, Annie. That's—I don't even know what to say."

"That's a first."

"I know. Better send out the press release." They both laughed for a moment, shaky with tears. "Annie. I'm so—my God. And I brought you here, with the kids—I didn't know, I swear. I knew there was something but not this. Christ."

"Don't say you're sorry. Let's have a pact, okay? We're not sorry unless it was our fault." Annie squinted at her. "So, this was your life before? Everyone talking about, I don't know, quinoa and the *Human Rights Act* and arranging weekends in Norfolk cottages?"

"I guess it was. We must seem like a right bunch of pretentious twats."

"No. It's just—we'd have had nothing in common, if we'd met before all this."

Polly didn't lie. "Maybe not, no. But here we are, and I'm not sure I can get through this without you, so you're stuck with me now, Annie Hebden. Only person who's ever beaten me in a sob-story competition. Damn you."

"Damn you back," said Annie. She reached for Polly's cold hand, and squeezed it, and they sat there in the dark for a while, watching the lights of the boats, and the city around them with seven million hearts beating on and on.

DAY 25
Share something

"Annie! Back again? You could skip a day, you know. No one would think any less of you, and your mum…well, you know. She might not realize." Dr. Max was once again at the vending machine, a Twix in each hand.

"I know. I'm meeting a friend, in fact." The word sounded strange in her mouth. It was a long time since she'd said it. "Is that your lunch?"

He brightened. "Machine gave me two by mistake! Karma for all my hard-earned cash that's been swallowed up by that minion of Satan." He looked at her. "Oh, would you like the spare one?"

"Don't you want it?"

He patted his stomach. "I'm living off sugar as it is. Can't remember the last time I had a meal on a plate. You know it's not—"

"Not a nine-to-five job, I know. Would you…?" Annie realized she'd almost asked him around for dinner. "Um, well, in that case, sure, I'll take the Twix. I'll save it for after my lunch."

"Lunch," he said nostalgically. "I used to eat that. It's jerk day in the canteen. Of course, it's always jerk day when you work in a hospital. If it's not the management, it's the patients wanting your life's blood."

"You take their blood all the time," Annie pointed out.

He'd unwrapped his Twix and was already through one bar of it. "Metaphorical blood, Annie. I swear this hospital is killing me. There's a queue of ten people just waiting to get their heads scanned so I can tell them they have cancer. It's not right."

"Is there anything we could do? You know, a fundraising event or something. Dr. Quarani's running the London Marathon." She'd seen him on her way in, doing laps of the hospital, his face set and grim. "I thought you were, too?"

"I just wanted to get fit," he said defensively. "I don't believe in fundraising for public services. The government would love that, making us raise all our own cash from bloody jumble sales. They need to fund the NHS properly from taxes, not sell it off to their fat-cat mates in private health care. It's a disgrace, Annie, that's what it is. Anyway, see you, got to go look into someone's brain now." He'd sounded furious, but he waved jauntily as he left. She couldn't figure him out.

The canteen was busy with doctors and families, and it took her a while to spot Zarah. Today she wore a blue scarf with butterflies, edged in blue sequins. Annie wished she'd suggested meeting somewhere they wouldn't be seen by one of Polly's many spies. But Zarah only got a short break and since Annie was there every day, anyway, it made sense. "Hi."

Zarah wasn't alone at the table, and for a moment Annie thought they'd have to share it with a random, but then she saw who it was. Zarah caught her look. "I hope you don't mind, Annie. I just think the three of us need to talk. This has gone on long enough."

"Agreed," said the other woman at the table, tall and striking in a red bodycon dress, her hair in a shiny weave. "Hi, Annie."

Annie swallowed. "Hi, Miriam."

Miriam met her eyes, frank and honest, just as Annie remembered. Too honest sometimes. It was why they hadn't spoken in so long. "Are you well? Zar said your mum was poorly?"

"Yeah, she's…" Annie couldn't bear to explain. "She's in the inpatients' ward. How's… Jasmine?"

Miriam looked surprised for a moment, as if she hadn't expected Annie to remember her daughter's name. But of course Annie remembered. She knew everything about Jasmine, another child that had been lost to her, but this time through her own fault. "She's fine."

"I'm so sorry about…everything."

"You mean her birthday?"

Annie nodded, staring at the greasy tabletop. "I shouldn't have even been there. I wasn't up to it. I just didn't want to… let you down." And so she'd made herself go, and the sight of all those one-year-olds smeared in cake had made her flee, weeping, and when Miriam had come after her, Annie had pushed her away, physically pushed her, and slammed her car door, pulling off and leaving Mike on the pavement, staring after her. Annie had often wondered if he would have left her if it hadn't been for the scene she caused that day. If that was the moment he decided to cut his losses and run, untether himself from the weeping mess of a person she'd become.

Miriam sighed. "Annie, the party doesn't matter. Jas won't even remember. But you just cut us off completely. All of us, not just Jane."

At the sound of the name Annie's teeth clenched. "I take it you're all still friends."

Zarah and Miriam exchanged looks. Zarah said, "Annie…

we're your friends, too. I missed you so much—you were always the first person I'd ring when I had a crisis. Remember? You were the only one who never panicked, who'd cheer me up if I had a terrible date or my car wouldn't start or my parents were giving me grief. I never wanted to stop being friends. You just wouldn't see us. You wouldn't see anyone. And Jane...she feels terrible, really she does."

"Not terrible enough not to do it."

"They fell in love," said Miriam. "I really think they did. I mean, obviously it was terrible for you. It's not like we were on her side."

It had felt like it, when Mike finally told her who he was leaving her for, and she'd called Zarah in total shock. When she'd told her friend what had happened, she'd heard the silence that meant everyone already knew. Annie was the last to find out. And so she'd packed her things and moved out and never spoken to any of them again, until now. What a mess it was. Everything—her child, her home, her husband, her friends—gone in one swoop.

She felt a hand on hers and looked up to see Miriam smiling at her. And the first tear splashed onto the dirty table. "S-sorry."

Zarah said, "What happened to you was awful, An. So awful. We just wanted to be there for you. But you vanished."

Annie shook her head, dislodging tears. "No one could help. There was no point."

Zarah nodded. "Well, maybe now the dust has settled a little bit...maybe we can meet up again, like we used to? I mean, the three of us." Annie felt how awkward it must have been for them, when one of their best friends went off with the other's husband. "I wouldn't expect you to... But she really does feel terrible, you know. Especially now that..." She fell silent. Another look between her and Miriam. "She feels terrible," Zarah repeated.

And so she should. "I can't forgive her. I just can't." Annie could hardly talk over the lump in her throat. It was too soon, too raw. Seeing the two of them brought back so many memories. Of old Annie, who had friends, who was even the sensible one. The one the rest came to when their boyfriends cheated or their bosses asked too much or they couldn't get their cakes to rise. That Annie had died when Jacob did.

She stood up, scraping her chair back. "I have to go. Sorry. Thanks for—thanks. I'd like that, if we could meet up. Soon. I have to go." And once again, she ran away, out in the corridor that was painted all the shades of misery there were.

DAY 26
Reclaim a hobby

"So do you come here a lot?"

Annie shook her head. "Sometimes I can't face it." What kind of person was she, that she didn't visit her own baby's grave? "It's just…it's very painful," she said. "And I'm always worried I might bump into Mike."

"I get that. So where is it?" Polly turned on her heels, looking around the vast municipal graveyard. She was dressed in denim dungarees and Converses with flowers on them; she looked like she was in an Abercrombie and Fitch ad.

"Third row on the left." Annie knew exactly. She could have walked here in her sleep—and she did sometimes, dreaming that she stood over his grave. Looking for him. It had been two years, but there were days when she still woke up expecting to hear his cry. She should have known, on the morning when he was silent. She wasn't sure she'd ever forgive herself for the brief relief when she thought he'd slept right through, for that moment of happiness. If only she'd checked on him sooner. If only she'd woken up earlier. Annie shut the thought down—she knew that if she carried on with it, the what-ifs would kill her. "This is it." She felt shame roll over

her. It was such a mess. Weeds were almost swamping the little gray stone that read Jacob Matthew Hebden, and the jam
jar she'd last brought flowers in was tipped on its side, full of
dirty green water.

"Matthew," Polly read. "Named after someone?"

"Mike's dad."

"Hmm. His, not yours."

Annie shrugged. "Why would I name my son after someone I've never met? At least, not that I remember."

Polly hunkered down on the grass. "You've never tried to
look for him, all this time?"

"I wouldn't know where to start. I don't even remember
him. He left when I was a few days old."

"Your poor mum. That must have been tough."

"Yeah. He was a bit of a loser, I guess. I always felt I didn't
need that in my life. Kind of ironic, isn't it, that my husband
ended up leaving me, too. A family trait, maybe."

Polly tutted. "I hope you're not expecting me to come to
this pity party you're throwing, Annie."

"No, no. I don't need him. It's just strange, listening to
Mum talk like he's still about. They must have been happy
at one point."

"I think that about my parents sometimes."

Annie frowned. "Your parents seem really happy."

"Yes, well, appearances aren't always the truth, Annie. But
listen to me! No pity party. We're here for Jacob, to remember him with love."

Annie bent to pull up a weed. "I... I guess Mike hasn't
been coming here much, either. You must think I'm awful."

Polly said nothing for a while. "You know, when I was
little, my grandpa died. He was cremated, and his ashes were
scattered at sea—he loved boats. I asked my mum once how we
would visit him, if he didn't have a grave. She said graves aren't

where the people are—they're just a place we go to remember them. I bet you don't need any help remembering Jacob."

Annie shook her head, trying to swallow down the ball in her throat.

Polly bent down, wincing with a hand on her back, and spread a purple pashmina under her knees. "We can sort this no bother. Weed it, tidy it up."

Annie wished she'd brought some garden tools. They'd all been left behind, along with her garden, at the house Mike and Jane were now living in not three miles away. She knelt herself, knowing she'd get grass stains on her jeans but not caring. She'd forgotten how the earth felt under her in spring, the gentle wet give of it. "Here." Polly passed over a mini trowel and fork from her tote bag.

"Where did you get these?"

"Oh, they're Mum's. She never uses them—she has a gardener in. Thought they might come in handy."

For a while they hoed and cut in silence, the sounds of the city far away. The only other people were on the other side of the graveyard, tending to someone else's plot. Annie looked up at one point and saw Polly digging intently, a smudge of soil on her pale cheek, and thought how strange it all was, gardening at her baby's grave, with this woman she hadn't even known a month before.

"You should forgive them, you know," Polly said quietly.

Annie didn't need to ask who she meant. "I can't."

"I know. What they did was crap, beyond crap. But…it's you who suffers when you don't forgive people. It's you who has to carry them around, day after day."

Annie pulled up weeds in silence for a while. "They almost destroyed me."

"I know. But they didn't. You're still here."

Barely. There'd been times over the last two years when

she wasn't sure she'd make it. The feel of Jacob in her arms, the same lightness as always, but cold and still. The day she moved into her damp little flat, looked around her and wondered how the hell she'd slid back down so far in life. The day the police called to say they'd found her mother, confused and wandering, and she realized she'd been losing another person, right under her eyes, and she hadn't been able to see past her own grief. She was barely living as it was—so what Mike and Jane had done felt insurmountable. She gave her standard response to most of Polly's suggestions: "I'll think about it."

"Ta-da!"

Annie looked suspiciously at the daffodils in Polly's arms. "Where did you get those?"

"They were just growing. Trust me, no one here will know the difference. Aren't they pretty?" She examined the bold yellow trumpets, the green stems oozing sap. "I love the way they come up every year, out of this cold dead soil, just when you think winter's going to go on forever. I think that's what I'll miss the most. I mean…not that I'll know, I guess. I don't know if I'll even know it's spring, or if I'll just be…gone. Can I leave some for Jacob?"

They rinsed out the jar and filled it with fresh water from the tap the parks office provided. For once, Annie approved of the organization she worked for. She'd never thought of how they were there to jam up the cracks in people's lives, take away rubbish, fix the holes in the roads, keep the parks nice. Polly shoved the flowers in, tidying them so the petals frilled out. "There. These are for you, Jacob. Nice to meet you."

Annie stood in silence. "Can I say something weird?"

"Always."

"I don't think he can hear me. I tried to believe it, after we lost him… It hurt too much to think I'd never see him again.

But I think he's just gone. I guess that's why I don't visit very often. I used to come with Mum—she believes in all that—but it would be too cruel now, to remind her he's gone. I'm not sure she even remembers she had a grandson, sometimes."

Polly shrugged. "We're not really built to understand death, I don't think. I sometimes imagine what it would be like to go up to people on the tube, or in the street, and tap them on the arm and say, 'Excuse me, do you realize you're going to die? Maybe not today or tomorrow but *one day*.' All those people rushing about to meetings and Pret and the gym. I wonder what would happen if they suddenly realized it. Let it sink in. Wouldn't you drop everything and do the one thing you'd always dreamed of? Jump out of a plane. Quit your job. Tell that person you fancy him."

Annie shot her a look. "This better not be about Dr. Quarani."

"He is gorgeous, though. So stern."

"He's got a family photo on his desk."

"Could be his sister."

"Poll-ee." Annie wasn't sure if Polly herself had let it sink in that she was dying. How could she flirt with people, make plans, even make new friends, when her life had an expiry date? "Maybe it's not possible to live being constantly aware you're going to die. Hard to get the motivation to wash the floor and stuff."

"I keep thinking I need to renew the car insurance or buy my summer bikini before all the good ones go," said Polly. "Then I remind myself…but I can't, you know? It's impossible to not think about the future." She hauled herself off her knees, with difficulty. "Anyway. Another thing you don't have to do if you're dying is quit sugar. In fact, I have actually taken up sugar. So, fancy a hot chocolate and cake?"

Annie looked down once more at the little grave. It was ti-

dier now, the worst of the weeds gone and the grass trimmed.
Jacob never got to make his mark on the world. He'd barely
been there before he'd gone from them. But to her, and to
Mike, and her mother—and if she was totally honest: to Jane,
as well—Jacob's short life meant nothing would ever be the
same again. There was probably some quite profound thought
in here somewhere, but she felt too overwhelmed to tease it
out, and Polly was looking pale and tired, and slumping on
the grass in a way that Annie now knew meant she was exhausted. "Sure," she said. "Let's go and have cake."

DAY 27
Change your bedsheets

"Annie! You are having someone over to stay?"

Annie snorted. "Some chance." In all the time Costas had lived with her, she'd never had anyone spend the night. She knew he did sometimes, but they always crept out before dawn, leaving only rogue hairs in the shower.

"Then why are you...?" Costas stood in her bedroom doorway, indicating the piles of linen all over the place. Buster was scooped in his arms, licking his face with a pink tongue.

"Don't let that dog down—I've just cleaned all this," she warned. Annie's usual beige-ish bedspread was lying in a heap on the floor, and she was putting on a new one, turquoise with pink flowers.

"He will not eat things. He's a good dog, aren't you, baby? Yes, you are. Yes, you are! So, Annie, why do you clean?"

"Oh, I just thought it was time for a change. Make things nicer." She'd slept in those bedclothes since she moved in here, broke and possessionless. She'd left all her nice things behind, turned her back on her old life, bought the cheapest sheets she could find, scratchy and uncomfortable, and hadn't washed them quite as often as she should have.

Costas gave her a thumbs-up. "Good for you, Annie. I go out now."

He was dressed in a tight silver T-shirt and she smiled at him indulgently. "You have fun." Maybe she should buy some sheets for him, too. After all, it wasn't very nice in the little box room he called home. As she plumped and smoothed and admired her new bed, she thought about what he'd said. If, in some parallel and very unlikely universe, someone did happen to see her bedroom, it would at least now not entirely embarrass her.

She bent down to open the lowest drawer in her cabinet, looking for a pillowcase. Something rustled. Tissue paper. And too late Annie remembered what she'd hidden away in there, her most precious treasure.

It was the only thing of Jacob's she'd saved. The rest had been clothes bought from shops, that anyone could have, but this little cream cardigan had been made by her mother, knitting solidly in front of the TV for two months. The buttons were shaped like lambs' faces. Annie pressed it to her face and breathed. Out of it fell a small plastic hoop, with the name Jacob Matthew Hebden printed on it. His hospital ID.

And she was back there. In her old bed, early in the morning. Mike bringing Jacob to her for a feed, his small body sliding in between them. The baby they'd made. A miracle. Usually when she thought about that time, it was blackened with the anger she felt. But Mike, too, had lost all that. Even if he had Jane now, Annie was not so blinded by rage she didn't realize it could never make up for what had happened. Nothing could. Mike was the only person who could really understand how it felt for her to hold this little cardigan and remember the baby who was no longer inside it. And maybe, after all, that counted for something.

Annie sighed to herself. Bloody Polly. Try as she might, it was very hard to stay immune from that irritating positivity of hers.

DAY 28
Forgive someone

"I think I've changed my mind. Can we turn back?"

"Come on. You know the saying 'bitterness is like drinking poison and expecting someone else to die.' And you, my dear Annie, have drunk a whole gallon of it."

Annie scowled. She liked her poison. It was like strong coffee, dark and stimulating and keeping her going. But here she was, all the same, sitting in the Volvo Polly had borrowed from Milly. "How come we aren't forgiving someone for you, then, if it's so important? I bet you have someone you're angry with."

Polly screwed her face up. "I'm not quite ready yet."

"I'm not ready, either."

"You've had longer. And trust me, mine is an utter, utter bastard."

"You were the one saying we have to forgive people, let go of the poison and so on." Annie looked at her. "Is it Tom that you won't forgive?" she risked. "Not that you've actually told me who Tom is."

Polly made another face. "I'm not ready, I said. Anyway. It's you today. Then I'll think about me. Come on, it's the per-

fect time for it. You've seen your old friends, they said Jane
feels awful—it's fate."

"It's not fate, it's you meddling. I wouldn't even have seen
Zarah if you hadn't set it up."

"You'd have run into her sometime."

Annie sighed. Useless to protest. "Fine. But I'm only going
to talk to them. I can't forgive them. Not yet." Not ever,
probably.

After a moment, Polly said, "Tom really is a massive bastard. Trust me."

"I'll have to take your word for it." Annie didn't like to
pry, but did Polly not trust her enough to share her secrets?
She knew all of Annie's. It seemed a little unfair, cancer card
or no cancer card. "You can definitely drive, yes?" she said
suspiciously as Polly ground the gears.

"'Course I can! Now, which way am I going?"

"Right, then next left. Look where you're—Christ!" She
winced as Polly lurched into the next lane. "Then go straight
on." She remembered the directions to the house so well
she could have walked there with her eyes shut: 175 Floral
Lane, Ladywell. Even the address sounded auspicious, she used
to think. Because this had been *her* house once. It was des-
tined to be hers when Mike had phoned in excitement, saying he'd found the perfect place, and they'd gone after work
to see it, their hands sweaty in each other's as they viewed the
black-and-white hall tiles, the clutches of daffodils in the back
garden—Annie's favorite. She'd even tried to call it Daffo-
dil Cottage for a while, but Mike thought it was daft and the
postman could never find it. It had been hers when they'd
found a chesterfield sofa in an antiques shop and when they'd
sanded down the wooden floors with a big noisy machine
they'd hired, so powerful it pulled Annie off her feet. And it

had been hers when she brought Jacob home from the hospital, his rose-petal face peeking out from his bassinet.

But now it wasn't hers; it was Jane's. Jane and Mike. "What if they're not home?"

Polly swung the car around the corner, almost knocking down a lamppost. "It's Sunday, of course they'll be home. They'll be doing flat-pack furniture and Jamie Oliver recipes, like all suburban couples."

"Thanks for reminding me. And watch the road! Jesus!" A small terrier narrowly avoided death under the wheels. "When exactly did you get your license?"

"Years and years ago. Relax, would you? I have cancer, car accidents hold no fear for me."

"But I don't!"

"Now who's rubbing things in? Look, you'll just say hello, and that you wanted to speak to them because it's been a long time and you're sorry you fell out and you think it's time you all healed and let go of the past. Then you hug."

"I am *not* saying that. They'll think I've joined a cult or something." Which she had, in a way, she thought, reflecting on the last few weeks. The cult of Polly. "Anyway, I'm not sorry we fell out. It was entirely their fault."

"Annieeeee—this isn't in the spirit of reconciliation, is it? You must have done something you regret."

Annie thought of the long angry emails she'd sent them both, when she'd drunk too much wine, saying how much she hated them and hoped they'd catch ebola. "Um, I don't know."

"Just say you forgive them, then. It's the greatest gift you could give."

But Annie didn't forgive them. And as they drew nearer to what had been her home, the familiar streets and shops, she felt the anger she still carried inside her like a dark child. But she'd come this far—she'd started something—and she knew she couldn't be friends with Zarah and Miriam again unless she at least tried to talk to Jane. "Turn here. It's the last one on the left: 175—*175*, I said." Polly had massively overshot. Annie saw the way she was screwing up her eyes and a horrible thought occurred. "Can you not see or something?"

"It's fine!"

"Polly!"

"Okay, okay, I'm having some sight problems. Bob is pressing on my optic nerve, that's all."

Annie closed her own eyes briefly. "Jesus. I'm driving home. This is it, anyway."

"It's cute! I love the bay windows, and the slate tiles."

Annie used to curl up in those windows and daydream on cold winter days. She'd imagined Jacob doing the same when he was older, reading a book or watching a film. And maybe another kid or two, as well. Ghost children now, just like Jacob, never to be born. "Too bad I don't live there anymore. Well, I guess we better get this over with. Are you coming with me?"

Polly shook her head. She'd parked with one wheel up the curb. "I'll stay here, and listen to the top tunes of Magic FM. Life really was too short for Radio 3. I wish I'd known."

What would she say? What if they threw her out? On the path she looked back nervously, to see Polly headbanging away to the radio. She noticed with a sort of strange mix of satisfaction and sorrow that they'd let all her flower beds overflow, weeds crowding out the delicate bulbs and seedlings she'd nurtured. She raised her hand to ring the bell but it stayed frozen in midair. She glanced back to Polly again, who had wound down the window, letting out the banging beats of the Backstreet Boys. *"Cancer card!"* she hollered. Annie cringed and pressed the bell.

No one answered for ages, and a terrible relief was growing in Annie's stomach, when suddenly she heard steps approaching on the other side of the door. "Coming!" Jane's voice. One that she'd once heard every day, on the phone if not in person. Dissecting boyfriends, jobs, Annie's wedding plans and the plot of the latest *Grey's Anatomy.*

This was a terrible idea. Then it was too late, because Jane was opening the door, and Annie didn't know what to look at first. Her former best friend, two years older, a little more lined and gray, in pajama bottoms and a big baggy jumper. Or the swelling bump beneath the jumper, which Jane's hand rested on, her wedding ring glinting. Oh, God. Why hadn't Annie considered this possibility?

Jane was pregnant.

It was a strange thing, to go into a house that used to be yours and now wasn't. The furniture and even many of the books in the living room were the same, but a framed picture of Jane's wedding sat on top of the TV instead of Annie's. Same groom, too. But it was a lot untidier—Annie had once been so house-proud, strange as it was to remember—and there were empty coffee cups and magazines strewn around the room. There was also a mat that was clearly for a child on the floor. It was designed like a garden, with embroidered butterflies and birds and flowers. Getting ready for their baby. Mike and Jane's baby. When Annie spoke, her voice was thin ice on a river of tears. "I didn't know."

Jane looked stricken. "No. We tried not to put anything online, in case... I told Mike he should tell you. But...you know."

We. The two short letters knifed at Annie. "I'm sorry to just turn up like this."

Jane busied herself tidying up some magazines. "Have you come...um, did you come to pick something up?"

"No. It isn't that." Oh, God, how to explain. "Could I sit down a sec, Jane? I just want to chat. Is that okay?"

Jane paused, and Annie shamefully relived the last time she'd been at this house, the day she'd left, screaming and shouting on the front path about how Jane was a home-wrecker and Mike a dirty cheat. "Okay. I guess it's about time." She nodded to the sofa. "Why don't you...?"

It was the same sofa. Annie had paid for this, a lovely cracked red leather, and yet the only sofa she had now was that awful pleather one she'd got from a British Heart Foundation shop. She tried not to mind as she sat down. Mike had felt so bad he'd offered her the house and everything in it, but she'd been too proud to take a penny. When she'd first moved out she didn't even own any spoons; she'd been so determined to walk away from her old life and leave everything behind.

"Tea?"

"Um, no, thank you." Annie wasn't sure how long Jane would let her stay once she started talking. "So I suppose you must be wondering why I—"

"It is a bit odd, yes." Jane bent down to pick up a dirty cup, hair hiding her face. It was still blond, but showing more gray in the roots now. Once it had been Jane on the sofa, Annie the flushed and happy hostess, getting ready for the birth of her child. It was the only time in her life when she hadn't felt secretly jealous of Jane—who, after all, had grown up with siblings, a nice house and a father—and when she'd felt at peace. If anything, Jane had seemed slightly lost, the name of a different man on her lips every time, tears catching in her throat when she talked. And Annie was always there to listen, provide tissues and tea and hugs. Funny. When Jane stopped moaning about her love life Annie had thought she was finally happy with being single, moving on. But really she was moving on to Mike.

Annie said, "Well. I guess I've been doing sort of…a lot of soul-searching recently."

"Oh," said Jane.

"So I wanted to come and ask you…try to understand what happened. With you and me and…him."

"You saw Zar and Miriam. Right?"

"Yeah. They said you—that you felt bad."

"Annie, I feel so bad I could just die. But you have to know I didn't plan it. Mike and I…" Annie winced. She used to say that same phrase. *Mike and I. My husband, Mike.* "You and him were already…just so broken, and so was I, and you were gone, out of reach somehow, and he just needed someone to talk to, and before I knew it we were…and now I'm…well."

"I can see." Annie stared at the bump. "How long?"

Jane put both hands on her belly, a gesture Annie recognized so well. "Seven months or so."

The baby inside would be fully formed already, fists and feet curled in on themselves. Jacob's little feet had been like that, tiny mice inside his blue and green socks. Everything safe, and cozy, and pastel. Annie swallowed, hard. "I know you didn't do it on purpose," she said (though she wasn't entirely convinced). "But I'd lost everything. My baby, then my husband, my house…and you, too. I had nothing, Jane."

Jane wouldn't meet her eyes. "I know. I'm sorry. I'm so sorry about Jakey…you know how much I loved him. I was such a mess afterward."

Annie felt like screaming, *Don't you say his name!* But she bit her tongue. Jane had been a brilliant godmother, visiting every week, taking hundreds of adoring pictures.

Jane sniffed. "It must have been horrendous for you. I can't even imagine it. But what happened with us…it was an accident, and I didn't mean it. I just fell in love. I know that was selfish. I just loved him so much. I fell so hard and I didn't know what to do."

"You're happy? The two of you?" It would be three soon. She wondered if they were using Jacob's room. Painting over the stencils she'd done of happy ducks and teddies.

Jane hesitated, then nodded guiltily. "I think so, anyway. I mean, I've been sick and knackered..." She stopped herself, as if aware of who she was talking to. "I'm sorry. I guess you don't want to hear it's hard being pregnant."

"I remember." It was hard having a baby, too. It was easy to forget that sometimes, so deep was her longing to have Jacob back. It felt like a betrayal, to even remember the feeling of walking around this very room with him, screaming in her ear, depositing snot and tears all over her, as 3:00 a.m. turned into 4:00. A deep sorrow came over Annie. "It wasn't your fault, what happened to Jakey. But, Jane—I think it was the final straw, what you did. The final thing that broke me."

Jane made a noise, a sort of ugly snort, and Annie saw she was crying, her face screwed up. Her own river of tears was shifting, moving dangerously under the ice. But no, she and Jane weren't going to cry in each other's arms, and they weren't going back to being best friends. "I'm so sorry," Jane said in her strangled crying-voice. "I miss you so much. I did such a terrible thing."

Annie's heart was so heavy it felt like a full bucket of water. "I better go." She couldn't stay here any longer, in this lovely house that was once hers. It was all so bloody unfair. Jane had her house, her husband and now a baby. And Annie had...nothing. For a second she imagined another world, one where Jane was pregnant with someone other than Annie's ex-husband. How happy Annie would have been for her. The loss of it—not just Jacob but Jane, and this baby to come, too—squeezed her heart in its fist. Could she imagine a time when she was part of their life? Went to the child's birthday parties, sent gifts?

She looked up at the ceiling. "Are you using...will you be using his room?"

"There's nowhere else." Jane was biting her lip. "I'm sorry. We'd have moved except for, you know...house prices and—"

"It's okay." Of course they'd use it—where else would they put the baby?—but all the same it hurt. It stung like an open cut.

As Annie went to the door it suddenly opened with a scrape, and standing there was Mike. He held the key in midair, almost comically, his face an O of surprise. Annie quickly took in that he, too, had aged—his hairline was farther back, and his stomach larger under his polo shirt and jeans. "Annie?" His hands were full of Waitrose bags-for-life. So he'd finally started remembering to bring them.

"Hi, Mike."

His head swiveled to Jane. "Babe, has she...?"

Babe. That was like a blade in Annie's stomach. She watched them have a quick silent conversation, the kind she used to have with him.

Did she cause a scene again?

No, it's fine.

Annie couldn't face another emotional showdown. She forced her mouth into a smile, or at least a pointing-up direction. "I need to go. Thanks for chatting to me, Jane. Con—" The word thickened in her mouth. "Congratulations. Bye."

She left them standing in the doorway, soon to be a little family of three, and as she walked down the path she heard Mike say, "There's some madwoman singing along to the *Grease* megamix in that car over there."

DAY 29
Have a Facebook cull

"Good for you," Polly said as Annie presented her phone, a little sulkily, for inspection. "Both of them gone?"

"Both of them." But it didn't feel good. She'd been friends with Jane since long before the internet, before periods and boys, before either of them could even tie their shoelaces. And now she'd erased her for good. Annie couldn't help feeling it might have gone differently, if she'd given it another year or two. Maybe if Polly hadn't pushed her into going before she was ready…but no. Those bridges were on fire, people screaming and jumping off them into the raging water. There was no point in what-ifs.

Polly squeezed her arm as they sat in the hospital café. "Come on, I'll buy you a cake. Do you think Dr. Q would like something for when he's done his run? I saw him earlier, going around and around and around the hospital. He's, like, really fit."

Annie frowned. *"Polly."*

"It's just cake."

"Sure it is. Anyway, any more cake and I'll develop type 2

diabetes and then I'll be in here with you and you won't be able to play that cancer card anymore."

"Fine, fine. Let's get out of here. I spy Dr. McGrumpy and I need to avoid him. He said I needed to get a white stick, my eyesight is so bad! Can you imagine? Me with a white stick. I'm not *blind*."

Annie saw Dr. Max at the counter, queuing for what looked like a triple espresso, and she waved. She found herself wondering idly if he was on Facebook.

DAY 30
Listen

Annie took a deep breath. She'd rewritten the email five times now and it was getting ridiculous. It was only seven words. Why not just click Send? But what if the recipient laughed, or ignored it, or forwarded it to everyone else? Her hand hovered on the mouse, paralyzed. What would Polly say? Something meaningless about it having to be dark to see the stars, no doubt. A lot of these inspirational sayings were about astronomy for some reason.

She sighed and clicked. Would you like to have lunch today? Then she stared down at her desk, the bottom dropping out of her stomach. This would be awkward. What would they even talk about? Assuming she said yes. She probably wouldn't. But when she risked looking up, Fee was nodding enthusiastically back at her.

"What a nice idea, Annie. I always just eat at my desk and work through."

"I know. But we're not paid for that, are we."

"You're right. And I didn't know this place was here." They had Styrofoam cups of coffee and bacon rolls, and were sitting on the metal chairs outside the park coffee kiosk. Fee closed her eyes against the weak spring sunshine. "This makes me feel better. Thanks, Annie."

"Is everything…everything okay?" she asked timidly. She didn't want to pry, but Fee hadn't been herself recently. She hadn't tried to get them all to do karaoke for at least a month.

"Oh, things at home are a bit tough. My partner, Julie, she's going through IVF and it's costing a fortune. And they keep muttering about redundancies at work. It makes me nervous, I suppose."

"I'm sorry to hear that. I know it can be tough when you're trying." A flashback knifed her—Mike begging, *Please, Annie, we have to stop trying. It's killing you*—and she tried to hide her wince with a sip of coffee.

"I just feel so helpless. Like it should be me doing it, but she's younger and it made more sense…" Fee trailed off. "You must think I'm awful bringing this up, Annie. After all you've been through."

"Oh! Because of…my son?" Everyone knew, of course, though no one ever mentioned it. She'd been off work for months, feeling like she might die herself from the sheer pain of it. "Honestly, I don't mind. For ages after no one would talk to me about their kids at all, or bring them to see me. I felt like a leper." As if dead children were catching or something. "So please. I'm happy to listen."

For the next half an hour she listened to Fee talk about the stress she was under, how Julie was sleeping in the spare room, how they'd maxed out their bank accounts, how worried she was about losing her job, and it made a change, Annie reflected, to for once not be the one who was falling apart.

DAY 31
Dance like no one is watching

"But should you be doing this, Poll? I mean, are you well enough?"

"What are you talking about, I'm totally fine!" Polly was already dancing along to the music as people got changed, pulling off jumpers to reveal tight leggings and vests. Annie hugged herself—she was wearing so many layers it was impossible to tell whether she was a woman, a man or the Honey Monster.

"This is going to be a nightmare," George said, chugging down Diet Coke. He had dark shadows under his eyes and an underlying reek of vodka was emanating from his pores. "I bloody hate this kind of hippie stuff. When I'm not off my tits at least."

For once Annie agreed with him. Hugging strangers and rubbing up against them was probably fine when you were on drugs, but not when it was 6:00 a.m. on Wednesday morning and you were stone-cold sober. Fear gripped her. She was doing her best to avoid eye contact, pretend it wasn't going to happen, but at some point in the next few minutes the contact dance class was going to start, and she would have to touch people, let them put their hands on her waist—if they could

find it—and her legs and arms and maybe even her face and…
oh, God. She grabbed his arm. "I can't do this. I just—I really can't. I can't dance, I hate people touching me and I just
really, really can't do it. I'm sorry."

"Don't say sorry to me, I'm in the same boat." He raked his
fingers over his exhausted face. "I hate dancing sober. I hate
wearing tight clothes. I hate smiling."

The other attendees were all glowing with health, smiling
earnestly at each other, greeting the teacher with hugs. Annie
was backed into the corner as far as she could go. A pulse of
horror was beating in her stomach. "Oh, God. I can't."

"Why didn't I actually join a gym instead of pretending?"
George moaned, sucking in his abs. "I thought the bloody
gays were fit and buff. This lot are just so…healthy."

Polly came twirling over. Although she was thin, she was
not healthy. You could see it in her fragile hair under her
headscarf, her jutting bones and tired skin. She was already
panting and they hadn't even started. Annie and George exchanged a quick look. "This is going to be great. You guys
will join in, won't you?"

"Of course!" trilled Annie.

"Can't wait!" George smiled, giving a thumbs-up. When
Polly turned around he grimaced at Annie. "Come on. We'll
get through this somehow, and earn ourselves like a million
good friend and brother points. In?"

"In," Annie said reluctantly, thinking that it was nice to
have an ally, even if it was from an unexpected source.

"And now grasp your partner by the arms…look deep into
their eyes!" Annie was currently partnered with a middle-aged
man, all noxious breath and flowing gray hair.

"It helps if you really open up to it, Anna."

"It's *Annie*." And who made him king of the contact class?

"And pushhhh…" sang the teacher, a willowy redhead called Talia, who looked as if her spandex had been spray-painted onto her slender limbs.

Bad-breath Man shoved hard at Annie. "You're meant to push back," he said helpfully.

"I am pushing," Annie gasped.

"Wow. You really need to work on your quads, Anna. I could suggest a great gym…"

"And chaaange partners!"

"Bye!" Annie scarpered before the inevitable high five. She did not high-five. It was a matter of principle. George grabbed her, wide-eyed. "Help. I just had to put my *head* between a woman's *legs*. I haven't done that since I was *born*."

They looked over to Polly, who was spinning, her turquoise scarf fluttering like a banner, cannoning into people. She was breathing hard, and Annie suspected she couldn't see very well. "Is she okay?" she said to George.

"Dunno. She's in total denial about this sight thing. Come with me." They danced over. "Hey, Poll, how about resting for a few songs?"

"I don't need to…rest," she panted.

"No, but you're showing the rest of us up. Give me and Annie time to connect with people, eh?"

"Fine," she said, sitting down quite quickly on a nearby chair. She put her hand on her back, face twisted in pain. "Just for you."

"Stick with me," George muttered to Annie. "We'll just pretend we're doing it."

And so, for the next fifty minutes, they spun and grunted and rolled on the floor and flung their arms out embracing the energy of the universe. Annie got hotter and hotter in her multiple layers, until she could feel sweat rolling down her back under her bra. George was unnervingly close, the stubble of his chin sometimes scraping her, the sound of his breath wheezing in her ear. How long was it since she'd been this close to another person? Not since Mike, surely. She kept her eyes firmly on the floor, the dented yoga mats with their faint smell of sweat, and tried to count the seconds, like when enduring a painful and undignified medical procedure. Which was something she had plenty of experience at. Eventually, it was over. She removed her head from under George's armpit, which smelled like someone had spilled a whole Glade PlugIn in it. "I think...it's finished," she said, hardly able to believe it.

"Is it?" George sounded broken.

"Hiii!" Polly came over. She looked tired but happy, dark circles on her pale face. "That was amazing. I just wish I'd done it years ago. I felt so...connected."

To Annie it had felt like being on a crowded tube, pressed up in someone's crotch, for a full hour. Only with everyone staring at you and aggressively smiling a lot. "It was...an experience," she tried.

George was more honest. "Jesus Christ, Poll. You better be actually dying, because I am never, never doing that again. I'm going to need years of therapy to get over this."

Polly waved her hand. Taking offense was one of the many things she'd decided she didn't have time for, along with worrying about her calorie intake, queuing and trying to look cool. She slung a cardigan over her thin shoulders; Annie noticed how her hands shook. But her voice was bright. "I might go with some of these guys for a hemp smoothie, fancy it?"

George and Annie clashed eyes. "I've got to work," she said quickly.

"On the weekend?"

"Um, it's Wednesday, Poll."

"Is it? Oh, well, it's all the same to me these days. What about you, bro?"

"I have a big audition…possibly."

"What for?"

"Um, I don't know," George vamped. "Agent forgot to tell me, ha-ha."

"Okay." Polly waved a hand. "See you guys soon?"

"Tomorrow. Remember?"

"Of course I remember. Duh, I've still got some of my faculties. See you then."

As she left, Annie looked at George again, and the two of them burst out laughing. "Dear God," she said. "I've had general anesthetics that were more enjoyable than that class."

"Let's never go again. Even if she begs. Pact?"

"Pact," she agreed. "Do you really have an audition?"

"Ha, no. The way things are going, I couldn't even get picked for a police lineup. Unless someone's casting for the role of 'battered husband.'"

Annie fell silent. She suspected there was more behind his black eye—now almost healed—than he was saying, but was afraid to ask.

He slung his man-bag over his shoulder and pushed his hands into his gilet pockets. "Bye, Annie. See you tomorrow for yet more ridiculous antics with my sister." And he leaned over and kissed her cheek. Annie blushed. She would never have even spoken to someone like George—so grouchy, so opinionated—in her life, if not for Polly and all this madness. Unless he rang up to complain about his council tax. And yet here she was, on a weekday morning, giggly and glowing, with an hour left before she had to be at work. Time to buy a latte somewhere, and maybe a croissant, and sit for a while in the spring sun. She thought of the city spread out before her, and she thought of Sharon and Jeff and Fee all cooped up in that smelly little office in Lewisham, and she heaved a deep sigh of something that might have been close to contentment.

DAY 32
Volunteer

"This is the worst yet," George said. "I mean…look at me."

"You look great. That yellow really matches the whites of your eyes."

He glared at Polly. "May I say it again, if you weren't already dying…"

Annie plucked at her own costume. "I get that George is the Easter bunny, but what are we?"

"Chicks, of course. Groovy chicks."

That explained the fluffy yellow dress and the orange tights. At least she got to wear a beak headdress that would hopefully hide her identity.

George was still moaning about his costume, which was made of pale yellow fur, with floppy ears. "This is so humiliating. I'm in Equity, you know."

"Think of it as a top acting gig," Polly urged. She managed to make her own chicken costume look like couture. "Come on, guys. This is really important."

Annie and George exchanged grouchy commiserating looks. "At least you're not dressed like a dumpy showgirl," she said. "You've got the starring role."

"Hmph. What's my motivation for this part?"

"To give Easter eggs to the poor suffering kids on the children's ward," Polly said sternly. "The ones who can't go outside because they're so ill it will kill them?"

"Fine, fine." He adjusted his ears. "I'm going to play it as an Easter bunny that missed out on the lead role in *Watership Down* because of a tragic brush with myxomatosis, and compensates by bringing a depth and pathos to even this gig."

"Whatevs. Right, we've hidden the eggs around the ward already, so you just have to help the kids find them and be nice and stuff. Think you can manage that?"

"Yeah," mumbled Annie and George.

"Och, it's Bugs Bunny!" Oh, no. Scottish accent. Dr. Max was approaching, today in a shirt and tie, both crumpled, as was his face with tiredness. With him was Dr. Quarani, neat as always.

"Hi, Dr. McGrumpy!" shouted Polly. "What do you think?" She gave a minitwirl, adding, faux-nonchalantly: "Oh, hi, Dr. Quarani."

"Hello," he said. Polite but distant. Annie saw Polly's face fall. "How is your mother, Ms. Hebden?"

"Much better, thanks. I found her doing the word search in her magazine earlier. It's been months since she could manage that."

"Interesting outfit." Dr. Max was looking at Annie.

Annie blushed, pulling down the edge of her fluffy dress. "It's for the kids," she said.

"Is it, or is it to make the adults feel better about themselves? I hope the costumes have been sterilized. Seriously, Polly, some of these wee ones are *vairy* sick indeed."

She rolled her eyes. "Stop fussing! It's going to be great."

"Well, sorry, but it's my job to fuss. Hand hygiene, everyone. If they're on 'nil by mouth' that means *nothing* by mouth.

Don't give them chocolate. If they're on 'limited contact,' *do not* cuddle them or pick them up. I know it might make you feel all fuzzy inside, but it could actually kill them. Aye?"

"Do you want to join us, Dr. Quarani?" Polly said innocently.

"I tend to deal with the older patients."

Dr. Max glanced at him. "Sami is a serious doctor. I doubt he'd want to be associated with grown-ups dressed like farm animals."

"Rabbits aren't farm animals." Polly adjusted her beak. "Come on, the kids are really cute!"

"I must go. It's time for my run." Dr. Quarani hurried off without a backward glance, fiddling with his Fitbit.

"Well, isn't he a barrel of laughs," muttered Polly.

Dr. Max frowned. "I'm serious, Polly. Leave Sami alone. And be careful around these kiddies. They're *vairy* fragile."

"Are you coming in?" said Annie.

He shook his head. "I've to excise a brain tumor. It's not a—"

"Not a nine-to-five, yes, we know." Polly rolled her eyes again. "That really is your catchphrase."

"Well, petition the government for more funding if you want things to change. Have fun, though."

Funny how he could always make her feel frivolous and stupid, even when she was trying to help. Annie pulled her hem down again. Polly stuck her tongue out at his retreating back. "Never mind Dr. McGrumpy. Come on, let's do this."

Annie was strangely nervous as the doors buzzed open, rubbing a layer of hand sanitizer into her palms. Sick adults she could cope with. At least they could understand their situation. But what did you say to a small child who might die before they'd even lived? At least there wouldn't be any babies. She couldn't have coped with sick babies.

There were six beds on the ward, each with a face peeping out. At the end, one little boy in Superman pajamas stared hopefully from a plastic tent. Annie swallowed hard. Tried to smile. The color palette in there was brighter, but awful somehow. The yellow of lying hope, the pink of pointless love.

"Hi, everyone! It's the Easter bunny and the awesome chicks!" Polly ran into the ward, flapping her wings. There was silence.

"They're a bit shy," said the nurse, a strapping young man whose name badge said Leroy. "Hiya, Polly."

"Babes." They exchanged cheek kisses. Annie raised her eyebrows at George. How did Polly know *everyone*?

"This is Leroy, who basically runs this place, and that's Kate, the pediatrician." This was a freckled young woman with plaits and scrubs who looked about twelve.

"Hi, guys. Did Dr. Max run through the infection control? I know it's a pain but some of them are pretty sick."

"What's—I mean, what do they have?" George made a rather subdued mythological figure, staring at one kid whose head was wrapped in bandages.

Kate went around them, pointing her stethoscope. "Bilal there had fluid on the brain. Amy has a hole in her heart— she's getting her fourteenth surgery soon." This was a little girl with pigtails to match Kate's, in a pink elephant onesie, who looked all of three. "Matty has brittle bone disease—this is his tenth fracture." A kid playing on a Game Boy, both legs in plaster. "Matty!" She mimed taking headphones out and he did, reluctantly. Kate moved around the room. "That's Anika—she has a brain tumor."

"Snap," Polly said with the disconcerting smile she wore whenever she talked about her illness. She'd told Annie, "Oh, it's just everyone says 'cancer' in that same way, like they have to swallow the word down in case it kills them. Like it's Volde-mort. I'm just trying something different, is all."

Kate came to the final two kids. "That's Roxy. Fifteen going on fifty, doesn't think she should be in the children's ward."

Roxy was a Goth-looking teen in a black jumper and leg-gings, with a black scarf around her bald head. She'd drawn her eyebrows back on with dark pencil. She tutted. "I can hear you, you know. And this is lame."

"Yes, Roxy, we know you hate everything. And in the little tent there is Damon. Poor kid was born with basically no immune system."

Annie tried not to look horrified. "So, he has to stay in there?"

"We're prepping him for a stem cell transplant, so we can't risk infection. Even his parents have to talk to him through that, sadly."

Annie felt something tug on her feathers, and looked down to see Amy, the smallest girl, standing there shyly. "Is that the Easter bunny?"

"Sure is! Um, maybe he'd like to talk now?"

She could almost see George give himself a pep talk, getting into the role. His voice came out high-pitched, with a slight American accent. "Hi, kids! I'm the Easter bunny! I know you've all been a bit poorly, so I'm here to lead the Easter egg hunt. Let's see what you can find!"

"What a pro," muttered Polly.

Annie would not have believed six children—one inside a tent—could cause so much mayhem. Eggs were located under beds, in the medicine store, in bedside cabinets, in the pocket of Kate's white coat. Even Roxy joined in, pushing Matty in a wheelchair so he could take part, too. Polly was chatting to Anika. "Did you know we're brain twins?"

Anika looked at her shyly. "I have a bad lump in my head."

"Me, too." Polly lifted up her chick headdress to show the bald part of her scalp.

Kate nudged Annie. "I think Bilal could use a little help. He's a bit woozy from his surgery."

Bilal, half his face obscured by the bandage, was feeling carefully around the edge of a set of shelves that held toys. Although *toys* was putting it kindly—there were some grubby colored blocks, a doll with one eye and cuddly animals with the stuffing knocked out of them. A bit like the kids. "Hello," Annie said, desperately nervous. She had no experience of children past the age of two months. "Um, I'm Annie. Are you Bilal?"

He stared at her.

"How old are you, Bilal?"

"Five." He looked so small, so sick.

"Look, I think there's something hiding around the back there. Inside the stacking blocks."

He reached in and brought out a small egg, wrapped in purple silver foil. His small face, so wan and scarred, lit up. "The Easter bunny!"

"That's right, he left you an egg!" She looked to Kate for confirmation; she nodded. "Why don't we have a bit?" As Bilal smeared his face in chocolate, Annie looked about her. There was George, letting tiny Amy slide around on his feet/ paws. Polly, with Anika by her feet dissecting an egg, was chatting to Roxy, miming putting on eyeliner. Her eyebrows had mostly gone with the chemo, too. Matty was over chatting to Damon, showing him the eggs he'd found, while the other boy looked out. He was bald and pale but Annie saw he had a lightsaber hung over his bed. Would Jacob have been into that, if he'd lived—would she have had to learn about Storm-troopers and football and Lego?

Annie blinked. Bilal was staring at her from under his bandage. "Hey, I know," she said, trying to sound cheerful. "I bet you could wear some really cool hats over that bandage. Polly, do you have a hat in your bag?"

"Of course! I never go anywhere without a hat. Let me see." She rummaged in her large print bag, pulling out a beanie. "How about this? This is the coolest one I have." She set it on Bilal's head, stepping back to look at him critically. "Oh, no! I made him look too cool. We can't let him wear this, Annie, can we? He's stealing all my style."

Annie played along. "Oh, come on, Polly, just because he's cooler than you, there's no need to be jealous."

Bilal giggled. It was far too big for him, but it hid the stark whiteness of the bandage, made him look more like an average kid, if a scrawny one wearing *Doctor Who* pajamas in the daytime.

George came over, pushing up his bunny ears. He was flushed and smiling. "Guess what? They want me to come back, maybe every week. They've got a whole rack of costumes apparently. Who'd've had thought Easter bunny would be my breakthrough role! I must go and prep for my motivation as Coco the Clown."

Annie met Polly's eyes, and they started to laugh. "He's going to be insufferable now," said Polly. "What about you, Annie? Any life lessons learned on the children's ward? Did they teach you the true meaning of things?"

"I wouldn't go that far." Annie looked back at the sad rack of toys. "But I might have an idea what we can do next."

DAY 33
Get organized

"Right, so Milly's going to sort out the social media and on-line stuff—she says if I just stay away and let her do everything she can make a go of it. Suze will do PR and press. Dr. Max is going to clear things with the hospital and—"

"He is?" Annie interrupted. "I thought he didn't believe in fundraising."

"Well, something's changed his mind," Polly said innocently. "Can't think why that could be, can you, Annie?"

"No," she said hurriedly. "I can sort the tickets, getting the money in and so on. We should set up a fundraising page, too, in case people want to donate online."

"Good idea. It's going to be great."

Annie wasn't so sure. Whenever she thought of what they were planning, she got the same feeling as when she'd climbed to the top of the biggest playground slide as a kid—that going back would be too embarrassing, but going ahead was absolutely terrifying, as well.

DAY 34
Let out your artistic side

"What's that meant to be?"

"It's a child. You know, like the ones we're meant to be helping?"

Annie regarded the screen Polly was painting. "Looks like a bear to me."

"A bear?"

"Yep. People will think we're raising money for Paddington."

"Okay, okay, I failed art at school, that's why I ended up doing history of instead. At least I'm having a go."

Annie patted her shoulder. Today Polly was wearing her dungarees again, the remnants of her hair tied back in a silk scarf. Annie had to hand it to her; there was nothing she didn't know about dressing for an occasion. "That's okay, we'll tell people the kids painted it. Maybe you should get that white stick, after all?"

Polly pouted for a moment, then drew back her brush and flicked a dollop of blue paint at Annie. It landed on her jeans and for a moment Annie gaped, then she stuck her fingers in the pot and threw some back. It hit Polly square on the face, and Annie for a second was terrified she'd hurt her, and then Polly burst out laughing and flung some more.

"Och, for God's sake," tutted Dr. Max, who was passing. He was just passing a lot, it seemed, for someone so busy. "Are you two twelve or something?"

She felt it, Annie realized, around Polly. Like she was young, and she'd found a new best friend, and everything was ahead of them, exciting and fresh and new. Except, of course, it wasn't. She passed a tissue to Polly. "Here. Sorry about that. Why don't you let me finish this one, eh?"

"Okay," Polly said, surprisingly acquiescent. "I might just... sit down over here for a minute."

Annie watched her friend drag herself to a chair, her face set in pain, and a flicker of alarm came and went in her stomach.

DAY 35
Help someone

Annie stood outside Costas's door, her hand hovering an inch away from it. Buster was snuffling around the edges of the door, unused to seeing it shut. She should knock. She knew that. But she'd never done it before, preferring to text him or leave passive-aggressive notes (actually, she wasn't much better than Sharon in that respect). On the other side of the door, she heard another gulping sob. It was unavoidable—Costas was crying.

"Maybe we should give him some space," she whispered to Buster. The little dog cocked his head at her and gave out a soft whine.

"Fine, fine, okay." Sighing, she knocked gently. "Costas?"

Instantly he went quiet. After a moment he said, "Yes?"

"Um, are you okay?"

"Fine, fine!" It was like a parody of his usual chirpy tone.

"Listen, I heard you. I know you're not."

The door opened and there was Costas in his work T-shirt, his face red and swollen. "What happened?"

He wiped a hand over his face like a kid. "Is nothing."

"It's not nothing."

Dejected, he said, "Is work. I was in kitchen, dancing to the—the Magic FM, you know. My favorite song."

"And what was that?" As if she didn't know.

"Mariah Carey, of course. And these men, the one who delivers the cups, they laugh at me—call me a bad word." He lowered his voice to a whisper. *"Fag."*

"That's horrible. I'm sorry, but they're just a bunch of bigots."

"I did not think it would be like this here. I thought was okay to be gay, you know." His face wrinkled up, his breath hitched, and she recognized the symptoms of someone on the verge of a full crying jag. "And all I do is make the coffee. I wanted to work in fashion, Annie. This is why I come to London, you know. We have no fashion in Athens. But instead I just learn to make the swirly patterns on the latte."

"Well, that's good, too."

He snuffled some more, his gym-honed arms folded over his chest. "I miss home, Annie. I am missing my mother and my sisters. They are so far away. I come all this way away from them and I get nowhere in my life. Just the pictures in the coffee." He sniffed. "I... I am sorry, Annie. I know this is a stupid thing, when your friend and your mama are sick, but... I am sad."

And all this time he'd been on the other side of the wall, and Annie hadn't been able to hear him over the sound of her own heart breaking. "I'm so sorry, Costas. That really sucks."

He nodded, more tears coming up. "Is okay. I will be okay. Is just...a setback. At least we have the puppy. Come here, baby." He lifted Buster in his arms, and the dog began to lick his tears, making Costas giggle. They'd have to get rid of the puppy soon; he couldn't live in a flat forever. But how could she do that to Costas?

Annie looked at her watch—two o'clock. She'd been plan-

ning to spend the day in bed with her favorite fictional doctors (and not think about her favorite real-life one). "Listen,
shall we go out? This flat is depressing enough to be in, no
wonder we feel down. How about I treat you to the British tradition of Sunday lunch in the pub? We can even bring
Buster if you like."

DAY 36

Get your hair done

"Honestly, Annie, you need to say goodbye."

"But I'm attached to it!"

"That's the problem." Polly leaned over and seized a hank of Annie's lank brown hair. "Cutting your hair is symbolic. Letting go of the past, freeing yourself—think Rapunzel. Delilah. Britney Spears."

"I'm not shaving it off."

"Just get a few inches cut, for God's sake. If you're speaking in public you need to feel confident."

Annie's stomach lurched at the thought. Why had she agreed to this? "Oh, all right, then. Just a few inches."

But as everyone knows, "just a few inches" is hairdresser code for "I want it all off, please," and an hour later Annie was regarding herself in the mirror with her hair just below her ears, blow-dried into soft dark curls.

"We should have done a color too," Polly said, running her fingers through it proprietorially. "Maybe we can—"

"Nope." Annie pulled herself away. "Look at me! I look totally different!"

"I know!" Polly gave her the thumbs-up. "Goodbye negative energy hair, hello new bob! I wish I could do the same. One blast with a drier and mine would all fall out."

"My hair didn't have energy in it. It was just…hair." And now it was on the floor.

Annie stared at herself, the way the bob curled below her ears, making her face looked heart-shaped. She was wearing one of the dresses Polly had forced her into, a green frock with little flowers on it, and Converses on her feet. She looked okay. She looked like a normal person. In the mirror she could see Polly smirking. "All right, all right, it's just a haircut. Nothing's changed."

"You sure about that?" said Polly.

DAY 37
Give something back

"Where do you want these guns, Annie?"

Annie checked her clipboard, flustered. "Um, I guess those are for the *Guys and Dolls* number. If you can find some people dressed as gangsters, give them to them?"

"Okay." Zarah, who was helping out backstage, rushed off.

It was hectic. Dozens of people were coming up to Annie, asking her questions. Amazingly, she did know the answers to most of them, because somehow, against all the odds, they had pulled this fundraising concert together inside a week. They'd kept it as simple as possible, roping in the staff to sing songs or do skits, as well as George's acting friends who were dancers and performers in West End shows. Annie had been amazed how many people were willing to help at short notice, and even more amazed when the tickets starting selling to rich members of the hospital board and their mates.

It kept growing. Polly's former corporate clients from when she worked in PR wanted to help, booking up rows of seats. "Cancer card," she'd explained. "Everyone feels bad for me, so I can ask for whatever I like." And it went on. Suze knew everyone in the media. Costas was very happily sorting out

costumes borrowed from Polly's stylist friend or Valerie's am-
dram group. Miriam's husband, an electrician, was doing the
lighting. And Annie herself had pulled it all together, creating
spreadsheets, delegating tasks, handling the money.

She'd even stood up in front of the hospital board—seriously formidable men and women—and explained her idea.
Word had got out, fast. The goodwill had grown and grown,
from patients, from their families, from everyone who knew
Polly. So now they were expecting a hundred people to watch
the variety show they'd somehow cobbled together. Annie
was doing her best not to think about it, in case she threw up
all over the front row. How did she, Annie Hebden, Annie
Clarke, end up doing this?

Polly. Polly was the answer.

"Annie." Dr. Max was approaching down the aisle of the
hospital's lecture theater, squinting at her in the dark. "New
hair?"

"Oh, yes." She touched it self-consciously.

"Thought so. Very...bonny." He stooped, picking up a large
yellow feather. "I see you got Big Bird in to do a turn."

"Oh, that must be one of the burlesque dancers."

"There's going to be burlesque? You know we have some
quite-senior board members coming tonight?"

"Polly says it's tasteful. Not like stripping. She once did the
PR for a cabaret club or something."

"Taking your clothes off to music? That sounds like the
dictionary definition of *stripping*. Not that I would know."
He rubbed his hands over his head, making his hair stick up
again. Once again he looked exhausted, in rumpled clothes.
Did he ever look in a mirror? Annie wondered. How could
someone perform brain surgery and yet not be able to do up
the buttons on their shirt right? "I guess this was Polly's idea.
Where is she, anyway?"

"It was my idea actually. She's up there." Annie waved to where Polly was up a ladder, stringing fairy lights.

Dr. Max gritted his teeth. "For the love of God. She's not well enough for this, Annie. I've told you. She needs to rest."

"She doesn't want to rest!" Annie tried to keep her voice low. "She knows she doesn't have a lot of time, and she doesn't want to spend it lying in a hospital bed! Okay?"

"I know. I know that. But trust me, she'll need her strength. When the time comes."

Annie shrugged off the cold chill his words gave her. "Look, maybe instead of moaning you could get involved? We're trying to raise some money for the children's ward. Buy them some toys and so on."

Reluctantly, he tucked up his coffee-stained tie and stooped to move some of the boxes littering the stage. "That's all very laudable, Annie, but what those kids need is proper NHS funding. Time spent researching cures. Nurses and doctors who aren't knackered and demoralized."

Stung, Annie bent down to pick up a box herself. She'd thought he was on her side since he'd helped sway the hospital board. "I'm just trying to do something."

"I know. I know you're trying to help. But really—things like this? Where everyone has a nice time and goes home feeling good about themselves? I worry that it's just a way to not ask the hard questions. The bigger ones. But you carry on. It won't do any harm, I suppose."

Carry on. Like he was patting a child on the head. Annie glared at him. "At least I'm trying. I'm not a scientist or a doctor, but I can do this small thing, and so I am. Okay?"

He held up his hands. "Annie, I didn't mean—"

"Let's just leave it." She turned back to her clipboard, hiding her face.

"It's Dr. McGrumpy!" Polly called down, swaying on her

ladder. "Come to tell us we're violating health and safety or something?"

"You certainly are, up a ladder in those shoes. Would you ever get down, woman?"

"In a minute." She was peering hard at the loop of the fairy lights, trying to secure it with some tape. It seemed to be taking her ages.

Dr. Max was watching. "Do you want a wee hand with that?"

"'Course not, it's only tape. Bugger!" The string of lights fell to the floor, fusing out. Dr. Max met Annie's eyes, with a clear *I told you so*.

"Polly," she called, "I need your help with something here. Um, the burlesque dancers have run out of…hairspray. Can you come down?"

"Oh, okay." Dr. Max rushed to hold the ladder as she wobbled down it in her silver stilettos and floaty pink dress. "I'm not an invalid," she grumbled. But she looked like one. She was so thin, Annie saw. Even thinner than a few weeks ago. How could you lose so much weight so quickly? The dress hung on her, her body lost inside the floating layers of chiffon. But she was still smiling. "Now, what's this hairspray… Oh, my God."

"Pollleeeeee!" Two voices chimed as one. Milly and Suze had flung open the door of the lecture theater. They were both in high heels, both in skinny jeans and both snapping away with iPhones.

"Who are those?" Dr. Max was staring as they approached, aiming their phones like a SWAT team sweeping a crime scene.

"Those are my friends. The PR Platoon." Polly waved to them. "Ohh emmm geeeee, you came! Let me do introduc-

tions. This is my neurologist, Dr. Max, and this is Milly and
Suze. These women basically run the UK media."

They fell on him.

"Omigod, I love your look. Noble yet careworn. How
would you feel about doing a quick to-camera?"

"Er, ladies…"

"Omigod, he's *Scottish*! Even better. I'm thinking radio.
Give Sunil a bell over at *Today*."

Their fingers tapped at their phones, unceasing. Milly said,
"The fundraising page is racing ahead, P. We're already at 5K.
It's all over Facebook, Twitter is blowing up. The *Telegraph*
want an interview."

"I'm going to bell Ivana at the *Guardian*. Human interest,
caring, etc., etc. They'll love it."

Milly caught at Polly's chin. "Babe, you're a bit pale. We've
got a photographer coming by—shall I contour you up a bit?"

Suze was snapping pictures of Dr. Max from every angle.
"The surgeon, too. Keep the shadows but blend out the nose
a bit and—"

"Ladies!" he roared. "I will not be interviewed, and I will
not have makeup put on me! I have paperwork, and sick patients to visit, and wounds to check. I don't have time for this."

"Love the anger." Suze sighed. "Maybe we can harness that.
I'm thinking Channel 4 News. I'll bell Liam."

"The money's coming in." Milly waved her phone. "Big
Twitter surge. But we need a personal story, Polly babes. So
people can relate. Quick video diary?"

"Money," Polly said to Dr. Max. "Wouldn't that go toward
the new scanner you wanted? The extra MRI machine? So
people don't have to wait as long for diagnosis and maybe you
can catch their cancer earlier?"

He considered it for a moment. "No makeup. I draw the
line there."

"Ace!" They spirited him away, tapping and snapping and chatting all the while.

Polly sighed. "Those two could run the world. I shouldn't have shut them out, I guess."

"It's your cancer. You can shut people out if you want."

Polly laughed. "That's why I like you, Annie. No pressure to be positive or organize fun runs or write long blog posts about how I feel."

"I thought that's exactly what you wanted to do?"

"On my own terms. Not because people expect it of me."

"But tonight, though, we have to pretend we're all positive and happy and that we can make a difference?" Whatever Dr. Max said.

"We do. Except I think we might have a small problem."

Panic gnawed at Annie's stomach. "What?"

Polly checked her watch. "Well, I know he has the lead role and everything, but have you actually seen George at all tonight?"

Annie had sweated all the way through her black vest top. Backstage was full of people—comedians running through their routines, dancers limbering up, singers going through scales, even someone juggling with IV packs. But of George, who was meant to MC the whole night, there was no sign. "Call him again?"

"I've tried." Polly was even paler. "Oh, God. I bet he's bottled it. That's what happened, you know, when he got his West End break—back of the chorus line as a soldier in *Miss Saigon*. He couldn't go on. Got fired after one night. I bet he's with fucking Caleb. I'm going to kill him."

"His ex-boyfriend?" But Polly wasn't listening. "Look, maybe there's an explanation. Maybe he got stuck in traffic or—"

"He's coming on the tube!" Polly was starting to lose it, something Annie had never seen before. "It's all going to fall apart. All those media people—we're going to let them down, Annie. The kids. The hospital. We're going to fail."

Fail. The word stuck in Annie's throat. Of course she couldn't pull this off. Why had she even tried? She wasn't the kind of person who could change things. She was the kind of person who got dragged along by life, and eventually towed under. But through her cloud of yammering thoughts, she could hear something. "What's that noise?"

"What noise?" Polly's hands were squeezed together so tightly they'd gone white.

"It sounds like…" It was crying. She was sure of it. She hunted around the small backstage corridor, eventually throwing open the door to the disabled loo. In there, perched on the seat, in his spangly red MC suit, was George. His hands hid his face and his shoulders were working. "What happened? Are you okay?" She rushed forward, but Polly stood where she was.

"Let me see your face," she said coldly.

He shook his head.

"George! Let me see it."

Slowly, George looked up. Annie gasped. His left eye and the side of his face were covered in another purpling bruise, blood matted in his hair.

"Did he do this?" Polly demanded. George just nodded. Polly swore. "We're calling the police this time. Okay? You promised."

George spoke in a tiny voice, one Annie had never heard before. "I can't go on. Look at the state of me."

"But you have to!" Polly said. "You have to do it!"

George sobbed. "Look what he did to me. I—I loved him. And look what he thinks of me. I—I'm nothing. I'm a no-body. I'm a fat nobody. And he's this big TV star and I'm just a failure and…" Annie suddenly put it together. Of course, *Caleb*. He was that guy in that thing about the vet.

"You got back together?" Polly sounded livid.

George shook his head, ashamed. "He wouldn't take me back. We were just…seeing each other sometimes. But now it's…" Fresh tears drowned his voice. "I'm sorry. I'm so sorry, Poll. I wanted him to come tonight. I wanted him to see me do well. So I called around and…this is what happened."

Polly strode in, kneeling in front of her brother. "Listen to me, George. You're not nothing. He's the one who should be ashamed. He should be in jail. But you're my brother and I need you right now. I really need you. This is your big night. But it's more than that—we could raise thousands tonight. We could help so many people, people who are sick like me. We could catch cancers earlier, give people a chance… Look." She pulled at her bag. "Where is it, where is it…here." She took out her hat of the day. "Fedora today, luckily. Put this on, knock it into a rakish angle, and we'll get someone to patch you up—that lovely nurse Leroy is about—then a bit of makeup and no one will know. It'll be dark. I promise."

He just swallowed, so hard Annie could hear it from where she stood. She heard herself say, "The show must go on. Right?"

Shakily, George stood up. When he turned to the light, the bruise was livid, and Annie winced. "I'm not wearing a fedora," he sniffed. "I'm not a bloody men's rights activist. See what else you can find and get me the buffest nurse and the best makeup person we have, and we'll try to pull this off."

"Done." Polly held out her hand. "Come with me. We don't have much time."

"Annie?" She turned to see Dr. Max standing in the corridor. "Is everything okay?"

Annie was distracted, watching some dancers get their tail

feathers perilously close to the lights. "Look, I know you think this is stupid, but it's really not helpful if you just keep criticizing things and—"

"I don't think it's stupid. I shouldn't have said that. I'm sorry."

She gave him a look.

"Fine, okay, it's not my thing. But...you've done a good job. An amazing job, really, in the time you had. It'll be good, I'm sure."

"Will it?" Suddenly Annie's own panic showed. "I don't know, because we really didn't have much time at all and it's all a bit thrown together, and you're right, there are important people here, and George is having a meltdown and there are seminaked dancers about to go onstage, and, oh, God. You're right. I shouldn't have done this."

"Hey, come on." Awkwardly, he held out his burly arms. "It's going to be fine. Calm down. Deep breaths."

Annie found herself squashed up against him, his lanyard digging into her cheek. Dr. Max was hugging her. She was hugging Dr. Max. She pulled back a little, dazed, and his face was very close to hers. As if in a kind of trance, he put up a hand, one of his capable surgeon's hands, and stroked her cheek. "Annie. It's going to be okay. I promise."

"I..." Was he going to kiss her? Surely not. He was Polly's doctor, and the show was about to start any minute, and no one had kissed her in years, and why would he fancy her, anyway? But he wasn't pulling away.

The moment continued. Annie held his gaze. Thought of Mike, and Jane. Her heart still felt like a raw piece of meat. What if she kissed him and fell in love with him and got hurt again? She wasn't sure she could stand it. But shouldn't she take a risk? He was just so nice. He smelled of soap, and coffee. His arms were so solid around her.

"Annie!" *Damn it.* Polly was standing behind them, frowning. "What are you doing?"

Annie stiffened and pushed at his chest. Dr. Max stepped away, clearing his throat. "Annie wasn't feeling well. Just a bit of nerves, I think."

"We're ready to start now."

She pulled herself together. "Great, great. I'll just…"

"Um, I better…" Dr. Max began to shuffle away.

"Okay…" She watched him walk away.

"Are you ready?" Polly was still frowning.

"Sorry. Yes, yes, I am. Let's do this."

Afterward, Annie could only remember the night as a blur. Sequins, lights, laughter and sighs from the audience, applause. The sound of tapping feet on the stage of the lecture theater, which normally only showed slides about disease. A place full of death, death and more death, and they'd filled it with life, loud and bright and shimmering. At least on the stage. Behind it things were a little more fraught, everyone losing their costumes and makeup and cues and dance partners. Annie raced around with her clipboard, barely seeing any of it. By the end she was doused in sweat, sure that she had a damp oval on her back, and her feet were aching. She could hear the final applause now, as George stood making a speech. He'd been onstage the whole night, smiling, entertaining, totally in control. You'd never have known he was the same man weeping in the loos. It was so easy to put on an act, Annie realized. She wondered what would happen now. Would he ditch Caleb, as Polly wanted? Or keep going back for more? She knew it wasn't as simple as leaving the minute someone hurt you.

She stopped to listen for a moment.

"Ladies and gentlemen, nurses and doctors, parents, patients.

Tonight, we've done something wonderful. With online donations, we've raised an incredible sixty thousand pounds."
There were gasps. Annie's mouth fell open—how could it be
so much?

The lecture screen behind George flickered into life, and
Annie saw a fundraising page, the target exceeded hundreds
of times over.

George was saying, "To explain why this money is needed,
I'd like to introduce possibly the most annoying patient in the
history of this hospital—my sister, Polly."

Thunderous applause. Annie's head swiveled, and then she
saw Polly come onstage from the other wing. She was moving slowly, as if her back hurt, but she was waving and smiling. Annie saw Milly and Suze standing up in the front row,
ready to film the whole speech and put it online.

"Hi!" said Polly. Annie could hear her voice was cracked,
her throat dry. "I won't keep you, as I'm sure you all need
to get home." Meaning, Polly needed to get home. "A few
months ago I was diagnosed, right in this hospital, with a brain
tumor." More murmurs of sympathy. She barreled through—
that would have annoyed her, Annie was sure. "I know, I
know, that sounds awful—and I guess it is—but I can honestly say I'm not brave, I'm not a noble cancer sufferer. The
people who are brave and noble are in this room—and also
not in this room because they're still working, changing IVs
and updating charts and bringing people drinks and cleaning
operating theaters." Polly looked around at the audience, the
staff members crowding into the wings and the aisles of the
theater, and she was smiling, despite her exhaustion. "When I
imagined where I might die, it wasn't in Lewisham. It would
have been on a tropical island somewhere, maybe in a tragic
speedboat accident at the age of ninety." Laughter. "But now
that it's happening, I feel truly lucky. If I have to die, I can

think of no better place to do it than here, with these people taking care of me."

Annie's hand went up, shaky, to wipe her face. Was Dr. Max here? She hoped he was hearing this. But probably he was off twiddling with someone's skull or fighting with the vending machine or drinking one of his horrible triple espressos. She hoped he wouldn't be angry with her after that weird moment. Maybe he hadn't been about to kiss her, anyway. Why would he, when the hospital was full of pretty women who all thought he was God's gift to neurology? It was all so unsettling.

Then she realized everyone was staring her way. She shrank back into the shadows. Polly beckoned to her. "So, as I was saying, the whole credit for dreaming up this amazing night goes to one person. Everyone, please thank my friend Annie."

Oh, God. She had to go onstage. Oh, Lord. And she was sweaty and her hair was all sticking up. She shuffled forward, blinded by the lights. An impression of hundreds of faces watching her. Everyone was clapping. Polly was pushing her to the microphone. Oh, God. She had to say something. She could feel all the sweat up and down her back. "Er, hi." This was being filmed. *Argh!* "It's not really down to me—it's everyone who took part, who spread the word, who donated to the online fundraising, who bought tickets...uhhh. But I just want to say that Polly was right. Even in my lifetime of being reasonably healthy, this hospital has so far helped me have a baby, then sent an ambulance to try and save him when he died." She was aware of George's sharp double take. He hadn't known. "It's also helped my mother when she can't remember who or where she is. And it's helping my friend Polly. So, I just want to say...we will probably all need a hospital at some point in our lives. If you haven't yet, you will, one day. So please support them. All of them. Please don't let them be destroyed. Just—please. We can't live without them. Quite literally." She stepped back, shaking with adrenaline. She'd said too much. She'd gone political.

Someone was coming onstage, taking the microphone from her, gently, murmuring over the storm of clapping. Clapping who? It must be her. They were clapping her. "Well said," murmured Dr. Max. He'd smartened himself up a little since earlier, in a new shirt and tie, and he'd dampened down his wild springy hair. "So unless you want to say more—and I think that was perfect—do you mind?"

She stepped back. *Perfect.* He'd said it was perfect. Dr. Max cleared his throat. "Hello, everyone. I'm the chief neurosurgeon here. What Annie just said—it's why we all go to work every day. We don't go for the money or the prestige—although it's fun when people try to sue you..." Nervous laughter. "But I promised I wouldn't rant. And as I've just lost a bet, I'm now going to sing you a song."

And Dr. Max began to sing, his voice low and rich. She couldn't place the song for a moment. Something about stumbling and a cup of ambition and... Oh, God. He was singing Dolly Parton's "9 to 5." A joke, a private joke. Singing it slow and mournful, almost like a ballad, then speeding up until people were on their feet, stamping and cheering and singing along, until his voice was drowned out. Then, just when she thought it couldn't get any more surreal, a piper came onstage, in full Highland dress, blowing into a set of bagpipes, playing the bass line. Annie recognized one of the nurses from Intensive Care. More clapping. More singing. Annie was looking at Polly, almost strangled with laughter, feeling lifted up by it—the joy of the moment, the silliness, the kindness, the relief—and Polly was smiling back.

Then a look crossed her face. Later Annie would think it was as if a shadow had swept past her friend. A shadow in a long black cloak. Polly's face seemed to fall in on itself, and Annie was already racing across the stage, as the final applause died down and Dr. Max was thanking everyone. She was already running as Polly's legs crumpled, and so she was there to catch her friend as she fell to the ground, unconscious.

DAY 38
Visit a sick person

"How is she?"

George just shook his head. He looked as if he hadn't slept all night; when Polly collapsed they'd sent everyone home from the concert, saying she needed to rest, but Annie hadn't slept, either, for worry, and had taken the first bus back in the morning.

She looked at the giant stuffed bear she'd brought, feeling stupid. She'd tried to avoid the "get well soon" stuff, as surely Polly was not going to get well at all. "Have they said anything?"

"Not a word. Dr. Max is avoiding me. And Mum and Dad..." He sighed deeply. "They're driving me completely mad. Come in, will you? They might stop if you're there."

Annie followed him into the private room, registering that Polly lay there—that frail body disappearing beneath sheets and hospital gown—hooked up to the machines. Heart monitor. Breathing mask. IV. Annie had been in the hospital enough times to know that the more tubes you had, the worse things were for you.

Valerie and Roger sat either side of her, arguing in stiff quiet voices. "I told you we shouldn't let her gad about the place. She's sick, Valerie!"

"It's what she wanted. And she was so well."

"She wasn't well at all! Why can't you just face things? Polly's dying, George is...how he is, and—"

"He's just confused, Roger! He doesn't know what he wants! And you're one to talk. I was so ashamed last night—having to call a taxi to get here because you weren't fit to drive and—"

"Annie's here," George said loudly.

They both stuck on fake smiles. "Oh, how nice. Come in, dear."

Annie stood in the door. "I don't want to intrude. I just needed to see how she was."

Valerie's eyes were bright were tears, her voice strained. "She had some kind of crash last night, but we don't know if it's...if it's temporary or not. We're still hopeful, of course! She's probably just tired." Roger tutted.

The door opened and Dr. Max came in, brisk and rumpled. Had he been home at all? Annie doubted it. "Hi, everyone." His eyes flicked over her, and the teddy bear she was holding.

"I'll go," she said hastily. "Give you some privacy." After last night, she didn't know what to say to him.

George grabbed her arm, squeezing subtly. "I think Polly would want you here, Annie."

Reluctantly, she stayed. Dr. Max cleared his throat, arranging X-ray films on the wall holder. "Right. This is a scan of her lungs. You see that white bit?"

Annie knew by now what white bits meant. They meant not good. They meant *oh, shit.* They meant Polly was getting worse.

"A tumor," George said in a small voice.

"Aye. A secondary, on the lung. It explains the breathless-

ness and back pain she's been trying to hide for weeks now."
He glanced at Annie and she felt a stab of guilt, thinking of
Polly up that ladder.

Valerie's voice was wobbly. "Can we…is there anything…?"

"Radiotherapy should shrink it. Reduce the pain a bit, let
her breathe. But it'll take its toll. She's so weak."

In the spaces between the words, in the silence of the four of
them—five if you counted Polly, out of it on the bed—Annie
understood what he was saying. It had started. The beginning
of the end. She had to do something—move, speak. "I…" Everyone turned to look at her. She fumbled the teddy into Dr.
Max's arms. "I shouldn't be here. I'm sorry. I'm sorry." She
pushed the door open and ran out into the corridor. This place.
Full of death and terrible news and just endless bad things,
going on and on. When would there be good news? When
would something normal happen to her, like falling in love
or going on holiday or taking up Zumba?

"Annie, wait!" She turned to see Dr. Max padding after her,
with his long loping stride. He was still holding the teddy in
his hands, as if he didn't know what to do with it.

"I can't be there, I can't, it's not fair, she's so young and so
alive and it's not *fair*. Dr. Max, why can't you do something?
Why can't you fix her?" She swallowed down hysterical tears.
"I'm sorry. Shit. I'm sorry."

Gently, he said, "Okay, only dogs can hear you now."

"I'm s-sorry."

"Look, I wish I could do something. I've thrown everything I have at this bastard tumor. Chemo. Radio. Surgery.
Drugs. And it just keeps coming back. I've done everything."

"I know you have. I'm sorry. I'm sorry I said that. And I'm
sorry…" She wanted to say she was sorry about last night, but
was she? She felt so confused.

"Och, everyone says it at some point. But we're not magic, Annie. We're just people."

She wiped a hand over her face. "This…this is it, isn't it?"

"Not quite." His voice was kind. "But…yes. It's the start of it."

"Oh."

"It was always terminal, Annie. There was no cure. Maybe in a few years, if trials go well, we might have something more to throw at cases like this. But there was never any chance for Polly."

It was happening. It was happening. Polly was going to die. "Will she…is this all, then?"

"Have a bit of hope, Annie. Just a wee tiny bit. We might get her out for one last hurrah. You'll see." He hesitated for a moment, and she wanted to throw herself into his arms. She was desperate for someone to hold her, hug her close. Who else was there? Even her own mother didn't know who she was.

But he hesitated, and so did she, and then he said, "I better go."

So she leaned against the wall and cried. For Polly, for herself, for Jacob and her mum, but mostly because hope, when you let it take root in you, was such a hardy little bugger.

DAY 39
Hope

"But just read the studies, please!"

Dr. Max's voice was calm. "I have read them, Polly. It's my job to keep up with the research."

"Well, then! The stem cell treatment's shown good results."

"In a very limited trial. For one type of cancer, which you don't have. And two patients died from it. They're a long way off an available treatment. Two years at least. I'm sorry. You don't have that kind of time."

"But... I'll sign something! I'll agree to have it early, before it's ready. I can be the tester!" Her voice cracked. Annie couldn't bear it. She got up to leave from her post outside Polly's room, but blundered into George, arriving with a bag of snacks from Waitrose. Annie knew Polly wouldn't be able to eat any of it, but they kept trying to bring her things, tempt her appetite back.

"What's the matter?" he whispered, seeing her face.

"I—" she waved at the door "—can't stop listening. Sorry. It's awful."

"...can't let you do that. The ethics board would never pass it."

"Well, then, I'll go somewhere else. I bet someone in the States offers it, or somewhere else, or—"

"Polly." It was as stern as she'd ever heard Dr. Max be. George's eyes were wide-open, listening in. "Please try to understand. It may be that some hospital somewhere would give you this stem cell treatment, in return for thousands and thousands of pounds of your money. There is no evidence it would even work, and in my opinion you're not well enough to travel overseas. You'd need a letter from me, which I wouldn't give."

"Why?"

"Because it would kill you."

"I'm dying, anyway, for fuck's sake! Why won't you give me a chance?"

"I have done. I've given you every chance there is. This treatment—if it even becomes that—is too far off for you. There's nothing else we can do, Polly. I'm so sorry."

The sound of sobbing. "I just want more time. Please. Just a bit more time."

"I… Christ, Polly. I'm sorry."

Annie and George jumped as Dr. Max opened the door, trying to look nonchalant. "So, yeah, it's burrito day in the canteen," George babbled.

Dr. Max raised a bushy eyebrow. "I guess you two heard all that."

"Mmmaybe."

"Please try to talk her out of this. Has she been holding out hope all this time? That there's a magic last-minute cure we're going to find?"

Annie thought of the research papers Polly had been reading, her mother's insistence on acupuncture and herbs and creative visualizations. "I think she's sort of been…in denial. She couldn't take it in." She could see it now. Polly cheerfully reciting the words: *I'm dying. I have three months to live.* Like someone acting a part, not really believing it.

"Jesus. So that's why she handled it so well. Listen, both of you. If I believed there was anything more to do, I would do it. But there is no cure. There is no miracle. The sooner she accepts that, the better."

George was shaking. "I think we all thought… I think we all believed there was something…" From inside the room was the sound of frenzied sobbing. Polly, positive, upbeat Polly, had finally broken. "There's really nothing?"

"Nothing," Dr. Max said firmly. "I'm sorry, I have to go check on another patient. I'll see you later." He went stomping off.

George bit his lip. "Jesus, Annie. What do I do? What do I tell my parents? Mum's in total denial."

"I don't know. I really don't know."

He was still shaking. "Oh, God. What will I say to Poll? How can I even talk to her, now that we know—what will I say to her?"

"Um…" Annie's head was reeling. "Maybe lead with that thing about burrito day?"

He looked at her, shocked, and then burst out laughing. Half sobs, half laughs. What they'd all been doing a lot of recently. "Oh, God. Oh, Jesus fucking Christ. She's dying, Annie. She really is dying."

"I know," Annie said, feeling it sink into her, too, like a lead weight around her ankles, pulling her down.

George ran his hands over his face, pulling on the skin. "I mean, they said it was hopeless but we didn't believe it, I guess, or…she seemed so well. You saw her. Didn't she seem well?"

"She did. But I think…maybe she was trying to convince herself, too. That if she just kept going it wouldn't catch her." And now it had. Annie realized she'd closed her eyes to it, too. Polly gasping for breath. Her back pain. The weight that seemed to melt off her overnight.

George was looking to Annie for answers, like a small child wanting to know *why, why, why.* "Do you think he's right? Are we really out of options?"

"I..." Annie could see Dr. Max at the end of the corridor, bashing the vending machine in irritation. "I think he is right, yes. Let's leave her be for now. She's going to have a lot to come to terms with."

DAY 40
Be honest

"She doesn't want to see anyone today." Dr. Max shook his head, closing the door of Polly's room behind him.

"She seemed so well," Annie said again, knowing how pointless it was. As if some stubborn part of her brain kept on insisting Polly couldn't be dying. She'd been up and laughing just days ago. How could she have so little time?

He ran his hands through his hair, making it stick up. "It was the tumor, Annie. She hadn't accepted it at all. That's how it works. Your mind sort of shields you from taking it in at first. People can keep going for a long, long time on auto-pilot. Hope is the last thing to die." He tucked his hands into the pockets of his white coat. "I'll see you."

It was there between them, the awkwardness of the night of the concert, pushing them apart at the moment Annie most needed him. "Listen," she tried. "I'm sorry about…what happened. You know. That night."

"Oh." He looked down at his feet. "It's nothing, Annie. You just seemed like you needed a hug. No big deal. Bye."

She stood looking after him as rain lashed the windows of the corridor and she realized Polly was dying, really dying and really leaving them, on the other side of that door. And somehow the rest of them would have to find a way to keep on going.

DAY 41
Go outside

"Where are you taking me?" Polly said sulkily. "I'm not allowed to leave this prison."

"Dr. Max said you can go outside for half an hour." George was pushing her in a wheelchair, Annie following behind laden with bags.

"I don't want to go outside. We're in Lewisham, it's horrible."

"Just come. You might be surprised."

They pushed her out the back of the hospital, past the maternity wing and outpatients and over a small bridge, where suddenly they were confronted with a small river and a wide-open field. "What is this place?"

"Ladywell Fields," said Annie. "I used to come here a lot. It's beautiful." It was near where she and Mike had lived, and had been one of Jacob's favorite places. Even though they knew he wasn't old enough to have favorites, not really.

"Hmph. Well, you've changed your tune, Little Miss Sunshine."

George and Annie exchanged glances. This was going to be harder than they'd thought. "Come on," said George, easing Polly out of her wheelchair. "Put your arms around my neck. Bit harder."

Her arms hung limp, with barely the strength to hold on. "I used to carry you when you were a baby," she said. "And now you have to lift me. I dropped you on your head once actually. Probably explains a lot."

Once they'd spread out the picnic rug Annie had brought, they arranged the food on it. "Look," coaxed George. "Your favorite, Roquefort. And there's olives, and ham, and all kinds of picnic swag."

"I can't eat that, duh. I'm on high-level infection control." She sat hunched in her cardigan, smearing sanitizing gel onto her hands. "It's like I'm pregnant, only I'm not and I never will be now. I'm pregnant with a big old tumor instead."

"Listen, P..." George began. "I know this is a setback—"

"I'm dying. That is kind of a big setback, yeah."

"Nothing's changed," Annie said quietly. "You told me when we met you were terminal."

Polly stared down at the rug, with its cheery shades of pink and blue. It was sunny outside, and nearby some children waded in the river, shrieking as the mud squelched between their toes. It was a happy scene. Wrong somehow. "I know. It's like... I knew it in my head, but not inside me. Not really. I thought I'd just get through these hundred days and then think about the rest after that, and then maybe by then there'd be some new treatment or something. But it's too late. I'm out of time."

"It's not over yet," George said. "Dr. Max said—"

"Dr. Max. What's the use of him? What has he actually been able to do for me? Two months ago I was totally fine and now look at me. I can hardly even pee by myself." She screwed her face up tight, as if she was trying not to cry. "What do I do? What do I do now?"

"You keep going," said Annie. "What else can you do?"

"But what's the point? I have so little time."

"You said you wanted to help people. You've already helped me, Poll. You can do more. Milly said the social media stuff's really taking off, loads of people commenting, and—"

"Social media. What does that matter? I'll never meet any of those people. They don't care if I live or die."

Annie held up her phone. "Scroll. Go on."

She watched Polly read the screen. "These are all donations?"

"Yep. A hundred yesterday alone. And look, they've all put comments, too. People do care, Poll. Even if it's just an illusion that they know you. You're making a difference to them. Look, they've started posting their own happy-days things."

George stretched back. "Someone chose 'cleaning the bath' as one, can you believe it? These people need you, P. Show them how to actually have fun."

"*We* need you," said Annie. "Have you seen what I'm wearing today?"

"Yes," Polly said grudgingly. "Did you get lost on your way to an ABBA tribute concert? I mean, really, Annie—fringes?"

A brief flare of herself, back from under the suffocating fug of despair. Dr. Max was right. It wasn't over yet.

"All right," Polly said after a while. "I'll try. I don't know if I can but I'll try. If you do something for me in return, George."

"I'm not doing that dancing thing again. Not without class-A drugs."

"It's not that. I want you to stand up to Mum. Tell her once and for all that you're gay, and as such you and Annie won't be getting it together anytime soon."

"She thinks that?" Annie felt herself blush.

George sighed. "She keeps dropping hints about how well

we get on. It's just—I mean, she knows it, really. I've tried to tell her. But she doesn't *want* to know. She still thinks I'll meet the right girl and settle down, buy a house in Surrey, get a BMW."

Annie looked between them. "But…your parents are so cool. They can't have an issue with gay people, surely?"

George said, "Oh, Mum's just…she thinks she's so liberal, but really she wants everything to be picture-perfect. This wonderful happy family, complete with cute grandkids. Before Poll was sick, the pressure was off me to reproduce, but now…"

"Now I won't be giving her any," Polly supplied. "It's down to Georgie here. She's not homophobic, not really. George being gay just doesn't fit into her dream family."

"Nor does me being a failed actor." His smile twisted.

"My God, your family's good at denial," Annie murmured.

"Well, she's about to lose a child, so that should put paid to it," said Polly. A short silence. "Please will you just stand up to her, Georgie? Life's too short to lie. I would know."

"Okay, then. In the same vein, are you ever going to call Tom?"

She scowled. "George, don't."

"He deserves to know."

"He doesn't deserve anything. Come on, take me back in."

Annie knew better by now than to ask who Tom was. Besides, she already had a pretty good idea.

On their way back in, they saw a lone figure in Lycra jogging around the hospital buildings. "Dr. Quarani!" Polly shouted. "Dr. Quarani!" Except her voice came out as a croak, and he didn't hear, and soon he was gone, leaving only dust at his heels.

DAY 42
Do something spiritual

"Amazing. Did you ever see Bowie there?"

The sound of a hacking cough. "Oh, yeah. He was a regular, so he was. Say hi to him when you get up there, will you?"

"Oh, I'd be far too starstruck."

Polly looked up as Annie stood awkwardly in the door of her room. An older man was in the chair beside her, wearing black silk pajamas. He was so thin. Annie blinked, trying not to stare. "Hey! You're better." Polly seemed composed, in contrast to the weeping mess of previous days.

"Just about. Dion, this is my friend Annie."

She raised an awkward hand. "Hi."

Dion stood up, which took a while. Annie could see the ridges of his spine under the silk of his pajamas. "I'll leave you to it, lovely girl. The eye-candy nurse is bringing the meds around soon—don't want to miss that." He blew Polly a kiss. As he passed Annie he quickly rearranged her pink scarf into a sort of snood. "There you go. Looks much more chic that way."

"Um, thanks."

Polly patted the chair, managing a smile. She looked

terrible—dark bruises under her eyes, her skin gray and wan. Annie could see how thin her hair was, the scalp showing underneath. But she was smiling. That was something. "Dion used to work in costume design at the Old Vic. There's nothing he doesn't know about clothes."

"What's he in for?" Annie sat down, noticing that the teddy bear she'd brought was propped on top of Polly's heart monitor.

"Oh, it's a fascinating story. He was the fourth person in the UK to be diagnosed with AIDS. In 1984. Imagine!"

"Wow, and he's still alive?"

"Just about. It's starting to attack his brain, and he forgets things a lot. All his friends are dead, two of his boyfriends—you name it, everyone gone. Can you imagine?"

"That's sad." Polly's mood was clearly swinging back up, buoyant as a balloon. Annie waited to hear why.

"I mean, can you imagine living like I am now, thinking every day's your last, only for twenty years? He's got no savings. Can't afford his rent now they've cut his benefits. No family, most of his friends dead." Polly patted a book on her bedside table. "He's given me this to read. *Man's Search for Meaning*. It's by this guy who was sent to Auschwitz and his wife and family died, but he still says it's possible to be happy in any situation. That we can always control our response to anything, inside ourselves. Do you believe that, Annie?"

"Sure." Annie didn't. There were some things she just didn't think you could get past.

"And have you seen the fundraising site? So many comments from people doing happy things. I need to keep doing stuff. Whatever happens to me. I need to keep going with the hundred days. But I'm stuck here. I can't leave the hospital until they've shrunk this new tumor down. Did you know I had an exciting new tumor? I'm going to call this one Frank."

"Yeah. I knew. Listen, George and I can do the happy-days stuff, if it means so much to you. Costas, too."

"Really?" Polly raised the place where her eyebrows used to be.

"'Course. I mean, as long as there are no marine animals involved."

Polly laughed, which turned into a storm of coughing. "I'll…just ring SeaWorld and…cancel. Would you really do that for me? See, if you could film yourselves doing things, we can upload it to the fundraising site, and Milly reckons it'll help 'drive traffic' or whatever. That's good, isn't it? That would mean something. Some kind of…legacy."

Annie wondered what would happen if Polly gave up on the plan entirely. The energy of it seemed to be the only thing holding her together. "Of course. Listen, I can't stay long, sorry. I've missed so much work recently, and I need to see my mum."

"Oh, can I come with you?"

"Er, you're bedridden."

"I'm not. Push me in the wheelchair. Pleeease. I'm so bored here."

"Well, okay, if you think a trip to the geriatrics ward is fun."

"In my world, this is what passes for a night out clubbing."

"Stop trying to get sympathy. Shall I call a nurse?"

"No, no, they're busy saving lives and stuff. We can manage it."

With much shuffling, Annie got Polly out of bed and into the wheelchair, which was sitting in the corner. She weighed so little Annie probably could have picked her up in her arms. "There. Where to, miss? I'm not going south of the river, not at this time of night."

"Is there an Uber wheelchair option? Maybe I can start one from my deathbed."

Annie wheeled her into the lift and they went to Geriatrics.
As she squeaked Polly down the hall she nodded to people she
recognized: the handsome pediatrics registrar, the motherly
woman who pushed the books trolley, the receptionist from
Patient Records. You could get used to anything, really. A
hospital could start to feel like a home. A stranger could start
to feel like your very best friend. And your mother—well, she
could become a stranger.

"She's sleeping," said Dr. Quarani, barring the way. The
ward was quiet, the only sign of the patients the tiny mounds
in the beds. Funny how you shrank back into yourself, at the
end.

"Is she okay?"

"She's fine, I think. Earlier she thought I was Omar Sharif,
but apart from that..."

"Oh, my God," Annie muttered, mortified. "I'm so sorry."

"It's quite all right. She seemed rather pleased to meet me.
Asked me to join her in a hand of bridge."

"Er, my face is down here," Polly said from her wheelchair.

He looked down. "Hello, Miss Leonard. Should you be out
of bed? I understood you had a secondary and were on bed
rest awaiting radiotherapy."

Polly pulled a face. "You make me sound like a garden or
something. I can't just lie there. I have to do something."

He frowned. "Does Dr. Fraser know you're up?"

"Oh, I'm sure he does. On some level. Anyway, enough
about me. How are you?" Annie could have sworn that Polly
was trying to bat her eyelashes. Not that she had any. She
leaned her cheek on one hand, the one with the catheter still
in it.

"I'm rather busy." He started reaching for the ward phone.
"I really think I should speak to Dr. Fraser..."

"Oh, leave it, please. He's so grumpy. Tell me more about

you. You have any family over here or...?" Annie looked away. This was totally cringe, as Polly would say.

"Family? No." He looked at his watch. "Miss Leonard—"

"It's Polly, please. I'm not a defendant in court. Not yet, anyway, ha-ha. What about back in Syria, family there or—"

Dr. Quarani snapped his chart shut. "Please. I must ask you to go back to your ward. The nurses will be looking to take your bloods and if you're not there it just creates extra work. Ms. Hebden, your mother is stable for now. I suggest you get some rest, attend to your own job and come back tomorrow."

Polly stared as he strode from the ward. "Hold the front page, I think we have a new contender for grumpiest doctor of the year award."

Annie started wheeling her away. "Seriously, Poll, what was that? Were you flirting with him?"

"So what if I was? Just because I'm in the hospital doesn't mean I'm dead inside."

"But he's a doctor, and you're—"

"What? I'm sick? I know I'm sick, Annie. For God's sake. Is that all I am to you?"

Annie pushed her faster, hissing through clenched teeth. It was hard to argue with someone when they were in front of you. "You know that's not true. It's just...not appropriate, that's all."

"But it's fine for you to flirt with Dr. McGrumpy?"

"I *do not* flirt with him."

"'Oh, Dr. Max, show me more brain scans. Oh, Dr. Max, someone should really iron your shirts and make you a decent meal!'"

"I don't sound like that." People were starting to look up at the sound of their bickering. Annie pushed faster. "Come on. Back to bed with you. Unless you want me to see if they can check you into some kind of ward for inappropriate behavior."

"I have a brain tumor, I'm allowed," Polly said, folding her thin arms.

"It's hard to tell what's the tumor and what's your personality, sometimes."

"Oh, charming. Shit! Dr. Max! Reverse, reverse! Duck in there! Quick!"

"But that's the—"

"Now!"

Annie turned the chair sideways, and shut the door behind them. She looked about them at the quiet, warm space, the light filtered through a blue stained glass window. They were in the chapel. One place in the hospital she had always refused to go, even when her mother asked to be taken. She just couldn't. Her hands clenched on the rubber handles of the wheelchair. "Come on, Poll, let's go."

"Why? Let's just sit for a minute. It's nice and quiet."

She was going to be late for work yet again. Reluctantly, Annie parked the chair and sat on one of the wooden pews. It didn't feel like part of the hospital. You could hardly hear the rushing feet outside, and the smell of disinfectant was overridden by a gentler one of incense.

Polly sat in silence for a while. "I've been putting off this bit, to be honest."

"What bit?"

"The one where I turn to God, or Allah, or the mystical universe, or whatever you want to call it. The one where I look for a loophole."

Was Polly sinking back into denial, looking for miracles? "A loophole?"

"That's what religion is, isn't it? It's just a way to put off accepting that you're going to die, and that's it. To not face the fact that when we die we just…disappear."

"Is that what you think?" They were speaking quietly.

Polly's gaze was fixed on the altar, her face colored blue by the shifting light. "It's what I always thought before. I didn't want to change my mind just because I had cancer. I guess... all this happy-days stuff, the reason for it, was I wanted my life to mean something now, not just after I die."

"Your life does mean something. You have to know that it does, Poll. You've reached so many people already."

"Does it?" She rubbed a hand over her head, grimacing as it came away with a fistful of gold strands. "God. I'm falling apart. Is this it, Annie? Will I ever get out of here again?"

"Of course," Annie said, trying to sound confident. "This is just a...setback."

"Sometimes I wish it was over. That's terrible, isn't it? I mean, here's Mum and Dad and even Dr. McGrumpy doing their best to keep me alive, and some days I wish I could say *stop*. Stop all the needles and tubes and pumping poison into me. Let me go somewhere nice, where it's sunny and hot waiters can bring me mai tais in the pool and I could just slip away. I don't think I want to die in Lewisham, Annie. No offense. I mean, I know it's a really vibrant borough and has some of the lowest council tax in London, but it's not exactly Bali, is it?"

"Not exactly," she agreed. "Although is Bali going to have Crossrail? I think not."

"Damn, Annie, I'm going to miss Crossrail. Isn't that typical? All of the disruption and I won't even get to ride the bloody thing. Ooops, sorry for swearing." She directed the "sorry" toward the altar. There was no reply. She gave a juddering sigh, and put her hands on her thin thighs, resolute. "Right. Here's what we're going to do. I'm not dying yet—I was promised a hundred days and I haven't had it. So I'm going to get well, or at least less dying-y, and come out and we'll do something lovely. I'm not sitting around here waiting to die."

"Sounds like a plan. But for now you better rest, or you won't be able to order us about, and then what would you do?"

"I'll order you about with my dying breath, Annie Hebden née Clarke. Now wheel me back to bed."

As they went out they were clocked by Dr. Max, who was checking a patient's chart at the nurses' station. "There you are! For the love of God, Polly, we almost had search parties out for you!"

"I was praying," Polly said piously. "Praying for you, Dr. Max, that you'll have the strength to do your duties with patience and forgiveness." She crossed herself ostentatiously.

He shook his head. "Bloody woman. I'm surprised at you, Annie."

"Sorry, Doctor," she said, chastened. "I'll get her back to bed."

As they wheeled off she heard Polly whisper, "'Oh, sorry, Doctor, I'm such a baaad girl. Why don't you tell me what you've got under your kilt?'"

"The sooner they put you on a ventilator, the better," Annie muttered, slamming the door behind them.

DAY 43
Ride a roller coaster

Annie stopped in the corridor, the bunch of yellow roses rustling in her hand. She could hear voices from farther down, just outside Polly's room. Valerie and Roger again, hissing at each other.

"Your daughter is dying, Roger, and you can't even leave your phone at home for one day?"

"It's work, Valerie! Someone still has to earn the money around here. What if Polly needs specialist care? I don't want my little girl in pain or discomfort, and Lord knows you haven't earned a penny in years."

"Isn't that just like you. Using work as an excuse to do nothing at home for nearly forty years now. But this isn't the time, okay? She needs you home! Not in the office or the pub or swigging whiskey in your study and—"

"Christ, Valerie, why must you always make it about you? I'm not the one upsetting Polly, yelling like a fishwife."

Annie felt a light hand on her shoulder. She turned to George. "Sorry for intruding," she said quietly.

"They've been like this for days. It's awful at home. Snipe snipe snipe."

"I should go. I brought these—can you take them to Polly?"

George shook his head. "Leave them with the nurses. She's pretending she's out of it, but she's not too bad. Just can't take Mum and Dad anymore."

"So what are you going to do?"

"Well, you and I have instructions."

"What? I have to go to work in a minute."

"Call in sick."

"But I can't, I—"

"Please, Annie. I need to do this. I can't sit around here feeling useless, watching her die, listening to Mum and Dad fight. And Polly was insistent. I know it's stupid, this hundred-days thing, but it seems to be kind of giving her hope. Or if not hope, then something, anyway. A reason to not give in. To wake up in the morning."

Annie had thought the same. She looked at her watch—8:00 a.m. "What's the instructions?"

George held out a piece of paper. Annie looked at it. "Are you serious?"

"Yup. And she wants us to film it. Since she can't go herself, she says. So, can you call in sick?"

Annie hated doing that—her fake sick voice was deeply unconvincing. "I'm the world's worst actress."

"Isn't it lucky you have a celebrated actor right here, then?" George held out his hand. "Give me the phone. Who am I asking for?"

Annie passed over her mobile, scrolling through to the number. "Sharon. Ask for Sharon. Say I've had a nervous collapse or something."

She had to stuff her sleeves in her mouth to keep from laughing during the phone call. "The thing is, Sharon—can I call you Sharon?... Thank you. You have such a kind voice, Sharon. The thing is, poor Ms. Hebden's just been working so

hard with her mother and her sick friend, we've had to keep
her in for observation. We think she needs a tonic for her poor
nerves." He was alternating between a noble Noël Coward
voice and a stoical Cockney one. "You know what I'm talking
about, Sharon. I can tell that you do... Me? Oh, my name's
Kent Brockwood. Chief staff nurse here at the hospital. We
do admire Ms. Hebden ever so much. She's so *noble*. Upper
lip stiffer than a big steel girder... Thank you. God bless you,
Sharon." He hung up, handing the phone back with a flourish.

She mimed a miniround of applause. "Give that man a
Tony Award."

"I try."

"Where were you even from, Kent Brockwood?"

"Bow by way of Letterkenny, I think. She'll leave you
alone for a few days now, I reckon. And you can stagger in
full of noble suffering, and if you're really lucky you'll be sent
home." Being sent home from work was the ultimate win.
You'd made the effort to go in, but you were really too sick
to be there, so you could leave with impunity.

"'You have such a kind voice, Sharon.'" Annie giggled. "It
was brilliant. So, now we go to Thorpe Park?"

"Now we go to Thorpe Park. She said we should pick up
Costas on the way."

Annie looked toward Roger and Valerie, who were still
arguing, voices lowered. "Should we—"

"Nah. Let's just go. Lucky Polly. At least she gets to fake
being in a coma."

Outside, George raised an arm to hail a taxi. Annie held
back. "Isn't it kind of far? Train, maybe?"

"Polly's given me a load of cash. She wants us to have a
good day out. And if we pick him up in a black cab—think
how his little face will just light up."

She studied George as they sank into the comfortable interior, shutting the door on rainy, gloomy Lewisham. "You like him, don't you?"

"Zorba the Greek? He's adorable. Too nice for this city."

"Do you *like him* like him?"

"He's a kid. And he spends his days foaming milk."

"Come on," Annie chided. "He's doing his best. He works really hard."

George looked guilty. "I know. He's just—he's so happy, you know? It makes me feel guilty. He's alone over here, away from his family, getting nowhere with his career. But he's cheerful. He's sunny. Even when he's having a shit time at work."

"How did you know about that?"

"Oh. We—we're in the same gym, it turns out."

"You joined a gym? I thought that was just a lie you told your mum to get out of the house."

"Yes, yes, I thought it was time to start fulfilling gay stereotypes. We're going to a Barbra Streisand concert next. Anyway, like I say, he's too young for me."

"He's twenty-two. You're twenty-nine. And haven't you only been out for, like, two minutes?"

He shrugged it off. "I was in a small uncomfortable closet for some time. As you've seen, my mother is very much not okay about her precious boy associating with nasty gays in leathers and drag. That's how she pictures it, anyway. What's your point?"

"So, Costas might be older than you in gay years. Is that a thing? Like dog years?"

"Oh, it's a thing. I'm practically ancient at my age."

"You don't look a day over twenty-eight." She nudged him. "What would Polly say? 'Seize the day! Jump off a cliff! Pee in the wind!' And so on."

He sighed. "Maybe. I hear you, okay? But for now, with Polly, and since I'm trying to stay away from Caleb, it's just nice to have a friend, you know?"

She smiled at him. Pictured rolling up to get Costas, how happy he'd be at the prospect of a day out. "I do know. Yes."

"Ready?"

"Oh, God. I'm going to be sick."

"I should not have eaten the floss of candy." Costas was pale. The roller coaster—an utterly terrifying one that dipped and twisted—was slowly winching them up, and up, and up. Annie felt her stomach churn with the burger, fries and milkshake she'd also wolfed down. She wasn't eighteen. This would have consequences. Down below, the people on the ground were so small. So far down.

"Here we go!" They were picking up speed. Her knuckles turned white. She felt Costas gripping her hand and, on his other side, George's. In his free hand George held up his phone, secured to his wrist by a strap. "Right!" he shouted, over the growing noise of the machinery. "Big smiles and don't swear—ahhhhh! *Fuck! Fuck! Holy Christ! We're going to die!*"

DAY 44
Reaffirm your goals

"F★★★! F★★★! Holy Christ! We're going to die!"

George peered at the screen of Polly's iPad. "You can hardly hear me over those beeps Suze put in."

"She had to," said Polly. "This baby's going viral. Ten thousand views already of the YouTube video. The fundraising site's getting mad traffic because of it."

"Really?" George perked up. "I better add a link to my casting page."

"Yeah, you can be that brother of brave cancer survivor Polly Leonard—what was his name again, the one who swore on the roller coaster?"

He stuck his tongue out. "It was bloody scary, wasn't it, Annie?"

"I threw up in a bin afterward," she said. "Can you see me on the video? I don't think work will believe that the cure for my sudden nerve condition was going on the scariest roller coaster in Europe."

"It'll be fine," said Polly. She was looking much better, her cheeks flushed from laughing at the video, sitting up in bed. "No one in your office can even work the internet, can they?"

"Only *Farm World* on Facebook," said Annie. "I better go, though. I can't be late again."

Annie couldn't stop smiling to herself, thinking of the roller coaster video. It was so stupid. So funny.

"You look happy," said a dour Scottish voice. Dr. Max was standing at the vending machine again, staring into it as if great wisdom was to be found between the Twixes and Bountys.

Annie felt ashamed. She shouldn't be smiling when Polly was dying. "Are you trying to decide what chocolate bar to get?"

"Hmm? Oh. Yeah. Patient just died on my table."

"Oh, my God! I'm so sorry."

"Ten years old. Couldn't do a damn thing for him, the tumor was so big." She could see his face reflected in the glass of the machine, exhausted and disappointed.

"At least you tried," Annie said timidly.

"Tried. Tried and failed." He shook himself and began stabbing buttons until a Mars bar tumbled out. "Better get back. See you, Annie."

Going out, she saw Jonny, the homeless guy, sitting at the bus stop. He caught her eye and she felt too ashamed to look away. "Hi."

"Hello. Rough time?"

"My friend's pretty sick."

"I'm sorry to hear that," he said politely. His fingers in raggedy gloves were dirty and sore.

"Um, is there anything I can get you?" Annie said it in an embarrassed rush. "Anything you need?"

He looked around at his meager collection of belongings, the cardboard box he was sitting on to keep the damp out. "Jacuzzi'd be nice." He laughed at her face. "Seriously, you don't have to give me stuff. I'm just passing the time of day, like anyone else. It's fine."

"Okay. Thanks." The bus came then, and Annie got on it, but she looked out of the window as they pulled off, Jonny's forlorn figure sitting by himself on the ground.

DAY 45
Be silly

"Ready? Set—go!"

"Are you sure this is safe?" Annie called.

Polly and her opponent ignored her, racing past in wheel-chairs, hands frantically spinning. They sped the length of the corridor, screeching to a halt beside a rack of sheets. A passing nurse dropped a pile of bedpans, swearing like a trooper.

Dr. Max stuck his head out of his cupboard-office, irate, hair sticking up. "I might have known it was you, Polly. But, Ahmed, I thought better of you?"

"I'm sorry, sir," Ahmed said meekly. He was seventeen and totally bald, wearing Action Man pajamas. He had a brain aneurysm which was threatening to burst at any moment.

"Don't listen to him, Ahmed. You're the terror of the neurology ward. Faster than a speeding bullet." Polly raised her hand to high-five him.

Ahmed smiled, aiming for her palm and missing it—loss of depth perception was one of his side effects. Dr. Max met Annie's eyes down the corridor, and she shrugged. It was all Polly's idea—the Great Neurology Ward Pentathlon. Next event: bedpan curling using a mop as a stick. Dr. Max rolled his eyes, offering a small blink-and-you'd-miss-it smile, then ducked back into his office-cupboard.

DAY 46
Raise money for charity

"Would you like a cupcake?" asked the French maid. He was six foot four with hairy knees.

Annie squinted. "Is that you, Yusuf?" Yusuf, or Dr. Khan as he was better known, was the head of cardio at the hospital.

"Yes, it's me. It's fancy-dress day. Everyone's raising money—bake sales, dressing up..."

"I see." She dropped a fiver in his basket and took two cakes, which were iced in pink ripples. Much like the one Polly had given her that first day. "Is this by chance anything to do with Polly?" The money from the fundraising event was still rolling in, and she'd become determined to raise enough for a new MRI machine.

"Do you even have to ask?"

"Good point. So what else is going on?" she mumbled through icing. It tasted like strawberries, the sugar hitting her bloodstream.

"We're auctioning off some of the radiologists, and the nurses from the NICU are doing a conga. Oh, and some of the hairier staff are getting waxed in the cafeteria."

"They are? Um, which staff?"

"The hairiest ones, I guess. I'm supposed to be doing it, too, but I felt the hair just added to this costume."

Annie arrived just in time to see Dr. Max with his shirt off, lying across one of the tables, which had been covered in blue hospital paper. His back, like the rest of him, was indeed rather hairy.

He saw her. "Oh, for God's sake. What are you doing here? Don't you have a home to go to?"

"You can talk. I thought you hated stupid fundraising things?"

"I do. I hate them with every fiber of my being. Almost as much as I'm going to hate this waxing."

"Oh, it hardly hurts at all."

"Really?" He cocked his head, hopeful.

"No, it hurts like hell." She stepped aside as one of the surgical nurses—used to de-fuzzing patients for operations—applied a long strip of gauze to his waxed back, then pulled. His howls could probably be heard all the way on the third floor, where Polly was no doubt masterminding the whole thing.

Annie checked her watch. "Much as I'd love to stay and watch this, I need to get my visits in, then go to work."

"There'll be pictures," he said gloomily. "Bloody Polly."

Outside the geriatrics ward, Dr. Quarani was running sprints up and down it, resetting his Fitbit each time.

"Not joining in with the fundraising?" Annie asked.

"I do not have time for that. Only five minutes between rounds." His white coat flapped out behind him as he ran the length of it, counting under his breath, every muscle rigid and controlled.

After she'd finished her visits, Annie went to the bus stop again. Jonny was in the same clothes. He must only have one set, she thought, then realized how stupid that was. Where would he keep the rest of them? He literally had nowhere else to go. "Hiya," he said. He was turning the pages of a Terry Pratchett book.

She pointed to it shyly. "I've read that one, too. It's good."

"Oh, yeah. Gives me a laugh, anyway. How are you today?"

"I'm okay." Compared to him, she had to say that she was. At least she had a home to go to, and friends, and a job. She wished there was something she could do for him. "Um, do you like cake?" she said awkwardly, holding out the brown paper bag. Cake was a small thing, in the scheme of things, but she knew from her first meeting with Polly that it was still something.

DAY 47
Meet new people

"You look so much better."

Polly beamed at herself in the hand mirror Annie had propped on her bed tray. "I do, don't I? Just as well, that whole cancer pallor thing wasn't doing much for my complexion. Pass me the eye shadow."

"Which one?" Annie had Polly's massive vanity case open in front of her.

"The sparkly green one. I feel in a sparkly green mood today." She shut her eyes. "You do it. My wrist strength isn't what it was. But don't spread that about, okay? I don't want the boys hearing."

"*Polly.* You really want me to do it? I'm hopeless."

"You have to learn. I won't be around forever to do your makeup and pick your clothes. Although I'm liking this ensemble. Let me see."

Self-consciously, Annie stepped back to let Polly admire her suede skirt and boots, worn with a stripey Breton jumper.

"Nice. Very nice. You won't even need me much longer."

"Shh now." Annie didn't want to talk about the end. Not today, when Polly had color in her cheeks—and not just from the generous application of blusher. Not when she seemed better, even if it was just another of cancer's cruel tricks. "There you go. Hope you like the 'drag queen having chemo' look because that's what I've given you. I'll need a few more makeup tutorials before..." She'd almost said, *before you go*. As if Polly was just setting off on a long cruise or something. It seemed impossible, however many times Annie reminded herself, to take in the fact that her friend would not be coming back from the final journey. And that it was almost upon them; maybe not today, maybe not even this month. But soon.

The door opened in a whiff of Chanel. "Darling, how... oh, hello, Annie."

"Hi, Valerie. We're just getting Polly all dolled up."

"That's good. I think George is around somewhere. I'm sure he'd like to see you." Annie just nodded. George clearly hadn't had "the talk" with his mother yet.

Polly said cheerfully, "Did you bring me more of those anticancer herbs, Ma? Because I have to tell you, they taste like horse pee."

"Er, Polly, darling, you have a visitor." Valerie was wearing an ankle-length cardigan today, her makeup fresh and her hair shining, but she looked exhausted all the same. This was taking its toll on everyone.

"Who's that, then? Milly? I told her, no more cancer videos for a while. Positive things only. The fundraising site's doing fine on its own—twenty thousand uniques yesterday!"

"It's not Milly. Er. I think... I think you should be on your own for this, darling."

Annie got the hint. She started packing up the vanity case. "I should go, anyway."

Polly's hand snaked out and grabbed her arm. "Don't go. You just got here. Unless it's Ryan Gosling visiting, in which case, Annie, don't let the door hit you on the arse as you go."

Valerie was twisting her hands together. She sighed, then stepped back, holding the door open. She spoke to whoever was outside. "Go in. I'm not getting involved." She was replaced in the doorway by someone Annie had never seen before. A man, in a suit that was obviously expensive—none of your polyester here. Polished shoes. Red tie. Tall, handsome in a catalog-model kind of way, with short dark hair. Big arms and chest. A gym-goer.

Polly was staring at him. Her hand was still clenched on Annie's arm, and the color was draining from her face, leaving the makeup on top like a gross joke. "Fuck."

"Hi," said the man. His voice was croaky. "Are you...? Christ...you look... I'd no idea."

"I'm fine. I'm totally fine. What the hell are you doing here?"

"What am I... Christ. Have you any idea how worried I've been? I didn't even know you were alive until I saw your bloody fundraising site!"

Annie tried to bolt for the door but Polly hung on to her for dear life. "Don't go."

The man moved closer. "Poll. Please talk to me. Please. You can't just drop a bombshell like that and take off."

"I can do anything I want, I have cancer," she said in a strangled voice.

The anger between them seemed to erupt then, like someone throwing a grenade and running off. "Cancer. It's not the cancer, it's you. You always did exactly what you wanted. Painting the house. Going on holiday with your mates. What about me? What about what I wanted?"

Annie's head swiveled between them. Who was this? What was going on?

"I don't care what you want!" Polly barked it out, as if she was using up the rest of her voice and strength. "Just get out of here! You've got no right! You didn't want me, so you don't get to stand at my bedside when I'm dying. I have other people for that."

"What, some weirdo you've only just met!" Annie blinked. That was a bit harsh.

"Annie's my *friend*, and she's been *here* for me, unlike some people—"

"Oh, like you gave me a choice!"

"Close the door, Annie," Polly said shakily.

"Er, wh-what?" Annie stammered.

"Shut the door on him. Kick him out. I haven't got the strength to do it myself but I can't listen to this."

Right. So she would just kick out the six-foot-tall, gym-honed man who was glaring at her like she was something nasty on the pavement. "Um, I'm sorry. Polly isn't supposed to get tired out, so if you could just—"

"Who the hell even are you? What gives you the right?" He turned to Polly. "Look, please, I really need to talk to you. You can't just send me away."

"I can," she said in a small voice.

Annie lifted her chin. "She wants me here. And she doesn't want you. So…" She held the door open for him. "Like she said, don't let it hit you on the arse as you go."

He went, slamming it hard behind him. Annie sagged. She'd really done it. "God. What was all that about?"

Polly was gray-faced, panting for breath. "Thank you. You were…amazing."

"Are you okay?"

She nodded as a storm of coughing shook her frail shoulders. "I bet he's never been thrown out of anywhere in his life."

"And…are you going to tell me who he is?"

Polly sighed, and lay back on the pillows, closing her green sparkly eyelids. "Urgh. That is…" She broke off to cough again.

"Tell me, Polly. It's not fair otherwise. Oh, God. He's not a doctor or something, is he? I haven't just kicked out the chair of the hospital or something? Tell me."

"All right! God, let me draw breath. That, Annie…that was Tom. My husband." And her face crumpled in on itself, and Annie realized that Polly was crying.

"Okay," Polly said when she could talk without wheezing or sobbing. "I'm going to tell you what happened. But only because you told me all your stuff, and we have no secrets now."

"We have some secrets."

"Well, whatever. But I need to say it all the way through without you interrupting, okay? Even to say, 'God, that's so awful,' or, 'Poor you,' or anything like that. It's just what happened. It's not a tragedy, or an epic story, or even important. It's just what happened to me." Her breath hitched. "Because I can't *do* this. I can't spend any more of my life crying about it. I don't have time."

"Right," said Annie. "I won't say a word. Er. After this."

She sat quiet on the orange plastic chair, while Polly heaved herself up on the pillows. "Okay. Chapter one. I got my cancer diagnosis like most people do, kind of out of the blue. Busy life. Couldn't possibly happen to me. I was—well, you see what Suze and that lot are like. She has an app to rotate her pants drawer and Milly schedules in sex with her husband six months in advance. I was like that. Up early, kale smoothie, Blackberry on the commute, press press press, angle angle angle. PRing the hell out of things. Yoga. Meditation. Weekends in Cornwall and Val-d'Isère. Out at plays, exhibitions, the latest restaurant where you get your food in a minihammock or something. That was my life. And I had the husband to go with it. Handsome, rich—stockbroker in the city, of course. Some might even say I married my dad—a man who'd always work even more than I did. We were headed down a one-way freeway that led to one or possibly two overscheduled children, a holiday house in Devon and me going freelance while he raked in his bonuses."

Annie nodded, trying to follow. Polly was gasping for air. Her hands were clenched in the blankets. "And then suddenly I was sick. I was at home after the results, getting myself in character—brave cancer sufferer, noble expression, that sort of thing. In total denial, of course. Can you blame me? And then, well—my life fell to pieces. I could almost hear the sound of it, you know? Shattering around my ears."

"I know. What happened?"

"I'll tell you."

Was that the door? Yes, he was home. Jesus, why was she so nervous? She smoothed her dress over her knees. As soon as she'd got in from the hospital she'd showered for a long, long time, until her skin was pink and raw, then put on her favorite dress, the one with the sprigs of cornflowers on it. She found herself running her hands obsessively through her long blond hair.

Tom was in the hallway, staring at the smeary screen of his phone. Shoulders hunched in his Saville Row suit. "Did you ring the plumber? That bloody toilet's still leaking. What are you doing in there?"

She'd even lit a candle for some reason—perhaps thinking it was finally a moment worthy of the forty-eight-pound Jo Malone mimosa-and-cardamom one. She was sitting in the living room in her nice dress, makeup done, instead of her usual yoga pants and skiing socks ensemble. Maybe if she looked nice, the universe would realize it had the wrong person. She was too busy for this. She had appointments all the way to next Christmas. Move along, please, nothing for you here.

He looked up briefly. "Have you not started dinner yet? I'm starving."

"I've been out." Part of her thinking, He's going to feel so bad when I tell him. "Could you come in here?" Calm. Noble. Rising above such petty issues as a leaking loo and a late dinner.

He opened the door—crumpled shirt, tie askew. Hair graying over the temples. And she thought, How did this happen? How did we lose each other like this? *"What? I need a shower—the journey was hell as usual."*

"I had my appointment today. Remember?" She'd told him, but in a passing way that she knew he wouldn't register. Because it was going to be nothing. Everyone got headaches, even if it was every day, even if she hadn't been able to see the display board on the train on her way to the hospital. She'd almost canceled the MRI when the meeting about the cereal account ran over. She probably just needed to try glasses or drinking more water or sleeping or Nurofen or acupuncture or decluttering or quitting work and starting a blog about it.

"Oh." His face—guilt immediately hiding in defense. "You should have reminded me." Tom didn't realize how bad the headaches were, or that she was having to write down everything she did each day so she wouldn't forget to brush her teeth or put her shoes on. He wasn't worried. Not yet.

"It's okay." She sat there, poised. Pulse hammering like she was almost excited. Waiting to shatter their lives. "I... Sweetheart..." (She never called him this but it seemed like something her new noble self might say.) "They found something. In my brain. The headaches..."

"What?" His eyes had already swiveled to the phone again. She would have liked to stamp her foot on it. Listen while I give you my noble speech, you selfish bastard.

"They think—it doesn't look good."

His face. "What are you saying?"

"I'm saying I have a brain tumor."

"Shit. Really? What?"

So she said some words: "Stage four glioblastoma. Very aggressive…rapid growth…"

"Shit. Shit. Poll, there must be something—"

"They'll try things. Chemo and that. But he wasn't hopeful. He looked…kind of grim." That was the right word, she decided, for the grouchy consultant she'd seen. Grim.

"Oh. Shit." Tom put his hands—the phone still surgically attached—on his head. "I'm so— Shit. Shit. Why now?"

"Is there ever a good time?"

"I'm sorry. I need—" And he bolted from the room. Maybe he was just overwhelmed, with love, with pain. She waited. Her own phone buzzed on the table and she picked it up. Thinking: How will I tell everyone? Facebook message? Brave cancer diary? Whatsapp group?

It was from him. It said, Shit. Bad news here. She's sick. Really sick, I think. Need to sort things out.

Clearly, in his sorrow, he'd sent it to the wrong person. It was meant for his mother, maybe.

And she might have overlooked it, not realized what was going on, because she was a tiny bit distracted, after all. If he hadn't made the effort, gone the extra mile he never went for her anymore. I love you, I promise.

He came back in, still holding his phone. He'd been crying. His shirt was untucked. "I can't believe this. I can't. Is it—is it true?"

She held up her own phone. She was still in orbit around cancerland. Calm. Noble. "Who is it you love, Tom?" Because she knew it wasn't her. She'd known it for a long time, she realized.

His face collapsed like wet paper. "Oh, shit."

"Wow," Annie said after Polly had told the whole sorry tale of how she'd come home with her cancer diagnosis, and Tom had accidentally texted the woman he was having an affair with. "Sorry. Am I allowed to say 'wow'?"

"Yeah. He didn't want to tell me, but I played the cancer card—very useful card, that. Eventually he came out and said:

"Yes, he had been seeing another woman.

"Her name was Fleur.

"Yes, when he said 'seeing' he meant 'fucking.'

"Yes, he had 'thought about' leaving me.

"Yes, Fleur was in her twenties.

"She was a yoga teacher and interpretative dancer.

"She worked at the gym I made him join."

Annie nodded slowly. "So you just left him?"

"Without another word. If life's too short not to burn the Jo Malone candle, it's certainly too short to worry about my cheating iPhone-addicted husband. So I went, moved back in with Mum and Dad, and I spent approximately two weeks in bed sobbing my eyes out. Like I wasn't even crying about the stupid cancer. I was crying about him. Him and her. Isn't that daft?"

"Not at all," said Annie. "Sometimes our brains can't take in the biggest thing. It sort of masks it, to protect us. I once cried for three hours because I couldn't find my left shoe."

"I hear he moved her into the house as soon as I was gone. Nice, huh." Polly stopped, wheezing. "So. That's it."

"Um, am I allowed to give my verdict now?"

"Yes, you may speak. My tale of woe is finished."

"I... Jesus, Poll."

"You better not say what a brave cancer sufferer I am."

"I wasn't going to. I was going to say, well done. You win the 'most pathetic story' competition. You just have to be best at everything, don't you?"

She was relieved to hear Polly laugh-cough. "You better believe it, Hebden."

"So, the day we met, when you seemed so happy..."

"I was fucking miserable, Annie. I'd just left my husband and I had cancer."

"So what...?"

Polly smiled. The smile Annie recognized, the one that said, *Aha, look at what I've taught you.* "Of course I wanted to be angry, and miserable, and impatient...like you, my dearest Annie. But I have so little time left. I wondered what would happen if I just didn't. If I just made myself be happy, despite everything."

"And that works?"

Polly spread her arms, indicating her tubes and monitors, her wasted body, her balding head. "Do I seem miserable?"

"Well, no, but—"

"Happy is a state of mind, Annie."

Annie's head was a mess. The Polly she'd met at the reception desk forty-seven days ago, that woman's life had just been crushed to pieces, too? She couldn't believe it.

Polly lay back. "I hope you're taking note of all these inspirational sayings. I expect at least four memoirs about life with me, after I'm gone."

DAY 48
Contemplate mortality

"Hello, I'm here to see—"

"She's busy right now," Annie said resignedly. She was basically Polly's unpaid PA at the moment.

The gawkers had started showing up the day after Polly was admitted. Old friends, casual acquaintances, people she'd once done a course with or met on holiday or dated their brother. They came with grapes—Polly joked that she could start a fruit and veg shop from her room—or chocolate, or flowers, or massive cards with cartoon elephants on them clutching ice packs to bruised heads. Polly made Annie throw these in the toxic waste incinerator. "For God's sake, I have a brain tumor, not a bump on the arm. What's the matter with these people?" But she always saw them. Annie didn't know why.

The most recent visitor was a very skinny middle-aged woman in a drab navy anorak, clutching a hemp bag to her chest. "Who shall I say it is?" Annie said brightly, heading her off in the corridor. Maybe after all this was over she could get a job as a receptionist. Experience—helping a very popular narcissistic friend to die.

"I'm Emily."

"Emily…?"

"Oh, she'll know me." They always thought this.

"But just in case…you know, she's very tired."

"We used to work together, years back. I was the office manager."

Annie shuddered, thinking of Sharon. "And did you keep in touch?"

"Oh, no. I saw her on the World Wide Web, and I said, *That's Polly! Polly the PR girl!* And I wanted to bring her this." She extracted something from her handbag—a badly printed pamphlet that read Heal Yourself with Food. Annie could smell her whiff of patchouli and sweat. "You see, there's still time, but it has to be now."

"Time for what?" Annie strained away.

"To go vegan. She always ate a lot of that posh stringy ham, didn't she, drank too much, had milk in her coffee? If you show her this pamphlet, though, she can cure herself with fasting and herbs and—"

Annie pasted on a smile. "Thank you, Emily. The thing is, she's only allowed so many visitors per day. Doctor's orders. But I'll make sure she gets this. Thanks now. Byeeee!"

"No, no, you have to let me see her—it's really important. Who are you, anyway?"

"I'll handle this, Annie. Thank you." Valerie had appeared, paper cup of tea in hand. "What's going on?"

Emily rushed over to clasp Valerie's hand. "You must be her mother! There's such a likeness. Hello, hello, I've come to give her some pamphlets."

"*Her* has a name," Valerie said tersely. "What sort of pamphlets?"

Emily pressed one on her. "I've got a cure for her cancer right here. It's very simple. She just has to avoid meat, sugar, alcohol, gluten and all additives."

There was a pause as Valerie read the pamphlet. "Do you actually know my daughter? Have you kept in touch?"

"Not for some years, but I heard what was happening and felt compelled to come down! I mean, it's so easy to heal yourself without all these dreadful toxins and poisons." She looked around at the hospital corridor with distaste. "They just keep the truth from us because of 'big pharma.'" She did air quotes, dropping some of her leaflets.

"So let me get this straight. You, a virtual stranger, took it on yourself to come to my little girl's hospital bed and tell her she has cancer because, what, she ate a chocolate bar once?"

"Not just that. Meat, alcohol, dairy—they all lead directly to cancer. But she can still save herself! She just has to leave hospital, come off her treatments and start intermittent fasting immediately." Emily beamed.

Valerie took a deep breath, swelling with rage. "How... dare you? How dare you come here, to where they're actually trying to save her life, and suggest she's suffering like this because of...ham? Get out!"

"But—"

"No. I said go, or I'll call security!"

Emily scarpered, uttering some decidedly non-Zen curses on her way. "Are you okay?" Annie asked Valerie, who was shaking.

"Yes. No, not really. These people just won't leave her alone. Everyone wants something from her, thinks they can tell her what to do. It isn't fair."

Annie wondered if that was how Valerie saw her, too. And maybe it was true. "Can I get you anything...do you need to sit down?"

"I'm fine. I'll just—I don't want Polly to see me like this." She was clutching her cup so tightly beads of beige liquid were rolling down the side and puddling on the floor. Valerie stooped to rescue the leaflets, gazing at them. "It's really happening, isn't it. She's not going to be saved by massage or reiki or some amazing new cure or any of this stuff."

"I don't think so," Annie said as gently as she could. It was so tempting to lie, say there might still be a last-minute miracle, but she knew there wouldn't be.

"I thought it wouldn't hurt to try. To have some hope."

"It doesn't. But… I think she's ready to face up to it now. To make the rest of her life as good as she can."

Valerie bit her lip. "Thank you for all you do for her, Annie. Please don't think we haven't noticed. I know it isn't easy."

"It's fine. She does more for me, far more."

"All the same. We're very grateful."

Leaving her alone—she thought Valerie might need a little private cry—Annie went back in to Polly, who was looking ruefully at her latest floral tribute, an arrangement of cacti in a Hope Your Temperature Doesn't Spike pot. "What do you think these symbolize? My spiky personality?"

"Maybe. Here." She dropped the pamphlet on the bed. "Your mum got rid of a hippie for you, though I'm sure she'll be back. Emily from your old work."

Polly had to think about it. "Dear God. Vegan Emily? Saving your spirit, not your documents. She was hopeless with IT, we lost the entire server three times."

"Don't they realize it's not cool to come here and hound you?" Annie dropped into the chair by the bed.

Polly shrugged. "They're sort of thrilled by it. Terrified it might happen to them, relieved that it isn't. It's voyeurism, really. And if they can think of a way it might be my own fault, that makes them feel safer."

"Why do you even see these people?"

"What else do I have to do in here? And besides, people really listen to you when you're dying. It's one of the perks.

Who knows, maybe I'll inspire some of them to change their lives and be happy."

"Or maybe they're just coming to have a gawp at your bald head."

"Maybe." Polly smiled. "Good job I have you here, Annie. Things might get dangerously positive otherwise, and we wouldn't want that. What would I do without you, eh, Betty Buzzkill?"

"You're welcome. Now, it's time for your commode, Baldy."

DAY 49
Support someone

"Woo! Go, Dr. Quarani! Go!" Annie jumped up and down, waving enthusiastically. She'd waited for over an hour to catch him jogging past, lean and focused. He didn't seem to hear her, just kept pounding forward. His running gear wasn't even sweaty. She turned the phone around so Polly could see via Skype. "That's him." All around them people were pressed against the marathon barriers, waving charity banners, shouting encouragement. The atmosphere was alive with positivity—Annie was worried she might even catch it. She'd brought Buster along on his lead, and he barked ferociously every time someone in costume went by. Annie hadn't realized that being with a dog made people smile at you. It was disconcerting, but she couldn't say it was unpleasant.

Polly was still mooning after Dr. Quarani. "He's got such a nice bum in that Lycra."

"Poll!"

"Well, he does. Where's Dr. McGrumpy?"

"Not sure. Oh, look, here he comes now! Woo! Go, Dr. Max!" Dr. Max was struggling up the final stretch. His face was so engorged with blood Annie wondered if he was going to burst. He was absolutely plastered in sweat, the logo of the hospital trust obscured by dark patches—despite his grumbling, he had, of course, been raising money for it all along. "Keep going!" she shouted. "You can do it!"

"I don't think he can do it, you know. I'll tell them to clear a bed in A&E," Polly said, her voice coming tinnily out of the phone.

"Shh," Annie chided. "He's doing his best." She waved at him as he limped on, brows knit fiercely and shoulders pumping forward.

"'Oh, I love you, Dr. McGrumpy! I definitely won't look up your kilt if you collapse!'"

"Shut up, Polly!"

DAY 50
Quit your job

"I'm sorry, Annie, but we do need to get to the bottom of this."

Annie's stomach fell away. She'd been called into Jeff's office, where Sharon was sitting at the Chat Area, an expression on her face like she was chewing a rotten sardine. Today she wore outfit three—an oversize jumper printed with pictures of puppies, and sprinkled all over with hairs from actual dogs. Annie tried not to sneeze just thinking about it. "What's the trouble, Jeff?"

Jeff looked even more awkward. "Um. Annie. I've just seen an online film thing."

Oh, no. Her stomach sank so far it was knocking about in the region of her ankles. Not the stupid Thorpe Park thing. "Oh."

"Is that you?" Jeff spun his laptop, which had the YouTube video on it, paused on a shot of Annie, mouth open, screaming.

"It's hard to say," she said evasively. "It's quite blurry."

"I have it on good authority that it's you. That you went there, to a theme park, when you were supposedly off sick."

"I don't know who that Kent fellow was what rang up," Sharon muttered. "Sounded so nice and all."

"But you can't prove that's me," Annie said, keeping her voice light and distant.

"No. We'd have to go through an official disciplinary process, and give you a written warning. It would take months. If you'd own up, however, we could leave it with a verbal warning. Three verbal warnings equal one written warning. Two written warnings mean a hearing..."

A familiar feeling was coming over Annie. Sitting in Jeff's office with its smell of protein shakes and Pot Noodles, being told off for not smiling enough, or being sad, or not wanting to talk about other people's healthy babies. In short, for being human, in a place that wanted to turn her into an invoice-processing robot. It sat on her chest, the knowledge that she could never change this place, its red tape, its rules. She wouldn't even be able to get the dead plants taken away without a health-and-safety briefing. She couldn't face one more day of lifting up her hand to key in the door code. Not one more day. "I can't do this," she heard herself say.

"Own up? I must say, Annie—"

"No. All this. Jeff... Sharon...why do we do this, day after day? Come into the horrible office—your homes are nicer than this, I hope? Don't smell of gone-off food and have dirt on the desks that hasn't been cleaned off in four years? They must be. But we spend most of our waking hours here—more than we're even paid for—and we don't even like any of the people we have to work with."

Jeff opened his mouth as if he was going to protest this, then didn't.

Annie went on. "What's the point? Why do we commute for hours on crammed trains, with everyone angry and miserable, and sit at a desk all day in a dirty nasty place, and eat limp sandwiches and Cup-A-Soups, and ignore each other, and get sciatica, and then go home and sit in front of shows about baking and dancing and other people watching TV?"

"We ain't all made of money," Sharon sniffed. "Some of us need the cash."

"No, we're not. But why do we live here in London, where we just work to pay for travel and rent on horrible damp flats on the tenth floor? And surely we can find something else to do with our lives, something that pays? You, Jeff. I know you have dreams. You want to be the big man in local government. Big salary. Move out to Surrey. Propose to one of the women at your gym, with the spray tans and boob jobs. Send your kids to private school, give them what you never had."

He gaped. "How did you—"

"But is it worth it? Is it worth spending your thirties pretending to care about dish rotas and photocopier etiquette and who stamps a little bit of paper? Just to get a good pension one day?"

"Annie! I must ask you to stop—this is very unprofessional."

"I know. I know it is. It's being professional that got me in this mess in the first place." Annie felt like she was falling, and sliding, like gravity had her and she couldn't stop even if she wanted to. Her fears were clinging to her legs, shrieking. How would she pay the mortgage? How would she look after her mum? How would she buy chocolate? But as Polly said, when you were dying, it really focused your mind. And Annie was dying, too. Maybe not in the next one hundred days, sure, but sometime, and in that context spending even one more hour in this office was too many. "I quit," she heard herself say. "I can't work here anymore. I'm sorry. It's not your fault. Well, it is sort of Sharon's fault, but I guess she can't really help it."

Sharon gaped. "You cheeky mare!"

Jeff was blinking hard, trying to keep up. "Annie, there's a process, there's a notice period, and—"

"I know that. But if I walk out right now, for example, is there anything you can do?"

"But…references…your final pay…"

"I don't care about those." If she was going to burn her life to the ground, she may as well douse it in petrol. "So, can you stop me? If I literally just go now?"

"No, but—I mean, leaving dos! We usually get a card and a whip-round…"

"That's kind, Jeff. But I can't go through it, pretending we all loved each other and you'll miss me. I need to start being more honest in my life. So…bye."

"But…but…"

Annie stood up. "Hey, by the way, you know those redundancies you've been holding over our heads for months now? Getting everyone to toe the line and work extra hours and keep their mouths shut? How about you give me one of them? Oh, and you'd be mad if you let Fee go. She's the only one who does any work about here."

She left the room, her vision swimming, her steps wobbly. Oh, God. *Oh, God.* She had to speak to Polly. Polly would think it was great.

No one looked up from their desks. They all stayed slumped at their screens, playing Candy Crush or scrolling through Facebook. Annie picked up her bag and coat, and powered down her computer. She looked around for one last time— the dead yucca plant, the invoice tray with the smear of ink, the dust ingrained in her keyboard. The square foot of the earth where she'd spent most of her life for the past four years. Her hands were shaking. She picked up the sparkly pens and posh tea bags and the little hyacinth Polly had given her. She opened her mouth to say something—*Bye, everyone, hope you have nice lives, hope you get out of here, too, unless you actually like it, of course*—then she closed it, and quietly walked to the exit, shutting the door behind her for the very final time.

"Okay, okay, stop whooping. I still got fired." Annie held the phone away from her ear.

"You didn't get fired," said Polly. "You stuck it to the man. You made a break for freedom! Annie, this is awesome news."

"Is it? Every time I think about the rent I want to throw up."

"Rent, schment. You'll find something. You've got some savings, yes?"

"A bit." Things did add up when you never went out or bought anything nice.

"You can do whatever you want now. Shoot for the moon, Annie! Even if you miss you'll be among the stars."

"You do know the stars are millions of miles farther than the moon? That saying makes no actual sense."

"Whatever. Never mind about work now. What you need is time to think it over. Regroup. Relax."

"Uh-huh," Annie said suspiciously. "What's the plan this time?"

"Scotland," Polly said happily. "Picture the scene, Annie. Herds of Highland cattle. Majestic snowcapped hills. A wee dram of whiskey to warm your cockles…"

"Are you working for the tourist board or something?"

"We're all going. The doctors say I'm well enough to come out now, take a treatment break, and I'm not spending any more time in Lewisham. You, me, George, Costas and Dr. McGrumpy. We're going to stay on his mum's farm in the Highlands."

"But won't it be freezing? We couldn't go to, say, Barbados?"

"I tried. He says I can't fly, spoilsport, and can't be too far from the good old NHS. Anyway, it'll be nice. There's tons of cool things to do up there, and we can cuddle up by log fires. It'll be great. We might even see the northern lights. I always wanted to but I've missed it every time. Even went to Norway, Iceland—no lights. This'll be my time, surely."

As if the aurora borealis themselves would show up at Polly's summons. After all, everything else did. "Well, okay. My diary's suddenly become very clear."

"Great. I'll tell McGrumpy. He's going to drive us all up."

Annie had a brief vision of a blazing log fire, a fur rug and Dr. Max beside her, whiskey in hand, kilt on and...

No. Dear God, what was she thinking? She couldn't have a crush on a scruffy grumpy doctor, especially not one who held her friend's life in his big hairy-knuckled hands.

"Oh, and pack some warm clothes," Polly added. "You can ski, right?"

DAY 51
Plan a holiday

"Mum, I've got some news."

Annie's mother was fidgeting, her hands restless on her lap. "What is it? Are you the dentist, dear?"

"No, I'm not the… Are your teeth sore, Mum?"

She peered over Annie's right shoulder, at nothing. "It was the toffees did the damage. Sally always did like them, but they pulled her teeth right out!"

"Right, okay, Mum, but try to listen, okay? I'm going away for a few days, but I promise I'll be back soon. It's only Scotland."

"Oh, you can say hello to Andrew, then."

Annie frowned. "Andrew? Mum, what do you mean?" Why was she suddenly mentioning him all the time? When Annie was growing up her father had been almost a taboo subject, brought up only as an answer for why Annie couldn't go to university or on the school ski trip. *We aren't made of money. Don't wish for the moon.* "Mum? Did you understand what I said?"

"Of course," she said crossly. "You're going on holiday."

Her mother used to always come over when Annie and

Mike went on holiday, to water the plants, collect the post and doubtless have a good snoop in the cupboards. They'd usually come back to find every piece of china taken out and washed in baking soda. It had been annoying—Mike had always rolled his eyes—but at least there was someone looking out for her. Now she wasn't even sure her mother would notice she was gone. "That's right. You see, I've been fired from my job. Well, I quit."

"Your job?" Her eyes passed over Annie, watery blue.

"I'm sorry, Mum. I promise we'll be okay. I just couldn't stay there for another second."

"Quite right, too, dear. Why should you be working, a young girl like you? You should be at home looking after your kiddies."

Annie watched the hands. "Mum, are you all right? You seem restless."

"Oh, I just wish I'd brought my knitting. The queue is so long in this dentist's. I feel like I've been here for weeks!"

She hadn't knitted since her diagnosis, but before that she'd been an expert, capable of intricate patterns—socks, hats, jumpers, the works. "I can get some wool, Mum. If the doctors say you can have knitting needles."

She saw Dr. Quarani approach. "Hello, Doctor. I'm just trying to explain I'm going away."

"So I hear." He made a mark on the chart. "Dr. Fraser, too. It's his first holiday in five years. Try not to worry, Ms. Hebden. I'll take care of your mother. She won't be distressed if you don't come for a few days."

No, because she still had no idea who Annie was. Sometimes she didn't even remember she had a daughter at all. Sometimes she thought she was five, or eighteen. "Thanks. I appreciate it."

She wondered when he'd last had a holiday himself. He was always so controlled, so distant. It was hard to imagine him having a life at all.

DAY 52
Buy new clothes

"No way," Polly said decisively.

"But I like it!" Annie held it protectively. It was her favorite hoodie; she'd had it since she was seventeen.

"There are literally teenagers who are younger than that jumper. Get yourself something new, for God's sake! There's a whole world of clothes out there. And don't tell me you can't afford it, because you can't have bought anything new since 2003."

Annie scowled. "I hate shopping. Those changing rooms are always so tiny, and the light is so bad, and nothing ever fits me. Anyway, I'm unemployed now. I have to save my pennies." Polly might only have a few months left, but Annie had to somehow manage for the rest of her life, and take care of her mum, too. When she thought about it, her stomach felt like it was back on that roller coaster.

Polly was sitting on Annie's bed, her head covered in a floppy straw hat. She sighed. "Annie, I wish I could make you understand. I'm not saying blow all your cash. Just that, maybe, some of your clothes are past their best, and maybe, replacing them might give you a little boost?" She looked pointedly at Annie's saggy black top, the fabric all bobbled around the neck. "Anyway, won't you need some things for interviews?"

Interviews. Of course. Annie began to nod, reluctantly. "I suppose."

"And look, if you feel guilty spending money on yourself, get someone else a present, too. That's what I always do. Used to drive Tom nuts. He had more pairs of socks than a millipede in winter. Anyway," she said, nodding to the corner of the room. "I'm afraid that jumper's a goner."

Annie leaped to her feet, pulling her hoodie away from Buster, who had somehow sneaked into her room and chewed the pocket off, all in the past minute. "Bad boy! Don't eat my clothes!"

"Oh, he's not a bad boy, he's a good boy, a good boy." Polly took him, crooning and kissing. "Don't listen to nasty old Annie, you're not a bad boy." Buster coughed, and spat out a scrap of fabric.

"Easy for you to say, Polly, he hasn't eaten all of your shoes, has he?"

"All the more reason to buy new ones." Polly smiled triumphantly.

"Well, okay. But I meant what I said about going to the shops."

Polly set Buster down on the bed—Annie tried not to wince at the thought of dog hairs on her nice new sheets—and held out a thin hand. "Give me your laptop."

"Why?"

"Just give it."

Annie complied, passing over the dust-covered hulk. Polly winced. "We'll talk about accessories after. But for now, let me introduce you to the delights of next-day delivery."

DAY 53
Give a present

"So I was just getting a few things for myself and I thought I'd... Does it fit?"

Jonny was speechless, looking at the jacket she'd bought during her online shop. Fleece-lined and waterproof, it seemed like something you'd want if you were stuck outside all the time.

"Is it okay?" Annie felt wretched. Was it patronizing? Would he rather have money?

Jonny made a sudden movement, and she realized he was crying. "I'm so sorry!" she said. "I just noticed you had holes in your jacket and I—"

"I haven't had anything new in two years," he said in a strangled voice. "It even smells new. Not like jumble sales or old people or damp." He stripped off the old rag he had on— Annie tried hard not to wrinkle her nose at the stink—and buttoned up the new one. "How does it look?"

The blue fabric just set off his pallor and thin face, but Annie said, "Great. Looks good."

"Thank you, uh..."

"Annie. I'm Annie."

"Jonny."

"I know, yeah."

"Thank you, Annie."

"It's nothing. Really, it's nothing." Compared with everything she had, it really was nothing. Even if she'd lost her job, she was so far away from the street. She still had friends. A mother. Polly. "Listen, I'm going away for a few days, but if you need anything, will you let me know? I mean, I know you need...lots of things, I'm sure, but..."

He waved her away from the awkwardness. "I will. Have a good time, Annie."

DAY 54
Take a road trip

"Absolutely, categorically no way."

"But whhhhhhy?" wailed Polly.

"Because it's my car. We are not having ABBA on. I forbid it."

Polly, who was of course occupying the front seat, turned around to the others. Annie, Costas and George were all squeezed in the back of Dr. Max's Renault, padded about with Polly's things. Polly raised her eyebrows at Annie. *You ask him.*

Annie shook her head. "So what music do you like, then?" she asked him. Polly mimed sticking fingers down her throat. Annie ignored her.

"Your usual dad-rock. Clapton, Fleetwood Mac. And jazz, of course."

George groaned. "Dear God, not jazz. How about show tunes? I've got the *Miss Saigon* soundtrack on my Spotify."

"Why not some disco?" Costas said, muffled by Polly's ski coat. "Donna Summer! Frankie Go to Hollywood!" At his feet Buster squeaked in agreement. Dr. Max had reluctantly agreed to bring him as long as he sat on newspaper. "As if a bit of puppy wee could make that car any worse," Polly had remarked.

George ruffled Costas's hair. "That's so passé. You're cute."

"No show tunes," Dr. Max said firmly. "I'm sorry, George. I'd literally have to give myself a lobotomy if I listened to show tunes for the next ten hours." He met her eyes in the mirror. "Annie, why don't you pick? You're sensible."

"Um…" Annie tried very hard not to look at Polly. "To be honest, I love ABBA, too."

"Fine, I'm overruled." He sighed and jabbed a finger at the stereo, which began pumping out "Dancing Queen." As everyone—even Dr. Max—lifted their voices to the chorus, the glorious rise of notes that couldn't help but tug your heart up with it, Annie looked up to see Polly had her eyes closed, a blissful smile on her wan face.

DAY 55
Overcome a fear

Annie eyed the procession of skiers traveling slowly up the mountain on a sort of moving walkway. Dr. Max had called it a magic carpet, but it didn't look like anything from Aladdin, creaking along as it was in the driving snow, which was already making Annie's face feel numb and frozen like after a trip to the dentist. "It's very *high*." She should have known the trip would involve various terrifying feats. Bloody Polly.

"Not really. No' but a hundred feet." His Scottish accent had broadened now they were over the border, and he sounded cheerier, less gloomy. He was kitted out in sensible black ski gear, sleek as an otter. Annie, who obviously didn't own any ski stuff, felt stupid in her walking trousers and raincoat. It was worn over so many jumpers she worried she might roll down the hill like a ball if she fell over. Which was very likely. She shifted nervously; the skis felt heavy and clunky on her feet, like hobbit paws.

"I'm not sure about this. I only did it once before, on a school trip to the indoor one in Milton Keynes. Do you think she'll mind if I bail?"

There'd been a fierce argument between Polly and Dr. Max

over whether or not she could ski. It was too cold, he said, and her bones were so weak a fall could finish her off. But she was adamant. She wasn't going to die without going skiing one last time. She'd never fallen in her life, and she would stick to gentle slopes and take lots of hot chocolate breaks. Of course she had won. Polly was already swooping elegantly down the nursery slope, rosy-cheeked in a pink ski suit, her remaining blond hair held back by a cute bobble hat. She looked like the popular girls at school, the rich ones who went to the Alps at half-term while Annie and her mum sat watching Doris Day films. The ones who'd never have spoken to Annie in a million years, who laughed at her frumpy vests and home-sewn clothes. And yet here she was, twenty years on, part of Polly's inner circle.

George slammed past, churning up powder. "Might try that black run next. Up for it, Max?" Costas, who came from sunnier climes, had refused to even try, and was drinking Baileys-laced hot chocolate in the café with Buster.

Dr. Max looked at Annie, still struggling toward the lift like a newborn foal. "I'll stay here for now. Not for Polly, either! A broken leg won't give her too many happy days." Polly stuck out her tongue as she glided past on another run. Annie still hadn't gone up. She was frozen at the bottom of the lift, holding up the queue.

"Excuse me."

She moved aside to let the next person on. "Oh, God. That kid can't be more than four."

"Aye, they start them young." How good might Annie have been at it if she'd had parents who took her skiing, instead of starting now, like a clumsy adult baby? It wasn't fair. "You don't have to do it," Dr. Max said, looking longingly at the high slopes, smooth and white as hotel sheets. "Polly will understand."

"It's just it isn't making me very happy right now. More utterly terrified."

He shifted his skis. They were tangled in hers, like feet entwined in bed in the morning. "The thing about happiness, Annie—sometimes it's in the contrasts. Hot bath on a cold day. Cool drink in the sun. That feeling when your car almost skids on the ice for a second and then you're fine—it's hard to really appreciate things unless you know what it's like without them."

Annie looked up the slope. It seemed very high to her, and yet toddlers were zooming down it, little legs set wide and sturdy. She pushed hair from her face, her goggles steamed up in the cold. "Don't you want to try the harder slopes?" she said hopefully. If he left, then she could sneak off to the bar.

"Och, no, I can go anytime."

But Polly couldn't. This would likely be her very last chance to glide down, feeling the air rush cold and clear into her lungs, hearing the crisp *schwwoop* of the snow as she slid over it. And Annie could do it for the rest of her life and here she was, too afraid to go on the nursery slope. "Will you help me get on the lift?" she asked.

She was clinging to him for dear life. His hands, his precious surgical hands, must be in danger of dropping off. He kept up a soothing monologue as she lurched off the lift, walking like a drunk giraffe. "That's it. Good girl. On you come."

Annie felt the surface beneath her slip and slide as she ground her skis in so hard she left grooves in the snow. "Oh, God. Oh, God!"

"Annie?" he panted. "Can I give you some advice? Don't dig in so hard you never actually go anywhere. Okay?"

For a moment she thought he meant in life—that he was giving her a Polly-style inspirational quote. Then she understood. She slackened off her snowplow and felt the ground slide under her. "Don't let go. Don't let go!"

He let go. She was moving—she was flying. Gravity had her and she was sliding away from him down the slope. He yelled, "Snowplow. Snowplowwww!"

Annie tried to push her legs out, V-shaped as he'd shown her. But she didn't have the strength. She realized a second before that she was absolutely, 100 percent going to fall, arms waving, legs wobbling. Then he was beside her, shooting down in a blur of black. "Snowplow! Turn to the left! The left!"

Annie leaned hard on her right leg, and she turned. But she turned straight into him, and for a second his face went into a comical O of shock, and she fell in a heap on top of him. "Oof!"

Winded, they lay there on the snow, as toddlers shot past them. "God, I'm so sorry. Are you okay? Your hands!"

He was under her, struggling for breath. "I'll be...okay."

"I'm so sorry. I'm an idiot."

"Och, Annie. Everyone falls over. It's how you learn. Can you get up again?"

Polly zoomed past, seeing them still entangled. "Jeez, get a ski lodge, you two." Annie blushed, filled with some kind of strange guilt on top of her existing feelings of shame, fear and embarrassment. Dr. Max hauled her up, with difficulty.

"There you go," he said. "You skied!"

"Er, I fell."

"Don't worry. That's all skiing is—the bits between falling. You just have to get up again."

"Like life," Annie said shakily. "Except I can't get up by myself."

"Well, in skiing, like in life, you sometimes need another

person to help you up. Come here." He brushed snow off her back. "Ready to go on?"

She looked down the slope. She'd already fallen, so what else could go wrong? After all, people fell over all the time, and it didn't mean she was clumsy or stupid or useless. It just meant she was…learning. "Show me what I did wrong that time," she said, sticking her ski poles firmly into the snow.

DAY 56
See the wonders of nature

"I saw it! I saw it! That was definitely a tail!" Everyone ran over to the side of the small boat, making it rock alarmingly. Annie braced herself against the side.

Dr. Max was wearing a blue North Face jacket speckled with rain. Drops of it were caught in his beanie hat and the beard he was letting himself grow away from the hospital. It was already impressive; he didn't have a five-o'clock shadow so much as a 10:00 a.m. one. "Did you see it?"

She shook her head. "Just trying not to fall in."

"Here." He held out his binoculars, which were heavy and cold.

She peered in but the sea was just a gray blur. "I can't see anything."

"Let me show you." He leaned over her, and she held her breath. His voice was in her ear. "There. Over to the left. See the wee tail flick up? That's a pilot whale."

Annie looked. She couldn't see it. Nothing but gray, gray, gray, then… "I saw something!" So quick you'd miss it, like a flicker of desire coming and going in your stomach. "And there's…oh, my God!" As she watched, three dolphins flipped out of the water and back in again, kicking up water. It was so fast.

He laughed at her astonished face. "They play with the whales, naughty wee buggers."

"Why do they do that, jump out like that?"

He took the binoculars back, looping them around his strong wrists. "Just for fun. For happiness, you might say."

"Jumping for joy," she said, eyes fixed on the water.

"Aye. Never understood why people are always so keen on swimming with them, though. Must be horrible for the poor beasties. They're intelligent creatures."

Annie nodded so vigorously her hat almost fell off. "I couldn't agree more."

"Oh, God. Why do you all look so happy? Oh, God. This is horrendous." George stumbled past, ashen-faced, and puked loudly over the side. His orange life jacket clashed horribly with his gray face.

"These Londoners," Dr. Max said, shaking his head. "No sea legs."

"*I'm* fine," Annie pointed out, conveniently forgetting that it had taken her half an hour to go near the side of the boat.

"Aye, well, maybe you're special." He said it offhandedly, and then moved over to Polly, who was sitting on a deck chair, all wrapped up in coats and blankets. "Don't let yourself get cold now, hear? It could be catastrophic."

God, Annie liked the way he said it. *Catttasstroooophic.* She looked out at the sea, spotting the dolphins again and the larger slow flick of the whale's tail. There was no way to tell from the gray choppy surface anything was there, but she knew that beneath them the sea teemed with life, and the dolphins were so happy about it they couldn't stay put in the water a second longer.

DAY 57
Eat something different

"What is in this haggis?" Costas was staring at his plate, prodding at the mass on it. It did resemble a tumor or something, Annie thought, underneath its translucent skin.

"It's just lamb," Dr. Max said, hefting another one over with an oven glove, and sticking it on Annie's plate. Buster was sniffing about at their feet, driven wild by the smell of meat. "You eat a lot of lamb in Greece, right?"

"Don't listen to him, Costas," George said, grimacing. "It's sheep stomach."

"Stomach?" Costas's eyes went round. "Maybe I will just eat these potatoes here."

"Haggis, neeps and tatties," said Dr. Max. "National dish of Scotland. Just try a wee bit, you'll love it."

Polly was already scarfing hers. "I'll eat anything, me. Life's too short to turn your nose up."

"I once ate a live grub," Dr. Max said cheerfully. In fact, he'd been cheerful the whole time they were in Scotland, Annie realized. Perhaps it was London that made him grumpy. "I was on a placement year in Brazil. Tasted like coconut."

"Bleurgh." George mimed retching. "I love you, really, Dr. Max, but is there a pizza delivery place around here?"

"Not for fifty miles. Just try it. Annie?" He held up a gravy boat filled with creamy whiskey sauce. He was wearing his mother's flowery pinny, and his hair was even more disheveled than usual from the heat of the kitchen.

"I didn't know you could cook." She pushed her plate over. Maybe it would disguise the taste of the sheep stomach. "Thought you lived exclusively off Twixes."

"Och, aye, lots of surgeons cook. Good hands, see."

Annie studiously did not look at Polly.

"I suppose you're used to seeing the insides of bodies," George muttered, poking at his haggis.

Polly tapped his plate. "Eat it! Don't be rude."

Annie poked at hers. He was watching her. "Go on. It's honestly delicious. My favorite food."

Annie cut into the skin of her haggis, and out tumbled black mulch, a bit like potting compost. Gingerly, she took a tiny forkful to her lips. Her mouth was filled with a rich, meaty, spicy taste. "It's really nice!"

"Told you. Try it with the whiskey sauce. I used ten-year-old Lagavulin for that."

"Maybe I can just have toast," George said with quavering self-pity.

Dr. Max relented. "That one's vegetarian haggis. Also verra tasty. Not been near a stomach. Promise."

Eventually they all ate theirs, and drank their whiskey, either neat or in whiskey sours, which made Dr. Max curse and mutter under his breath about them being a pack of philistines, and Edna, his mother, a tiny lady with a helmet of blue-rinse curls, came to say good-night (her bedtime was 9:00 p.m., no exceptions). She was buttoned up to the neck in a pink quilted dressing gown, as—no surprise—it was absolutely freezing outside the kitchen. "Och, did you enjoy your haggis?"

"Delicious," George said, smiling broadly. Maybe he would make it as an actor, after all, Annie thought. "Are you off to bed, Mrs. F?"

"Oh, aye, verra late for me to be up. Your beds are all made up and I've put in a wee hot water bottle. Are you laddies okay bunking in together, aye?" She said the last to Costas and George, and Polly winked at Annie across the table.

"You didn't need to do that, Mrs. F," said George. "We don't want to put you to any trouble."

"No trouble at all," said Edna. "Stay put and have a wee dram. Maximilian never brings any friends here. It does my heart good to see you all."

"Everyone gone up?" said Dr. Max. He and Annie had just washed the dishes, listening to the radio in comfortable silence. He sang along when songs he liked came on. The Eagles. Smokey Robinson. Even ABBA, surprisingly. "Say nothing," he told her when she'd raised her eyebrows at that. "Maybe they're not so bad, after all." Now they were done, and back in the living room. Buster had fallen asleep in front of the fire, his paws twitching as he chased dream rabbits.

"Polly's in the bathroom, I think." George and Costas had said something about "looking for the northern lights," and disappeared off. Annie was sleeping in the living room on the sofa bed. She'd planned to sit by the fire, nursing the whiskey. She thought she might be acquiring the taste for it everyone went on about, for the warming afterglow and the peaty smell that reminded her of heather and streams on a spring day.

He waved a hand at the sofa he'd sat down on. "Is this okay? I realize I'm in your bed right now."

Annie hoped her blush would be disguised as heat from the flames. "It's fine. Just enjoying my drink."

After a few moments, he hunkered down by the fire, stirring it with the poker so the orange center of it flamed up. The smell of peat was the same as Annie's whiskey, warm and clean somehow, like fresh air and earth and the outside. She could see the top of his head, where his untamed hair was starting to thin a little. He'd be bald when he was older, she thought to herself. Not yet, not till he was fifty or so. He'd age well, his beard graying and… She stopped herself from imagining anything more. "I'm glad you like it," he said. "I mean, not just the whiskey but Scotland in general. You do, don't you?"

"Of course. I can't believe I never came before. It's so beautiful."

"I always think more clearly up here. In London everything seems so loud. Not just the streets but even my thoughts, my head. Here I can just…be quiet."

"I know what you mean. So, if you don't mind me asking, how come you don't work up here?"

He sat back on his heels, swirled his own whiskey. "I've thought about it. It would have to be a big city, of course, and so far the jobs haven't come up. Plus, we're doing more cutting-edge work down there. But yeah, I've thought about it. And with Mum getting on a bit, you know."

Annie really didn't want him to move to Scotland. "I guess London has more…plays and things."

"Sure." He scratched Buster's tummy, absently. "When did you last go to a play?"

"Um, about six years ago, probably."

"Me, too. So. Why do we stay?"

"Mum's there. I grew up there. Work—well, it was there. Now, who knows."

"The world is your oyster. I've never understood that expression. Oysters aren't interesting, are they? Sort of gloopy and gross."

"Gloopy and gross sums up my world pretty well." But not anymore, Annie realized. Right now she was in the most beautiful part of the country, with a good friend upstairs, good food in her stomach and a good scruffy man sitting at her feet. He was close enough that she could have reached out and stroked his head.

"Annie?"

"Hmm?"

"Have you thought about what might happen—you know, after?"

"After?" She didn't understand at first.

"Polly. She's still very sick, you know. This is just…this is the last hurrah, I think." He was speaking very softly. "What will you do?"

She sighed. "I have no idea. She sort of threw a grenade in my life. I'll have to find another job, and somewhere for Mum to live."

"It doesn't have to be London?"

"No, I guess not. Somewhere cheaper would be good. But I need to work, too."

He raised his glass to his mouth. He was facing away from her, staring at the fire, and she suddenly had the impression he was about to say something important. Her spine tensed. "Well, maybe—"

"Not interrupting, am I?" Polly called from the doorway. Annie's heart sank. "'Course not. You all ready for bed?"

Polly was wearing fleecy pajamas with hearts on, and you could see how thin she was, how worn out. But her chin was raised and her eyes bright. "Just about. Dr. Max, can I have a word with Annie?"

"Oh. Sure. I'll go and lock up the gates. See where the boys have got to."

Polly came to sit where he'd been, curling her legs up toward the fire. She lifted his glass and finished the dregs, an intimate little gesture that somehow stabbed at Annie. "Yuck. No idea how he can drink this stuff."

"What's up?"

"Well, you know how tomorrow is our last day here?"

"I can't stay any longer, I'm sorry. I know I got fired but there's still Mum—she has no one else."

"That's kind of what I wanted to talk to you about." Polly held up the now-empty glass, squinting at the trails left by the whiskey. *Legs*, Dr. Max had called them. "What if there was someone else?"

"What do you mean?"

"Don't be mad." Polly smiled brightly.

"Well, I'll try. What is it?"

"When you first told me about your dad, how you'd never met him and so on, I thought that was a shame. Seeing as you've sort of lost your mum now, in a way. I didn't want you to be alone. That's why I did it. I hope you can see that?"

"What did you do?" Annie sat up straight, panicked.

"Well. All I did was look for your dad, really." Polly spoke so casually.

"You...what? Polly. Why did you do that?"

"So you wouldn't be alone, like I said. Look, Annie, we've had fun, yeah? But I won't be around forever. And then where will you be? Back in that flat with your poor mum who doesn't know who you are, stalking Mike and Jane online, never going out? I don't want that for you."

"I..." Annie was speechless. "I'm not a child, Poll. I can look after myself."

"Can you? You weren't doing that good a job before you met me."

She's dying, she's dying. With supreme patience, Annie said, "So. You looked up my dad. Did you…find him?"

"Oh, yeah. It's easy to find people on the electoral register. He lives quite near here, in fact. Well, in Scottish terms." So that was what her mother had meant about seeing Andrew. He lived here. But…how did her mother know that? A pulse began to beat in Annie's stomach. Polly was still talking. "So I thought tomorrow, Dr. Max could drive you over while we go for a stroll in the town. Visit the distillery and so on." She was still beaming.

"Just like that." She'd handed Annie a father she'd never known, never even thought about finding.

"Yeah, just like that. I'll clear it with Dr. Max but he'll do it, I'm sure."

"Right." Because transport was the only problem in this situation.

Polly frowned. "What's the matter? Aren't you happy?"

Where could she start? It was one thing giving her make-overs, forcing her to miss work over and over until she got fired, making her take part in bizarre dances and go on roller coasters. But interfering in her family, as if Annie couldn't have found him by herself? "Polly," she began, hearing the wobble in her voice. Then the door slammed and in came Costas and George, bringing a winter chill with them, hats and coats dusted in snow.

"We saw many, many stars!" Costas said happily. "Cassiopeia, Pleaides…names from Greek!"

"What he said," George said, also grinning. "Haven't a bloody clue about stars, but man, it is stunning out there. Still no northern lights, though. Sorry, Poll. What's up with you two?"

DAY 58
Connect with your roots

"Why have you stopped?" she asked nervously.

The engine had died, and Radio 2 had abruptly been silenced. Dr. Max said, "Because. We're here."

Panic shot through her. "Are you sure? The sat nav—"

"I'm sure. It's the only house on the road." *Road* was pushing it; it was more of a dirt track and a lone house. The windows were lit up already. It had never really got light that day, and they'd been driving for most of it, all the way to this little house on its own beside the forest. Her father's house. Maybe.

Annie scrubbed a patch in the steamed-up window. "I suppose I have to do this."

"Well, we did drive two hundred miles to get here."

"In a blizzard."

"Och, that wasn't a blizzard. It was only a wee flurry."

A wee flurry indeed. The sky was cloudy with snow, falling white and sticky, covering the car even as they sat there. Annie took a deep breath. "I bet he's not here, anyway. It was probably a different Andrew Clarke. It's a common name."

"Maybe." His tone was noncommittal. "I think I better stay here, Annie. Come and get me if you need me."

"Will you not be freezing?"

He gave a dismissive look. "This isn't cold. I'll put my coat on if it gets chilly." He took out a book.

"Jilly Cooper's *Rivals*?"

He looked sheepish. "I got into them when I was a resident. You only get wee bits of time to read, so you need something gripping that you can pick up and put down. And I guess… I liked the glamour. You know, everyone not covered in boke and blood and dying all over the place." He opened the book. "On you go now. Don't disturb my reading, someone's about to bonk in a horse box."

Annie opened the car door, feeling the rush of cold air. "God. It's freezing." The snow fell on her face, like the touch of icy fingers. Inside her stomach there was also a nervous flurry. What was she doing? Her father had left when she was two days old. She didn't know if he'd ever changed her, or given her a bath. If he'd loved her, or if he couldn't wait to get out the door. Her mother never talked about him, except to imply it was his fault they couldn't have nice things. How could she do this—go up to the door and ring the bell, and smile, and introduce herself, and then have it out with him about missing the last thirty-five years of her life?

She'd have bolted, but there was Dr. Max in the car, reading his bonkbuster, waiting for her. Annie began to crunch across the yard, the stones already slippery with snow. She wiped it from her eyes as she rang the doorbell. No answer. Relief surged through her. They must be out; they must just leave their lights on—

"Hello?" The door opened an inch, on a security chain. Behind it, she could just about see a woman's face, wearing big glasses.

"Um…" Annie's mind went blank.

"We don't buy door to door. There's a sign…"

"No. That's not— Um. I'm sorry. I don't know how to..." *Deep breath, Annie. Deep breath.* She could imagine Polly rolling her eyes. *Try not to sound actually mad, Annie.* "My name's Annie Hebden," she said. "I mean... Annie Clarke."

There was a silence.

She tried again. "I'm sorry to interrupt. It's just I'm looking for...someone...and I thought he might live here."

The door rattled, then swung open wide. The woman there was about fifty, and dressed in a long cardy and jeans, glasses on her nose, long undyed graying hair. "Come in."

"But—"

"I know who you are, hen. Come in out of that snow."

Unnerved, Annie followed her into the kitchen of the house, which was blissfully warm after the chill outside. Logs burned in a fireplace, and the table was set for dinner, with round gray bowls and tumblers the colors of stained glass. A teenage girl was curled up in front of a TV, her face sulky. She was watching *Countdown,* and Annie had a sudden lurch of memory, her mother in front of the TV with her quick pen, finding the sense in the jumble of letters. It felt like a betrayal just being here. "Turn that off now, Morag," said the older woman, who had to be her mother. They had the same long pale hair, same glasses. The girl wore a black T-shirt with Nirvana on it and ripped jeans. She stared at Annie. Annie stared back.

"Can I get you a wee drink, cup of tea?"

"Um, I don't..." Annie had no idea what was going on.

"Take a cup of tea, hen. It'll help."

"All right, then. Um. Milk, please."

"Morag, make the tea."

The girl gave a theatrical sigh and flounced to the kitchen area, flicking on the kettle. She caught Annie's gaze as she passed and Annie felt a deep jolt run through her. She had blue eyes. Familiar ones.

"Sit." The older woman patted the sofa, which was comfortable and squashy. Annie did. There was a framed family picture on the TV, but she couldn't examine it in detail without being obvious. "So. Annie. You came."

"Well, yes, but how… I'm sorry—you're…?"

"Oh! I thought you knew. I'm Sarah, that's Morag over there."

Morag busied herself reading the packet of tea bags.

Annie said, "You must be wondering why I've just turned up out of the blue."

"Och, no, dear, we thought you'd come sooner to be honest. I'm sure you must be busy, down in that London."

They did? And how did she know Annie lived in London? She plowed on. "The thing is, I'm looking for someone called Andrew Clarke. Does he—does he live here?"

The woman—Sarah—blinked hard. She looked at Morag, and the two seemed to have a hurried silent conversation. Sarah sighed and turned back to Annie. "Oh, hen. You don't know, do you?"

"Know what?" Annie felt rising panic again. Her hands clenched.

"Well, Andrew—your dad…" Annie thought she might be sick. "I'm sorry, hen, but he passed away two years back."

Annie didn't understand. There were words, and they were in English, but somehow the meaning of them could not sink in. *"Oh."* There was a noise from the kitchen, and the girl—Morag—let out a choking sob and dashed from the room, throwing the box of tea bags into the sink.

Sarah sighed again. "Poor wee thing. She was very close to her daddy."

Her daddy. Her *daddy*. So that meant… "I'm sorry. I'm not

really… A friend of mine—well, I say 'friend' but I'm actually pretty cross with her right now—she tried to find him for me because she knew we'd never met, well, not that I can remember, anyway, and she gave me this address and I came and—"

"So you really knew nothing. Dear God, hen, what was that mother of yours thinking? I wrote when he got sick. I thought you should both know. She didn't tell you?"

"My mum's not well. She…she gets confused." Had her mother known he was dead? Was that why she kept talking about him? "But…did Mum not reply?" Annie wasn't understanding any of this.

"Let me explain, hen. I can see you're all at sea. Andrew—your daddy—he lived here, yes. You've come to the right place. And I'm—I was—his wife, and Morag there, she's your sister. Half sister. Your dad, he got sick a few years back, and I wrote to your mum. And your mum, she wrote back, all about you and that you'd had your baby. She wanted him to know."

Jacob. Her father had known about Jacob. "Oh."

"He was ever so pleased, love. He'd wanted to get in touch for years, ever since Morag was born, but he thought—he didn't know what your mum would say. When she replied he thought he'd get to see you before he… She didn't pass it on?"

Annie shook her head slowly. "She already had it by then. The dementia. Maybe she forgot, or maybe…oh, I don't know."

Sarah looked stricken. "Oh, hen. I am sorry. Your dad wasn't verra well himself at the time. He didn't have long left. If only—ah, well. It can't be helped."

Annie wasn't sure what happened next. All she knew was she needed Dr. Max, needed him like you need a life buoy when you're drowning in the ocean. She got up, upsetting her tea over the beige carpet, and ran out, crunching over the ground to him, waving her hands hysterically. He opened the car door, laying aside Jilly Cooper. "What...?"

She didn't realize she was crying until she felt the tears cold on her face. "He's dead. He's dead, Dr. Max. My dad is dead."

Annie was vaguely aware of things. The warmth and crackle of the fire on the backs of her hands. Sarah and Dr. Max in the kitchen, murmuring to each other in low Scottish voices, the kettle boiling, the clink of cups. He had, she thought, tactfully explained the situation with Annie and her mum and Jacob. The light was fading outside—they wouldn't make it back now before the real weather set in. Snow was already whirling around the windows, until Sarah whisked the curtains closed. She pushed a mug into Annie's hands, which were cradling her head. "Drink that. You've had a shock."

"I'm sorry. I just—I never thought I'd even meet him. I thought he was gone, and then suddenly I thought I might meet him, after all, and... I never will now."

"He wanted to meet you. He knew he'd not done right by you, love. I tried to get him to write for years, but he was afraid."

Dimly, Annie felt the blow, and knew she would suffer for it later. Her mother hadn't told her they were in touch, for whatever reason—and now it was too late. That was what death meant. It meant it was too late for everything. There was no way back. No wonder Polly was trying to do so many things, be so many different people, all in the space of a hundred days. Once she was gone, it would be as if she'd never existed, and the rest of them would have to turn around and keep trudging on. Annie swallowed some tea, hardly tasting it. "I'm sorry, Sarah. I wouldn't have come if I'd known."

"We wanted you to, love. I wrote inviting you to the funeral."

Her father's funeral. He'd been buried and she hadn't even known. If she'd found out in time, she could have met him. Forgiven him, maybe, for running out on her and Maureen. So many emotions were swirling in her head, she felt like she was in the middle of a blizzard. At least one person could understand. As Sarah and Dr. Max busied themselves in the kitchen, making yet more tea, just for something to do—Morag crept back into the room, her eyes red. "Hi," Annie tried.

"Hmph."

"I'm sorry about this. I had no idea—I didn't know about you. I swear."

"So...you're, like, my sister or something?"

"I guess so." It was so strange. A lifetime of being an only child, of having only her mother, and now there was this girl, sneaking looks at Annie out of the corner of her eye. A sister. "How old are you?" asked Annie.

"Fifteen." Reluctantly, she flicked her eyes to Annie. "You?"

"Way older. Thirty-five." So she'd been twenty when this girl was born. Working already, dating Mike. Morag could have been her flower girl at the wedding. But no, it couldn't have been like that. There was no point in all these what-ifs. There never was.

Morag leaned in, lowering her voice. "Is that your husband? Or your boyfriend or something?"

"Dr. Max? Oh! No, no, he's not. He's..." She looked over at him, moving around the unfamiliar kitchen like he moved around his operating theater, picking up mugs and spoons, totally focused. His hair was damp with snow and his fleece was old and ratty. He must have felt her look because he glanced up, and mouthed a quick, *Okay?* Annie tried to summon up a smile back, but couldn't quite manage it. She was going to need time. There was so much to explain. That she'd had a husband, but didn't now, and Dr. Max definitely wasn't it. And it hit her, suddenly. Jacob had been part of this family, too. He'd been her father's grandson, and Morag's nephew, but they would never know him. A fresh wave of loss slammed into her and she leaned back slightly, as if from a physical blow. "He's just my friend," she said.

Morag was watching her carefully. Her eyes were the same as Annie's own—blue, watchful. Their father's eyes—she'd never known. Annie wondered what else they'd inherited. His inability to stay in anything, not a job, not a marriage? At least, that was how her mother had described him. But he'd stayed here, hadn't he? Morag was fifteen or so. Fifteen more years than he'd had with his other daughter.

The feelings were swamping her. That her father had chosen this other life, other family, other child. That she had no one now. He was dead; her mother was lost in the darkness. And Polly. Soon Polly would be gone, too. She stood up, shakily. "I'm sorry," she said, raising her voice so they could hear her over the boiling kettle. "I think we better go."

Sarah looked disappointed. "Oh, hen! I thought you were stopping for dinner? You can stay the night, too, if you like."

"No. No, we can't. Our—my friend's ill. We need to leave early tomorrow."

"Are you sure?" Dr. Max had a flowered tea towel over his shoulder—it seemed he'd been washing up. "It's no trouble to stay awhile, Annie."

Why couldn't he understand? She started looking around for her bag, ignoring the hostile expression that had crept back onto Morag's tearstained face. "No. We should go. Will you take me, please?"

Much, much later, in the wee small hours of the night, as Dr. Max described it, the car pulled up at the gate of his mother's house. It was icy cold, and still, not a breath of a mouse stirring around. Annie was stiff and freezing, her eyes sore. She hadn't spoken the whole way back, over dark hills and rivers, the headlights catching the glowing eyes of nighttime animals. "We could have stayed, you know," he said, turning off the engine.

She stared at her cold hands. He must be disappointed in her. She'd been cold, she knew, and awkward. "It's a bit much to take, okay? Finding out my dad lives here, only then I find out he's dead, and guess what, he was trying to meet me only Mum never passed on the letters, and I can't ask her why because she thinks I'm her friend from school, oh, and I also have a sister I never knew about."

"I know. I know it's a lot. But…they were really trying. It's not their fault."

"Yeah, well, it's none of your business."

He paused for a moment. "I know it isn't."

"Look, I'm grateful to you for taking me. It's just—it doesn't seem fair. That I could have seen him, could have known him, but I'm too late. Story of my life. Nothing ever works out."

She had the impression he was trying very hard not to snap at her. "Annie, I know things have happened to you, bad things… It must have been dreadful. But you're not the only one, okay? Polly's dying. Her family are going to lose their sister, their daughter, at thirty-five. And Dr. Quarani—you know he's from Syria? Came here on a work visa but they wouldn't let the rest of his family in, so he's working all the hours he can to try and get them out. His sister's stuck in Aleppo with her two little kids. He's got their picture in his office—you might have seen it. No one's heard from his brother in months. He's basically all alone here, in a country that thinks he's a parasite, while he works himself to the bone trying to save lives."

Yet more sadness, yet more suffering. "I didn't know."

"I'm not trying to make you feel bad."

"Well, you are."

"Sorry. But it's just the facts."

They sat in silence for a while. Annie wiped her hands over her eyes, willing the tears to stay in. "That's terrible. He must be so worried."

"It's how life is there. Don't tell Polly, okay? She'd only blab to the whole hospital or try to organize some kind of rescue mission. He just wants to do his job."

Annie saw that one light was still burning in the living room. "We should go in. Thank you for driving me."

"That's okay. Will you maybe think about contacting them sometime? Once things have settled a bit?"

"Maybe," she muttered. She couldn't imagine that things ever would settle. "Let's just go in, okay? I'm tired. You must be, too."

Inside, the warmth hit them like a wall. Polly was curled up on the sofa, wrapped in a blanket, with her ski hat on her head. Buster slept in the crook of her arm, snuffling away. It must have been thirty degrees in the room, and she was still cold. Not a good sign. Her blue eyelids fluttered as they came in. "Oh, there you are. Good trip?"

"Didn't exactly go to plan," Annie said stiffly.

"Why not? The weather? Thought you'd be fine with your famous snooow tirrrres." She put a cod Scottish accent on the words.

"Annie's had some bad news," Dr. Max said, closing the door. "Maybe you shouldn't—"

"What's happened now?" Polly yawned. She actually yawned. What did that mean, *what's happened now*? Did she mean Annie was always finding problems, reasons to be sad?

"My dad's dead," she said stiffly. "He died two years ago."

"Oh, God! Annie, I'm so sorry. That sucks."

"Yeah. I've also got a half sister I never even knew about."
She heard her voice tremble. "She's fifteen."

Polly beamed. "But that's awesome! A sister! I bet you're
glad I did all that digging now. And there you were all grouchy
with me."

Annie's hands clenched. "Polly, you shouldn't have done it.
It was up to me to look, if I ever wanted to."

"You wouldn't have. You were too scared to shake things
up. She wouldn't, would she?" Polly appealed to Dr. Max,
who was shutting the curtains and putting the fireguard on.

"Leave me out of this," he said shortly.

"So what if I was?" said Annie. "It's up to me. You can't
control every aspect of my life. You can't just decide when it's
time for me to meet my dad, or find out I have a sister. What
am I supposed to do with that? My dad's gone, and she had
him all her life. I had him for, like, a day and I don't even remember. How am I meant to deal with that?" Polly rolled her
eyes. Annie felt icy rage pour into her veins. "What?"

"Oh, Annie. You're so determined to feel miserable. You
were sad you had no family left, and here I've found you a
sister and you aren't even grateful."

"You haven't found me anything! You're not God, Polly!
You don't get to push us all around!"

"Annie, keep it down," Dr. Max said reasonably. "Everyone's in bed."

She turned on him. "You agree with me! You know she's
always interfering. You were the one who said she was un-
stable." Annie was quivering all over. Polly was just staring at
her, unmoved. She heard herself say, "I'm leaving. First thing
tomorrow."

"We're all leaving tomorrow. Don't be so dramatic, Annie!"
Polly drawled.

"I'm leaving without you. I'll get the train."

"Fine. If you want to make me do the journey by myself, when I'm ill."

"You've got your brother, and your neurologist, who incidentally is taking time off from saving lives to hang about in Scotland with you. Because everything always has to be about *you*."

Finally, Polly snapped. "Is that so much to ask for?" Her eyes blazed. "I got three months, Annie. That was all. One hundred days, to do everything I ever wanted. This cancer, it's taken so much away from me. My hair. My dignity. I can't eat, I can't sleep, and no one will look at me except to see if I might be dying soon or stick needles in me. I have nothing, and you begrudge me a few days of attention? Jesus, Annie. I thought we were friends."

Annie gulped. She wasn't going to let Polly play any more cancer cards. "Friends don't push each other around like... like...a puppet on a string."

Polly laughed. A hard and unfriendly sound. "You're mixing your metaphors, Annie. And where would you be if I hadn't pushed you? Stuck in that job you hated, miserable, hating every day? Feeling sorry for yourself, wasting your life? You've no idea how lucky you are! I just helped you along."

"What do you mean?" Annie frowned. But as soon as she said it she realized she knew. The link to the YouTube video. Jeff never went on YouTube; he was far too dedicated to the job. What were the odds he'd just stumbled across it? Someone must have sent it. "You didn't. Polly! Did you get me fired?"

Polly shrugged. "Someone needed to. You were going mad in that place. I just gave you a little boost."

"You got me fired! How could you? You—you...you're unbelievable. You're the most selfish person on the planet."

"Good," said Polly. "I want to be. At least that way people might remember me when I'm gone."

She felt Dr. Max's hand on her arm. Not the way she would have liked him to touch her—gentle, loving—but warning. "I think you should stop this now. Go to bed, both of you."

Polly snarled, "Don't think I don't notice you two making eyes at each other. I bet you're delighted—me dying's worked out great for you. Fall in love over my dead body, why don't you. It's not *fair*. Everyone else will get to go on with their lives and I'll be gone, dead and gone!"

"No one's in love," Dr. Max said coldly. "You're acting like children. Both of you. Now go to bed and we'll sort this out tomorrow."

"I won't be here tomorrow," Annie said, making her own voice cold, too. "Like I said, I'm going. I have a life to get back to and a job to find. Thanks to her."

DAY 59
Travel

"Ladies and gentlemen, we apologize for the delay to this service, which is due to, er, cows on the track."

A loud groan went up.

Annie hadn't been able to get a seat on the packed train from Edinburgh, so she sat on her case near the loo as far as Doncaster, sniffing bleach and wee with every breath, people stepping over her. And what did she have to go back to? Costas and George were going to stay on in Scotland for a few days, because "Buster is so happy here." So she'd be going back to her empty, damp flat—all those nights she'd longed for Costas to be miles away, and now she would miss him singing to himself in the room next door. Alone, it would be just her, a frozen pizza, a boxset, and back into the hospital to visit her mother again. She'd have to start staggering her visit times with Polly's—although everyone in the damn place loved her so much, it would be hard to avoid her name. It wasn't fair. Polly was doing a better job of dying than Annie ever had of living—popular, cool, making the world a better place with every day she had left. Whereas Annie just ruined it. She'd lost her best friend and husband and son, and now a father and a half sister, too. Her mother would go soon, as well, and then where would she be? Anchorless. Orphaned. Divorced. Annie felt it rise up in her, a wave of sadness, of hopelessness.

"Are you okay, dear?" An old lady peered over her *Take a Break* at Annie.

Annie stared hard at the grimy train floor. *Make something up.* Allergies. Peeling an onion. But there were no onions there, and so she let it go, a sob ripping out of her stomach. "I'm so sad. I'm just so *sad*."

"Oh, pet! Whatever's the matter?"

How could she explain all of it? Her mother, Mike, Jacob? "My…my best friend is dying," she whispered, and then she was lost in an incoherent sobbing mess, snot running down her face.

Everyone was so kind. The old lady—Patricia—said her best friend had died the year before—"Bless her, she made eighty-four, though she was furious she missed Wimbledon"—and that she understood how alone it made you feel. A squaddie with arm tattoos gave Annie his seat, and a student with dread-locked hair fetched her tea from the buffet cart. She couldn't drink it, she was crying so hard, but the gesture made her sob even more. "You're all so niiccce. Thank. You," she hic-cupped.

She didn't understand what that woman in that play had been on about. Sometimes, you could hold it together in front of everyone you knew, but it was the kindness of strangers that cut you right to the bone.

DAY 60
Take some downtime

Costas did not come back for several days. So, alone, Annie's first day went like this:

11:00 a.m.–1:38 p.m.—lying in bed staring at the damp patch on the ceiling, replaying the conversation with Polly.

1:38–2:07 p.m.—replaying the conversation with Dr. Max. Bashing her head into the pillows, groaning loudly.

2:07–3:45 p.m.—thinking about going to shops for food. Not actually going.

3:45–3:59 p.m.—rooting about in the kitchen cupboards, tearing off bits of bread and shoving them into her mouth, wolfing down an entire bag of Costas's pistachios. Throwing the shells all over floor. Crying more because he'd probably move out soon and she'd always been mean to him.

4:00–6:00 p.m.—crying, lying on the cold kitchen floor. Finding one of Buster's disgusting chewed-up dog toys, sticky with drool, and crying because she'd always been mean to him, too.

6:00–8:45 p.m.—running a bath in an effort to cheer up but lying there crying some more until the water went cold. Rummaging in the dirty fridge, past moldy peppers, for a bottle of rosé wine. Drinking the lot lying in tepid bathwater, weeping.

8:45 p.m.–3:00 a.m.—watching old episodes of *Grey's Anatomy*, crying afresh any time something sad happened (approximately every three minutes).

DAY 61
Start a new healthy habit

The next day: same except for one quick trip to the corner shop—the horrible estate one where the milk was always out of date—for rosé wine, crisps and Ben and Jerry's. Wishing Costas had left Buster with her so she could at least have something to cuddle. She'd gladly have cleaned up his wee if it meant a bit of nonjudgmental company. Thinking about calling Polly, clearing the air, then remembering her words—*wasting your life, feeling sorry for yourself*—and realizing she couldn't face it.

DAY 62
Shop local

"Sorry, love. Ain't got none left. You 'ad the last tub yesterday."

"What?" Annie looked around the grimy shop in a panic, past the trashy magazines and off-the-back-of-a-truck beer. "You must have something. Chunky Monkey? Phish Food?"

"Ain't got no Ben and Jerry's left, told you. Could do you a Carte D'Or?"

"What flavor?" Annie's voice wavered.

He peered into his freezer. "Vanilla?"

She bit her lip hard to keep from crying in the middle of the shop. On her way out—ice cream–less, because she still had some pride—she caught sight of herself in the security monitor. Crazy, unbrushed hair, with what looked like a pistachio shell caught in it. Greasy, open-pored skin. Mad, swollen eyes. She'd have crossed the road to avoid herself. She went home, and got back into bed, where she stared at her phone for almost an hour without doing anything. Polly wouldn't want to speak to her, anyway. She'd have called if she did. *Wasting your life. Feeling sorry for yourself.* Who would want to be friends with someone like that?

DAY 63
Learn a new skill

"It will be fun!" Costas pleaded. He'd finally come back, staggering under the weight of shortbread and haggis (apparently he now loved it) and tartan throw pillows. Buster leaped and pawed at Annie's legs, and she was so grateful he was pleased to see her she almost cried. Even though Buster would be pleased to see a cardboard box. "Come on, Annie. You have not left the flat in all this time?"

"I have," she muttered. "I've been seeing friends...local friends. I don't need Polly. Um, is she okay?"

He shrugged. "Same, I think."

"Did she say whether she might... Whatever. I don't care."

He gave her a pitying look. "Please, I would like for you to come with me tonight."

"It sounds horrific. Isn't it full of hipsters?"

"What is hipsters?"

"You know. Trendy middle-class types with beards and checked shirts?"

His eyes lit up. "You have been!"

"No, no, I... Never mind. But seriously. I don't want to go

to ukulele class. I can't even play the recorder. That's a sort of flute, by the way."

"It's fun! We learn tunes, and we play along, and we sing, and it's nice. Nice people. Nice pub. Nice music. Nice glass of wine."

She glared at him. "Stop enabling me. I can't go out. I haven't even showered in three days."

"No kidding," Costas said, wrinkling his nose. He'd been spending too much time with George. "Come on, come on. One hour only. I will buy you much wine, I promise."

"Oh, all right, then," she said sulkily, but only because she'd run out of biscuits and couldn't face another trip to the shop after her ice cream meltdown. "It better be a really big glass."

Half an hour later they were leaving the house, Annie blinking in the fresh air like a newborn baby. Costas, with his ability to dress for the occasion, was wearing a jumper with penguins on it. Annie was back in her standard: black, and more black. At least she was clean, though. "I don't even have a ukulele," she tried.

"They give. Come on! Small-guitar time!"

She felt her old familiar nervousness as they climbed the stairs in the pub—the sweat on her top lip and the feeling her head was too heavy, like she couldn't look up. She'd have run away at the door but Costas pushed in, waving at the crowd of people gathered in a semicircle, all holding ukuleles. Ironic jumpers were much in evidence. "Hi, hi!" Costas found them two seats. "My friend Annie, everybody."

She managed a grimacing smile, eyes fixed on the opposite wall. Someone put a ukulele into her hands, and sheet music in front of her.

"Nice easy one to start," said the teacher, a man with a beard that stretched past his nipples. Annie wondered what Polly would have to say about that. Then she remembered they weren't speaking, and clutched the stupid little instrument closer. She tried to make out the notes on the illustration. Of course the song was "Over the Rainbow." Gah. There were no happy little bluebirds or troubles melting like lemon drops in Annie's world. She felt like the Wicked Witch of the West.

"So? You like small-guitar night?"

"It wasn't so bad," Annie admitted. For a while she'd been absorbed in plucking the right notes, and she'd almost forgotten everything that was going on. "Do you go there a lot?"

"When I don't have work or gym or basketball practice or dressmaking class," he said cheerfully. "So much to do in London."

"Do you like it here?" She'd never thought to ask him before.

"Sometimes, when I first come, it was lonely. I miss my sisters and Mama and Greek food. But there are many good cafés here in Lewisham, and many fun things to do! Also, is better for being gay. Everyone is not so prejudiced." Annie couldn't imagine how it was, to move to a different country when you were only twenty-two, knowing nobody and with a sketchy grasp of the language. And look at him. He knew more people and did more things than her, who'd lived in the same postcode all her life. She had to do better. She would do better.

"Do you, uh, do you want to get a pizza or something?" she asked carefully. "We could take it home, watch a film?" All that time living together, she'd done her best to keep walls between them. Not just physical but social, too, emailing him instead of knocking on his door, refusing to watch TV with him or go for a drink or eat his cooking. And now she realized he was one of the best friends she had.

Costas lit up, like a small child. "I want the pepperoni on mine, please. And please can we watch the *Dirty Dancing*?"

DAY 64
Put yourself out there

"Come on, Buster. Please. Do your wees! Please!"

Buster wagged his tail obligingly, but then wandered off to sniff an abandoned chip wrapper. Annie shivered—she'd thrown a coat over her pajamas to take him downstairs, but it was 3:00 a.m. and freezing. The straggly patch of grass between tower blocks wasn't inviting by day, and by night it was downright terrifying. "Come on, please. I'm begging you. I'll give you a dog treat. Two dog treats."

Buster came over and licked the side of her foot. Annie sighed. "Right, fine, let's go inside." She carried him into the lift and back into the warm flat, gratefully shutting the door behind her. Costas was out on the graveyard shift, getting ready to make coffee for commuters. What a crap job. At least Annie, being now unemployed, could devote herself full-time to lying in bed feeling miserable.

She switched the kettle on for tea, knowing she'd struggle to get back to sleep, and pulled her laptop onto her knee. She clicked on Polly's Facebook page, feeling vaguely ashamed, but there were no updates since their Scottish trip. She should call. She knew that. You couldn't just fall out with a friend who had maybe only weeks to live. But every time she picked up her phone, she remembered what Polly had said, and she chickened out. She didn't think she could bear it if she reached out and Polly wouldn't speak to her.

Instead, she clicked on a jobs website, knowing she should really do something about that. Many of the finance officer jobs were in charities, she noticed, scrolling down. Badly paid, but at least you'd feel you were doing something. And she had to start thinking about the future. After Polly. It was impossible to imagine. But life would still go on. And she had to be part of it. As Buster padded over and climbed into the crook of her arm, Annie went through the different charities, starting to think about maybe planning some kind of future for herself, until the soft snores of the little dog filled the room.

DAY 65
Visit the library

Annie pushed open the door, breathing in the smell of old books. The library was full of people sheltering from the rain outside, cold and gritty. Funny, she hadn't been in for so long, not since she was at school. She used to go with her mum every Saturday morning, choosing books in companionable hush, then going for a milky coffee and a bun and looking at what they'd picked. Her mother loved Mills & Boon, Catherine Cookson, gory true crime, family sagas and anything that was chunky and comforting. It had been several years now since she was able to follow a book, but Annie had the vague idea she might find her some knitting patterns. Her eye was caught by a New Additions stand with a book on it called *Learning the Ukulele*. Costas would like that. She picked it up. Then she saw it: the section labeled Gardening. Five whole shelves on planting, bedding, pruning and garden design. All the things Annie had once loved to read about. She'd always felt having a garden was a sign of truly being grown up. Literally putting down roots, in a place where she planned to stay forever. Where Jacob and his brother or sister would play among the plants she nurtured. And now none of that would happen—Mike would probably put in decking so he could invite his insurance-salesman buddies around for barbecues. That life would not be Annie's. She had no garden now, no soil to stand on and call her own.

But all the same, she had windowsills. She had indoor pots, which she'd never got around to filling. She picked up a book called *Window Box Gardening* and hurried to the reception desk, almost furtively.

On her way out, her tote bag stuffed with reading material, she noticed a sign in the entryway. Guerrilla Gardeners: Improving the Urban Landscape. Annie stared at it for a long time, and then quickly took out her phone and snapped a picture of the flyer.

DAY 66
Say sorry

"Annie. Annie!"

"Ugh?" She came awake slowly, realizing that Costas was standing over her. In her bedroom. "What are you doing in here?"

"I am sorry!" He backed off, hands up. "You would not wake up when I knocked. Sorry, Annie. But you have to get up now."

She yawned widely. "No, I don't. I got fired, thanks to Polly, so I may as well have a lie-in."

"Annie, Polly is sick. Very sick. Yesterday, she have…" He shook his hands, trying to think of the word. "She got bad. Very bad."

Annie was bolt upright in a second. "Her lungs?"

"No, no, her head. George says her head tumor is back. Bigger."

Shit. It had grown. Annie threw back the covers, momentarily ashamed that Costas could see the tea stains on her pajamas. "How bad?"

"Annie, she cannot see. She wake up and she can't see at all.

Please, you have to come now." He was opening her drawers, finding jeans and a clean jumper. "Wear this."

"Okay. I'll come right now. Shit."

He held the clothes out to her. "Maybe you have shower first?"

An hour later, all the crisp fragments washed from her hair and clothes, Annie was scurrying down the neurology corridor after Costas. The walls seemed to be tilting and swaying. This couldn't be it. She'd just had a fight with Polly—you didn't have fights with people who were about to die. It had only been two months, not three. There was still time. There had to be time.

At the door of Polly's room, Dr. Max was standing with a chart in his hands and a grim expression. Annie did her best to push away the thoughts of what she'd said to him in Scotland. *Idiot.* "How is she?"

"Stable. For now." He didn't smile. "This is it, Annie."

"Oh, no. Please, no."

"I'm sorry. The tumor's grown again, and it's pressing on her eyes. I've put in a shunt and drained some fluid, so she might get a bit of vision back, but it's a temporary fix." She recognized the voice he was doing—soothing, but honest. The bad-news-for-relatives voice. Her stomach fell.

"Oh, God. Can you not—"

"No." He put the chart back in its holder by the door. "Believe me, Annie. I've done everything I can. There's nothing else to try."

Beside Annie, Costas was crying. "How long, Dr. Max?"

"I can't say for sure. A week or two, maybe."

"But it's only day sixty-six. She didn't get all her days!" Annie said stupidly.

"I know." Dr. Max looked exhausted. "I'm sorry. You can

go in if you want. She'll be coming around soon. But the surgery was fairly brutal, I'll warn you. She won't look…like she did."

How could that be? Annie had only seen her a week ago. She wanted to kick herself. How selfish was she, wallowing in her flat during what might be Polly's last days? Why had she let it go this far? Why hadn't she battered Polly's door down, forced her to be friends again? She put her hand to the door, then took it away, frightened by what might be on the other side. Dr. Max nodded. *Go on.* She pushed it open.

Polly was tiny in the bed, her head shaved all over, a livid red mark on one side with scabbing-over stitches. Annie's hand flew to her mouth. Costas went white beside her and he began backtracking. "Annie, I go… I find George. He text me he's in the canteen. Sorry. I leave you."

Annie stared at her friend, horrified. Her beanie hat was too big for her, falling down over her shrunken face. Her hands were like claws, bristling with tubes, purple with old and new bruises. "What did they do to you?" Annie murmured. She laid her hand gently on the bed, which was piled with extra blankets despite the heat of the room.

"I'm not…dead…yet," Polly wheezed without opening her eyes. "Annie, is that…you? I'd know that smell of crisps and… desperation anywhere."

Annie sniffed. "Hey, Baldy."

"Like it? It's very…'retro Sinead O'Connor.' Everyone says the…nineties are back in style." She opened her eyes, wincing as if the light hurt her. "I can't really see. Come over."

She beckoned. Annie sat in the orange chair, leaning on the bed. "Sorry, I didn't have time to get you anything. Costas made it sound like you were at death's door, so I just came."

Polly coughed, making her tubes rattle. "I told him to. Knew...you'd be wallowing around in your flat."

"Well done, Sherlock Baldy. So you're not at death's door?"

"Maybe...on its garden path." She groped for Annie's hand. Her skin was icy cold. "Annie. I think this is it."

A lump rose in her throat, choking her. "I'm so sorry."

"Hey, come on, no sorry. Remember the pact. But it is a... shame. I didn't get to do all the...days."

Tears pricked Annie's eyes. "It's okay. We had a lot. I wouldn't have had any of them without you. Poll—I'm so... God. I can't believe I said all those things to you. You're sick, and there was me shouting at you, making a fuss. I'm a terrible person."

Polly waved her other hand. "Fuggedaboudit, as they say in... New York. I was out of line. I'm sorry, too. I just get so angry, you see, watching people...waste the time they have, when I don't have any. I really am...sorry about your dad. And your job! What was I...thinking? *I'm* a terrible person. Christ, will you be okay?"

"Honestly, I don't know. I don't have rich parents to fall back on, see." Annie sighed. "Listen. I know why I've been sort of hostile to you at times."

"Hadn't noticed," wheezed Polly. Sarcasm even with her last breaths.

"I was just so—if I'm totally honest, and I know this reflects really, really badly on me—I was jealous of you sometimes. All the things you had. Great family, cool parents, lovely house growing up, all your friends and your education and clothes and coolness. Even down to your name. A Polly would never end up doing admin for the council, or in a poxy former council flat in Lewisham. I just kept thinking how unfair it all was. I know that sounds awful, when you have cancer, but...there it is."

Polly cracked open one eye. Still so blue, despite the yellowing and bloodshot whites. "I was jealous of you, too. You've got time, Annie. You've got time to be anything you want. And I could see you getting on so well with McGrumpy. Whereas I tried to throw myself at Dr. Quarani and he just looked at me like...a tumor on legs. Not a person. I panicked—you don't need me anymore. You'll be fine after I go. You'll have a future. But, Annie, I need you. I can't do this without you."

"You don't have to. I promise, I'll be there. All the time, until you get sick of me."

"Pro-mise?"

She clutched Polly's hand more tightly. "God, of course I promise. I'll be here. Right till...right to the end."

"Well, let's not be too dramatic. You can still go home to shower and stuff."

"Meh, showering is overrated."

"There's the Annie I know. Oh, and, by the way...my name isn't actually... Polly."

"What?"

"I wasn't born Polly."

"What? What's your real name, then?"

She coughed. "You have to promise you'll never tell anyone. Even after I'm dead, or I swear to the great...spaghetti monster I'll come back and haunt you."

"How bad can it be?"

"Bad." She shuddered, almost dislodging her cannula. "My real name is... Pauline. After some great-aunt. I changed it when I was five—I always hated it."

Annie gaped. *Pauline.* A Pauline could easily end up doing admin for the council. A Pauline could be overweight, and sad, and obsessed with *Grey's Anatomy.* A Pauline could be left by her husband and could most definitely live in a horrible flat. "My God," Annie said, her brain falling apart. Polly hadn't been born Polly. Polly had *become* Polly.

"You ever tell anyone, I'll kill you with my…bare hands."

"You'll be dead first, Pauline."

"True," she said. She started to laugh, a deep gurgling sound, and after a few moments Annie joined in, too.

DAY 67
Meet a newborn baby

"Oh, God, not another blood sample," moaned Polly. "Why not just cut out the middleman and install a permanent pump between my veins and the lab? Sorry, Khalid. I know you're only doing the bidding of the evil Dr. McGrumpy."

The green-clad nurse smiled uncomfortably. "I'm not here for you, Polly." He looked at Annie. "Are you Mrs. Hebden?"

"Well, yes. But it's Ms. now."

"There's another Mrs. Hebden down in Maternity and she's asking for you."

Annie didn't understand at first. Mike's mum? Then she did. So did Polly. "Oh, no, she didn't! She's having her baby here?"

"It is the nearest maternity ward." Annie marveled at how reasonable she sounded. After everything that had happened.

"And she wants *you* there? Jesus! The cheek of the woman!"

"Er, I thought you said we had to forgive people and let go of the past?"

"Well, yes, but there are limits."

Khalid looked puzzled. "Will I tell her no? She's kind of… She was screaming a lot."

Annie got up. "Poll, I'll see you later, okay?"

"You're ditching me for her? I won't forget this, Annie Hebden." She mock-pouted.

"It's your fault, anyway. Making me all forgiving and saint-like, like Mother Teresa in nylon slacks. See you."

"She won't stop screaming," said the harassed-looking midwife. "I tried to tell her it'll go on for a lot longer. You're the friend?"

"Well...yes." It was easier than trying to explain. "She's in labor, then?" It was too early, surely.

"Barely. But she's hysterical. Do you know where Mike might be?" She consulted her clipboard. "That's the husband, yes?"

That's my *husband.* It was hard to shake the impulse, even now. "Yes. You can't reach him?"

"He's not picking up. She says they had a row and he stormed out. Baby's not due for another month. At least, I think that's what she said. She was screaming a lot."

"Okay. Thanks. Should I go in?"

"If you want. I'd wear earplugs if I were you."

Annie advanced cautiously down the corridor. Sure enough, she could hear guttural howls, like an animal in pain. Which was true, really. One thing she'd learned from all this hospital time was that people were no more than animals under a thin veneer, and how quickly that was stripped away by pain and fear. She pushed open the door. Jane was leaning against the bed, gripping its rail in her hands, wearing a hospital gown that gaped and showed her back tattoo. It was one of a lotus flower, which she'd got in a dodgy place in Croydon when they were seventeen. Annie had chickened out of getting one, too, like she'd been doing all her life. Until now. "Jane. Jane!"

"*Arrrrrgghhhh.* Annie, is that you?" Panting, she stopped screaming for a moment.

"You wanted me?"

"Come here. Come here." She held out her hands and grasped Annie's in a death grip. "Oh, God. The pain. How did you do it?"

"You'll get through it. Are you having an epidural?"

"I wasn't, but holy Christ! I think I'm going to break in two. Where's Mike? Where the fuck is Mike?"

"I don't know." Mechanically, Annie rubbed her ex–best friend's back. Her breath was heaving, shallow and terrified. "They'll find him. There's loads of time left. How did you know I was here?"

"Called...your house... Some kid...said you were...here."

Bloody Costas. Incapable of lying, and why would he know to, since Annie'd never told him what had happened to her?

Jane was sobbing. "I'm going to die, Annie. I'm literally going to die and it will serve me right for what I did to you."

"Oh, come on, you're being silly. You aren't going to die. They'll take good care of you."

Tears were streaming down Jane's face, her forehead creased in agony. "But you forgive me? Please say you forgive me, Annie. I don't want to die without you forgiving me."

"You're not going to die."

Jane sobbed a little. Annie rubbed her back, feeling the racing of her heart. She was terrified. Annie remembered that all too well. That fear you might split apart. That you'd never be the same again. That your body and your heart would be crushed by it, by sheer bloody exploding love. And how could she stay angry with Jane when she was so terrified, so scared and hurting? "It's okay," she said soothingly. "It's fine. It'll be fine. I promise."

She looked around, catching the eye of the nurse and waving frantically through the glass panel in the door. When it opened, she hissed, "Why won't you give her some drugs? She's in pain—look!"

The nurse shrugged. "Sorry, miss. She's had all the drugs we can give her for now."

"Well, what about an epidural?"

"Far too soon for an epidural. We'll send in some ice chips." The door closed again.

"What did she say?" sobbed Jane. "Are the drugs coming soon? Oh, God, I need all the drugs they have. I said I didn't want them. What was I thinking? Why was I so stupid?"

"Everyone thinks that before it starts. Come on. You'll be fine."

Jane clutched at Annie's hands again, cutting off the blood supply. "Oh, God. Where the hell is Mike? You won't leave me, will you? Please don't leave."

Annie kept rubbing her back, feeling the baby roll and move beneath the skin. Her ex-husband's baby. This was the weirdest situation in the world. Luckily, thanks to Polly, she'd had quite a bit of experience with weird recently. "Come on," she said. "Let's do the special breathing, okay?"

Later, Annie would remember that day as informative, terrifying and completely overwhelming. During the birth of her own child she'd been mostly out of it, alternating between screams and giggles as the drugs kicked in and they wheeled her off for a cesarean. She'd woken up to find a clean baby swaddled on her chest, Mike looking on with adoration. If only they'd known what was coming.

As a bystander, by contrast, she was there for every screaming bloody tearing moment of Jane's daughter's birth. Annie did her best to stay away from the business end of things, feeding ice chips into Jane's whimpering mouth, holding her hand and trying to wipe the terrified sweat from her friend's forehead. "Where's Mike? Where the fucking hell is Mike?" Jane kept saying.

And Annie would say, "I don't know. I don't know."

Jane lay back on the pillow, exhausted by the contraction that had rippled along her. "I'm glad you're here. I always thought you'd be here, if I had a baby."

And Annie remembered something from the happy fog when she'd had Jacob—Jane had been the first one there, almost before Annie had held him herself, bursting in with balloons and a blue teddy the size of a small dog. Hugging Mike, delightedly. Had it been there, even then? Should Annie have seen it, the thing that was growing between Mike and Jane?

No. She wasn't going down that road again. She couldn't let every good memory turn black in her hands, like rotting fruit, tainted by her own misery and pain. Jane had been her best friend. Mike had been her husband. It hadn't started until after they lost Jacob and everything fell apart. She had to believe that.

The doctor between Jane's legs looked up, her face tense behind her mask. "Okay, Mrs. Hebden."

Annie almost said, *Yes?* She bit her tongue.

"Jane, I need you to give one big last push. She's ready to come out."

"But Mike isn't here! Where the fuck is he? I'll never forgive him, never."

"We can't wait. On you go. One last big push."

Jane screamed, a sound so loud Annie thought it might tear her in two, and she felt the strain in her own hand, crushed almost to the bones, and all the way down her arms. She yelped, and then suddenly, just like that, there was another voice, and another person in the room. A slithery lump was slipped onto Jane's chest, all blood and mucus, a little tuft of dark hair, eyes crumpled shut. "A little girl," said the doctor. "Congratulations, Mum."

Mum. Annie found she was sobbing. No one had ever called her that. Jacob had never said it, never would. They were all crying, her and Jane and the baby, too, red-faced and squalling. "Is she okay?" Jane groped at the baby, blindly pulling her close. "Is she all right?"

"She's beautiful," said Annie. "She's the most beautiful thing in the world."

Later—she wasn't sure how much later—she was sitting in the chair by the bed while Jane slept, conked out. In Annie's arms was the baby, as yet nameless, wrapped in a white waffle blanket. One hand was clenched in a little fist. Annie was rocking her, very gently, jiggling her against her body, when the door opened.

Mike stared at her—his ex-wife—holding his baby. "What…?"

A thrill of fear went through Annie. What must he think, her being there? She jumped up so quickly the baby stirred, making a small mewing sound. "They couldn't find you. I was here—my friend's sick—so Jane asked for me. I… Here!" She held the baby out like a Christmas present.

Mike was staring, oscillating between Jane and Annie and his child. "I—I'd turned my phone off. We had a row… Jesus. It wasn't meant to be for another month!"

"Well, here she is!"

"She?"

"Yup. You have…" Annie's mouth suddenly filled with tears. "You have a daughter, Mike. Here. Look at her. She's perfect."

He took the baby in his arms, looking at her the way he'd

looked at Jacob. "I can't believe this. You were here, the whole time?"

"I've got the broken hand to prove it." She held hers up, then jumped again as Mike grabbed it.

"Annie, I wasn't here. I can't believe I wasn't here. She must hate me. I'm sorry. I'm struggling to take this in."

"I don't know if she'll remember most of it," Annie lied.

"We had a fight—I said she shouldn't have let you in the house that time. She felt so awful about it! She's been miserable ever since. She thought we'd be punished somehow, for what we did to you...and now here's the baby coming early..."

"She's fine, the doctor said. Just a bit small."

His face twisted in on itself, and Annie realized he was going to cry, too, just to complete the set. "What if it happens again, Annie? I can't bear it. I..." He bent his head to the baby, a sob tearing from him. "I didn't even want another one! I can't stand it if I lose her, too!"

Annie took the baby back, gently. "You won't, Mike. What happened to Jakey—it was just terrible bad luck. It won't happen again."

He bawled into his fists. "How can you even talk to us?" he said, muffled. "After what we did? What I did? You must hate us."

Annie shrugged helplessly. "I... I hated everyone for a while. You. Her. Me most of all. But... I guess things have changed recently. You and me—we couldn't have got through it, anyway, could we?"

"I just couldn't reach you. I felt so hopeless. I never meant to hurt you."

"I know," soothed Annie (though she didn't think she'd ever be entirely sure). "We were broken, you and me, and you just got on with your life. It isn't a crime. Just because I didn't know how to."

"She was so desperate for you to forgive her."

"I do," said Annie. "I do, really." It might even have been true. Even if it wasn't—even if Mike had done the worst thing imaginable to her—it didn't seem to matter now. Not when there was a whole new person in the world.

He was still sobbing, incoherent. Annie directed him to the chair, then walked the baby around the room, soothing her back to sleep. She looked up to see Polly peering through the door, leaning up from her wheelchair and shielding her eyes to see. Quietly, Annie eased the door open, holding a finger to her lips. "You shouldn't be out of bed!"

"I got bored. What the hell's going on? You've been gone hours."

"This happened." Annie hoisted the baby in her arms.

"Is that...? Holy God. You were her birthing partner?"

"Didn't have much choice. Mike was AWOL." They were whispering.

"That's him?" Polly nosied around the door at heaving-shouldered Mike and zonked-out Jane. "Annie, you're going to have to tell me every single detail of this."

"I will. But...look at her." She held the baby out for Polly to see.

"Oh, my God. She's so small."

"I know." Annie felt the rush of tears again. "She looks just like him. She really does. Jacob."

"Oh, Annie." Polly's strained face was kind. "You're going to have another baby one day. I just know it. Lots of cute babies, maybe with kilts on."

"Stop." Annie wiped her face on her sleeve, as her hands were full of the baby, who looked up with dark blue eyes. Seeing everything for the first time. A whole world in front of her, shiny and new. "I'll be okay. I promise. But for now... say hello to someone who was, for a little while earlier at least, the world's newest person."

DAY 68
Bring people together

"So then it's into the bunny hole, run around the tree, out of the bunny hole, away runs he!"

"It's harder than you make it look, Mrs. C," Polly said, struggling with the needles and wool. Annie knew she didn't have the strength in her wrists to even hold them up.

"No one can knit nowadays. You young girls just buy all your jumpers in the shops! So expensive."

"I can knit, Mum," said Annie. "You taught me, remember?" Another thing they'd done on long Sundays at home—a hobby that didn't cost much, and saved buying clothes. It wasn't right, she thought. Her mother looked better than Polly, who just months ago had been so vibrant and colorful. It was all leached from her now, the white hospital gown, the white sheets, her pale face, her bald head. Whereas Annie's mum had perked right up. She'd put on a little weight around the face, her leg was better and her mood was sunnier and less confused. But she still didn't know who Annie was. Maybe she never would.

She was looking puzzled now again, as if trying to work

things out. "I taught you? But when… Who are you again, dear?"

Maybe it was cruel, reminding her over and over that she wasn't herself. "Never mind," Annie said soothingly. "It's good of you to show us, Maureen."

"I taught children, you know, in a school. I wanted to train as a teacher but we weren't made of money."

She'd been a classroom assistant, part-time, after Annie was at secondary school. Accepting so little. A small life. Asking for nothing, getting nothing. It felt cruel, sitting with her mother, knowing that her father was dead, but she couldn't begin to explain her visit to Scotland, or her anger that her mother had never told her he was trying to get in touch. Annie pushed it all away, and forced a smile. "Show us that again, Maureen, will you? You're so good at it."

DAY 69
Cut loose

"Annie!" Costas was standing outside Polly's hospital room, flapping his hands in agitation. "Thank God you are here. We have a problem, Houston."

"What's the matter? Is it Polly?" Annie tried to see over his shoulder but he was blocking the way.

"Annie, I have done a bad thing."

"I'm sure it can't be that bad."

He raised his arms over his head in surrender. "You look. Go and see. Is very bad."

Inside the room, Annie could see the back of Polly's head, poking out the window she had open. Not that it was doing any good, because the room stank of weed. George was sitting in the nearby chair with his eyes shut. Annie turned back to Costas, who had closed the door behind them, his eyes wide with fear. "You got them this?"

"A friend at work has some... I did not know they would smoke it here, Annie! We will get in big trouble!"

"Lighten up, Costas from Costa," Polly slurred from the window. "I just wanted to get high one last time. What's so wrong with that?"

"You're *smoking*," Annie hissed. "In a hospital! When you have a tumor in your lung! Would you come inside?"

Polly ducked her head back in, a fit of coughing racking her ribs. "It's hardly going to give me *another* tumor, is it."

"That's not the point! Look at you. You're freezing." And she was, shivering and goose-bumped, her eyes bloodshot and swollen in a way Annie recognized from boys at school who used to smoke behind the bike sheds.

She chivvied Polly into bed, plucking the glowing joint from her fingers and dousing it in a glass of water. "Come on, get yourself warm. George, how you could let this happen?"

No answer. "Er, Annie," said Costas. "He is…sleeping."

She turned to see George slumped in the chair, apparently out cold. Costas was fanning him with his hands. "Oh, for God's sake. Costas, go and find Dr. Max."

"No!" wailed Polly from the bed. "He'll shout at me!"

"With good reason. Go, Costas."

He went. George let out a loud snuffly snore. Annie stood with her hands on her hips, glaring at the tiny figure in the bed. "This was your idea, I suppose."

"I just wanted to do it…one last time," wheezed Polly. "To feel alive. To feel normal. Stop being such a Betty Buzzkill, Annie."

"Polly, I'm worried about you. Listen to your breathing." It was rattling like a penny sucked up into the vacuum cleaner.

Polly coughed. "It doesn't matter. I'm dying, anyway. What does it matter if I take drugs, or drink myself into a stupor, or shag everyone in the hospital? Tell me that, Annie. What difference would it actually make if I lived as hard as I could for the rest of the days I have?"

Annie tried to think of something. "Well, no one wants to die with cystitis," she said.

Polly let out a loud sound, half sob, half laugh. Annie had

heard a lot of this cry-laughing over the past few days. Then Polly was just cry-crying, her face twisted and wet. "Shit, Annie. I've already had my last times. To get high, to get drunk, to get laid even. I'm never going to do any of that stuff again. I'm never even going to lie in bed with anyone ever again. I'm going to die here, in this horrible hospital room with these sheets that are definitely not four-hundred-thread-count Egyptian cotton."

Annie thought for a moment, then slipped off her Converses. "Budge over."

"What are you doing?"

"Getting in beside you."

"Huh. No offense but I was thinking more along the lines of Ryan Gosling."

"Well, you've got me. So, tough."

The bed was narrow, but Polly had shrunk now to the size of a child. Annie lay beside her, thinking of sleepovers with Jane and the girls as a teenager, trading secrets in the dark, giggling so hard Jane's mum would come and bang on the door to get them to be quiet. Polly's breathing was labored, the sheets damp from her tears.

"I'm sorry."

"It's okay. No harm done. Well, probably."

"Will Dr. Max be cross?" she asked pathetically.

"Yup."

"Maybe you can reason with him. He likes you, you know. Like, a lot."

Annie didn't want to think about that now. "Shh. It's okay." She stroked Polly's hair, or what was left of it, off her shrunken face. She looked like an old woman, the skin stretched tight over her bones. Melting away, minute by minute.

"Annie," Polly said in a very small voice. "You're my best

friend now, I think. Did you know that? Thank you for—thanks for being here. Will you stay?"

"Of course. I'm not going anywhere."

"Because I need you. To get through this. I know I've been selfish, and awful, and… I'm sorry."

"Shh," she whispered again, swallowing the lump in her throat. "It's okay. It's okay." Even though it wasn't.

"What the hell's been going on?" The door flew open and Dr. Max barged in, followed by an anxious Costas. He had a crease down his cheek as if he'd fallen asleep on his desk.

"Shh." Annie raised a finger to her lips. "She's sleeping." Because Polly's breathing had calmed, and her eyes had closed. Her fists were curled under her chin like a child's.

Dr. Max lowered his voice. "Is she really sleeping or just pretending so I don't shout at her? Smoking weed, for God's sake! Is she okay?" He approached to check her vitals, lifting her limp wrist to feel her pulse. Annie lowered her legs off the bed and got up.

"I am sorry," Costas said, wringing his hands. "She is okay?"

"Well, she's no worse than she was. But seriously—we can't have that here. Understand? I'd have to call the police next time."

Costas looked like he was going to cry. "I don't think he realized they'd do it here," Annie said. "He was just trying to help."

"With *illegal drugs*." Dr. Max raised one of Polly's eyelids, very gently.

"You've never dabbled? Come on. Give him a break."

"Not in a hospital, and not when I had a tumor in my lung." He relented. "I suppose there's no harm done, but really George should have known better, and—eh, where is he?" They all turned to look at the empty chair, and the open door to the room.

"*Skata,*" swore Costas.

★ ★ ★

George, however, hadn't got very far. The three of them stood over him, where he was slumped on the ground by the vending machine, one arm inside it. "I'm stuck," he said mournfully.

Dr. Max knelt down. "I don't know, George. What will we do with you? First drugs and now trying to steal a KitKat?"

"I *paid* for it. It didn't come out."

"Aye, I know that feeling. Let me see." Dr. Max squinted into the coin slot, pressed a few buttons and held out his hand to catch the thing that was spat back out. "Well, you see, George, here's your problem. This machine doesn't take gym locker tokens."

"Oh," said George. "Um, can you help me?"

Dr. Max rolled up his sleeves. "Aren't you lucky that you're here with the world's foremost expert in vending machine extractive surgery?"

"Surgery?" His lip trembled.

"Aye. Nothing for it but taking the arm off, lad."

George started to cry. Dr. Max rolled his eyes. "Lord, people take things seriously when they're high. Come on, grab his legs. Costas, you're skinny, see if you can get your hand inside there."

A short time later, with some pushing and pulling and George whimpering like a puppy, he was free, minus a Kit-Kat but at least in possession of all his limbs. "That was horrible. I thought I was going to *die*."

"Maybe you should knock off the drugs, lad. Seems you don't have the temperament for them."

Costas was kneeling beside George, tenderly examining his swollen wrist. "Please, George, you must be more careful. You will hurt yourself."

George squeezed his good hand over his eyes. "It was her

idea. She wanted to cut loose one last time, she said. How could I say no? Oh, God. How can it be the last time? My sister. She's my sister. I'm going to be a…a…what's the word for like an orphan but not an orphan?"

Annie and Dr. Max exchanged looks. "An only child?" she ventured.

"It's not fair." George was crying again. "It's not fair. Why Polly? She's a good person, she's so smart and alive and amazing, and now she's dying. It's not fair."

Costas hugged him, murmuring words in Greek. Annie looked at Dr. Max, and a strange current seemed to run through her from her head to her toes. A sweep of blood so powerful she was surprised she was still standing, still fully clothed. He scratched his head, blushing in a way that she knew meant he could feel it, too.

"Listen," she mumbled, unable to look him in the eye. "About Scotland. I don't know if I ever said sorry about…everything. But I am. Really. You were such a good friend to me, and that's how I repay you."

"A friend."

"Well, yes. You were." And she wanted him to be more, much more, but she didn't know how to say it, how to find space in her heart around the huge boulder that was Polly dying. "I…"

There was a moment of silence, stretching on longer than she would have thought possible. "It's fine," he said. "It doesn't matter. Come on, let's get young George here into a bed so he can sleep it off."

DAYS 70 TO 80
Let go

Toward the end, during Polly's last days, Annie felt like a cave dweller. She only went home to shower and change, and otherwise spent all her time in the hospital, shuttling between one bed and another.

Jane was discharged, with her baby strapped to her chest, still crying and begging Annie to come and visit. Mike repeated the offer, though rather more nervously. Annie said of course. And maybe she even would. It was hard to see more than one day in the future at the moment. For now, she was letting them go, Jane and Mike and their baby, letting them drift out of sight like a boat sailing over the horizon. And that was enough.

The MRI machine they'd bought for the hospital was delivered, paid for with money raised online and through the charity concert. It was unveiled and the local press came and Dr. Max awkwardly cut the ribbon, and Milly pitched the story to the *Guardian*, who did a piece on how inspirational Polly was. The machine had a plaque on it that read Donated by Friends of Polly Leonard. Polly herself was too ill to get out of bed.

Annie began to catch her mother looking at her suspiciously, as if she was in some kind of unconvincing disguise. As if she recognized her, but the name was gone, on the tip of her tongue...

George got another audition for the chorus of a West End show—*Guys and Dolls* this time. He mentioned he might not go to it because Polly was ill, and at Polly's request Annie threw grapes at him until he changed his mind.

Costas was named Employee of the Month at Costa and got them all free pastries. Most days he sneaked in Buster to see Polly, until Dr. Max noticed that his gym bag was woofing and banned it. "Fascist," Polly wheezed.

Milly brought in her twins, Harry and Lola, who scribbled all over the walls of Polly's room with eye pencil, then ate the chocolates Polly had been sent until Harry was sick behind the heart monitor. Suze came with neck pillows and hot water bottles and her latest terrible boyfriend, Henry, who ran a start-up coffee company in Shoreditch (Polly whispered, "My dying wish is that you will never again date anyone who runs a start-up anything"). They had to ask people to send donations to the fund instead of flowers, as there were so many Dr. Max grumbled he felt like he was in *The Day of the Triffids*.

There was Valerie, brushing Polly's remaining tufts of hair and putting cream on her dry skin. Holding scented tissues for her to cough blood into when spots of it began to come up, scarlet as poppies. "There you are, darling. Cleanse, tone and moisturize, that's what they say, isn't it?"

There was Roger reading to her from women's magazines. "Here we go now. Top ten mistakes you're making with mascara—good God, what is this rot?"

The two of them were practically camped out, bringing clean pajamas and books Polly couldn't read and home-cooked food she couldn't eat, but notably they were always there at different times.

There was Dr. Quarani, too, who seemed to be on Polly's

floor a lot considering he worked on a different one entirely. "How is she?" he asked Annie whenever he saw her.

Annie just shook her head. "Still here. For now." There was nothing else to say. One day at a time.

Annie passed Dr. Max most days in the hospital, buying quadruple espressos in the café, checking charts, feeling pulses, asking patients to follow his fingers with their eyes, peering at scans, shaving in the loos, eating Twixes, sitting on gurneys reading medical books or Jilly Cooper. There was, she felt, a lot that needed to be said between them—enough to fill one of those massive books he read—but for now she could only see a few paces in front of her, like walking in fog at night. She could only get up, and shower, and change, and try to take care of Polly and her mother.

Then there was the day Polly sweet-talked the man who ran the hospital radio—"DJ Snazzy Steve"—into playing "Is This the Way to Amarillo," and made everyone in the ward—staff, visitors and any patient well enough—do a conga up and down the corridor, weaving in and out of rooms until they got a visit from the bemused security staff, who Polly then somehow inveigled into joining the end of the conga.

And there was the day she ordered pizza for everyone in the hospital, delivering it to their beds in a Santa costume even though it was May, George wheeling her chair and dressed as an elf.

And there were visits. From Dion, who'd been discharged, and came gaunt and elegant in a pale gray suit and carrying a polished cane. From Polly's stylist friend Sandy, fashionable and almost as thin as Polly; she smuggled in Amaretto in a hip flask and told scurrilous tales from the catwalk. From friends old and new and real and fake and crying and laughing and stoic and selfish, and the whole thing went by, because that's the thing about time. It always goes. It always runs out, eventually.

DAY 81
Make your peace

"I don't understand," said Tom. "Why are you here?"

Annie tried to be understanding. It was, as she knew, quite disconcerting to have a strange woman turn up on your doorstep. "Polly sent me. She's ready to talk to you now."

Tom was wearing a navy toweling dressing gown, although it was 10:00 a.m. on a weekday. He hadn't shaved in a few days, either, and he scratched at his beard as he stood there. "But…last time she sent me packing."

"I know. She wasn't ready. She is now."

"I don't even know who you are."

"I'm—look, does it matter? I'm her friend. I haven't known her long, sure, but… I'm her friend. And I really think you should come with me now. Trust me. You'll regret it otherwise."

He looked back into the hall. "I'm not dressed. I—well. I took a bit of time off work. They sent me home actually. After what happened at the hospital, last time. I wasn't myself. There was…a bit of scene. I smashed something."

"You did? What?"

"A coffee cup. And, er, a photocopier. I was a bit…frustrated."

Annie knew that feeling. "Is she here—Fleur, was that her name?"

He shook his head. "She—she moved out. I was too much of a mess, she said."

Annie sighed. So many casualties in this ongoing war. "Why don't you have a quick shower and get dressed, and come with me. Polly's really sick, Tom. This is it."

She watched the news hit him, percolating down like milk into coffee. "Oh. I thought somehow—shit. I'm not ready."

"I don't think anyone is. But it will happen. Soon. So come with me, and make amends with her. It's the least you can do."

Annie waited in the kitchen while he showered. It was messy, with dirty plates stacked around the sink and takeaway pizza boxes piled by the bin, but she could see how nice it had been before all this. The floor was tiled in gleaming marble, the furniture carefully chosen antiques. One wall was covered in pictures of Polly and Tom's life, in a variety of shabby-chic frames. With her parents, with George. She recognized Milly and Suze in another shot, wearing bridesmaid dresses. No chiffon and puffed sleeves here, just sheer slips of red silk. In the center was Polly, in her wedding dress. She looked so beautiful Annie could hardly take it in. Like a film star, her hair in a messy braid studded with daisies, the lace dress clinging to the curve of her hips. It was hard to believe this was the same woman in that hospital bed, shrunk down to the size of a small child, bald and pale and covered in a scaly rash. Annie swallowed down a lump. She'd been right—Polly *had* had the perfect life, before the cancer, at least on the outside. But all the same it wasn't perfect. Not at all.

"That was our wedding day." Tom was in the doorway, smelling of lime and dressed in gray jeans and a thick navy jumper. Catalog man again. The perfect husband, too.

Annie didn't know what to say. "It looks lovely."

He rubbed his eyes. "I can't believe this is happening."

"I know. But it is. Let's go."

"Are you staying?" Tom hovered in the doorway of Polly's hospital room, looking supremely uncomfortable. She hadn't opened her eyes when they went in. Her breathing was slow and noisy, the machines beeping and humming around her.

Annie said, "I'm sorry. She asked me to—she's struggling to talk these days, with the ventilator, but she's told me what to say. I know it's hard."

He looked wretched. "But I...we need to say things. Private things."

Annie could tell Polly was awake. There was something subtle about the way she held her eyes. You'd have to spend a lot of time with her to notice, and Annie had barely left the hospital in the last two days. Polly took a deep breath in, coughing out into her ventilation mask. "Tom," she said, muffled. The plastic steamed up.

"Hey. Are you...?" He trailed off. "Jesus, Poll. I'm so sorry. I'm so, so sorry. I'd no idea it would be this fast. I thought they'd fix you, see, and..."

Polly squeezed Annie's hand, the faintest pressure, like the pulse of her veins. Annie said, "She doesn't want you to apologize. She knows she should have told you what was happening and she's sorry for that."

Tom just stared. "Can they not do something? Why don't they do something?"

"They've tried everything," Annie said gently, aware that she was echoing Dr. Max's words. "Radio, chemo, surgery. It's aggressive and growing and they can't hold it back anymore. She has a secondary tumor in her lungs that's pressing on her spine. She can't walk and her speech and sight are going. She's in a lot of pain."

"I'm so sorry," he said again. His face was shiny with tears.

Polly removed her mask, her frail body racked by a spasm of coughing. "F-Fleur…"

"She's not there. I'm so sorry I moved her into the house. I don't know what I was—but she's gone."

Polly tapped Annie's arm. "I know. Shh," said Annie. "Tom, she wants to know if you're happy with Fleur? Or if you were at least?"

"Um, I guess, but I didn't—"

"L-love?" Polly got out.

"Did you love her? Did she love you? She wants to hear the truth, Tom."

He nodded. A sob tore out of him.

"Then Polly wants you to get back with her, and be happy. Because you and she weren't happy, not really, and she's run out of time, but you haven't. And life is too short for any of us not to be happy." Annie glanced at Polly, who nodded faintly. She was getting it right. "So, go home and call her and be together. And if you want to come to the funeral you'll be welcome, she promises. You can even bring Fleur." Polly had insisted she add the last bit, though Annie winced for Tom. From the look on his face, you would have thought something was pressing on *his* spine.

"But I can't… How can she just…? Jesus, Polly! This can't be it! You're my wife!"

She tapped Annie, who said, "That's okay. Consider yourself divorced, Tom, but without all the paperwork. I'm sorry, she made me promise I'd say all this." Polly glared at her, which was hard to do when you'd no strength left in your face. "She doesn't mean to be cruel. She just thinks we're all wasting our lives, being unhappy, when we could be happy. I know it's not as simple as that, but there you go."

Polly tapped Annie's hand again, imperious, and shut her eyes. Her breathing was labored. "She's tired now. I think that's all she needed to say."

Tom pushed past Annie, grabbing Polly's thin hand, pressing it to his face. Polly tensed for a moment, then let him gather her into his arms, and her own feeble ones went around him as he rocked her, choking out sobs. Annie quickly left the room, hearing the quieter sound of Polly's crying mingle with his. Weak, worn-out sorrow. The tears of someone who'd almost cried themselves out. That had been her, once. Would Tom ever be able to forgive himself? Would it spoil any future happiness he had, knowing what he'd done to Polly? Annie realized she had to make herself truly forgive Mike and Jane, once and for all. For herself more than anyone.

Soon Tom was back in the corridor, the one that was the color of pain, openmouthed, shoulders heaving. "Is there really...there's nothing they can do?"

"No. We have to let her go now."

He slumped against the wall, still giving out loud heaving sobs, as if he was about to be sick. "There's a chair behind you," Annie pointed. "Sit down a minute."

He did, crashing into it as if his legs had given way. He wept into his cupped hands for a few moments, then lifted his wet face. "You must think I'm awful. Cheating on my sick wife."

"You didn't know she was sick."

"It's just... I did love her once. I think. I can't remember. Isn't that awful, that I can't remember if we were happy? We were sort of—we had a good life. Nice house. Holidays and that. I thought we were happy. Both of us working all the time, seeing each other when she was off to yoga and I was back from golf, on our Blackberries in bed, working till three in the morning. Then one day I met Fleur—and I realized we weren't happy, not at all. We were just like strangers, living together in a show home."

"Do you miss her, this Fleur?" Annie was picturing a twentysomething in spandex.

"So much. I cried the other day when one of her gym socks turned up in the wash."

"There you go, then. Go get her. And, Tom—I know you'll probably feel really shit about this—Polly dying and you cheating on her and everything—but it's just bad luck. She really meant what she said. All of us—me most of all—have to let her go, and then we have to do something even harder."

"What's that?" He was wiping his face, trying to tidy himself up. She imagined a man like Tom hadn't cried in about thirty years.

"Live our lives. Try to be happy. That's all." As Annie walked away she could hear his ragged sobs follow her all the way down the corridor.

DAY 82
Write your own obituary

"No, no, no, no, absolutely no way."

"But…why?" wheezed Polly.

"For God's sake, Polly. I don't want to write a eulogy for you when you're still alive!"

She was sitting up in the bed, her bald head covered by one of her wigs, a short pink one. Aside from her thinness, she looked all right. Was this the "last good day" that they talked about in cancer lore? "Why not? This way I'll get to…hear it."

"Because it's—it's mawkish, and it's attention-seeking, and God, it's like real-life Instagram or something."

Polly was calm. "I just want to know…what people thought of me, before I die. What's the good of saying nice things once I'm…gone? Why don't we tell people we love them while they can still…hear? You do realize I'm…dying, yes?"

Annie tutted. "How can you say that? Everything we've done, all of us, for months now, it's been about you dying. You're so busy dying you forget that we're all living still."

Polly tried to roll her eyes. "If anyone forgot they were living it was you, Little Miss… Boxsets and No Chill."

Annie hated it when Polly was right. "*Fine*, then. You'll

only get your way on this, like you do on everything. What do you want?"

Polly smiled. "I want a...mock funeral. I guess in the chapel here, since I can't really...go out. But *zhuzz* it up a bit, will you? You know, flowers and candles and...stuff. It's so... depressing in there. Ask Sandy. She has...a degree in interior design. Also don't let anyone wear...black. Especially not you. It's so depressing. I want color, color...and more color."

"Anything else?"

"List of all the music I want." She tapped a leather-bound notebook on the bedside table. "For God's sake...don't let my mother play 'The Wind Beneath My Wings' or anything... cheesy like that. Mum will probably want...a vicar. She's secretly a real...traditionalist. But I want my mate Ziggy to officiate, as well. He's a...humanitarian Zoroastrian and lives in a tree. She'll *hate* that. Tell her it's what... I want."

"But you'll be there, won't you? You can tell her yourself?"

Polly waved a hand. "Sure. Next, food—not from the canteen. It's too...hideous. Ask Tom for the company who did our...wedding. Tell them...no gherkins under any circumstances."

Annie made a note on her phone. "This is going to be the weirdest event ever."

"Classic Polly, am I...right?"

"You can't say that about yourself. It just makes you sound totally narcissistic."

"Why change the habits of a lifetime...darling?" She stretched out her feet under the blankets. "I could use a... pedicure. Can you see if anyone will come to the hospital? Not someone who does people's awful...corns. One who knows about gel nails. I want them to really...*pop*."

Annie wrote, *Popping toenails*. "What am I, your PA?"

"Do you have...anything else to do?"

"No, since *someone* got me fired."

"What do you think I should…wear? Do you wear black to your own funeral?"

"You can wear whatever you like. You will, anyway."

"True. Right, ring up Sandy. Tell her I want a once-in-a-deathtime outfit. Like…the best dress she can imagine me ever wearing. At least I'm skinny enough to…pull it off right now."

Annie made notes. It was easier to just go along with it. "Pedicure, clothes, food, music, decor. What else?"

"I want a slideshow of my life. Get me some numbers for… video people. And I want everyone to say something about me. Like a toast at a…wedding, only I won't have to share it with anyone else."

"Have you always been this narcissistic? Were you just holding it in for years?"

"I believe my imminent death has reduced my stores of… giving-a-fuckness." Polly looked at her dried and cracked feet again and sighed. "You know what I really wish I could do?"

"Hot-air ballooning over the Sahara? See a performance of *Les Mis* done by cats?"

"I wish I could go on a…date. That's silly, isn't it? I just haven't been on one since Tom, and I've forgotten what it was like. If I'll be all…glammed up, I wish I could go out somewhere…nice. With a man. But who would take me? I can't even leave this…stupid hospital."

Annie made some more notes. "Well, you never know, Poll. If you've taught me one thing, it's that everything's possible."

She nodded. "Maybe I can go on… Tinder and see if there's anyone else in the hospital who's dying and wants a last-minute date. It might appeal to all those…commitmentphobes out there."

"Sure," Annie said, turning an idea over in her mind.

Polly leaned back and closed her eyes. "So what are you going to say in my...eulogy?"

"Oh, that you were power-crazed and got me fired from my job and made me dance in a freezing dirty fountain and fall down a mountain a hundred times."

"You're...welcome."

Annie paused, rolling the pen in her fingers. It was a sparkly one, same as Polly had given to her all those weeks ago, to brighten her dull desk. "Polly... I've been meaning to ask. Why did you do all this for me? I mean, I'm horrible. I'm grouchy, and scared all the time, and I'm mean."

Polly laughed, a rasp in her dry throat. "When I saw you in the hospital that day, way back, you looked so...miserable, so broken, I thought to myself, *Here's someone who sees it like it is. Who knows that life is...truly shit and it all comes down to dying in small, crappy rooms all alone.* I didn't want...platitudes. My friends—they're great, but they're always so positive. They'd have liked all my Facebook posts, and never talked to me honestly about the fact I was...dying, and they'd have taken selfies at my funeral and put up sad-faced emojis and somehow it wouldn't have sunk in. Even Milly and Suze, they didn't really want to hear anything...negative. They'd have wanted to look for a meaning in it. Even my parents. They were so scared, they couldn't face it. They mean well, but I needed...reality, I guess. To try and be positive while facing the truth. You see, I wasn't like this before. I was the same as you—spent all my time in the office, grumbled about the...commute, barely spoke to my husband or family, angsted about how many likes I had on... Instagram and what kind of face cream I should be buying. All that...rubbish. But you—I thought if you could start being happy, after all you'd been through, then it would be real. I'd know it was really possible to change things. To actually become...happy."

"So what, I'm like your legacy or something?"

"To start with, maybe. And then, well, you know, you kind of started to grow on me. Betty… Buzzkill. I mean…it's so weird. I won't even be able to call or email you from…wherever I go. How will I tell you what to…do? Find out if you ever got it on with McGrumpy? Or just ask you how you are?"

Annie looked at Polly, whose eyes were still closed. She'd gone pale again, the color of the pillow. It was all too easy to imagine what she'd look like with those eyes closed forever. "Poll, did I ever thank you?"

"Nope. I'd…remember that."

"Well, thank you."

"Even for getting you…fired?"

"Hmm."

"You'll be…fine, Annie. There's so many things you can do for a job, so many places you can go. Trust me, when you're lying where I am—and you will be, one day—you'll be…glad of it."

"I know," Annie said quietly. "I know. Thank you, Polly."

Her thin hand came out from the covers and caught Annie's. "Thank you, Annie Hebden-Clarke. I don't think I could have…done this without you. I'd have been a…screaming wreck otherwise. You showed me that when something is really shit, it's okay to be sad. It's not a disease you have to cure. You can just…be sad."

"Well, you were a screaming wreck, some of the time."

Polly laughed, very softly, and after a few minutes her breathing grew flat and regular again. Annie held her hand for a few more moments, then gently detangled herself and slipped out.

DAY 83
Go on a first date

"Hey, look at those toes!"

"Good, right?" Polly wiggled her feet, the nails of which were now painted bright tangerine. "Popping all over the… show." She waved her fingers, which were each done in a different shade of neon. Lime, sherbet, acid lemon. "I'm gonna be the most on-trend…corpse in the mortuary."

Annie winced. She wished Polly wouldn't say these things, but she knew she had no right to feel upset. Polly couldn't be expected to spare other people's feelings, when she was the one dying. "How are you?"

"Good. I feel good. Got my hair done, got my threads. I'm ready to…rock." She did look better—her wig was styled to look like her own hair, the blond curls baby-fine and shiny. Makeup gave her some color, and she was smiling. "Sandy sent over the most…amazing dress. Shame I have to wait for the fake funeral to wear it."

Annie checked the clock—almost time. "Well, maybe you don't have to."

"What?" Polly was wrinkling her nose over her dinner tray, which held a bowl of tinned vegetable soup and some slices of white bread. "Dear God, what is this? I seriously doubt it's made in a... NutriBullet."

"Don't eat that. You're going out tonight. Well, not *out* out. Out of this room, at least. They wouldn't let us take you out of the hospital, sorry."

"Us? What's going on?" Polly set down the spoon with a rattle.

Here goes. This could all backfire so easily. "Well, when you said you wanted to go on one last date, I...arranged it for you."

"What? Who...with?"

"Who do you think? Your hospital crush."

"Not... Oh, Annie. For Christ's...sake. I made a total fool of myself flirting with him. He wasn't interested."

"Well, he is now." At least she hoped so. She still couldn't believe George had got him to say yes. He was so professional, so reserved.

Polly tried to fold her arms, but they were too weak. "This isn't fair, ambushing me...like this."

"Oh, as opposed to when you got me fired? Or told Dr. Max I fancied him—"

"—which you do—"

"—or made me pose naked or any of the other hundreds of daft things you've had me do? You owe me, Polly Leonard."

"Hmph. I don't want some manky...pity date."

"Think that's all you're gonna get at the moment. Sorry, babe."

"Don't you...'babe' me, Annie Hebden."

"Oh, stop moaning and get out of those gross PJs and into your frock. He'll be here soon."

Polly seemed to consider it for a moment, chewing her lip. Then she held her arms up. "Bollocks, I suppose it is my... last chance. Help me, will you? I'm afraid you're on...pants-pulling-up duty."

★ ★ ★

"You look beautiful."

"Thanks. Beautiful in a...dying-of-cancer way, I assume."

"Nah. All the models look like they're dying, anyway. You'd fit right in."

Polly looked at herself in the small mirror of the bathroom, twisting and turning. It was the first time Annie had seen her standing up for weeks. The dress was made of heavy red silk, with a boat neck and tight sleeves to the elbows. It swelled out at the hips, hiding her thin legs and ribs, giving her pale face warmth. Annie handed her a lipstick. "Here. Red, to match."

"Thanks." She slicked it on her dry lips, still staring at herself. "I look... God, Annie. I look...normal. I look like me. Me after a month-long...juice cleanse."

"You'll knock him dead."

Polly narrowed her eyes. "Ha-ha."

"Sorry. Omigod, he's coming!" Annie peered out the glass panel in the door. "It's him!"

"Jeez, Annie, I'm not going to...prom." But it felt that way. Polly clutched her hands, grinning widely. "I'm going on a... date! In the romantic hospital!"

"Shh. Okay, are you ready?"

There was a knock on the door. "Keep him waiting," Polly muttered. "One, two, three...oh, sod it, I don't have time to play...hard to get." She pulled the door open. "Dr. Quarani."

"Sami, please." He was dressed in a navy suit and pale blue shirt, and smelled of something lovely and musky. "Polly. You look very beautiful."

"Oh, this old...thing. So, Sami. Where are you taking me?"

"We're going to...a little place I know."

"Is it the canteen?" Polly whispered.

"Of course not. It's a lovely restaurant that just happens to be in the same place as the canteen. Shall we?" He held out his arm and Polly swept forward, her dress swirling about her ankles, leaning on him heavily. She'd refused to use the wheelchair tonight. It was only ten steps to the lifts so maybe she'd make it.

"Walk slowly," Annie said, scooting past them. "I happen to know for a fact your waitress isn't there yet."

"So tonight we have a special Greek menu for you. To start with, stuffed vine leaves, followed by moussaka. May I take your wine order?" Annie had to avoid Polly's eyes, or she knew she would laugh. She had a tea towel draped over her arm, and had shoved a waistcoat, borrowed from George, over her white shirt. The lights were dimmed and candles flickered on the canteen tables, which had been covered in red cloth. She'd set up an iPod dock playing Michael Bublé. It almost looked nice. If you squinted and ignored the strong smell of bleach, which even a bunch of pink lilies hadn't been able to shift.

"We have wine?"

"Champagne." Annie indicated the ice bucket Costas had nicked from his friend's restaurant.

"Am I allowed?"

"Apparently, yes. One glass."

Dr. Quarani shook his head. "Not for me, thank you. I don't drink."

"Not a problem. We have grape juice for Sir."

He raised his glass once she'd poured it from the carton. "Congratulations, Polly. How old are you?" Polly shot Annie a look: *What?* Dr. Quarani saw. "Oh, I'm sorry, that's a rude question, isn't it. What is it you say—cheers."

Annie poured Polly's wine and retreated. "I'll leave you to chat."

In the kitchen, things were steamy, and not in a good way. Costas was wrestling with something on a chopping board, his face red. He swore in Greek. "It does not look like this when my mama makes."

George was also sweaty, his white T-shirt drenched. "Goddamn vine leaves won't stay stuffed. Did your mother get back to you, Costas?"

His phone beeped and Costas grabbed it, getting meat all over the screen. "She say why am I doing woman's work. Classic Mama."

"Not very helpful, though. Bollocks." George sucked his finger, which he'd nicked with the knife.

"Problems?" said a Scottish voice. Dr. Max was leaning in the doorway, hands in the pockets of his white(ish) coat.

"Vine leaves will not stay stuffed," Costas said miserably. "I cannot follow what my mama says."

Dr. Max rolled up his sleeves. "Someone care to tell me what's going on here?"

"Um, we cleared it all with the hospital," Annie said guiltily. "She wanted one last night out, you see. One last date."

"And you made Sami the fall guy? Sami who never puts a foot out of line professionally? He's on a date with a dying patient?"

George wiped some rice off his cheek. "Um. I maybe didn't use the word *date*."

"What did you tell him?" Annie glared.

"Maybe I said something about just having dinner with her...and maybe I implied other people would be joining them. Look, I told him it was Polly's birthday party, okay?"

"You *what?*" Annie felt stupid under the ironic gaze of Dr. Max.

Dr. Max sighed. "Right. And none of you considered that Sami could be struck off for dating a patient? And that if he's struck off he'll be sent back to a war zone?"

"How were we supposed to know that?" George flounced

away. "Honestly. Cooking, asking out straight men… I didn't sign up for any of this!"

Costas looked confused, wiping meat off his hands. "We are not cooking the dinner?"

"Don't worry," Dr. Max said dependably. "I can do these." Deftly, he began trussing up the vine leaves.

"How did you know how to do that?" Annie watched, half annoyed, half relieved.

He shrugged. "That's all surgery is, really. Taking out things that don't belong, making sure other things stay in." He threaded a skewer through the leaf, as neatly as he sewed up wounds. "There. How's the rest coming on?"

"Moussaka is in oven," Costas said anxiously. "George is making baklava."

"Not that I'll get any thanks for it," George said from the other end of the kitchen.

Dr. Max washed his hands, turning off the taps with his elbows. "Right, then. Annie, come out here with me."

"Why?" She untied her apron, now splattered with rice.

"If this is Polly's last chance to have an evening out, it's up to you and me to save it. Well, me mostly, but you can make up the numbers."

Make up the numbers indeed. Fuming, she trailed out behind him.

"…it was quite a tricky procedure, because the patient's bowel had perforated and fecal matter was leaking…" Outside, Dr. Quarani was sipping grape juice and telling Polly about a particularly gruesome surgery. Polly's champagne was untouched, and she gave Annie a furious look. *What the hell?*

Annie avoided her eyes. Dr. Max swept over. "Sami, Polly! Isn't this nice? What's this god-awful rubbish you have on?" He switched off the iPod. "We can do better than that, I think." In the corner, under a red cloth, was a piano. "The Friends of the Hospital put this here, thought it would boost morale or something. Ah, here we are." He pulled off the cover and sat down on the stool. "Any requests?"

"You can play the piano?" Annie said, breaking character in her surprise. Was there anything the bloody man couldn't do?

"'Course," he said. "It's all in the fingers. How about some Frank—not your tumor, Polly—to get us started?" And he began to sing "I Get a Kick Out of You," the notes rippling in the empty room, his voice ringing out deep and throaty. At the line about getting no kick from champagne, he nodded to Dr. Quarani, who actually smiled. Annie was glad he didn't do that more often—no one in the hospital would get any work done.

Costas and George crept out of the kitchen to listen, and Dr. Max played, and Polly picked up her drink at last, and Dr. Quarani lifted his glass in a toast. *Oh, God, don't wish her a happy birthday.* "Here's to you, Polly," he said. And that was all.

"Want me to help you with the dress?" The date/not-date didn't last for long, as Polly was too tired to stay sitting up, but at least she ate a vine leaf and two spoonfuls of moussaka and half a baklava.

"There are literally a million layers of pastry in that," George had said. It seemed silly for them all to hide on the sidelines, so it had ended up with the six of them around the table, in the candlelight and with Bublé back on, under protest from Dr. Max, and they'd eaten the food and talked and laughed, and it had actually been fun.

Polly shook her head. She was lying on her bed, still in the red dress, staring at the ceiling. "I think I'll keep it on. It's too...beautiful to take off."

"Was it okay, your date?"

"He didn't actually know it was a date, did he? I wondered why he'd...agreed to it."

Annie busied herself smoothing the pillows. "You need to talk to George about that."

"It's okay. I got what I wanted—a handsome man...picking me up, a pretty...dress and an evening with the best people I know. Maybe all first dates should be...group dates." She paused. "He told me what's happening over there. His family."

"Oh."

"Will you keep an eye on him? You and Dr. Max? I think he's lonely. Imagine being stuck in Lewisham, of all places, and not even able to drink. Poor man."

"I will," she said. Polly hadn't added *after I'm gone*, but Annie knew what she meant. "Do you want me to stay with you?"

"Oh, no. Get some...sleep."

"If you're sure." Annie moved to the door, dimming the light. "Ding if you need a nurse to take your makeup off or something. That's what they're paid for, after all, to wait on your every whim."

"'Kay. Annie?"

"Yeah?"

"Thanks for this. It was the...best not-date I've ever...had."

"Night."

"Night... Annie Hebden-Clarke." As she left, Annie looked back at Polly—lying above the covers in her scarlet dress, still and white as a statue, the remains of her golden hair gleaming in the dull light.

DAY 84
Say goodbye

Ringing. The phone was ringing. Annie groped under her pillow, eventually finding it and stabbing at buttons. The ghostly blue light filled her room. "Uh?" What time was it? Still dark out.

"Annie?"

"Uh?" It was George. Why was George calling in the middle of the... Annie sat bolt upright. "George?" Her voice sounded remote, as if coming from outer space. "Is...?"

He didn't answer. She heard a small watery choke. He didn't need to say anything else. Annie was out of bed, throwing on jeans, looking around for her keys. "I'm coming. I'm coming right now."

She could never remember much about the journey. The burn of orange lights as she sped through Catford, the silence of her Uber driver, who seemed to pick up on her anxiety and drive fast, braking hard at every light. She got out, thanking him and running inside, into the green glow of the nighttime hospital, the beeps and harsh lights and shuffling people, tired-eyed doctors and nurses keeping watch. Rather than wait for the lift she panted up the stairs, huffing and puffing. At the end of Polly's corridor, she could see a gathering of people. Her eyes took it in but her mind couldn't grasp at it. Valerie, crying into George's shoulder, while he patted her back, his face ruined with tears. Roger standing to the side, shoulders vibrating like a shaken-up bottle of champagne. Annie skidded to a halt at the door of the room, looking in the glass panel. For a moment she didn't understand—they'd moved her? Why was everyone just standing there if they'd moved her and...

"Annie." Dr. Max was there, in the same clothes, the same smear of tomato on his sleeve of his shirt. He clearly hadn't been home.

"Where is she?"

"Annie. I'm sorry—she just slipped away..."

"No."

"It must have been not long after you left. She was still wearing the dress, and she looked peaceful, she really did."

"No."

"You gave her a good last night. But she's gone, she's gone, Annie. I'm sorry. Polly died, about an hour ago. She went in her sleep, and she wouldn't have felt it. I promise you. It's the best we could have hoped for, under the circumstances."

"No!" How could she be gone? It was only two hours since Annie had left her, happy and alive, talking, laughing, drinking champagne. How could she be here one moment and gone the next?

Dr. Max had his arm around her waist, moving her away gently but firmly. "Come on now. There's nothing you can do. We need to get everyone out of here."

"But...it's her pretend funeral in a few days!" Annie said stupidly.

"I know. I think—I think maybe she always intended it this

way, Annie. I think she wanted us all to be ready. She knew
she wouldn't make it that far. Come on now. Please."

Annie stared back, in disbelief, at the room Polly had oc-
cupied for weeks now. The sheet of the bed was pulled neat,
the machines dark and dimmed. It looked as if she had never
even been there at all.

DAY 85
Lie in bed and cry

Polly was dead.

DAY 86
Take the packet of pills out of your bathroom cupboard, stare at them, but then put them back again

Polly was dead. She was dead. Dead. How could she be dead? It was so unfair. So bloody, bloody, fucking unfair.

DAY 87
Sit mindlessly on your living room floor, staring at the turned-off TV screen

Polly was dead. She was dead she was dead she was dead she was dead she was dead.

"Annie?" Costas's light hand on her shoulder. "I take Buster for walkies now." The little dog was snuffling around Annie's feet, but her heart felt too heavy to pick him up. "You want I bring a pizza?"

She found her voice, deep inside her. "No. Thank you."

"You must eat, Annie."

Why must she? Polly was dead. Polly was dead and there was no point to anything. Polly was dead. No matter how many times Annie said it to herself, it still wouldn't sink in. This time, she didn't know how she would ever put herself back together.

DAY 88
Speak in public

Was it possible one woman could have known so many people, in just thirty-five years of life? The church was rammed;
they'd managed to move it out of the hospital, but all the
other details of the funeral were the same. Except that Polly
would not be there. Not alive, anyway. Annie walked down
the aisle, feeling like a shy bride at a wedding. She'd spent too
long getting ready, thinking Polly would at least want her to
wash her hair, and put on makeup, and find tights that didn't
have ladders in. Plus, she wasn't used to walking in the new
silver slingbacks she'd bought a few weeks before. She hadn't
known it at the time, but she'd clearly been getting them for
Polly's funeral. And now here it was.

She found a seat near the front, behind the family, and
squeezed in, murmuring apologies. George was in front in his
spangly MC suit, eyes red and raw. On either side of him were
his parents, Valerie in a big red hat with a veil, and Roger,
stony-faced, in a green tweed suit that needed dry cleaning.
And right in front of the altar, in that biodegradable hemp
coffin—that was Polly. Her body, her mind, everything she'd
ever been. In a box. Forever.

She sat down, looking about her. There was Suze with her hipster boyfriend, chiding him to put his phone away. She looked thin and miserable, in contrast to her cheerful coral-pink dress. There was Milly in green, trying to control her toddlers, one in a blue dress and one in a little suit, while her husband shushed them ineffectually. And there were other people, too—Costas, dressed in a very nice suit indeed, char-coal gray worn with a pink tie. Dion, looking frail, leaning on a stick, in a pale blue suit that must have once fitted but now drowned him. And behind, taking up nearly half the church, were the hospital staff. Cleaners. Receptionists. Radiographers. Zarah had come, of course, and Miriam, too, even though she hadn't known Polly. Annie gave them a little smile. There was Dr. Quarani, as well. And beside him—her heart tripped over in her chest—Dr. Max.

He'd put on a suit for the occasion, but it still looked crum-pled, his hair sticking up like Wolverine's. His face was creased, too, with tiredness. He caught her eye; she looked away.

There was a motion at the front, and a vicar came out, flanked by a man with long gray hair and a rainbow-colored chasuble around his neck. This must be Polly's friend the hu-manitarian minister. Annie met George's eyes. He raised his to the sky and gave a small smile and shrug. It was Polly. What could they do but go with the flow?

"Dearly beloved, you are welcome here today," said the vicar, a friend of Valerie's from book group. "I'd like to also extend a welcome to Reverend, uh, Ziggy, who will be cel-ebrating this with me, in accordance with the humanitarian spirit Polly wanted us to bring today. As requested, you're all a riot of color, and I know she would have loved that."

Reverend Ziggy stepped to the lectern. "Peace, dudes. Let Polly's spirit shine like a rainbow, yeah! Can I get a *hell, yes*?"

The congregation made a vague mumbling sound. The

vicar went on, manfully. "We will now have some short eulogies from Polly's friends and relations. First, she has asked that we hear from her friend Annie Hebden."

That was her. Annie clutched her index cards, already creased from her sweating fingers. She walked up, feeling everyone's eyes burn on her. *Oh, God, Polly. You owe me. You bloody owe me big-time.*

Walking there seemed to take ten years. She was terrified she'd slip over in her heels. The lectern was too high, so the vicar had to adjust the microphone for her, and as he did she saw he'd cut himself shaving under one ear.

"Er, hello." The church was deadly silent, people in reds and greens and oranges staring up at her.

"Um. It's actually Annie Clarke now, or it will be—something most of you won't get, but I think Polly would like." Polly, who was in that box just in front, and wouldn't ever know. "I, uh, I met Polly fairly recently actually, compared to most of you. But we spent a lot of time together, and I think she asked me to speak today because she knew I learned the most from the way she approached her death. It was, quite simply, remarkable. She took most people's worst nightmare—a diagnosis of terminal cancer—and turned it into a chance to be joyful, and productive, and change her own life, but even more than that, other people's. And one of those people was me."

More silence. She plowed on. "When I met Polly, I was miserable. I hated my life and everything about it, and I felt like the loneliest, most put-upon person in the world. Well, naturally Polly couldn't have that, so she played her cancer card, as she called it. I didn't want to know at first—honestly, I thought she was mad—but she drew me in, and, well, here I am. So I want to share what I learned from the last eighty-odd days."

She took a deep breath. "Sometimes people say you should live every day as if it's your last. Well, I don't think that's

practical—you might live for another fifty years, and it's going
to get complicated really fast if you never wash the kitchen
floor or pay your taxes or eat salad. Not to mention sticky."
She looked around at the sea of faces. People were smiling,
dabbing at their eyes. She took another breath. "I want to
share something I've learned from Polly—who taught me,
through her dying, how to live. I think we should all live as
if we are dying, too—because we are, make no mistake. We
should live as if we're dying at some unspecified but possibly
quite soon time. We can't expect every day to be happy, and
there'll always be sickness and heartache and sadness, but we
should never put up with a sad or a boring or a depressing day
just for the sake of it. None of us have time for that, whether
we have a hundred days left or a hundred thousand."

Annie looked down at her scrawled index cards, suddenly
overwhelmed by it. At having to sum up all the things she
felt right now. To speak for her friend, so colorful and alive,
when all Annie had ever been was drab. *Damn you, Polly.*
What a thing to ask. She always asked too much. "Um..." In
the crowd, she caught sight of Dr. Max, in his suit and tie, a
horrible shade of tangerine. He wasn't crying. He must have
patients die on him all the time. Occupational hazard. "Um,
that's all, really. I just want to say that I only knew Polly a
short time, but she changed my life, and I won't ever be the
same again. And I miss her. I will miss her so much. That's all."

Annie stepped down, staring at her silver shoes, aware of
clapping above her head, like the roar of a plane, the chatter
of birds. People were reaching out to her, hands on her arms,
patting her and whispering words of comfort.

Spoke so well...

Thank you, Annie...

She'd have loved...

But she could only see one face, hear one voice, feel one pair of arms around her. Helping her into her seat. Dr. Max's clean soapy smell. "You did well, lass. You did it. It's over now."

The rest of the service was a blur to Annie. Dr. Max sat beside her, his arm around her, and she sobbed freely into his shoulder, breathing him in. Music, and flowers, and funny stories, and tears. George breaking down as he told childhood stories of Polly. Milly's little girl singing "Over the Rainbow," forgetting the words and running offstage. Reverend Ziggy making everyone move about the room and hug people. Annie saw Valerie locked in a very uncomfortable embrace with one of the hospital porters, and Milly's little Harry shaking the hand of Dr. Quarani.

As soon as it was over—"The Wind Beneath My Wings" soaring out of speakers—Annie pushed her way through the crowd into the sun, sucking in lungfuls of air as if she was suffocating. "God," she said shakily to herself.

"I know. I already bailed." She turned. Valerie was sitting on a gravestone, her red hat beside her, smoking a cigarette. "Don't tell George, okay? I just needed something. She was married out of this church, you know. All in white. She was so beautiful."

"Are you holding up?" It was a stupid question, but Annie didn't know what else to say.

She drew in more smoke. "Polly told me you lost your baby."

"Yeah."

"Do you ever get over it? Does it stop, this feeling…" Valerie tapped her chest. "Like you're dying, too? She was my little girl, Annie. My baby."

"I know. Honestly, I don't know if it does. I think you just…kick some layers over it, as time goes by."

"I don't want to kick over her. I want to remember everything." Valerie stubbed out her cigarette. "Why do these things happen, Annie? Your baby and my girl?"

"I don't know," Annie said, gently taking the cigarette butt from her. "I'm not sure we're meant to know. There's no reason. They just are. They just happen, and we have to live with it."

Valerie gave a great juddering sigh and put her hat back on. "Stupid thing. Typical Polly, making us all dress up like clowns."

"I quite like it," Annie said truthfully. "It's special. Like her."

"Thank you for what you said about her. It meant a lot." She stood. "I just have to get through today. Just have to hold it together." She stooped to look at some of the wreaths piled up by the wall. There'd been so many they wouldn't all fit in the church. "People are so kind. Aren't they? Total strangers, many of them. Look at this one. 'From Jeff and everyone at Lewisham Council.' I didn't think the council provided that kind of service. How nice."

Annie jumped up to read the card herself. A wreath of yellow roses. They must have taken up a collection, an envelope going around as it had so many times when she was there, for someone's baby or birthday or leaving gift. All the small gestures she'd once thought were pointless, when people didn't really know you. She must remember to send a thank-you.

George came across the churchyard. "Okay, Ma? Annie, were you *smoking*?"

Annie flashed Valerie a conspiratorial look. "Um, no, I just found it lying here."

He tutted. "Litterers. Ma, apparently there's some kind of bus taking us home?"

Valerie shrugged. "Another of your sister's mad plans."

"Typical." He held out his arm to his mother. "Come on. I'll find you a seat."

"Typical Poll," muttered George again, hoisting himself up into the Routemaster bus. "Hiring a wedding bus for her funeral. God, there's even favors." There were, too—little photo frames with a picture of Polly on one side and a poem on the other. "'Do not stand at my grave and weep,'" read George. "Sweet God. I wish I could tell her how twee this is."

"I might pitch an article," said Suze, who was swigging from a bottle in her handbag. "Are funerals the new weddings? Gin, anyone?"

"I'll need it to get through this," George said, drinking deep.

Costas was muttering, scandalized. "Where was prayers? Where was incense? And clapping and hugging in the church! Is not right."

"That's my little Orthodox gay." George put his arm around him. "Here, have some gin. You are over eighteen, yes?"

At the house, more abundance greeted them. The trees were hung with bunting, and Polly must have got someone to print This Way to the Funeral signs. A slideshow of pictures played in the living room. Polly graduating. Polly on a yacht. Polly on the Inca Trail. Polly running the marathon. A smiling blonde woman, lacquered and perfect. Annie could not imagine she would ever have been friends with that person. With Old Polly. She could only be thankful they'd met when they did, both changed so utterly by life.

Inside there was smiling catering staff in black waistcoats, dispensing flutes of champagne. "Fuck's sake," Annie muttered, taking it all in. "How much did this cost? You couldn't have just gone with Cava from Aldi?"

Then she realized Polly wasn't there to smile at her grumpy frugality, or roll her eyes or shout, "Cancer card!" while popping the cork with both thumbs. Where she'd been there was only a blank, a silence that would go on and on forever. She would never hear Polly's voice again.

"Hi!" said Polly.

Annie froze. She'd had a few glasses of champagne, but

surely not enough to start hallucinating her friend's voice. Then she realized it was real, and coming from the living room. She stumbled in, bits of the lawn caught in her stupid heels. A young man in a polo shirt was fiddling with the projector, and fending off Valerie. "Sorry, missus. She paid me to come and play the video, like. I have to do it."

"But it's a funeral! George, did you know anything about this?"

He shrugged. "Another mad Polly thing, I'll bet. What video is it?"

The hapless technician pressed Play, and Polly's giant face filled the screen. It had been filmed the week before—Annie could tell by the knitted hat she was wearing, and the background of her hospital bed. "Hi, everyone! Hope you're having fun at my funeral. Sorry I can't be there, after all. Try the salmon things, they're amazing." Everyone was staring. A video message from the dead person? That really was a first.

"So since I can't be there in person—though, really, I think live funerals will catch on now we're in the selfie generation— I want to leave some last words, from beyond the grave." She put on a spooky voice, then laughed, then coughed. "Crap. I better not be too funny. Okay. Last will and testament of me, Pauline Sarah Leonard—ha, yes, Pauline... I managed to cover that one up well, didn't I?—being of sound-ish mind and not-at-all-sound body. This isn't a will for my things. I don't have anything worth willing, since Tom kept the house—hi, Tom, if you're there."

Tom, who was eating a quail's egg, turned red and began coughing into a napkin. On-screen Polly went on. "So. What I'm going to give away today is not possessions, it's intangible things. Costas. Is Costas there?"

He waved, as if she could see him.

"Sandy—is Sandy there, too?" She was, drinking mineral

water, thin and elegant in off-white. "I want you to give my boy Costas a job. He's wasted making coffee. He's got the best eye for color I've seen and I think he'll do you proud. Bet he looks great today, right?"

Sandy nodded. "We'll talk, Costas."

"Now, George. Where is my lovely brother? Moaning about the food, no doubt." George paused with his hand hovering over the plate of crudités, which he'd been scowling at. "George, my dearest brother, you and I both know you've not been living an honest life. I don't really blame you—which of us does?—but now it's time to be who you really are. No matter what Mum thinks." Valerie, who was sitting alone on a sofa, stiffened. "So I give you Dion—is Dion here? I hope you were well enough to come."

"He was!" someone shouted. Dion waved his stick from the corner where he'd plonked himself, looking exhausted.

"George, look after Dion. What happened to him and his friends was awful, but because of their generation, it hopefully won't happen to you. He's someone who's had to fight to be himself—it won't be as hard for you, thanks to him. I know you're up to it, bro. Hear his stories. Find out what went on—you're part of a community, a history, and I want you to be proud of that and not ashamed. And, Mum, I'm sorry. I don't mean to hurt you. But it's true. Let Georgie be who he is and let him be happy, and maybe then he'll stop going out with utter losers who hit him. He's loved, and love is always enough, no matter where it comes from. I hope they didn't get back together, by the way, or this will be totes awks."

Everyone looked at George. "We didn't!" he said defensively. "Er, hi, Dion."

"Hello, darling boy," Dion said in his hoarse voice. "I don't know if I'll make it out clubbing, but let's do cocktails soon."

Polly on-screen was still talking. "Now to Mum and Dad.

I'm sorry I caused you so much trouble. I know it was hard, that I wouldn't die normally. Please look after yourselves, okay? And, George, look after them. It must suck to lose a child, especially one as awesome as me." Valerie gave a long sob. "But that's not what I want to say. What I want to say is— Mum, Dad, please will you get a divorce?" There was a crash as Roger dropped his wineglass. No one moved, spellbound by Polly. In death as in life. "You've never been happy, not really. You put up a good front—the nice house, the friends, the dinner parties—but George and I always knew you weren't really in love. Dad's always working, you're always nagging... it isn't right."

Roger was barreling over to the technician, who could be heard saying wretchedly, "Sorry, sir, I'm not allowed to turn it off."

"So, Dad, why don't you move on, be happy? I know you're drinking too much right now. I guess that's understandable at the moment, but keep an eye on it, okay? I don't want you joining me too soon. And, Mum, trust me, speaking as someone who tried to hold on to a husband who didn't love her, it brings nothing but misery. Let Dad go. Find someone who'll really love you. Do your pottery classes and your tae kwan do and whatever. You don't need Dad to be yourself. And, Dad, I know you'll feel guilty, but it isn't wrong to make yourself happy. Oh, I guess I should say the same to Tom, if he turned up..." Tom was scarlet now. "If you love Fleur, why don't you stay with her and be happy. Do interpretative dance or yoga or whatever. Just look after my Moroccan tiles, they cost a bloody fortune to ship from Essaouira." She smiled out from the screen. "Now for the rest of you. Milly, my love, you're the best social media person I know. Please go back to work. Harry and Lola will cope. Don't let Seb keep you at home forever. Hi, Seb, if you're there."

Lola piped up. "Mummy, is that Aunt Polly?"

"Shh, darling," said Milly, scarlet.

"Suze. Dearest Suze. You're so special and lovely. Please, please, ditch that awful boyfriend and find someone nice. Or be on your own for a while. It's better than being with someone who can't appreciate you and makes you pay all his bills while he starts some kind of lame pop-up café. Okay?" Suze and Henry were side by side, gulping down champagne, avoiding each other's eyes.

"Now Annie." Annie jumped. She hadn't expected to be included—such a late-stage friend. For less than one hundred days. "Are you there, Annie? I hope you did your eulogy or I'm going to haunt you from beyond. I want to say thank you. You may think I taught you things, and obviously I did— *loads*—but the truth is I learned something from you, too. I learned about sadness. It sounds daft but it was something I'd never really experienced. I grew up thinking that if you felt down you just needed a glass of wine or a self-help book or a yoga class or some pills from the doctor. I'd never had to think about what it's like when your life collapses into an almighty pile of shit. When you're not depressed, as such, you're just so sad you think you'll never be happy again. I might have had cancer but you, Annie—you're the brave one. You've had to live with the worst pain I can imagine. One that positive thinking and yoga could never touch. And you're still going. I admire that. That's bravery. That's a battle. Me, I was just… drowning with style. You were swimming against the current, every day."

All eyes were on Annie now. She looked at the screen, her friend's smiling face. "Er, thanks, Poll," she said, her voice wobbling. "You couldn't have told me that when you were alive?"

There was a small laugh, a brief easing of tension. The tech guy looked relieved. Annie guessed this was the weirdest gig he'd ever had to do. That maybe he'd go home tonight, to his housemate or girlfriend or boyfriend or parents, and tell them, and Polly would touch some more lives, like a comet burning across the sky. "So, Annie. I leave you my cancer card—you can turn it into a 'lots of really bad shit card' if you like. But it's only valid for another month, and then you have to get on with things. That's the rules. So here's what else I leave you. I leave you Dr. Max. And, Dr. Max, if you're there, I leave you Annie. You two need to get it on, and fast. Everyone else can see it."

"Amen," muttered George. Annie was staring at the screen, openmouthed.

"So go on. Do it. Seize life. And that's me done. In more ways than one. Everyone, please don't say I lost my battle with cancer. I didn't lose anything. Truth is, there are some things you just can't fight, no matter what you throw at it. Dr. Max did his best to save me, and no one could have tried harder, but it didn't work. That's just life. It can't all be positive. After you dance in a fountain you have to dry your feet. After you ride the roller coaster you might have to be sick in a bin. It's all a balance. And please don't worry about me—I'm really okay. I was so desperate to be remembered, but in the last few weeks I've realized I will be, no matter what. That you'll think of me when you hear a certain song on the radio, or smile at a joke I told you, or drink a coffee in the sun, or wear your favorite outfit. I know I'll be remembered, and that means I won't be gone from you. Not really." She made an ironic V-sign. "And so…peace out, dudes." And the screen went blank.

"Annie?" She turned, hearing his voice. Dr. Max was standing in the doorway, his tie loose and sleeves rolled up. "Did you put her up to this?"

"No! I had no idea. I swear!"

"Because I won't be pushed around by you two. All these

mixed messages, getting close, then pulling away. I won't have it, Annie." And he turned and went out the front door, slamming it behind him so panes of glass rattled in the windows.

She stood for a moment, frozen. "Run after him!" shouted Costas. "You have not seen any rom-com movie, ever?"

So she ran. She huffed up the street after his rapidly retreating back. He was pulling his coat on as he strode, the sleeves all tangled up. "Dr. Max! Wait!"

"What do you want, Annie?"

"Er, your coat's all…" He had the wrong arm in his sleeve. "Look, I'm sorry, okay? I'm sorry. I knew nothing about this, I promise. But I do know…she was right. About us. For me, anyway."

He was shaking his head. "It's too late. I'm just done, okay? I've given that hospital everything I have for the past ten years. My personal life. Any hope of cardiovascular fitness. Most of my friends, three relationships. And a large chunk of my hair. And what do I get back? Patients who die on me, over and over, who I can do nothing to help. Management who cut corners, and treat us like garbage, and families who threaten to sue us and moan and complain about everything we do, read Google and come in demanding second opinions. I'm done. I haven't been able to help Polly, and I sure as hell can't help you. She's gone now. You'll have to drag yourself out of the pit this time, Annie. We all do, in the end."

"But…but…" What could she say? He was wrong? He wasn't wrong. And the walls of her pit suddenly felt higher and slippier than ever.

He turned away again, disappearing over the hill, shouting back, "Tell Polly's parents I'm sorry." And he was gone.

DAY 89
Read old letters

Annie let herself into her mother's house, feeling how still and humid the air was. Motes of dust drifted in the sunlight from the smeary window, and the panes rattled each time a bus went by on the main road. This was the house she'd grown up in, spent her whole life in until she'd met and moved in with Mike. If Annie closed her eyes she could conjure up her mother as she used to be. Dependable, if interfering at times. Always there when Annie fell over and cut her knee, or had a fight with Jane, or left Mike and ran away. Until, suddenly, she hadn't been. Annie knew now that nobody would always be there.

"You were right, Mum," she whispered. "There's no such thing as a perfect life. But there is such a thing as a happy life. Maybe."

It was so familiar—the china figurines on the mantelpiece, now in need of a good dusting. The sagging armchair where her mother had sat doing crosswords, watching TV, reading her books. The worn patterned carpet that had been there since Annie was a child. They'd never replaced anything. *We can't afford it*, her mother would say. *We're not made of money. Because of your father.*

And now she knew that her father had tried, at least at the end. It was too easy to imagine things being different. Eyes closed, she'd spent weekends and holidays with her father, got to know him; they'd been close and she'd felt loved. She'd had a sister. Eyes open, she was back in the noisy living room, and her father was dead. And she knew her mother would not be back here again. Annie would have to find her somewhere else to live. This house, with all its sad memories, would have to be sold.

She found the letter in the bottom drawer of her mother's bedside table, inside a shoe box that had once held sensible flat shoes from Clarks. Annie laid her hand on it, breath held. Then, as if Polly was over her shoulder chivvying her on, she took it out of its envelope. Standard blue notepaper, scrawled writing. This was her father's handwriting. *Dear Annie. I hope your mother will pass this letter on to you…* Annie's eyes blurred, and she tucked the paper away carefully. Something to read later, maybe, when she felt stronger, when she could process all of this.

There was something else in the box, too—a scrap of fabric, the color of gone-off salmon. A fragment of the prom dress her mother had made so carefully, and Annie had rejected. The one she'd thought meant her mother didn't care, not seeing that it really meant the opposite. Annie fished something else out. A tiny bracelet of plastic, so small she could barely fit two fingers through it. *Anne Maureen Clarke.* Her hospital tag as a baby. Kept all this time, just as she'd saved Jacob's.

Burning tears choked her again, and the contents of the box began to blur. Annie sat on the pink shag carpet of her mother's room, choked with the smell of Anaïs Anaïs and damp, and she cried for everything she'd lost, and everything she'd never had to begin with.

DAY 90
Visit a grave

The grave was like an open wound in the ground, the soil churned up, the wreaths on top already starting to look bedraggled and rotten. "You'd hate this, wouldn't you? So unchic," Annie said out loud. Silence. "I suppose I better start coming more often. Keep you tidied up. You're in the same graveyard as Jacob, you know. I can visit you both."

The flowers waved in the breeze. Annie shoved her hands deep in the pockets of her jacket. "I better tell you the news. Dr. Max has gone. Turns out he wasn't interested in me, after all." Silence. She sighed. "Okay. You're right. He was interested, I know that, but I scared him off by acting like a madwoman and panicking when he tried to kiss me. My fault. Everyone's doing what you asked otherwise. Your parents are splitting up—your dad's looking at flats already. It all seems pretty amicable. Costas handed in his notice. George is going to report Caleb to the police. My mum's getting out of the hospital soon. I wish you were here to tell me what to do. Do I sell her house? Do I tell her I know about Dad? She might not even understand."

There was no answer, of course. There never would be. If

she thought she heard Polly's voice in her head it would just be her imagination, a projection, a ghost. "I wish you could send me that email, after all," she said. "Tell me you're okay. Tell me I'm an idiot. Just something."

Nothing. In the silence, Annie knelt down and began to prune some of the wreaths.

DAY 91
Reminisce

"What's the matter with you, love? You do look down in the dumps."

Annie watched as her mother's hands flew, knitting the soft yellow wool together. She hoped it wasn't more baby clothes. That was always hard to stomach. "I am down in the dumps, Maureen. You see, Polly died. She died and I don't know what to make of the world now she isn't in it. It feels like...staying too long at a party after the cool people have left."

"Who's Polly?" Her mother's eyes roamed the hospital room, unfocused, but her hands never stopped moving. So deft, so quick, never dropping a single stitch. How could she still do that, when she didn't know who anyone was?

"She's...my friend. She was my friend."

"Jane? Jane is your friend, isn't she?"

Annie froze. "That's right. Do you know me, then, Maureen?"

Her mother didn't look up from her knitting. "Of course I know you, Annie. Haven't I been sitting here talking to you? And what's this Maureen business? Call me Mum."

"Um, sorry." Annie's heart was racing. Dr. Quarani had

said there might be moments like this, when the clouds parted and she was lucid. When she came back to herself. But she'd almost given up hope. "How are you, Mum?"

"Oh, I'm all right. Bit sick of this place, to be honest. The food is terrible. Worse than when me and your dad went to Butlins in 1975."

She could have said it: *Mum, he's dead, and why did you not tell me he wanted to meet me?* But she didn't want to spoil the moment, break the spell. "Well, maybe we can get you out of here soon. Where would you like to be, Mum? Would you like to stay with me?"

"In that pokey little flat of yours?" So she remembered Annie had moved out of her nice house. "No offense, love, but I'd rather be at home."

"I know, but, Mum…it's not really safe. You had a fall, re-member? What if I could find you a really nice care home? Would that be okay? We could—I guess we could sell the house?"

"I suppose. I never did like that house, really." She went back to her knitting.

"As long as it's not in with a load of old biddies, though. I mean, I'm not exactly drooling into my porridge yet, Annie."

"I know, Mum. I'm sure there's a nice one." She decided to risk it. "Mum, do you remember everything that happened? With me, and Mike, and Jane, and…everything?"

She frowned. "You and Jane had a falling-out, is that right?"

"That's right, Mum. But that's over now. Did you know Jane had a baby? A little girl. They're calling her Matilda."

"That's lovely. Like that book you loved when you were little."

"Yes, Mum." She hoped her mother wouldn't ask who the baby's father was.

"That'll be nice for Jacob, won't it? A little playmate? Did you not bring him today?" She looked around vaguely, as if he might be there somewhere.

Annie's heart was like a stone. So she didn't remember everything. And Annie could not bear to remind her, over and over. Kinder to let her think her only grandson was still alive. "No, Mum. I didn't bring him."

"Oh, well. Another time. We can take him to the park!" She was beaming. It was funny, but when she had good days now she seemed so happy, in a way she'd never been before. As if the disease was stretching her, pushing her to the very edges of herself, tears and laughter and everything in between. And Annie realized the past few months had been that way for her, too. She had become bigger than herself. Big enough to contain all that sadness and laughter and joy and misery.

She looked at her mother. How could someone who'd given birth to you be such a mystery? She had to at least try. "Mum," Annie said. "I found the letter Dad sent me. Why didn't you tell me?"

Her mother went back to her knitting, as if she couldn't hear. And maybe she couldn't.

"I want to say, Mum—I don't want to upset you, and I know you tried your best, but all those years telling me not to get my hopes up in life, not to go to uni, always scrimp and save…" She swallowed down more tears. They were so near the surface these days. Did her mother even know her father was dead? Would it be cruel to say it? "It wasn't right to tell me not to wish for the moon. I know you wanted to protect me but—really, what's the harm in wishing for more in life? Some people say that even if you miss, you'll be among the stars. Although that makes absolutely no sense in astronomical terms."

Silence. She watched her mother, who was smiling down

at her knitting. "Guess what, Sally. I'm going to wear this sweater to the dance on Saturday!"

Annie sighed. She was Sally again now. "That's good, Maureen."

"Maybe Andrew Clarke will be there. Do you think so? He's just the most dreamy boy at school."

"Yeah. I bet he will." Annie paused. "Can you tell me a bit more about Andrew, Maureen? What's he like?"

DAY 92
Have coffee

George sighed. "It just doesn't seem right without her here, nagging us into doing something stupid and terrifying."

They'd met for coffee, the three of them—Annie, George and Costas—but as he said, something was definitely missing. "So you guys have news, you said?"

Costas and George smiled at each other. "You tell."

"No, you should do it."

Costas looked anxious. "Annie, I need to tell you I will move out—if okay with you? I will move into a flat with George."

Annie blinked. "You mean...together? Or to share?"

They exchanged another shy look, and Annie twigged. The flat would likely be a one-bed. "Oh! Well, of course it's okay with me, Costas. That's great. Really great."

George sipped his flat white, leaving a faint foam sheen on his mouth. Annie was reminded, painfully, of Dr. Max. "It would have happened sooner, I think, but, you know, with Caleb, and Polly, and everything..."

"It's what she would have wanted. I'm sure of it."

"But you will be okay for the rent?" Costas, who was wearing a slim black jumper and gray jeans, looked the epitome of continental chic. "We will take Buster to live with us, too, if you don't mind, Annie?"

Annie was surprised by the stab of regret she felt. Of course it made sense—she'd have to get another job soon, and then there was her mother to visit. All the same the little puppy had somehow wriggled his way into her heart. "That's okay. I think he'll be happiest with you." Under the chair, Buster flopped his tail lazily. "I'll manage for the rent, too. Maybe— well, my mum's going to need a care home. I might have to move, to be near her." Annie's heart sank a little more as she said it. Caring for her ailing mother, getting older, never going out—was that what her life would be now? Was this interlude with Polly just a flash, like driving through a lighted tunnel at night?

"What about you?" asked George. "Did you follow your instructions and go after the dishy Dr. McGrouchy?"

"Oh, no. You saw what happened. He couldn't wait to get away from me. He's not even working at the hospital anymore." Annie had accidently on purpose wandered down to the neurology corridor a few times, and the handwritten sign on his door was gone, his nameplate covered over. "They said he quit."

"What? Where did he go?"

"I don't know. He had loads of holiday saved up, unsurprisingly, so he didn't have to work any notice."

"Maybe he need some time," said Costas. "We are all very sad about Polly. Maybe he will come back."

She remembered the way he'd said, *I'm done with this. I can't do it anymore.* "I don't know if he will."

George sighed. "I'm trying to think what inspirational go-get-him advice she would have given you. But I can't."

"No. Me, either." Annie didn't say what she was really

thinking: that she was desperately afraid she didn't know how to have a happy day without Polly there chivvying her along. She finished her drink. "I better go, guys."

"Aw, stay! We're taking Dion and Sandy out clubbing later."

Annie smiled. "Thanks, but not sure I'm really the clubbing type. Anyway, I have to help clear out Polly's clothes and things." Her diary was actually looking quite full these days. Lunch with Fee, a night out with Zarah and Miriam. There were friends. Plenty of friends. Just no Polly. And no Dr. Max.

As Annie walked away she saw Costas and George were holding hands under the table. Costas reached over and wiped the milk moustache from George's lip, and she heard them both laugh, the sound rising up in the spring sun. There would always be people, Annie realized. People to laugh with and have fun with and drink coffee with and talk to. But would there ever be someone just for her again? She was happy for them, but she couldn't shake the feeling that the rest of her life was going to be a dull coda, and the main event was already over.

DAY 93
Have a wardrobe clear-out

"It's so hard." Suze sighed. "Every time I look at this stuff I think about her. Those bloody yoga pants. She practically lived in them. Look at the state of them. I can't bear it."

"I know," Annie said gently. She didn't have the same attachment to Polly's things, the years of knowing her. But all the same it hurt enough, looking at the shoes that would never hold her dancing feet again, the hats that would never go on her funny crazy head. What hurt the most was how normal all this stuff was. She'd known Polly as a rainbow, a comet firing up the sky, but these things—overstretched bras and bally jumpers and reading glasses on her bedside cabinet—these belonged to a woman who'd been exceptionally ordinary. In the same way that everyone was exceptional and ordinary all at the same time. "We better get this done before Tom gets back." They were in the old house, packing up the things Polly had left when she fled. By tactful agreement, Tom had taken Fleur out to buy a spiralizer.

"Coo-ee." Milly came in, knocking softly on the open door. "I managed to get a sitter, after all. Don't mind, do you?"

"'Course not!" Suze reached out to hug her friend, and for

a tiny second Annie felt left out, awkwardly holding a knitted purple hat, and then Milly extended her arms again. "Annie, darling, how are you?" As if she was one of them. A friend. Two more friends.

Annie hugged back, smelling Milly's perfume, something rare and hand-mixed no doubt. She'd lost weight, and felt angular under her Breton top. "Oh, I'm all right. Trying to get by."

"Done anything about that lovely doctor you were willed?" Milly asked innocently, opening a drawer.

"Oh! Well, no. He's gone. Also I don't think you can really tell people what to do in wills like that."

There was a brief silence, during which Annie saw the other two exchange a look. "I've decided I'm going back to work," said Milly. "Seb will just have to reduce his working hours. Or pay for a nanny."

"And I've broken up with Henry," said Suze. "You know..." She made a gesture around her chin, indicating a big bushy heard. "P was definitely right about that. He said me crying every day was 'really harshing his mellow.'"

Milly started to giggle. "Oh, dear, does he think it's 1997? Good riddance, darling."

"I know. Though, at first, I was really mad with her, to be honest—how dare she, bossing us all around like that? First she cut us off, when she got her diagnosis, and we hardly heard from her for months, and then suddenly she was best mates with you, Annie, and it was all one hundred happy days and living life to the full."

"And now she's gone," finished Milly. "And we can't be mad at her or laugh with her or tell her to get over herself anymore. It's all just...stopped."

Annie had never thought what it was like for them, losing their friend. She'd only seen them as sleek, stylish women who had their lives together. "Are you…are you really crying every day?" she asked shyly.

Suze nodded. "Oh, yes. In the shower usually."

"Me, too," said Milly. "Only time I get to myself. Although I've broken down during *Peppa Pig* a few times, too."

"It's the hospital that does it for me," Annie confided. "When I visit my mum. She can come out soon, though, luckily."

"Any help you need with settling her, you just tell us," said Suze. "Milly and I could move mountains, P always said. And we'll need a third musketeer now, you know."

Annie stared down at the tan loafer in her hands until her eyes stopped burning. "Cucumber slices," she said when she could speak again. "We all just need more cucumber slices. That's all."

DAY 94
Say thank you

"I honestly can't thank you enough for what you've done."

"It's only my job, Ms. Hebden."

"Are you back to calling me that? Anyway, it's Clarke again."

Dr. Quarani gave a small smile. "Habit. Sorry, Annie. It's been very helpful for my clinical trial—your mother responded well to the drug. Her lucidity periods have increased. But the disease…it's tenacious. I cannot guarantee we will hold it back."

"I know. I know that. But really, I never even thought I'd have this." Her mother had called her by name when she'd arrived. She seemed to think it was 2003 and Tony Blair was still prime minister, but it was progress.

The bathroom door opened and Annie's mother came out, with her coat on and handbag clasped. "Thank you very much, Doctor," she said formally. Apparently she no longer thought he was Omar Sharif, so that was something, too.

"It's my pleasure, Mrs. Clarke. I wish you good luck in your new home."

With his help they'd found a nice place in Kent, with green

gardens and a knitting club and other people under sixty who'd been robbed of their memories. They'd lost time, too, in a different way to Polly. And that might be Annie, too—she hadn't taken the test for the Alzheimer's gene yet, and wasn't sure she ever would. She hoped she wouldn't need the spur of a deadline to live the rest of her days to the full. Even if she only had twenty-odd years of good time left, that would be enough to do all the things she'd always wanted. See Machu Picchu in Peru. Visit the lost gardens in Cornwall. Even another baby one day—but she was afraid to hope for that. And there wasn't exactly a potential dad in sight. "I'm sorry for what happened," she said. "That last night with Polly, roping you in like that. I know it wasn't right. But thank you for it—it meant so much to her, even to pretend."

He shrugged, embarrassed. "She was very beautiful. That, I can say. Like…lightning in a bottle, or something lovely and brief, that cannot be held in your hand. But I cannot be involved with patients, Annie. This is a rule for a reason. And I cannot—I do not have space in me for anything like that. It's not possible, not yet. But perhaps it's time I joined the world again, just a little."

"Really?"

"I don't know." She saw his eyes were resting on the picture of his sister and her children. "I don't know if I can, Annie. There is still so much to worry about, to fight for. You know, when I first came here, I could not settle at all. All these people, living in such safety and with such wealth, and yet they still complain and criticize and ask for more more more. I just felt angry that they did not know how lucky they were. Meanwhile my family lives every day with bombs falling from the sky."

Annie nodded guiltily. She'd been one of those, she knew.

"But now…now I have some friends." He said it so shyly.

"Maybe I can start to think about making my home here. Maybe I can stop running quite so fast."

And that, she knew, was more than half the battle. "I hope so. Come on, Mum, we better get going."

Her mother's eyes seemed to snap and focus. "Are you the nurse, dear?"

"It's me, Mum. Annie."

"Who?"

"Mum, it's me. You knew me two seconds ago!" It was too much. The frustration. Nothing good lasted, even for a minute. "Why can't you try, Mum? Please just try to remember? Just try. Please!"

Her mother's lip was trembling. "There's no need to *shout*. Who are you? What is this place?"

Annie felt a hand on her shoulder. Dr. Quarani, gently warning her. Her eyes brimmed. "She knew me. She knew me and now she—"

"It will always be like this, Annie. Like the sun. Coming, then going. At least you had a moment."

Annie nodded, wiping her hands over her face. "Thank you, Doctor. Thanks for helping. I hope we'll see you again very soon."

He raised a hand in farewell. "Be well, Annie."

As she guided her confused mother out to find a taxi, she looked for Jonny at the bus stop, but he was nowhere to be seen. The little square of ground he'd sat on was quickly fading to the same color as everything else, as if he'd never been there, either. It wasn't right, Annie thought, how quickly the world moved on, forgot about you. Even someone like Polly would soon be left behind, with no trace of her remaining.

DAY 95
Go to a party

Annie hovered outside on the pavement, the huge gift-wrapped present slipping in her hands. She could imagine Polly urging her on. Just go in. What have you got to lose?

Luckily, the door opened as she stood there. Miriam was wearing a party hat and an adult Elsa from *Frozen* costume. "Saw you from the window. You coming in or what?"

"Um, I was thinking about it."

"We've got cake. And costumes. And fairy wings."

"Cake is good." Cautiously, Annie began to move toward the door. The memories of this same day two years ago were flooding her. Running out to her car, screaming in Mike's face, driving off without him.

Miriam put an arm around her. "Hey, it's okay. Today's another day, yeah?"

"Mummy, Mummy, can I have my cake now?" Behind Miriam, a small girl was dressed as a mini Elsa, a large badge with the number three on it pinned to her chest.

Annie's heart contracted: she was so beautiful. Huge dark eyes, red ribbon threaded through her hair. A little girl she might never have known, never have seen again, if it wasn't for Polly's interference. She bent down, still clutching on to the overlarge present. "Hi, Jasmine. I'm Annie. Happy birthday, sweetheart."

DAY 96
Join a club

"Hi," said Annie. "Is this, um, are you the gardeners?"

Stupid question. Why else would a group of people be gathered around a patch of waste ground behind a bus shelter, leaning on spades and pulling up weeds?

A woman with a baby in a sling said, "We sure are. Come to join us? I'm Kate and this is Finn."

Annie looked at the little face peeping out, and realized it didn't hurt as much as it used to. She could smile at a baby now without always seeing Jacob, his small body on that terrible morning, his skin already cold. It would never leave her, not really, and she didn't want it to. But at least she could function again. "I'm Annie. What can I do?"

"You could help Geoff pull up those weeds over there, maybe."

Geoff was an older man in a Rolling Stones T-shirt and white beard. He took off his soil-covered glove to shake her hand. "Welcome, Annie. Know your way around a trowel, do you?"

"I think so." She put down her mat and knelt, feeling the give of the earth beneath her. This patch of ground didn't look like much now—sprouting with cow parsley and nettles, filled with broken bottles and no doubt worse—but with a bit of work she knew they could make it flower again.

DAY 97
Take a step forward

"Hey, Annie!"

She turned, puzzled to see a man coming toward her on the high street. He was clean-shaven, with short dark hair, and she wouldn't have known him except for the blue coat. She'd no idea he was so tall standing up. "Jonny? Is that you?"

"It's me." He laughed at her face. "I just had a wash and shave, is all."

"Wow! You got into a shelter?"

"For now." He pulled a face. "It's not easy, as you know. I got a shower at least."

"I'm so pleased. I wondered where you'd gone."

"How's the old bus stop?" he said, almost nostalgically.

"I haven't been for a few days. My mum's out now."

"And your mate?"

Annie just shrugged in answer, and her eyes filled with tears again.

"Ah, shit, I'm sorry."

"It's okay. It was always coming."

"She seemed really nice. Like a really kind person."

"Well, she was sort of bossy, and self-centered, and a little crazy at times, but yeah, she was. She was really, really kind."

There was a short awkward pause. "Well, I have to go. We have a curfew. But thank you once again, okay?"

"I didn't do anything."

"You talked to me. Like I was a person. That means more than you know." He set off down the street with a jaunty wave, and Annie watched him go.

DAY 98
Decorate your home

Annie wished she hadn't bought quite so many tins of paint. She was struggling to carry them home from the shops. But it was so exciting—the pale greens, the light blues, the yellows and reds and purples. Her landlord had said she could paint the kitchen as long as she paid for it herself, so she'd gone mad collecting samples. It was the first time she'd made these kind of decisions on her own, without ringing her mother or Jane or Mike for backup. It was just her now. And that was okay.

She stopped to rest for a moment, huffing and puffing, feeling the sweat on her back. It was going to be a beautiful summer, she thought. She'd always loved this time of year—flowers bursting out and the days lengthening and just a sense of hope somehow. And Polly was not here to see it. Polly had had her last summer, and winter and everything else. But Annie had many more to come, hopefully, and she better start making the most of them.

Stooping to pick up the bag of tins, she saw a familiar figure come out of the church hall opposite. There was a printed sign tied to the railings that read Slimming World. The woman, who wore a kaftan with dogs printed on it, paused by the gate, looked around her furtively, then unwrapped a Double Decker bar from her bag and started cramming it in her mouth, smearing chocolate over her face.

Annie thought about walking away—after all, it was Sharon—but something made her raise a hand, and wave.

Sharon squinted, then raised one chocolaty hand herself, and waved back. Annie didn't go over to say hi. One thing at a time, she thought.

DAY 99
Send a letter

Ms. Annie Hebden, née Clarke. The letter looked official, printed on stiff cream paper. Annie picked it off the mat and recognized the logo of Polly's solicitor. She tore it open, heart hammering. Enclosed was another letter, in a lilac envelope that was stuck over in stars and hearts, as if Annie had suddenly acquired a ten-year-old pen pal.

She sat down at the table to open it, knowing it would be something important. After all, it was from Polly. Anything less than explosive wasn't her style.

My dearest Angry Annie, my Betty Buzzkill,
Don't worry, I'm not writing from beyond the grave. I've arranged to have this posted to you a little while after I go, because I know you'll need reminding of a few things. And I know how stubborn both you and Dr. Max are.

People say you should only regret the things you haven't done. This is clearly bollocks, because what if you started World War III or bought a load of Blu-ray discs or something? One thing I regret is that I never pushed you to ask out Dr. Max. I was a little jealous, you see. That you'd get to live and fall in love and it was all over for me. Forgive me for that? You are very sad and he is very angry, but I feel you could make each other a little less so. I very much doubt you will be speaking right now, if I know either of you, so here is my message from beyond: *go after him*. Be happy, Annie. You deserve it. You've had more than your fair share of the other thing.

If I'm wrong and you're already together, then fine, you win, and say hi to him for me. *Do not* start ironing his shirts.

I don't know if I believe in heaven or if I'd get in, anyway, but if I'm also wrong about all of that, then you can bet your sweet ass I'm going to find Jacob and your dad and give them big old hugs from you. Not that they will know who the strange lady with the bald head is. With all my love and all my life,
Polly xxxxx

Annie wiped away the tears that had fallen on the letter, smudging the bright purple ink. Bloody Polly. Bloody, awful, amazing, irreplaceable Polly. What would she do without her to argue with? She could even hear her voice in her head, urging her on.

But he went away. He said no.

He was just upset. He blamed himself.

But he might say no again.

Annieeeee—what do you have to lose?

But I don't know where he is!

Where the hell else could he be?

She laid down the letter, and picked up her phone, and started checking train times to Scotland.

DAY 100
Tell the truth

The tube was rammed again. Annie found herself crammed under the armpit of a sweaty businessman who had music seeping out from his headphones. She tried to channel Polly— *Don't get angry. Rise above it.* A woman with a pushchair fought her way on, bashing into Annie's ankle. She yelped.

"Sorry," said the woman, who looked wild-eyed with stress. "It's so busy." The baby looked terrified at the crush of people around him, his red face smeared in some kind of organic baby food.

Annie laid a hand on the businessman's arm. "What?" he said irritably, taking out an earbud. Annie realized she used to be that person. Burning with anger, drowning in sadness. Infecting everyone around her with her own toxic pain.

"Do you think you might move a little? Let this lady in? Only, it's very cramped. Thank you."

He shuffled up, guiltily. "Sorry, didn't see."

"You can sit here," called another man who'd previously been playing a game on his phone and studiously ignoring them.

"Or here if you want." Suddenly people were standing up all over the carriage, guilted into doing something.

"Thank you," said the woman to Annie, almost tearfully grateful as she sat down, unbuckling the baby from his chair. "Would you like to sit, too?"

"Oh, no." Annie stayed where she was. "I'm just fine, thank you. Just fine."

Since she was already doing something crazy, Annie had splashed out and bought herself a first-class ticket. She settled into the wide seats as the train pulled out of London, flashing past houses and towns and villages and fields, millions of lives Annie would never touch, millions of hearts that would beat and break without her ever knowing them. The attendants brought her tea and coffee, and she savored the comfort and quiet, the sense of forward motion calming her mind. This was a good idea. Even if nothing came of it, it was always better to be moving than standing still.

By the time she finally got there it was very late, dark as pitch and freezing. The ground was damp under her feet as she huffed over the field, raindrops delicate as diamonds beneath her walking boots. This time, she'd been ready for the cold, knowing that June in Scotland did not mean actual summer. With no pollution, the sky bristled with stars, a million tiny points of light. She almost couldn't see him, sitting alone on the hillside.

She cleared her throat. What to say after all this? Now that Polly was dead. Luckily at that point she tripped over a rabbit hole and went flying at his feet. He jumped. "Jesus! Annie!"

"Er, hi."

"Are ye hurt?" His accent seemed even stronger now.

"I'm fine. Well, my body is."

"Why are you—what are you doing?"

"Your mum said you'd be out here. Sitting in a field in the dark."

"I have a blanket. Sit down, you'll catch a chill on that grass."

"Is that really a thing?" She crept onto the soft checked blanket beside him.

"Well, no, but a wet bum does no one any good." He was facing away from her, his face in shadow. She could see his beard had grown back, practically to mountain-man or hipster length already. "What are you doing here in a more general sense?"

"Um. Well. Looking for you, since you ran out on me."

"Hmph. I didn't do that. I just had to go. I had to."

Annie took a breath, her teeth chattering. She'd rehearsed this moment over and over on the train. "I thought you were going to kiss me once," she began, launching right into it.

"Aye, I was. You pulled away."

"I didn't! I just—it threw me. It's years since I did anything like that, and that was a complete disaster. I got my heart stomped on like an overripe strawberry. I just...couldn't risk myself again. I didn't know you well enough, I guess."

"So the fact I spend my whole life trying to save wee babies and old folk and your friend, too, that counts for nothing with you?"

Annie sighed. "Can we not just blame it all on Polly, since she's conveniently not about to mind? She convinced me we didn't have time for romance."

"She was so bloody selfish," he said. "I mean, you didn't even know her before this. Why did you care for her so much, and nurse her, and listen to all her nonsense? I had to be there every day, but you—you did it out of love. I'm in awe of that, Annie."

Was. Did. The past tense still kicked. Polly had already been and done everything that she ever would. Their memories of her would crystallize like amber, and she would never be around to defend herself. "Because," said Annie. "Look what she did for me. I was so miserable when I met her. I was so angry, and unhappy. I'd basically stopped living. But Polly—she lived more in these last few months than I ever had. And that made me ashamed. To have all this life, and be wasting it. That's how she was." *Was.*

"And I couldn't save her. It was sort of the last straw. This amazing woman, this woman who was so alive, and I couldn't do a thing to save her. Cancer one, me zero."

"You did everything you could. She knew that."

"I lost. She died."

Annie sighed. "You must be used to patients dying on you. I mean—not to imply you're a crap doctor or anything. But brain tumors, that's a powerful enemy. Worse than Voldemort."

"Don't say his name," he muttered.

"Polly wouldn't want you to quit, for God's sake. Aren't there other people who need you? Cute kids? Helpless old ladies with large, loving families?"

"Annie. Did you come all this way just to make me feel bad?"

"Who says I even came for you? I do have family up here, you know."

She felt him turn to her. "You're going to see them? Morag and Sarah?"

"Well. Probably. Dad left me a bit of money apparently. Not that I really feel entitled to it."

He made a noise of irritation. "Annie, for the love of Christ. You didn't get a penny from him all your life. Don't be your own worst enemy. Go and see them."

"I know, I will. Maybe. It depends."

"On what?"

"Er, how the rest of this conversation goes?"

"Hmph. How did you hope it would go?"

Annie realized she didn't know. "I hoped you'd stop being mad at me. And come back, maybe. I don't know. If you want to." She sucked in all her breath. *Damn you, Polly.* Goddamn deathbed promises. "I hoped to just see you because I really, really miss you."

For a long time, they just stared ahead, into the dark. She shivered. "Cold?" Without asking, he put his arm around her shoulders. He was so warm, so big, the heat of him radiating out from his smelly old Barbour jacket. Annie leaned in.

"Oh, Annie Clarke." He sighed. "What are we going to do now? Now she's gone? I mean, what's next—a hundred miserable days? A hundred days of feeling crap? A hundred days of back to normal, and sleeping in the doctors' lounge and getting my hand stuck in the vending machine?"

She rested into him, feeling the beat of his heart through the seventeen layers of clothes she had on. "How about a hundred days of doing our best to be alive—even if it's sad, or ordinary, and we want to cry most of the time? That's what living is, I think. Letting it all in. The happy days, the sad days, the angry days. Being awake to it."

"You're starting to sound like one of her motivational books."

"Well, it's your fault. With you gone, there's no one to be grouchy and tell me all my ideas are doing more harm than good. Costas is no use—he's all sunshine and rainbows. And George is going that way, too. Very sad to see a bitchy young man cut down in his prime."

"Sounds like things are worse than I thought down there," he said. "You'll all be cleansing your chakras soon."

"Maybe you should come back," she risked. He said nothing. "Please come back," she said, almost whispering. "We need you. I—I need you."

His hand was stroking her neck, very gently. Annie could hardly breathe. How had she ended up here, freezing on the side of a mountain with a grouchy neurologist, her entire life hanging on what he said next?

"You said I tried to kiss you," he said. "Were you—was that a suggestion I should try again?"

Annie said nothing. She reached up and took the hand that was around her neck, squeezed it. She'd almost lost all feeling in hers. "Max."

"You've never called me that before. Och, here, you're freezing, lass."

Lass. She thought she might melt, if she wasn't so cold. "Maybe we can go inside?"

"Just a wee minute. You didn't think I was sitting out here for no good reason? Did you think I'd lost my wits, was that it?"

"Er…"

"Annie. You're going to have to start thinking the best of me. I'm not your ex-fella who ran off with your friend, the scutter. I'm me. And look." He pointed to the sky, which had turned an unusual shade. Like green lights were being shone on it. Like the luminescence from a large town, except there was no town anywhere near.

"Is that…?"

"Aye. I told you, you can often see them up here."

"She missed them. She bloody missed them."

She felt him smile as she rested her back against him, and together they watched the northern lights flicker and shimmer, all the colors of the rainbow. Purples and pinks and greens and blues, shining and shifting and the most beautiful thing Annie had ever seen. Unique. All-consuming. Like Polly. He said, "One of your motivational books might say she's like that now. Far away. Shining."

Annie tutted. "God veto, Max."

"Fair enough. But it's lovely, no?"

"It's lovely."

"So there's still that, even if everything is shite and depressing and people are dying all over the show. We're here now—admittedly with frozen arses—but we're here, watching this, and we're alive. Is that enough for you?"

Annie felt his arms around her, holding her close, just the two of them under the vast ceiling of the sky, the stars sending their light from so far away, even after they were dead and dark and gone. They still shone. Polly would shine, too, as long as they remembered her. Annie was here. There was no one like her on the whole of the planet, no one who had ever lived or ever would. There was not a single other person with her fingerprints, with the memories she carried in the tangle of meat and nerves that was her brain, no one with the blood beating in her veins. She was herself, and she was alive right now, despite everything. And so was he. "Yes," she said. "It's enough."

★ ★ ★ ★ ★

Author's Note

Dear Reader,

Thank you so much for reading *Something Like Happy*. I started writing this book because I was intrigued by the "100 happy days" concept that was flooding my Facebook feed. Usually, I would roll my eyes at such things and dry-heave a bit whenever I saw #blessed hashtags on my social media. I'm not a naturally positive person—I grew up in Northern Ireland, for one thing, and we love a bit of misery. But something about this idea made me think. Was it really possible to make yourself happy, just by noticing the good things in your life every day? Can you drag yourself up from the bottom and start again?

There've been times in my life when, like Annie in the book, I felt I had hit rock bottom. When I was twenty-four I was diagnosed with cancer, like Polly. Luckily it was caught early and I recovered fully, but I found it hard to restart my life. Later, I found myself broke and homeless after my marriage broke down—I even got hit by a car, as well! (Luckily I was okay.) Both times I realized that doing happy things did make me feel better. Going to dance classes, taking a trip to the beach, even just baking a cake. So yes, I think it is possible to find happiness and hope again, even in the darkest days. There are always good things in the world.

I hope that, if you are going through a tough time, you might be able to find the same. Thanks for reading, and I would love to hear your thoughts on the book, or if you've been through something similar. My website is www.eva-woodsauthor.com and I'm on Twitter, too, as @inkstainsclaire.

Eva xx

Acknowledgments

An awful lot of people are involved in taking a book from a random idea someone has on a train to the beautiful published thing you see before you. First, I need to thank my wonderful agent Diana Beaumont, who always steers me right when I'm a bit lost with a book, and pushes me to go the extra "10%," especially when I don't think I can. Sasha Raskin in New York has also done an amazing job with overseas rights, and it's so thrilling to know this book will be published in different languages. Thanks as well to everyone at UTA and Marjacq for their support in getting the book off the ground.

This book is my first time being published on both sides of the Atlantic, and it has been a fantastic experience. Thanks to everyone at both Sphere and Harlequin U.S./Graydon House, especially Margo Lipschultz and Maddie West for their enthusiastic, clear-sighted edits. And huge thanks as well to everyone who has been involved in copy edits, cover design, marketing, publicity, and more—it's truly overwhelming to see the support for the book.

I'm fortunate to have many wonderful writing and nonwriting friends, who have helped me at every step of the process.

I wish you all, and my family too, hundreds of happy days. Finally, this book is dedicated to Scott, who has accompanied me on many a happy day, mostly involving cake. Sorry for making you go to Scotland in February and forcing you to go skiing in a blizzard.

This (and every) book would be nothing without readers, so the biggest thank-you must go to you if you've picked up this book—I hope you've enjoyed it. If so, I'd love to hear from you. I'm on Twitter @inkstainsclaire, Instagram @evawoodsauthor, and online at www.evawoodsauthor.com. Drop me a line!

Lots of love,

Eva x

SOMETHING LIKE HAPPY

EVA WOODS

Reader's Guide

GRAYDON
HOUSE

QUESTIONS FOR DISCUSSION

1. At the beginning of the novel, Annie is angry, unhappy and bitter. Did you sympathize with her or feel she needed to change her attitude?

2. Polly and Annie become friends despite being very unlike in background and personality. Do you think friendship can blossom despite differences? Or do people need to have things in common to maintain a friendship?

3. Did you find Polly's "inspirational" quotes useful or annoying? Why? Were there specific quotes you appreciated or disliked most?

4. Annie has been through some terrible things—divorce, bereavement, a parent with dementia. Do you think that, as Polly says, simple actions like gratitude lists can help people cope with such hardships?

5. Have you ever tried a challenge like the 100 Happy Days? What was your experience? Would you try it again?

6. Who was your favorite supporting character in the novel? Why?

7. Which was your favorite day in the challenge?

8. Some of the happy day challenges, such as having a piece of cake or going for a walk, seem minor. Do you think small things like these can truly make a person happy?

9. Is Annie right to quit her job or is this decision reckless?

10. Polly creates a video message to be played at her funeral and tries to organize a memorial while she's still alive, so that in some sense, she gets to attend. What do you think of this approach?

11. Dr. Max says that Polly's happiness and outgoing personality are caused by her brain tumor. To what degree do you think this statement is true?

12. In what ways do you think Polly and Annie ultimately helped each other?

Read on for a sneak preview of Eva Woods's next novel!

Two hundred and fifty-three. That was how many people heard or saw it when Rosie Cooke stepped in front of the bus on a bright, cold morning in October, as it crossed a bridge spanning the gray, muddied waters of the Thames.

Another ten would have seen it, but they were so engrossed in their phones they didn't know anything was wrong until the screams started, and the traffic stopped and for a moment in the beating heart of London everything was still and quiet and terrible.

An office worker on the twenty-seventh floor of a sky-scraper saw it as he sat at his desk, thinking about leaving his job before it crushed him, but turning over and over in his head the size of his mortgage and the children's school fees. He frowned at the sound of screeching brakes that carried all the way up to him, and then went back to his spreadsheets.

Three people on the bus that hit Rosie were late for work. Another missed an interview for a recruitment job she hadn't really wanted anyway, and decided she was going to go travel-ing to Brazil instead. There on the beach, caipirinha in hand, she would meet her future husband, Cristiano.

A woman stuck on the bridge, which was closed off for hours, had to stay late in the office to make up the time and cancel a first date with the man she would have married, who six months from that day would have slammed her head against a wall when she shrank his jumper in the wash. Twenty-three people missed their trains. Two got fired. One of the paramedics who answered the 999 call decided this was the final straw, and he was going to quit his job and retrain as an art therapist. In the crowd, a party of hens from Glasgow got entangled with a bachelor party from Cardiff, and went on a riotous night out in the West End, after which more than one monogrammed T-shirt ended up on the floor of a Premier Inn. A small child who saw the accident happen became so afraid of crossing the road that for the rest of his life he'd have to count to three before taking the plunge, and eventually move out of London to that Channel Island that has no cars on it. The driver of the bus would take early retirement, and move with his wife to the Costa del Sol, where he'd never get behind the wheel again. His wife, who'd been thinking of leaving him, would decide to stay now that he seemed to need her more. She'd take her driving test and become very interested in vintage cars. Two young women on a different bus struck up a conversation after one burst into tears, and six months later would move in together. In two years' time, they'd be happily married and adopting a child from Romania. More than one person went home to their partner that night and held them a bit tighter, spoke a little more kindly, overlooked the dirty socks on the floor. At least one child was conceived as a result. As many as fourteen people decided to abandon their diets and have a biscuit when they reached the office (for the shock). The street cleaner who had to mop up the blood had a flashback to the war-torn country he'd fled, but got on with it anyway, because what choice did he have?

The doctor who met the ambulance, newly in post and on hour twenty of a shift, locked herself in the loos to cry afterward. The ripples from the accident spread out, across London, across the country, across the world, far into the future.

And as for Rosie, she knew nothing about any of this, because for several minutes in the ambulance she was actually clinically dead.

But she came back. In a fashion, anyway.

DAY ONE
Rosie

"…losing her. BP is falling…"

"Stats are very worrying. Where the hell's Andy?"

"Buggered off again…"

"…in front of a bus? Suicide watch?"

"Get the crash cart and page him now!"

How strange, she thought. She'd fallen asleep in front of an old episode of *ER*. She hadn't watched that since…she had no idea. What was stranger, though, was that hands were touching her. Gently, but in a professional, distant way. Someone held her wrist, and someone else kept pulling out bits of her hair. It hurt. *Ow*, she said. *Ow*. No words seemed to come out of her mouth. She tried to open her eyes but they felt stuck shut. Her face felt…gritty. That was strange. Had she blacked out? *What's happening?*

A strange bright light was shining through her eyelids, as if someone was interrogating her. She tried to move away from it, cover her face, but her arms didn't move. And breathing was so hard. As if someone was sitting on her chest, some small but very heavy person. Danny DeVito maybe. *What the hell?* For a moment, with great effort, she forced her eyes open a crack. This wasn't her room. It was too bright, and there were plastic curtains, and on the other side of them another bed and something happening on it. It took her brain a while to figure out what it was. A man in motorbike leathers, but his chest was open and red. People in masks pulling on him, packing things into him, attaching tubes and wires. *What's going on?* She thought for a second she could see his heart beating, right there, open to the air, and a surge of panic went through her. *Is he...am I watching someone die?*

The man had longish fair hair, and just for a split second his eyes, bright green, opened and he looked right at her. Her heart jumped in terror and her eyes fell shut of their own accord, like drawbridges slamming down.

"...responsive. Call Doctor Khan and have her transferred to the ICU."

Now someone was tapping her eyelids. How very rude these people were. "Rosie? Rosie, can you hear me?"

Yes, *Rosie*, that was her name. Her name was Rosie and she was...how old?...and...she couldn't seem to remember any more. Where was she? Why did everything hurt? *What the hell's going on?*

"Rosie, you're in the hospital. You've had an accident. A bus hit you but you've been very lucky, you're still with us."

A bus had *hit* her? *It's the drivers*, she said. *They drive like maniacs, have you seen them?* But again the words had no sound. Her mouth was frozen. And how could she be lucky if a bus had hit her? What were these people going on about? Who were they?

"...said a name in the ambulance—Luke? Rosie, who's Luke? Is he your husband?"

Husband. Did she have one? She didn't know. She didn't even know how old she was. Trying to remember hurt her head, and it was so comfortable in the bed she was lying on. Like a cloud. A cloud that was carrying her away from all this noise and brightness and pain and these strange people touching her. That was it, go to sleep and when she woke up again this would all be over. A cascade of untethered memories whirled through her mind as she sank, like watching a stranger's home videos. A grassy meadow, running over it as fast as her legs would carry her, white Clarks' sandals flapping…a fair-haired man on a beach, turning to her and saying something…standing on a stage in blinding lights, an unseen audience furiously clapping for her…

"Rosie? She's going under! Damn it, page Andy again!"

Rosie, she told herself firmly, as she slipped under again. *I am Rosie and I am… I don't know who I am.*

Daisy

Daisy had never quite come to terms with the fact she couldn't speed up time. As a child, she'd lie awake impatiently every night once December came, counting down the days to Christmas. What kind of stupid world was it where time always moved at the same pace?

Now she was a grown-up, and she knew the sad truth. Nothing went faster or slower because you needed it to. The tube still dawdled between stations. Train doors took an eternity to open. People milled about on escalators like lost sheep. She cannoned off them, fighting her way out of the tube station and up into the light. "Excuse me…excuse me… SORRY CAN I GET PAST!" Offended looks. Mutterings. For once, she didn't care. God, it had taken nearly an hour to get there. She'd run for the train on hearing the news, but was there a quicker route? No, a taxi would have sat in traffic for ages. There had been no way to get there faster, short of, say, a helicopter.

Had they taken Rosie in a helicopter? No, the hospital was so close to where it happened, the next street over. The best place to get hit by a bus, if there was such a thing.

Her feet felt weird. She looked down as she stumbled toward

the signs for the hospital. Her shoes were on the wrong feet.
She fought the urge to stop and change them round, dodging
her way through the crowds. Everything was all wrong. She
hadn't done any of her leaving-the-house checks, hadn't picked
up any clean clothes in case she was stuck there overnight, didn't
have her makeup bag or water bottle or the work she had to
do today. She tried to reset her brain, tell it she wasn't going to
get that report done. She wouldn't be in the office today at all.
Bollocks, she had to text Maura. Her boss would be livid—she
hated last-minute absences, especially in a week with a big pitch
looming. But who could argue with *my sister just got hit by a bus?*

A nasty ball of pain formed in her throat and she tried to
swallow it down. She'd asked her mother, on the phone, "But
what do they mean, hit by a bus? Hit a little bit—like clipped
by the wing mirror? Or hit a lot?"

"I don't know!" Her mother's voice had ricocheted around
the line. "She's out cold, they said. You have to go there now,
Daisy. It'll take me hours on the train. And I don't have anyone to look after Mopsy and there's nowhere to park at the
station and… Oh God. What if she's badly hurt?"

"I'll go," Daisy had said, already pulling on her coat. "I'll
go right now."

She had now reached the hospital, all fifteen floors of it, full of
illness and suffering and death. She found she'd ground to a halt,
her mixed-up shoes rooted to the pavement. What would she find
inside? It sounded pretty serious, being hit by a bus. What if Rosie
was dying right now, while she stood on the street dithering?

Rosie never dithered. She just decided to do something, and
then did it. *You're always so careful, Daisy,* her mother had said,
at the engagement party. *That's what I most admire about you,
darling.* But thinking of the party brought up jagged, uncomfortable feelings, and she pushed them down. Would that be
Daisy's last memory of Rosie, in her leather jacket and biker

boots, her ripped jeans, red curls wild and untamed over her shoulders? What would she look like now after...after?

Daisy dragged her feet forward, as if detaching them from chewing gum stuck to the pavement. The hospital was bright and modern inside, with a Marks & Spencer department store on the ground floor, not what she'd expected. She found the lift and got in beside two handsome young doctors in blue scrubs, talking loudly about nephritis, whatever that was. The doors opened and she rushed out into Intensive Care.

This place was more like she'd expected. Swift feet, beeping machines, a hot and oppressive atmosphere. Someone was crying in the waiting room, the jagged sobs like a bassline to the rest of the noise. She found the reception desk, which had a harried-looking young man behind it, with a tragus piercing and tattoos all up one arm.

"Um, hi, I think my sister is here? Rosie Cooke?" *Is it a question or a statement, Daisy?* she imagined Maura saying.

He consulted the computer and she saw him suddenly focus on her. Her stomach dropped away. Waiting for him to say, *I'm very sorry but...*

He called over a young woman in scrubs. Nurse...doctor? How did you tell who did what job? It was impossible. They all dressed the same. She heard him mutter the words "*bus jumper.*" What did that mean? *Jumper?*

The woman's face was calm and unreadable. "Will you come with me please, Miss Cooke?"

She went. A horrible thought was crystallizing in her mind, as she realized she'd feared this all along. Even before her mum's phone call. For years. Since Rosie was fifteen, really, and Daisy was only twelve, this precise worry had been at the back of her thoughts, every time the phone rang and an unexpected voice was on the other end.

Had Rosie done this to herself?

Rosie

Rosie opened her eyes. Except she didn't, because her eyes, like her voice, apparently no longer worked on command. *Come on, guys, open! After everything we've been through together! I'm sorry I forgot to wear sunglasses all those times and never take my mascara off. Please...move?*

A tiny crack of light opened up. She found herself in a private room, and with her was a small woman she recognized as her grandmother, sitting in a plastic orange chair, knitting. Which was weird, because she was pretty sure her grandma didn't know how to knit. God had invented Marks & Spencer for a reason, she always said. See, that was a memory. "Grandma?" she tried. It was so strange. She was sure she'd spoken the words, but the two doctors standing by her bed didn't seem to notice, carrying on their mutterings about BP this and systolic that, like actors in the background of a bad play. They seemed...muted somehow. Not quite real.

Her grandma said, "Rosie love. What have you done to yourself then?"

"I...really don't know."

Her grandma got up, leaving the knitting on the chair. It

was in some kind of lurid pink wool, and the shape of it was odd. Was it for a four-legged baby? Rosie's head hurt. "Hmm, yes," said her grandma, peering knowledgably at the chart on the bottom of Rosie's bed. The doctors did not turn around or even seem to notice the small woman in the navy drip-dry slacks. It was very strange, like watching two videos super-imposed on top of each other. "Massive head trauma. Retro-grade amnesia. That explains it."

"What?"

"I watched a lot of medical dramas after your granddad died, love."

"Why am I...why don't I know who I am?"

"You're Rosie. Rosie Cooke."

Rosie Cooke. Two names. That was twice the information she'd had before. Progress. "And you're my grandma." She knew that, somehow, deep in herself.

"'Course I am, love." Was this her mum's mother or her dad's? Who were her mum and dad? Oh God. There was so much she couldn't recall it was scary to think about, like when you look under the sofa cushions and it's so filthy the only thing to do is put them back and try to forget.

Was that a memory? Was she the kind of person who didn't clean under their sofa cushions? "Do you know what happened to me? Does it say on that chart?"

"Sorry love. Just says some complicated stuff they never covered on *Grey's Anatomy.* But it's okay. They're helping you. See, they're giving you something, a nice drug. I tell you, I wish they'd had all this when I was your age. Two kiddies and only a slug of brandy to get me through!"

Rosie focused hard. Okay. A hospital room, white, sterile-looking. Two doctors hanging over her, in navy scrubs. A young Asian guy and a blond girl, with fresh peach-like skin that looked good even paired with blue scrubs and no sleep.

She tried hard to hear what they were saying. *Ears! Guys, you need to come through for me, too, okay? Sorry about that infected piercing. That was my bad.*

She found she was able to hear if she listened with all her might, like a station on a badly tuned radio. The girl was saying "…should use the restraints really. It's protocol."

"Come on, Zara. She's hardly going anywhere. She can't even open her eyes. I wonder what made her do it?"

Do what?

"The family are on their way. And I guess the police will want to ask questions. Hey, maybe she was pushed."

"You watch too much *CSI*."

"It's all they ever have on in the doctors' lounge."

Yes, she could hear, but nothing helpful. Pushed how? Down something, or under something? She tried hard to speak. "Hello, can you tell me why I'm here?" Nothing. "You can hear me, Grandma, can't you?"

"If you say so, dear." She'd gone back to her knitting now, holding it up to the light. "What do you think? Will he like it?"

"Who?"

"Filou, of course. Who d'you think it was for, a four-legged baby?"

"No," said Rosie quickly. Filou was… "Your dog!" She had him in her mind, suddenly, a yappy little pug. Filou had come back to her memory, slotting into place like a jigsaw piece. Surely the rest would come too. It would all be fine. No need to panic just because right now she couldn't remember who she was.

"That's right. See, you'll get there, love. You just need to give yourself time to heal. It was a nasty accident, by the sounds of it."

"A bus hit me." She frowned, remembering the moment she'd been awake before. The lights, the pain, the man with his chest open and his green eyes looking right at her. Had that been real?

Grandma sucked her teeth. "A bus! How did that happen, then?"

Rosie tried to take stock of her body, searching for clues. There was something on her mouth, tape of some kind, a tube in her throat and going down the back of her nose. There were so many sore places she had to move through them, cataloging. Head. Left ankle. Right knee. Bum. Back. Shoulder. Both hands burning like fire. Arm. Ribs. And her nose felt wrong too. "I don't remember," she said, frustrated. "I don't know what happened!" Questions crowded her head. How had she got here? Who was she? Why had she said the name *Luke*?

"Look, here's Daisy. Maybe she'll know more."

Who was Daisy? How had her grandma got here first? And why was she wearing slippers and a cardigan? Wasn't she in a care home somewhere? Devon? Yes, Devon. Had she busted out of her home and rode here on a sit-on lawnmower, like that man in that film?

When had Rosie seen that film? No idea. She realized there was a noise in the room. A sort of dry, rasping sound, like when you tried to squeeze the last bit of shampoo from the bottle in the shower. The noise was coming from a young woman who stood in the doorway, with sensible shoes, A-line skirt and an old-lady handbag. There was something weird about her feet that Rosie couldn't quite put her finger on. A diamond engagement ring, too big for her, sparkled on one hand. The woman was sobbing, leaning against the doorway of the room for support. The girl doctor was speaking to her in low, cool tones, hands in the pocket of her white coat. Rosie strained to listen. "...sustained massive head trauma. There was an intracranial bleed which we've managed to stop for now, and we've put in a drain, which explains the shaved hair."

They shaved my hair! Dammit, didn't someone tell them my ears are too big to pull off a crop?

The woman in the doorway was still crying, gasping hard for breath. "But how did it happen? How could she walk in front of a *bus*? Oh God."

Rosie had a bad feeling. "Grandma? Who's that? Why do I feel...why does it make me feel terrible that she's crying?"

"That's Daisy, love. Your sister."

I have a sister? But as Grandma said the word it all came flooding back, Daisy, Daisy, Daisy. Daisy a tiny baby in a cheesecloth blanket, so light on Rosie's knee. Daisy in a graduation robe, refusing to throw her mortarboard in case it hit someone. Daisy climbing into Rosie's bed after a nightmare, a small child, scratching her with toenails and hogging the covers. Daisy, a teenager, stealing Rosie's CoverGirl lipstick but feeling so guilty she bought her a new one. A million index cards slamming into place in the filing cabinets of her brain, making her wince. Every memory stamped with *Daisy*. Daisy laughing Daisy crying Daisy screaming, "For God's sake, Rosie, you're so selfish..."

Oh. "We had some kind of fight? I... I can't remember why."

"You will. You have to. Anyway, look, she's here, she's crying. She still cares."

What did that mean, *you have to*? She looked up and saw Grandma was staring to recede, fade and grow smaller somehow. "Wait! Please don't leave me. There's so many things I don't understand!"

But the old woman was gone, and so was her knitting for FiIou. Who, now that Rosie had remembered him, she seemed to recall had been around when she was small and scared of him. How long did pugs live? How old was she now, for that matter? A grown-up, surely. Daisy, who was apparently her sister, looked to be about thirty, despite being dressed like a sixty-something librarian.

Something else had been bothering her too, hovering around the edge of her vision like a bothersome fly. "The thing is, Grandma," she said, out loud—although the doctors and her sister didn't seem to hear. "Didn't you die too? Like, years ago?" And as she thought about it the memory was there—Grandma waxy and cold in her coffin, Rosie crying in a church pew wearing a too-tight gray dress from Jane Norman. Yes, she was almost sure that her grandmother, who had just been here chatting to her and knitting a jumper for a long-gone dog, was dead.

What the hell is going on?